Silence in October

JENS CHRISTIAN GRØNDAHL

Silence
in October

Translated from the Danish by
ANNE BORN

HARCOURT, INC.
New York   *San Diego*   *London*

www.harcourt.com

This is a translation of *Tavshed i Oktober*

Library of Congress Cataloging-in-Publication Data
Grøndahl, Jens Christian, 1959–
[Tavshed i Oktober. English]
Silence in October/Jens Christian Grøndahl; translated
from the Danish by Anne Born.—1st U.S. ed.
p. cm.
ISBN 0-15-100399-8
I. Born, Anne.   II. Title.
PT8175.G753 T3813 2001
839.8'1374—dc21   2001024978

Text set in Bell
Designed by Linda Lockowitz

First U.S. edition
A C E G I K J H F D B

Printed in the United States of America

Silence in October

1

Astrid stands at the rail with her back to the town. The breeze lifts her hair in a ragged, chestnut brown flag. She's wearing sunglasses and smiling. There is perfect harmony between her white teeth and the white city. The photo is seven years old, I took it in late afternoon on one of the small ferries that cross the Tagus to Cacilhas. Only from a distance do you understand why Lisbon is called "the white city," when the colors flatten and the facades' glazed tiles melt together in the sun's afterglow. The low light falls horizontally on the distant houses rising behind one another over the Praça do Comércio up to the ridges of Bairro Alto and Alfama on the other side of the river. It is a month since she left. I haven't heard from her. The only trace of her is the bank statement showing the activity in our joint account. She rented a car in Paris and used her Mastercard on the route via Bordeaux, San Sebastian, Santiago de Compostela, Porto, and Coimbra to Lisbon. The same route we took that autumn. She withdrew a large sum of cash in Lisbon on the seventeenth of October. She has not used the card since. I don't know where she is. I cannot know. I am forty-four and I know less and less the older I get. When I was younger I thought my knowledge would increase with the years, that it was steadily expanding like the universe. A constantly widening area of certainty that correspondingly displaced and diminished the reach of uncertainty. I was really very optimistic. With the passage of time I must admit that I know roughly as much as then, perhaps even slightly less, and with nothing like the same certainty. My so-called experiences are not at all the same as knowledge. It is more like, how shall I put it, a kind of echo chamber in which the little I know rings hollow and inadequate. A growing void around a scant knowledge that rattles foolishly like the dried-up kernel in a walnut. My experiences are experiences of ignorance, its boundlessness, and I will never discover how much I still don't know, and how much is just something I believed.

One morning in early October Astrid said she wanted to go away. She was standing at the bathroom sink leaning toward her reflection, painting her lips. She had already dressed, elegant as always, in her usual dark blue. There is something reserved, discreet in her elegance; dark blue, black, and white are her favorite colors, and she never wears high heels. That is not necessary. After she said it she met my eyes in the mirror as if to see what would happen. She is still beautiful, and she is most beautiful when I realize once more I am unable to guess her thoughts. I have always been fascinated by the symmetry of her face. Symmetry in a face is not something one can take for granted. Most faces are slightly irregular, either the nose is, or there is a birthmark, a scar, or the divergent curve of a line that makes one side different from the other. In Astrid's face the sides mirror each other along her straight nose, which in profile forms a faint, perfectly rounded bow. There is something luxurious, arrogant about her nose. Her eyes are green and narrow, and there is more space between them than in most people. She has broad cheekbones and her jaw is angular and slightly prominent. Her lips are full and almost the same color as her skin, and when she smiles they curl in a subtle, conspiratorial way, and the incipient wrinkles fan out delicately around the corners of her mouth and eyes. She smiles often, even when there is apparently nothing to smile at. When Astrid smiles it is impossible to distinguish her intelligence from her skin's spontaneous registering of the environment, the temperature of the air, the warmth of light and coolness of shadows, as if she has never wanted to be anywhere other than precisely where she is. The years have discreetly begun to mark her body, but she is still slim and erect even though it is eighteen years since she had her second child, and she moves with the same effortless, lithe ease as when we first met.

I would have put out a search for her long ago if I didn't have the bank statement. But she didn't want to be found, I understood that much. I am not to look for her. I asked her where she was planning to go. She didn't know yet. She stayed there in front of the mirror for a while, as if waiting for a reaction. When I said nothing, she left. I heard her voice in the living room as she was phoning, but couldn't hear what she said. There is something lazy, laid-back, about her voice, and every so often it cracks, as if she is always slightly hoarse. Shortly afterward I heard the door slam. While I was in the shower I saw the sun's reflection on a plane passing overhead between the buildings in back. I had to keep wiping the mist from the mirror so as not to disappear as I covered my face with shaving foam. The same distrustful gaze always meets me in the mirror, as if wanting to tell me he is not who I think he is, that man with white foam all over his face. He looked like a melancholy, tired Santa Claus, framed by the frieze of glazed blue plant stems on the Portuguese tiles around the mirror.

She'd found them in a foggy village near Sintra, we had driven the mountain roads' winding green tunnels, I swore because I got my shoes muddy, while she fastidiously and capriciously inspected the detail on the blue tiles as if they differed radically, and the corners of my mouth trembled when I took a drink of the rough wine that a peasant with his jacket full of straw offered me from a barrel on the back of a donkey cart. At night we made love in a blue hotel, and against the shining blue petals and sailing ships and birds on the walls her muffled moans took on an enigmatic tone, making her remote and close at the same time. When I came out of the bathroom she had gone out. The apartment was quiet. Rosa had more or less moved in with her new boyfriend, and Simon was riding his motorbike somewhere in Sardinia. It wouldn't be long before we were really on our own, Astrid and I. We hadn't talked about it much, maybe because neither of us could quite imagine what it would be like. It was a new silence and we moved about in it with a new carefulness. Before, we had enjoyed the freedom when for some reason the children were away from home. Now the rooms opened out like a distance that we either put behind or allowed to grow between us.

A world of sounds fell silent. Sounds that the others made and sounds I made myself and which had surrounded me for years with their continuous themes, secondary themes and variations of footsteps and voices, laughter, weeping and shouting. A kind of unceasing music, never entirely the same and yet consistent through the years because it was the music I heard and recalled, not the instruments, the sound of our life together and not the individual words and movements of which it was made. Our life, which repeated itself day after day while it changed year to year. A life of disrupted nights and smelly diapers, tricycles, bedtime stories and visits to the emergency room, children's birthdays and class trips, Christmas trees and wet swimsuits, love letters, soccer games, joy and tedium, squabbles and reconciliations. During the early years it had kept growing, this hectic polyphonic world, until it pervaded everything. It spread out among us with all its arrangements and planning and routines. We each stood on our own side of a new world, and for long periods we could only wave and signal to each other through the noise and the bustle. In the evening, after all the chores were done, we collapsed together in front of the television set to watch the news and quiz shows and old films, and although neither of us ever dared say it aloud, I was sure that she too sometimes wondered whether all the details and precautions, all the wearying ordinary daily routine, had not eclipsed the supposed meaning of it all. Only much later did it occur to me that the meaning was perhaps not to be found in the selected moments I had photographed and pasted into the fat family album, but rather was bound up in all the repeated trivialities, the repetition itself, the patterns of repetition. In the midst of it I had only noticed the meaning as a sudden, fleeting ease that might spread through me when, stumbling with exhaustion, I stopped between the kitchen table and the dishwasher with yet another dirty plate in my hand, hearing the children's laughter somewhere in the apartment. In isolated moments it crossed my mind by chance that precisely there, in the passage through the days and evenings' repeated words and movements, I was in the center of what had become my life and that I would never come closer to this center.

It was in the silence that I understood it, in the void in which Simon and Rosa would by degrees leave us. The sounds in the apartment were no longer a music made by instruments combining in a shifting resonance. They occurred alone at the edge of the silence like hesitant signals; when I was in the bathroom with the hot water gurgling down the drain, while I shaved and heard her answer me from the kitchen against the barking of the juicer, the whistle of the kettle or the long sighs of the coffee machine. Now that we could at last make ourselves heard, we sometimes didn't really know what to say. I woke up beside her and gazed at her face, turned toward me in sleep, toward the first light of day. As I looked at her while she slept, expressionless, her features withdrew from their accustomed semblance, the register of her moods that I knew so well, and it might almost have been another face, this face I had beheld for so many years. I knew her as I had seen her in the thousands of days and nights we had spent together, but what of herself, as she was to herself? Before, we might quarrel over trifles, who should do what, who should have done this or that. Now we had suddenly become considerate, almost discreet. Even in bed we approached each other with a cautious tenderness. It was not quite the same tired or lazy intimate, drowsy exchange, or the same transition from spontaneous revival to all too determined passion, after the children were asleep, muffling our groans and exclamations so they wouldn't hear us. It was a little like meeting afresh, as if we were slightly surprised that it was really us, that we were still here. We have been together for over eighteen years, Simon was six when we met. We have never been alone for more than a day or two at a time, at most a week, except for that October seven years ago when we drove through Les Landes, Asturias, Galicia, and Trás-os-Montes.

Astrid left the next day. If she had not already gone out by the time I finished in the bathroom, I might have asked her why. But when she finally came home well into the evening and we sat having supper in the kitchen because the children were not at home, it was somehow too late. There are questions that can only be asked at certain moments, and sometimes you get only one chance. If you don't ask in time the chance has been missed. When I served the meal and poured her a glass of wine, her journey was already an accomplished fact, although she had not even packed her suitcase and might not have known yet where she was going. All day the thought that she wanted to go away had provoked so many new questions in me that the one asking why she was leaving had grown far too big, too momentous. I couldn't have asked it without all the other questions thrusting their confused and blushing heads into the silence that followed. For some reason I was sure there would be complete stillness in the kitchen if I asked the question. I did not want her to notice that her remark that morning, while she replaced the cap on her lipstick and quickly inspected her face in the mirror, that her casual utterance had kept me from getting more than half a page written of the article on Cézanne that I should have started a week earlier, and which I considered already planned out to the last sentence. I didn't want to sit there like some despondent youth airing his jealous paranoia. After all, we were both grown-ups, as they say. And maybe I had exaggerated my unease during the day, as I sat in my study trying to concentrate. In any case, surely there was nothing unusual about her wanting to be alone for a while to see something new, now that our duties had not only relaxed their grip but had actually released us, leaving us to ourselves and to each other.

She had phoned from the editing room late in the afternoon to say she would be delayed. I could hear the chittering, cartoon-film gabble from the loudspeaker as she quickly scrolled through a scene on the editing table. After I had put down the receiver I went over the brief conversation line by line, trying to find a hint of change in her tone, but every word sounded normal and reassuring, and she had been neither more detached nor more affectionate than she normally was on the telephone. Nor when we were in the kitchen was there anything between us to set this evening apart from all the others. I expected her to bring up her travel plans herself, but she seemed to have forgotten about them. Unless she was only waiting for me to interrupt her. She chatted about the film they had finished editing that day and, with her usual crinkled smile, described the young director, a very serious, quivering type who had despaired as his favorite shots vanished with the cuts. In a way her work was invisible. It consisted of extracting a story from the unconnected shots the directors brought her. She usually made them coherent by excising the greater part of them. That's how it is with stories, mine as well. I cannot include everything, I have to select from among the images I have, I have to decide on a sequence, and thus my story will be quite different from the one she could tell, even though they are supposedly about the same subject. While she talked I registered each movement in her face. It was the same face it had always been. At long intervals over the years I had noticed a gray hair I hadn't seen before, a line grown sharper, but otherwise they were the same eyes that met my gaze through everything that happened between us, the same mouth that spoke to me in all our conversations.

Later I lay awake and tried to remember the past weeks and months, searching for an expression, a gesture, a remark that could explain what was perhaps not a mystery at all. But either no change had taken place, or I had failed to notice it. Have I really become so distrait? Evidently. My memory is bad, the days run into each other, they blur so there is only the same well of time in which each day the sky reflects itself anew. Every day was much the same. She would go off in the morning and I would sit at my table looking out at the row of trees along the Lakes, which day by day was imperceptibly transformed from a wall of rustling green to a lattice of gnarled bare branches and withered foliage before the silent, shining water. She came home and lay on the sofa while I cooked; we ate, watched television or read, went to bed. The only change was the silence after Simon went away, and later in the steadily longer intervals between Rosa's visits; the consciousness that we were breaking a silence when we spoke to each other, that we were not contributing to the same continuing story as before. More than once I paused on my way from one room to another and watched her through an open door as she sat on the sofa with her legs pulled up underneath her, reading the paper, absentmindedly scratching the loose cover with a fingernail, or as she stood at the window looking out at the row of facades on the other side of the lake as if she had seen something or was waiting for something to come into sight over there. When I observed her like this, without her knowing it, apparently forgetful, immersed in a vision or a thought, she might suddenly look up from the paper or turn away from the view to meet my eye, as if she had felt it on her face, almost like a light touch, and I would hasten to make some casual practical remark to quash the moment's unspoken question.

I lay listening to her calm breathing and the distant cars. I thought she had fallen asleep but then heard her voice in the darkness. Perhaps she was surprised that I had not questioned her while we were in the kitchen. Perhaps she had expected

me to try to stop her from leaving. She lay with her back to
me, her voice calm and matter-of-fact. It might be for quite a
while. How long? She didn't know. I put a hand on her hip
under the duvet, she did not move. As I stroked her hip I
thought that my question sounded as if I knew what she was
talking about. I asked her if she was going alone, but she
didn't reply; perhaps she was already asleep. When I woke up
she was standing in the bedroom doorway looking at me. She
already had her coat on. I got up and walked over to her. She
continued to gaze at me as if reading a message in my face
which I myself did not know about. Then she picked up the
suitcase beside her on the floor. I accompanied her to the front
door and watched her walk down the stairs, but she did not
turn around. I could not understand myself. I did not understand why I had let her go away without giving the least explanation. Of course I had no claim on her to answer all my
timorous questions. The claims we had had on each other had
gradually fallen away as the children no longer needed us. But
I could at least have asked, and left it to her to decide how
much she would reply. She had announced her decision in such
a matter-of-fact, offhand way in front of the mirror, as if it had
been a matter of going to the cinema or visiting a friend, and
I had allowed myself to be seduced by the naturalness of her
tone. And later, in bed, when I thought she was asleep, there
had been a distance in her voice as if she had already left and
was calling from a town on the other side of the world. As if
by her cool announcement she wanted to tell me to leave her
in peace. On the other hand her reply in the darkness could
have been an offer which, only now, too late, I realized I had
failed to accept. Many times I had had to drag the words out
of her, one by one, with long pauses between them, when her
silence and aloofness told me something was wrong, that she

was feeling hurt or offended. It was an established ritual, her withdrawal in which I acquiesced, and my own familiar role, the forbearance of the humble questioner, I knew the tone and gestures by heart, sitting on the edge of my chair or bent over her turned-away back, as I mumbled my plea for mercy. When she stood in the bedroom doorway waiting for me to wake up, in that long moment when we stood facing each other, she in her overcoat, I in pajamas, she had perhaps given me a last chance to protest, to keep her from going, to confront her with my uneasiness and incipient jealousy. But her unmoving eyes had unnerved me. Without knowing why, I knew it would be futile, as I met her deliberate gaze, which seemed to regard me from a distant, unknown, and inaccessible place.

As I sat by the kitchen window with my coffee, contemplating the pattern of bricks in the opposite wall as I so often do, I gingerly touched on the thought I had skirted the previous day. While she was presumably sitting in a plane or a train, and I was again scanning the displaced patterns of the joints and the red-brown variations of the bricks, I forced myself to ask whether she was traveling by herself in that airplane cabin or train compartment. Whether in reality she was in a strange car next to an unknown driver somewhere on the highway south of the town. I reassured myself that she would have told me if she had a lover (both of us would have smiled at that word). And that if not, she would have taken pains to come up with a convincing reason for leaving. As far as I knew, she had never been unfaithful to me. As far as I knew. Anyway, I had never been jealous, which of course was no guarantee of anything but my own complacency, but if she really had had affairs during our eighteen years together, she was a more sophisticated and cold-blooded deceiver than I could imagine. However inscrutably silent she could be when I tried to get her to tell me what was wrong, she was equally bad at hiding her moods. But the thought that she had a secret life in addition to the life we shared seemed not only threatening, it fascinated me because it threw shadows where I had believed for years that everything was open and unconcealed.

As a rule I went away several times a year in connection with my work; in reality she had had ample opportunity to start an adventure or two. Perhaps her impetuous joy in our reunions, when we made love as passionately as in the first years, had more than once been a kind of compensation. Perhaps her renewed desire had been equally made up of smoke screen and bad conscience. I tried to imagine her in bed with another man. I saw her flushed, inflamed face turning from side to side and a strange body on top of her, locked between her knees. I could even see the strange room. Many years ago, soon after we had moved in together, she said that if I was ever unfaithful to her she would ask me to see that it was not in our bed, and I was sure that she would keep this rule herself, but as I said, I have never suspected that the occasion had arisen. I pictured her lying in an unknown room, I invented the furniture, the pictures on the wall and the view through the closed blinds onto a street in another part of town, but I could not imagine the strange man's features, and suddenly I realized that this exercise in jealousy was a blind alley, a trap. In any case our life together had surely lasted too long for a chance affair to be able to shake it, nor had she probably ever seriously thought she would sleep with anyone but me. The idea seemed absurd, and if she really had had an affair it was none of my business as long as it did not change anything between us. But it was just that which had disturbed me in the bathroom the day before, it was that uneasiness which had grown in the dark bedroom and in the doorway only a few hours earlier when she regarded me silently before picking up her suitcase. The growing sense that her sudden inexplicable journey, secret lover or no, affected the whole of our life.

I put my dirty cup into the dishwasher and went into my study, telling myself that I must try to live with my unanswered questions, to teach myself to live with uncertainty, at least for the time being, without filling the gaps in my knowledge with lurid fantasies. It was bound to be quite a while. That was all I knew, all she had said. Now that weeks have passed with no word from her, I no longer take her words as a warning, but rather an attempt to reassure me. She must have known what she was about to do when she said it, and perhaps she only said it so that I wouldn't lose my head and report her missing to the police. What is she doing? How can I comprehend the extent of my uncertainty? I leafed desultorily through my notes and followed the ducks' wedge-shaped tracks on the shining surface of the water or the running figures disappearing and reappearing between the dark tree trunks along the shore. I suddenly felt I had nothing more to say about Cézanne. After all, others had probably said what there was to say about him without my assistance. I had planned to finish writing the article and deliver it before going to New York, but I was supposed to leave in less than a week, and I had not even got halfway. The trip had been planned for several weeks. I have written a number of essays in recent years on American painters, and among other things there was a retrospective exhibition of Edward Hopper at the Whitney Museum which I absolutely had to see. Now I was not at all sure whether I should go. Astrid's sudden departure had paralyzed me. I could not think of anything but her mysterious decision and the equally mysterious resolve on her face as she stood looking at me in the bedroom doorway. I felt seen through as I stood there, sleepy and speechless in my creased pajamas, but I had no idea what she saw with that gaze that penetrated through me, itself impenetrable and impossible to interpret. I felt her eyes strike a core deep inside, how in a few seconds they lit up a place I myself did not know, whether it was because it had remained in darkness far too long or because at that moment she knew me better than I have ever known myself. I still have not found words that could open that glance for me, it was a look that came from the other side of words, and already when she was on her way down the stairs, already while I stood listening to her footsteps, I realized I would keep returning to those moments when we faced each other silently on the threshold of the room where we have slept beside each other for so many years. But I also knew she would not come hurrying back just because I was home keeping watch in her absence. It was all the same whether I walked around in circles in the apartment or in Manhattan, her gaze in the doorway would follow me everywhere.

I tried to pull myself together, and to concentrate on Cézanne. My rough improvised notes suddenly seemed vain and futile. One was an observation I had made several years earlier. I had never really known what to do with it because it introduced a distracting element of psychology into a purely aesthetic meditation on Cézanne's method. The note referred to one of his pictures of bathing women, who in fact are not bathing at all, but have come out of the river and stand or lie on the grass, naked, voluptuous and completely at ease, at rest in their sensual weight, as they yield to the observer's gaze as it shifts among their bodies and the branches and foliage of the surrounding trees, so that skin, bark, leaves, water, and reflections form part of the same flow of color, the same round of contrasts and gradations around the clearing, through which there is a clear view, behind the women in the foreground, of the river and the far bank. And right in the center of the picture, on the other side of the river, Cézanne has placed two small indistinct figures, almost invisible in the misty remoteness of color, a man standing on the riverbank with his dog beside him. He is too far away to have a face, but it is impossible to miss him, looking over at the opposite side, facing the spectator across the span of the river, and naturally it is the women he has caught sight of, it is their undisturbed nakedness he is spying on in the company of his dog. The indistinct little male person reflects the observer's gaze in the perspective plane, so that someone standing in the silence of the museum for a moment feels a vague, inexplicable shame, as if his gaze, which travels around in the abstract separation of colors, without distinguishing between flesh and plants, as if this passive and dispassionate gaze were also a hand furtively brushing the breasts and thighs of the unsuspecting women.

When I heard the telephone I was sure it was Astrid, but it was Rosa calling to ask what time they should come. I had completely forgotten that the previous week we had invited her and her boyfriend to dinner. She sounded so well brought up, like a proper dinner guest rather than the demanding, impatient child I had fed with yogurt, then frankfurters and inventive Indonesian dishes. I tried to write a page or two about Cézanne's discreet voyeur while thinking, between sentences, of how I would explain Astrid's absence. But she had thought of that, I saw, when during the main course Rosa narrowed her eyes teasingly and said that now she was probably up in the

Swedish Skerries with Gunilla, pulling me to pieces as deftly as the crayfish they were sure to be having for dinner. Rosa's eyes have always been narrow and teasing like her mother's, and the corners of her mouth curl just like Astrid's in a very sensual and sometimes almost spiteful way when she smiles, which she did when she saw my sheepish expression. I apologized for not serving crayfish as a starter, which merely made her laugh and stroke my cheek in a tolerant, comforting gesture. Gunilla is a lesbian child psychiatrist from Stockholm with dyed hair, almost copper-colored, and I have never really taken to her and her voluminous silk-screened dresses and her holistic Skerries Island with its outhouse and oil lamps and lumps of amber as big as cobblestones, even though she has known Astrid since she was married to Simon's father, or perhaps precisely because of that. When Rosa and her boyfriend had left I looked up Gunilla's number in Stockholm. Maybe Astrid really had gone up there to stay with her old friend, whom she knew I couldn't stand, maybe that was why she hadn't told me where she was going. I could not decide whether the thought was reassuring, and I was actually relieved when I heard how surprised Gunilla sounded on the phone. I even felt a touch of malicious pleasure. It was obvious she didn't know Astrid had gone away, although they called each other at least twice a week and never talked for less than an hour.

Rosa's new boyfriend must be at least five years older than she is. He was fairly silent during dinner. We had met only once before, but I still wasn't sure that his silence and abrupt minimal sentences were due to shyness and not to an abysmal contempt. He was one of those shaven-headed young men in black who, like some gang of renovators, has undertaken to

speed up the Fall of the West so we can get rid of all the out-
dated civilized shit. In him the dislike of culture had obviously
developed into a dislike of everything, with the possible sole
exception of Rosa; now and then he caressed her neck in what
resembled a stranglehold, while fixing me with his small gim-
let eyes. But as far as I could judge, not only my daughter but
also my gazpacho seemed to meet with his approval. Before we
ate Rosa had shown him around the apartment, she had even
dragged him breezily into my study, with the nonchalance
of a cherished daughter heedless of territorial limits, but he
chuckled ironically at my series of Giacometti etchings and
the open monographs on Cézanne on my table. Rosa had told
me he was an artist, and I hadn't known whether to be glad or
concerned about the enthusiastic glow in her eyes. As far as I
could gather he worked mostly on installations, and was the
man behind an exhibition that has aroused some interest on
account of its preserved human embryos embedded in ma-
genta plastic and flanked by a wall of video monitors on which
a German porn film with prepubescent Thai girls played in
slow motion. While Rosa helped me fill the dishwasher she re-
proached me for not having welcomed him more warmly, and
told me in wounded tones that he had read my essay on Jackson Pollock and had been looking forward to discussing it
with me. Before I could defend myself the phone rang, and she
went in to the installation artist, who in the meantime had in-
stalled himself in the living room. I could hear them kissing
in there, and the hallway to the kitchen is not exactly short.
Then they were drowned out by my mother's hectic stream of
words.

My mother is what is usually known as an exuberant
woman. Everything about her is luxuriant, almost tropical.

She asked if she could speak to my charming wife. She says that every time, she never tires of saying it, she has said it for eighteen years. I said Astrid had gone up to see her friend in Stockholm. She asked if all was not quiet on the western front. She uses expressions like that all the time, and I've often wondered whether she could have sounded so affected and false when she was young. She still surprises me, after so many years' acquaintance, not only with her unusually well developed sense of smell where "smoke in the kitchen," as she puts it, is concerned, but also with the intimidating lack of decency with which she oversteps all my boundaries and with an ingratiating "Hel-looo" thrusts her head past the door of my innermost sanctum. I'm sure I would have put her inquisitiveness to a hard test if I had invited her to camp out at the foot of our bed. Improbable though it may be, Astrid thinks she is sweet, and she still laughs at the flood of postcards and letters her tireless mother-in-law sends us when she is on tour in the provinces. Her need to communicate is insatiable, and she doesn't stop until she has used up the entire stock of notepaper in her hotel room. Naturally, her letters are always about herself and the present state of her personality in the midst of a cataclysm of development that makes her see everything in an entirely new light. This happens at least every other month. She is an actor and although she became too old to play Ophelia or Miss Julie a generation ago, she has never stopped acting the part of the skittish kitten she must once have been. She was calling to remind us of the premiere she had already invited us to seven times, of a play a young dramatist had written specially for her. She was hoping to see us both. Her tone was unmistakable, she saw through the situation, and I caught myself wishing she would tell me what she saw, but she had already thrown herself into a long, drawn-out account of the "friend of her heart" as she called him, a somewhat decrepit opera director with prostate trouble and a silk scarf around his neck. It has always amazed me that Astrid can stand her, that she will put up with being my "charming wife," but she just smiles tolerantly as if it was not her at all who was being described that way. On the whole Astrid is very forbearing, she just smiles away at fatuous remarks while she thinks her own thoughts.

As usual my ear was hot and swollen when I finally put down the receiver. Rosa and her installation artist left soon after. I would have liked to continue our conversation, it had been too long since we had been together. As she had gradually emerged a graceful young woman from her childhood gawkiness she too had pulled back from our old intimacy. She used to question me about everything, and I replied to everything she asked. I would talk on and on long before she herself could talk clearly or understand what I said, but from the time she was ten she was the one who talked, who stubbornly, permitting no interruption, told me about the world she saw and appropriated, as if she had to repeat her growing knowledge of it so as not to forget anything. We might still sit whispering together in a corner, but more and more often I noticed how my questions were left alone on the threshold of a new unknown room to which I had no access, and I thought of my mother, of her overbearing lack of restraint, and kept quiet. If I tried to teach Rosa about the pitfalls of adult life, she merely smiled patiently until I had finished. I had to content myself with observing her from a distance, secretly moved, both happy and sad at the sight of her arrogant but vulnerable beauty, which no one had yet had the opportunity to mar. Sometimes

I scarcely recognized her, when I saw her chatting and laughing with her friends, unaware that I was watching, and if she
suddenly looked up and smiled at me with those eyes and that
mouth, which were both Astrid's and her own, I was forced to
admit I knew less and less about what went on behind her
green gaze. It reminded me of what one of my older friends
had said when his children left home: that children know their
parents better than parents know their children.

I walked aimlessly around the apartment when I was alone
again. I couldn't decide if it seemed larger or smaller to me
than usual. I cleared the table and tidied up, but that was soon
done and it was quiet again. It was not our mutual silence
though, Astrid's and mine, which one of us could break at any
moment. It was a constricting silence that enclosed me after
every sound I made, after every car that passed along the Lakes.
I thought of reading but got no further than the thought. Instead I put on a record, one of my old John Coltrane records
that Astrid can't bear, but neither Coltrane's waterfall of notes
nor McCoy Tyner's thunderous chords seemed anything but
the crackling, slightly hollow, mechanical echo of an afternoon
in a sound studio in Manhattan far too many years earlier. I
did not know what to do with myself on that first evening of
Astrid's absence. I paced the apartment, listening to my own
steps and the creak of the floorboards. At one point I stood in
the hall with my coat on, I would go for a walk, have a glass or
two somewhere, escape the silence in the apartment and the
feeling of hemming myself in. Then I discovered I had left behind my cigarettes, and in the hallway on the way to the kitchen
it occurred to me that Astrid might call. I wasn't going anywhere. I sat on the sofa and edited my own meaningless film,
channel-surfing between panel discussions, golf tournaments,

car races, and tropical animals. Then I resumed my pacing, leaving the television on so as not to be the only person moving and making sounds amid the immovable stillness of objects and furniture. For the first time in eighteen years I did not know more or less when she would come home, or if. Of course we had quarreled like everyone else, but usually over trifles, and never for long. We had never gone to bed without making up. We had never, for more than an hour at a time, allowed the apartment to be the scene of one of those theatrical marital tableaux in which one person stands with her back to the window while the other sits in the foreground pretending to read a newspaper. Through all our years as a family, and even now, when the children were drawing away from home every day, we had moved in a sometimes harried, sometimes tranquil, but always flexible choreography of meetings and partings and meetings again. The hectic mornings when we sent the children to school, the busy evenings when we cooked, had all been more or less elegant repetitions with imperceptible variations of the same ballet, in which we moved with an intuitive knowledge of each other's movement patterns. Even after we were alone together more and more we would still anticipate each other's movements and compensate for each other's lapses, whether an electric lightbulb needed to be changed or a cup caught before it fell to the floor. We knew each other's bodies inside out, knew how to fall into one rhythm when we walked along the street or went to bed together. Even in our sleep we adjusted to each other's bent knees and elbows.

I looked around at our furniture and possessions, most of which she had found. It was she who had decided on the decor, with her unpredictable but sure taste. I have often been surprised by a lamp, a teapot, or a vase she brought home, but even her most eccentric discoveries soon inevitably became logical additions to our universe of intimate objects. The furnishings in the apartment did not merely decorate the frame of our life together, they are also traces of her whims and caprices, as characteristic of her as her drawling, crisp voice or the eager, still girlish way she walks on her long legs. Each thing in the room was in its accustomed place, but when I looked at the objects it was as if they repelled my intimate gaze. The dark red carpet we had once bought in Istanbul was suddenly any old carpet, the Japanese woodcut views of Mount Fuji at the end of an ice blue sea were no longer the familiar landscape of my daydreams but meaningless glimpses of a hostile foreign world, and the honey-colored mahogany bureau Astrid had inherited from her aunt seemed to me hideous, although its contours and the polished wood's age markings were as unalterably engraved in my memory as Astrid's mouth and eyes. There was nothing in the room to indicate that she would not come through the door any moment and sit down on the sofa with a newspaper. And I knew exactly how she would sit, in which corner, with her legs pulled up under her, erect and with her head slightly tilted while she read and thoughtfully stroked her neck with the palm of her hand. I lingered in the bedroom doorway in the same place where she had stood that morning. My duvet lay in a twisted bundle beside hers, smooth and long and airy. My pillow was crushed up against the wall, hers was plumped, full and without a fold, without the hollow her head used to leave. She had taken the time to make up her half of the bed, as if wanting to obliterate any traces of herself before she dressed and positioned herself in the doorway to observe my unsuspecting sleeping face. But she had forgotten to close the door to the wardrobe. She could not have taken very much with her, almost all her clothes still hung on their hangers, and the sight of her lifeless dresses and blouses struck me with sudden force, as if she were dead and all that remained of her were her clothes and her other things. The brushes on the small table below the mirror, with a few long, tangled chestnut brown hairs. The Chinese box with its black lacquer lid decorated with gilded herons over gilded rushes, where she kept her jewelry. The rows of shoes, the oldest showing the dark imprints of her heels. Although her clothes and her belongings displayed all the whims of her personal taste, now that she had left them behind they seemed strangely anonymous, and mute. They had so little to say in her absence. The more I had come to know about her, I thought, the better I knew her, although the opposite might well have been the case. For all I knew, there might well be even more to know. A bottomless thought. I couldn't remember when I had stopped imagining her secret, hidden sides, when I had grown used to her as she was with the children and me. I could not know whether she kept any secrets from me or had ever done so, or whether her hidden sides had been hidden from herself as well. Perhaps she had even become what I thought she was.

For the first time in ages I took out the thick album in which I had stuck the pictures of our life. The oldest have faded and their colors have blurred. Astrid breast-feeding a plump-cheeked Rosa. Rosa's chubby waddling body on the seashore one summer. Simon angling, with a cod in his arms almost as big as himself. Astrid in fur cap, posing with the children beside a lopsided and melancholy snowman. Astrid before a golden, tree-covered valley in Trás-os-Montes that autumn seven years ago, and by the ferry rail in the middle of the Tagus in the afternoon sun, her white teeth and windswept hair and flashing sunglasses, and behind her the dazzling facades of Alfama and Bairro Alto rearing up. I am seldom in the pictures, I took most of them myself, and it has struck me more than once that in a way it was my own absence I was photographing, as when I was in an airplane imagining what they might be doing at home. Rosa on the lawn by the sea, naked in the sun with a pudgy stomach and wild, wide eyes as she sticks a finger over the hose so the water refracts the light around her in a brilliant rainbow fan like the outspread tail feathers of a peacock. Simon with his cheek against the floorboards, lost in contemplation of the trafficated microcosm of his toy cars, like a gentle and lonely Gulliver daydreaming that there was room for him on their small empty front seats. It went by so fast, the children's growing up, as if our lives couldn't progress fast enough, and even the pictures can't stop time. On the contrary, they show how long it is since Simon played with cars and Rosa sprayed the hose. I am glad I took those pictures though, even if I often felt a bit clumsy squatting down with the camera. I felt like an intruder on their unselfconscious concentration or spontaneous delight, which I wanted to preserve. I don't know which of the pictures make me feel most wistful, those where the children don't realize they are being snapped, as if they were alone, or those where they laugh and look into the camera, completely present as they meet my gaze. In one kind of picture I don't seem to be there at all, in the other it is certainly not me they smile at, but the stupid camera I hide behind. Sometimes I think you take photographs instead of seeing, you forget to look in your eagerness to grasp what is seen, to capture it in time's flight. You are absent from your own pictures, not only because you took them yourself, but also because you betray the moments you want to save from oblivion. Before you get the picture in focus it has already become a different image, a different moment. Astrid hardly ever took photos, she left it to me, she even encouraged me to take them, and each time I did I had the feeling of being outside. She is totally present in them, at one with the moment I plucked out of time's blind growth and stuck into the album like the flowers Rosa pressed and stuck into an exercise book. Withered fragments of our life, where she buries Rosa in sand so only her little grinning head sticks up, or paints lines on Simon's face that Shrovetide carnival time when he was an Indian, while I spy on them through the lens, at a distance, like a doting detective in love.

One picture shows Astrid standing alone on the balcony early one summer morning, when the facade is still in shadow. She leans against the wall, which meets the row of trees beneath her at the vanishing point. She looks away, I don't know what at, as if hesitating between two seconds, between one thought and the next. A composed musing, perhaps on the years that have followed one another so rapidly, on the way her life has taken shape, as if it had happened in a moment when she was pondering as now, absorbed in following a bird's flight, the changing shape of a cloud, the wind's creased track on the bright trembling membrane of the lake or the way the leaves of the trees turn their shining and then their dull side to the wind and the light. If it was disappointment she felt, she could not have said over what, yet even so her happiness seems to her in a vague and indefinable way to be a betrayal. Even though she cannot decide, and anyway has not yet tried to decide, whether it is life that has betrayed her, or the other way around. Life: Can you speak of it this way? Can you talk about anything but the life that is hers? This life, which cannot be

thought of without the other lives, those of the boy, the girl,
and the man. Just as they too, as the years pass, cannot be
thought of differently, the way the years allow her to see them
or allow her to see herself in the mirror when she is alone.
They are hers, and she is theirs. Has chance or destiny shaped
it this way? When was one thing succeeded by another?
When did she stop distinguishing? When did it suddenly become too easy and too difficult, too all-encompassing and actually useless to ask if she really loves the man looking at her
through the camera's little aperture? As when the youngest
child asks where space ends.

I sat by the window looking onto the lake without lighting the lamp above my desk. The treetops, the mirror of the
water, and the row of houses on the other side merged in
the darkness. Only the lighted windows were visible between
the trees, like an elongated, uneven yellow mosaic. Here and
there a stone in the mosaic was missing, elsewhere the stones
looked as if they had been broken, because a dark ramification
of branches in the foreground splintered the distant square of
light. The lighted windows were dimly reflected in the black
water, and the ripples on the surface made the reflections
tremble. As I looked across the lake from my chair at the rows
of luminous windows, it seemed for a moment unimaginable
that behind the dark dolls' house facades strangers were living
out their lives. Perhaps some of them were watching the same
film on television, perhaps some lifted their coffee cups at the
same time, perhaps more than one stood just this moment at
the kitchen sink, watching the soapy water shine violet on a
plate in the light of the lamp above the sink, all in a slightly
displaced synchronicity of trivial everyday movements. How
many of them were thinking that their little world of repeti-

tions and changes, of trivialities and tragedies and sudden felicity, was merely one world among many in the great mosaic? Did someone on the other side also perhaps sit behind a window looking across the lake, thinking the same thought I did? Were there two of us thinking about all those windows, and doors, all those views and possibilities opening and closing on each other? Many years before, soon after I had moved into town, just starting out in the world, I would cycle around in the evening, along the Lakes sometimes, and think there would surely be enough doors for me to enter. I had cycled along the water, beneath the trees, passing door after door, longing to find a door, just the right door that would open onto something I could not yet imagine.

She has rented a car in Paris, somewhere on Avenue Foch. Then driven south. I have our bank statement, I can see where she has used her card. She reached Bordeaux late in the afternoon and registered at a hotel there. She drove along the river, in the stream of late-day traffic in front of the sooty facades. While I sat at dinner with Rosa and her boyfriend, she sat in a restaurant in Bordeaux, observing the other guests and vaguely listening to their conversation, a woman traveling alone. She followed our old route south through Les Landes, down through the endless pine forests in the drizzle to the Spanish frontier. The hours linked in a long tunnel of gray, misty light as she sat behind the wheel, unmoving and yet in motion, in a car among other cars in the branched delta of the highway. Perhaps she was conscious of leaving a trail every time she used her card at another gas station and various places en route. A trail of names she must have known I would recognize, even as I recognized their order. It was the same journey, the same time of year, when Europe fades to a palette of gold

and red brown and dusty green along the roads, and the suburbs, factories, power stations, and highway loops dissolve in
the rainy mist among the moving chains of car lights. Perhaps
it was even a delayed message she sent me through the list of
places, a reminder of something she wanted me to remember.
In San Sebastian she went into a bar at La Concha. I can only
imagine San Sebastian in the drizzle, the colonnade beneath the
row of hotels looking out on the little bay with its corn yellow
sand and the green water and rocking trawlers farther out, pal-
ing into transparency in the Biscay fog. I imagine her standing
in a noisy bar sipping *café cortado* while by turns she watched
the passing umbrellas on the promenade beside the sea and
the shaky, gritty, and somehow corroded image on the television screen above the bar, of a remote, incomprehensible war
between bearded militia in ragged uniforms, driven by an unimaginable hatred, an unimaginable desire to cut someone's
throat or get one's own throat cut in the Caucasian mud. The
same images I myself watched those autumn evenings, alone
in front of the screen in the apartment beside the Lakes and
later in the hotel room on Lexington Avenue, alone with the
numbed feeling that time withdraws from us and divides us in
the same movement, unaware of its own face while devouring
its children.

 We walked between the columns beneath the promenade
and over the wet sand. Even at this time of year there were a
few late bathers. Their freezing, glistening limbs resembled
stray summer memories when they ran across the sand, stooping and hugging themselves. Astrid jumped away from the
tongues of foam that reached after her on the beach, she
laughed euphorically after the long hours in the car, her hair
curly in the damp air, her cheeks cool and sticky with salt. I
told her that *concha* means both conch shell and cunt, and she

laughed again and pushed me away, so the foam from the
waves washed over my shoes. It wasn't that we felt young
again, as they say, it was not a reawakening of our once unin-
hibited playfulness. We were still the same people we had been
all along, while everything happened to us at breakneck speed.
Rosa was eleven and Simon was sixteen, and as I said it was
the first time we had been away for more than a week without
them. We were apparently the same, and yet we regarded each
other with curious, searching, and slightly anxious eyes. We
were still young, but we knew it wouldn't last much longer.
We made love in the afternoon in hotel rooms, which we had
not done in several years. We were in motion all the time from
one place to another, and with each town we stayed in on our
way south we grew a little more alone together, left to one another. I lay with my head in her lap, feeling her stomach rise
and sink with her breathing, I listened to the rain pattering
on the shutters onto La Concha, and she cradled me softly
against her thighs and asked if I could hear the sea. There
were other things she might have asked, but she didn't. I had
come back from New York a couple of weeks before we went
away, it had been my idea for us to go, I suggested it as soon
as we got into the car when she met me at the airport. She
smiled in surprise, considering the idea. For the first time the
children were not between us, conducting our love, and we
swayed slightly in each other's sudden undisturbed presence.
We felt our way forward, I did anyway, while I tried to deci-
pher, in the hotels and in the car en route, whether we were
still the people I hoped we were. We continued along the Bay
of Biscay between the sea and the mountains, without stopping, as if somehow we were in a hurry. We stopped only to
eat and sleep, Bilbao and Santander were nothing but names in
the rain.

2

I drove a taxi in the evenings the winter I was finishing my degree. I was twenty-seven. I drove all over the town, in every direction, wherever people wanted to go, or wherever the cool, slightly impatient women's voices over the car radio told me someone was waiting. To my customers their trip in the car was merely a necessary interim between what they had just left and what they were approaching on this particular evening of their life. To me the rides were a chance web of routes through the city as I took my passengers to their destinations. Disjointed insignificant moments of transition in their ongoing stories of which I caught a glimpse listening to the conversations in the back seat, trying to guess whether I had a pusher in the car, a married couple on a silver anniversary trip, or a businessman on the way to his regular appointment with a leather-clad mistress. Thus I spent my evenings crisscrossing among unknown, ever-new stories, endlessly in motion and yet unmoving behind the wheel, in going from one end of town to the other. One evening in January I was dispatched to an address in one of the northern suburbs. I waited at the curb until a tall slim woman came out of the house with a small boy in one hand and a large bag in the other. She looked about my age, in her late twenties. A man in shirtsleeves came running after them just as they were getting in. He kept repeating that she mustn't go, that she wasn't going anywhere, although obviously she was doing just that. His hair was rather long and grizzled, he looked at least twenty-five years older than her, and he clearly would be considered a good-looking guy when his face was not contorted into a grimace both menacing and pathetic. He tried to grab her by the arm, but she lashed out at him so he had to step back. She slammed the car door and called out to me to start driving. The boy began to cry and kept on while she talked to him quietly and calmly, I could see him in the rearview mirror, huddled in the corner hugging a large teddy bear, hiccuping as he wept. She gave me the name of a street downtown and started humming to him. Gradually he calmed down. She kept on humming the same tune, and I glimpsed her in the mirror, bent over the boy, when the light from a street lamp passed over her pale cheeks and narrow, flashing eyes.

When we arrived and I switched off the meter the graying man was standing on the sidewalk waiting for us, still in shirt-sleeves and with the same pathetic yet frightening expression. I was annoyed not to have anticipated the shortcut he had taken to get there before us, since I thought I knew the town so well. He must have driven like a maniac. He took hold of the door handle, but she had locked it, and he had to speak to her through the closed window, more calmly now, almost inti-mately, looking in at her with a somber, damp gaze. He turned around abruptly when a young woman came out on to the steps. She wore only a T-shirt and hugged herself in the cold, looking in alarm at the man, who pointed at her and shouted something I couldn't hear. The boy started crying again. My passenger rolled down her window and shouted to the woman that she would call later, then asked me to drive on. The woman took a step toward us on the sidewalk, but the man grabbed her arm and I started the car. They stood gazing after us, and he loosened his grip on her arm as they disappeared from the rearview mirror. I asked where we were going now. She didn't reply, she was trying to get the trembling boy to calm down. After a block or two we stopped at a red light and I asked again. Irritably she told me to just drive. I followed the traffic, improvising as I did when I had no customers in the cab, and listening to her reassuring whispers and humming. It occurred to me that we might spend the whole night like this, driving around the city, unless she thought of something soon, and I glanced at the pulsing digits on the meter. By the time we had passed the town hall plaza for the fourth time the boy was asleep and she had clocked up almost five hundred kroner.

I took the road along the harbor and switched off the meter shortly before the Hovercraft jetty. I pulled over to the side and turned toward her. What had she decided to do? She sat with the sleeping boy's head in her lap, looking out at the sea. She didn't know. Her voice was faint and cracked. I turned and studied the crowds of passengers coming out of the Hovercraft terminal, thronging the pavement. When the last passenger had gone and the waiting room was empty in the hard neon light, I turned again and asked if she had no place to go. She sat bent over so her dark hair hid her face. When she raised her head her cheeks were streaked with tears, but no sound came from her. I found a roll of paper towels that I used for wiping the windshield, and while she blew her nose I suggested a cheap but decent hotel I knew. She crumpled the paper and smiled, almost scornfully. She didn't even have enough money for the fare. What about her friend? He must have left by now. I was surprised to hear myself utter the words "friend" and "he" so naturally, as if I were quite familiar

with the situation. She said he would spend the whole night
outside her door, if need be. But was there no one else she
could stay with? I offered her a cigarette and lit myself one.
There wasn't. I studied her profile in the mirror as she sat
blowing smoke out the window, gazing out at the reflections
on the black water of the harbor, lost in herself. She seemed to
have completely forgotten where she was. I asked if he was her
husband. She looked at me coldly in the mirror. What business
was it of mine? I shrugged my shoulders and looked away. I
don't know whether I had the idea because I could not picture
sitting like that beside a quay with a strange girl and her son
while evening turned into night. At first she looked at me as if
I had suggested something depraved, and I smiled as normally
and trustworthily as I could as I explained that I drove all
night and didn't get home until well into the morning. She
would surely find somewhere to go tomorrow, but she could
have some peace until then. Her eyes narrowed even further
and stared at me for a long time, surprised and wary. It was as
if she was only now seeing me, as if she was sizing up who I
might be, this strange taxi driver so intent on rescuing her
from the mess she had got herself in. Finally she managed a
smile, suddenly quite shy, though not exactly grateful. I avoided
her eyes in the rear mirror as we drove through town one
more time. I carried the boy up and laid him on my bed, he
didn't really wake up, just mumbled a little before curling up
and going back to sleep. There were only two rooms in my
apartment, she was in the other one looking at the books on
my shelf. I gave her an extra set of keys and told her she could
slip them through the mail slot when they left. I felt a sudden
urge to get away, perhaps I was slightly alarmed by my own
impulsiveness. Looking at her as she stood there I realized she

must be rather beautiful when she was not so pale and red-eyed from weeping. She smiled again and asked my name. That was how I met Astrid.

I drove all night until there began to be long gaps between fares, and then I went on for another hour, annoyed at myself for handing over my bed to a strange girl and her child. When I got home I fell asleep the moment I lay down on the sofa. I woke when the sky had appeared behind the rooftops across the street. For some minutes I stayed there not knowing whether to get up, feeling like a guest in my own home. Then I crept over and opened the bedroom door a crack; the bed was empty. I undressed and slept all morning, as I usually did. If someone had told me that she was the one I would live with, this stranger whom I had rescued from an embarrassing and dangerous situation the night before, I would have smiled, as you smile at your friends' most grotesque or extravagant notions, with an indulgent and slightly distracted air, stubbing out your cigarette in the overflowing ashtray among the puddles of beer on the bar counter. But who would have told me that? The future was still far-off and indistinct, something you could at most talk wildly about, like discussing where you might go next summer. When I woke up I could barely recall what she looked like. Of course I was old enough to know how randomly people meet, but I was still too young to realize that the number of meetings is not infinite. When a beautiful unknown woman returns my gaze on the street I can still play with the idea that life is like a tree branching with possibilities and alternate paths, but it is only an idea. For I know full well that trees don't grow in the sky, as they say, and you can't move in one direction without cutting yourself off from the others.

When I met Astrid I was not yet old enough to have accumulated a history. I could still get dizzy thinking of the profusion of girls' faces in the city and the vague outlines the future might hold, but it was not a blissful dizziness, it sickened me. The seductive blinking of the casino of coincidences left me with a feeling of homelessness and aversion. I had already grown tired of nights standing swaying among warm, intoxicated bodies to pulsating noise and flashing lights, where it didn't matter who I was. Of bending over yet another strange girl between songs as she hoarsely confided her travel plans and mundane prospects for the future, until the music's punching beat parted us again, as if an angry child somewhere below us were jerking at his jumping jack. If she woke up in my bed it was only another nocturnal impulse, and I could barely remember the mirages my desire had projected onto her blank young face. When she looked around in groggy surprise I couldn't guess what she saw, not even on my face, if she could be bothered trying to interpret it from the scraps I'd confided to her. She was so alien herself, as I drew her close, rather conventionally, since after all she was there, warm with sleep, and I thought about how close one can be and yet know nothing. I looked at her naked body, oblivious to whether she was beautiful, completely preoccupied by its blind particularities, the shape of her breasts, the scars and birthmarks on her skin. Another body with its bundle of genes that a glazier or a clerk and his wife from out in the suburbs had passed on to the precious princess of this night. I stroked the hair back from her unknown face, made a show of examining her features, and she snuggled at my side and caressed me absently. A touch without content, like an imaginary language of words that meant nothing, just another sweet and absentminded little slide through eternity.

I awoke about noon with my back feeling strangely cold and clammy. The boy had peed in my bed, beside himself because of his parents' marital drama in the night. And now Simon's riding his Kawasaki, doubtless without a helmet, as Sardinia's rocks and cork oaks and flocks of sheep sweep past him, and it would never occur to him to call home, that boy I grew used to calling my son so many years ago. The dark wet spot on the sheet was the only visible trace he and his mother had left behind, but it seemed she had kept my keys. I tore off the sheets, and as I carried them into the bathroom I breathed the smell of boy's urine and the scent of her perfume. So she had taken the time to splash some on before she left the gray-haired man. If, as I unobtrusively passed her the keys the night before, there had been a moment when I thought she was actually the kind of girl I would have looked at on the street, the moment soon passed. I was still far too absorbed in my own private pain. As I lifted the mattress, between the slats of the bed I caught sight of the charcoal drawing that used to hang fastened with a thumbtack above the headboard. It must have fallen on the floor during the night, that rough sketch of a bird's skull which Inés had once given me, long before I stood at the window for the last time and watched her go down the sidewalk until I couldn't see her anymore in the snowflakes whirling upward in confused spirals. I saw her again a year or two ago, one evening as I was leaving a cinema with Astrid. We nodded and smiled through the crowd, Astrid asked who she was and I replied it was someone I had known before we met. True, in fact. Of course I'd told Astrid about her, back when we had still not finished telling each other our histories. But I didn't tell her that the woman in the cinema lobby was the Inés she had heard me speak of, a bit summarily and re-motely, as one speaks of the women one knew before the woman who is listening to one's story. I don't really know why. Was I afraid that somewhere inside me she still hid, that the image of Inés after I saw her again by chance would reemerge and make me suffer or dream in secret? She still looked beautiful and dramatic and Middle Eastern, but when I turned to Astrid to answer her curious if not at all inquisitorial question, I felt nothing of the pain I had once suffered. Inés was just a woman I had once loved, and in the meantime I had dreamed other dreams and nursed other wounds.

I picked up the sketch and searched for the thumbtack. She hadn't even finished it, my thumb had left an impression on one of the broad lines tentatively outlining the contours of the bird's skull. I rubbed finger and thumb together until the gray charcoal was gone. Eighteen months before, one hot late-summer afternoon, I had gone into the Glyptotek museum, mainly because it was cool. I thought I was the only visitor, but I noticed her in one of the small dark halls exhibiting Roman heads. Her back was to me, and she stood quite motionless, her black hair gathered into a soft casual knot on her long slim neck. At first she was only a silhouette in the distant, sun-flooded doorway opening into the last of the adjoining halls, a narrow black figure reflected in the polished stone floor. She was pale although we had had unbroken sunshine for three months. I stopped, apparently she had not heard me. She was wearing a long black dress, her bare feet were in black shoes with heavy heels and thin straps around the ankles, old-fashioned, rather somber shoes which brought to mind a slow tango in a brothel in Buenos Aires before the war. There was a honey-colored tinge to her pallor, and I knew immediately that I would touch her, that I would feel this pale and yet strangely smoldering, completely homogeneous skin with my hands and lips. She stood in front of a Roman emperor, or what was left of him, a tight-lipped face devoid of illusions, disfigured by time, balancing on an iron pole bored up through the stone, as if decapitated. His features were almost completely eroded, so that the veins and pores in the stone stood out along the fractured surfaces from which the nose and lips had disappeared. The face was like a picture which in the course of centuries had slowly faded to the anonymous eternity of the marble block. I said this or something like it to her, and she turned and looked at me with her large dark eyes, completely calm, her expression seeming to recognize me from somewhere, although we had never seen each other before.

Her face still shines through the years that followed, through the moving reflections and swirls and ripples of everything that has happened since. It shines down in the green darkness like the face on a coin that slipped from my hand, rare but not irreplaceable. Sometimes I can't see her, at other times she appears briefly among the changing reflections of the days, among other faces that I held in my hands one at a time as if they could tell me something I did not know. Her eyes have lost their terrible power to attract, turned greenish like tarnished bronze and wiped out in the current of time, but now and then she looks at me again, from a distance, with an inquiring gaze, with an ever more indistinct, incomprehensible question that year by year grows more impossible and irrelevant to answer. We left the museum together. We walked side by side in the low light, the shadows long between the hot walls, across the burning pavement of the squares, talking nonstop of everything that occurred to us, as if there were no bounds to what could be said, related, and replied to. We walked along the harbor and through the parks, we went on as if it was impossible to stop, while the last reflections of the sun dissolved in the upper windowpanes and the twilight trickled out from between the cobblestones and blades of grass and the calm folds of the water. By winding somnambulists' routes we arrived at her house on a side street, opposite the Jewish cemetery. We delayed what we both knew was merely a question of time, spoke more calmly now, with long pauses when we just looked at each other for as long as we could bear to, putting off the moment when we would have to touch each other there in her room with its view of the overgrown graves and crooked headstones with mysterious inscriptions.

There was something old-fashioned about her, about her way of speaking, and it was not only her accent. She seemed like someone from another era, as if she had come ashore from one of the great ocean-going steamships with tall funnels, long ago sunk or broken up. Her father was a French diplomat, her mother Persian, and she had remained in Copenhagen after her parents had gone on to Tehran, New Delhi, and Caracas. She told me she liked drawing, but I never learned whether it was just something she did while she was waiting for something else to happen. What else she did was never clear to me, regardless of how much I questioned her, but clearly she had never had to worry about money. Her apartment was furnished as austerely as a nun's cell and she apparently ate nothing but packaged frozen food, yet she spent a fortune on taxis, and I have never known another woman who bought so many shoes. Expensive, extravagant, crazy shoes, which she wore a few times before leaving them at the bottom of her closet. She showed me her sketches of skulls and fragments of bones. I didn't know what to say about them, about her obsession with death's gnawed leavings registered with wheeling, monomaniacally insistent lines, alternately vehement and fleeting. Her black eyes and black drawings seemed to open onto an alien darkness that I shrank from penetrating. At any second she might suddenly start and gaze at me in fear, as if I had terrified her with a sudden sound or an unexpectedly hard tone of voice. It happened often, and each time she looked literally shattered. It was one such moment that we gave in to what we had been damming up on our way through the town. Her body was long and almost lanky, her breasts were small and her feet were long and narrow with bones that protruded beneath the thin skin like the fine bones in a bird's wing. There was nothing in the least voluptuous or indolent in her figure, an insatiable hunger radiated through the avid restlessness of her hands and her mouth. Lovemaking with Inés was an unending battle, an ungovernable, merciless raging, as if she were trying to wrench us over an abyss into a free fall in empty space with her body locked around mine. It had been light for some time when we let go of each other and she suddenly asked me to leave.

It lasted just over a year. When it began to snow again the story had ended, if in fact it had ever become a story, the confused series of clenched embraces, outbursts of rage, philosophical escapades and rare moments of slow and silent gentleness. When we were not making love we mostly talked about art, chiefly older artists, Rembrandt, El Greco, Goya, and the sketches of Leonardo, his anatomical studies, which naturally appealed to her with their fearless, merciless precision. Among twentieth-century artists only Giacometti and Francis Bacon elicited her approval. She was as uninterested in modern art as she was apparently ignorant of the political realm, which surprised me considering her background. She once looked at me in sincere amazement when I mentioned

Charles de Gaulle in the past tense, she hadn't realized he was dead. I never saw her read a newspaper, and she had neither television nor radio in her apartment, only an old record player and a small eclectic selection of records including Orlando di Lasso and Gabriel Fauré, Serge Gainsbourg and Astor Piazzolla. But in spite of the huge gaps in her picture of the world I was struck over and over by her analytical perspicacity and knowledge of what interested her, whether it was Indian archaeology, Persian Sufism, or Goethe's theory of color. If I have ever succeeded in writing something about a painter that has not been said better by others, I trace it to those conversations in bed with Inés when we lay smoking, still breathless and sweating, while she philosophized her way to an unexpected point with the hair's-breadth balance between outspokenness and skepticism of the original thinker. She is one of the most cultured people I have ever known, because her education was of the kind you find only in those who have not studied but sniffed their way forward, out of pure and aimless curiosity, in antiquarian bookshops, libraries, and museums, greedily and without regard to scholastic categories.

The only thing she had no wish to turn upside down and dissect was us, what happened between us, where we were going. It was just too silly, she said, and when once in a tender, wanton moment I whispered something about having children, she laughed hoarsely at my flushed cheeks and timid eyes as she unscrewed the lid from the bottle of brandy she kept on the floor beside her bed. She went on laughing as she drank from the bottle, and I had to thump her between her fragile protruding shoulder blades so she didn't choke. When she straddled me with her back facing me to enjoy the sight of her own excitement in the mirror above the bed, her shoulder blades reminded me of the folded wings of a large bird. We would meet at my place or on the street beside the Jewish cemetery, but she insisted that I phone before I came to see her. I could call at any time, but she did not let me in if I arrived unannounced, even if there was light in her windows. She, on the other hand, might show up without warning, any time at all, always vibrating with the same suppressed ferocity that demanded to be immediately unleashed, often before we got any further than the hall. After our first meeting we went out together seldom and only at night, to bars and inns on the outskirts of town, never in the center where we risked meeting people we knew. It was Inés who wanted it that way. She wanted us to be a secret, that was how she put it, a secret from the world. I soon realized I was not the only man she was seeing. She didn't tell me about the others, but neither did she hide the fact of their existence when I finally summoned the courage to ask. She was amused at first by my jealousy and observed it with detached interest, as an anthropologist observes the strange behavior of natives. She knew I suffered, and she let me suffer, apparently without sensing that only she could bring my sufferings to an end. Later she grew tired of my questions and my glowering silences.

I was still thinking of her that morning after Astrid and Simon had stayed the night. My days were empty and idle, and she would invariably come back to me when I had nothing else to think about or do. I would remember her face and body during the lulls in my night driving, and I was in constant dread of running into her. The knowledge that we were in the same town turned it into a danger zone, in which both her absence and the risk of suddenly seeing her could produce startling jolts of physical pain, as if an unseen hand were squeezing my

lungs and stomach. That morning too I found myself several
times picking up the telephone, about to dial her number. I lay
on the sofa for hours smoking and listening to music, until the
gray winter light once more began to fade to blue. I went out
to get some air, wandered the streets aimlessly among people
on their way home with their briefcases, shopping bags, and
children, and when I stood outside my door again I could hear
Simon's little voice inside. He fell silent and pressed against
Astrid on the sofa, as if I were a stranger intruding on what in
the course of a day he had come to see as their territory. She
looked up from a comic book with a searching, uncertain smile.
Was it all right if they stayed another night? I said I supposed
it was, after all I had invited them, and really I didn't mind
being distracted from my funk. She apologized for the wet mattress, and I made light of it and said I'd wet the bed myself, you
know, until I was in high school. She laughed politely although
I hadn't said anything particularly funny. I recognized her perfume. She looked different, she had pulled her hair back into a
ponytail, and I noticed she was wearing black mascara around
her eyes, as if she was trying to make an impression. But it
probably wasn't for my sake, it was probably only the sort of
war paint women hide themselves behind when their lives are
falling apart. The black makeup gave her eyes a hard, challeng-
ing expression that was at odds with the playful, knowing way
she suddenly creased her lips into a smile, even when there was
apparently nothing to smile at. Maybe she was smiling from
embarrassment, maybe to draw me, confidentially, into her surprise at finding herself here with her little son in a strange man's
apartment, homeless and left to my unexpected hospitality.

She had been out shopping, and started cooking dinner
right away. I sat down and read to the boy, mainly because I

didn't know what else to do with myself. He looked at me suspiciously while I read the speeches in the balloons above the little blue men in white pixie hats who lived in a village with toadstools for roofs, but soon he moved closer, until finally he was leaning against me and let me put an arm around his bent little shoulders. Astrid glanced at us from the kitchen and smiled, and I looked down at the little blue men, suddenly shy, as if I couldn't acknowledge to myself what must be the touching sight of the taxi driver sitting and reading aloud to the pathetic child of divorce. The pan was bubbling and simmering, and there was already a scent of garlic and chopped basil, it was almost like playing at father, mother, and child, with myself as stand-in for the angry, gray-haired man we had run away from. It was a long time since I had cooked anything, I usually didn't eat until late at night when I drove past a takeout. I glanced at her standing there as if she were at home, as I had said she should, slightly embarrassed by the empty phrase. If you think about it, empty phrases often slip out of your mouth at the moments that turn out to be most decisive. But I didn't know that yet, I merely looked up at her between the speech balloons while I explained a word the boy did not understand. She was as tall as Inés but her hips were rounder, and her calves had a softer curve in the black tights she wore under her short skirt, as if she was going out. But strictly speaking she was out already. Everything about Astrid was different from the woman who had conformed my desire to hers. I hadn't so much as looked at anyone else since I met Inés, and now here I was stealing glances at Astrid, simply because she stood there with her back turned, chopping vegetables in my kitchen. Her movements were slower and calmer, even her voice had a lazy quality in contrast to my lost love's impatient, syncopated intensity. Astrid apparently not only had masses of time, she seemed to give herself over to the sequence of movements and their natural tempo without anything being left out. There was no urgency for her, there was a sleepwalker's inevitability in the way she dealt with things that resembled above all enjoyment, as when she let her knife-blade sink through a tomato's taut skin without using force, so that it looked as if it had opened itself to her, with its firm flesh, its moist cavities and green seeds.

While we were eating I didn't think about Inés. We talked, as strangers do, about what we did, and avoided mentioning the events of the night before, as if by unspoken agreement. I asked her about filmmaking, the same questions that everyone else doubtless put to her, and she talked about the directors she liked, Truffaut, Rohmer, and Cassavetes. I talked about abstract expressionism, about de Kooning and Jackson Pollock, and every so often Simon made us laugh with one of those penetrating short circuits only children can produce. On the whole everything flowed easily, and you wouldn't have guessed she had just left her husband or that I had recently been deserted. In the car on the way out to the airport, where I usually began the evening, I realized almost guiltily that for the first time in weeks I felt lighthearted and at ease. Only when I had crossed through the city center and passed the harbor did I notice that I had not made my usual detour along the wall of the Jewish cemetery, at a snail's pace, holding my breath. There had been nights when I had hardly any fares because I could not tear myself away from her neighborhood and kept going back there, hoping to see her. As my inquisitorial questions gradually poisoned our hours together, in a rare bout of sympathy Inés had tried to console me by saying she was not seeing any one particular man besides myself, and that she did not prefer any of her lovers over the others. From her perspective their number alone should assuage my torments and prove to me that my jealousy was both useless and out of place. The fact that there were so many of us should make each of us feel it was ourself with whom she was unfaithful to all the others. I pictured her giving herself to them one after the other in unknown rooms or in the room looking out on the graveyard that I knew so well. I could not bear to be just any man in the series of men she visited or opened her door to, and it was no consolation when she assured me that it was our differences, our assortment of bodies, faces, and histories, that fascinated her. I tried to imagine whether she was the same regardless of which of us she was with, or whether she was a different person to each of us, and I could not decide which possibility was crueler. When she straddled me on the floor, still in her coat, her ferocity was unchanged, and when she let me take her, lying passive on her bed, she wore the same distant gaze. The nights when she forbade me to come or did not answer the telephone, I haunted her street in the taxi or parked on the corner, staring uselessly at her door. I knew it was comical and humiliating, but I also knew that I could not resist the temptation to abase myself further.

It had made a difference, a decisive, all-embracing difference, our first meeting in the cool, dim hall among the battered Roman heads, when she turned and looked me in the eyes. When I went over the scene in my mind I was no longer sure whether it was she who met my glance or I who met hers, without knowing the question my eyes replied to. I knew how easy it is to catch someone's eye and then to vanish from each other's sight again, and perhaps it was in revolt against the whirl of chance meetings that I decided to love Inés. Perhaps it really was a decision, and not, as I liked to believe, that her unusual glance had torn me out of the familiar, stupefied routine of my days. Perhaps she hadn't after all seen any more, any further in, when she caught sight of me, and perhaps there was not so much to look for, perhaps I, like everyone else, was only an ever-changing reflection in the restless, foaming eddies of looks. Holding her face between my hands I tried to find that glance again, which had opened to me like a crack in which I appeared to myself, released at last, but her eyes, teasing, scornful, or preoccupied, held me in check at a distance. She eluded me when I tried to hold her fast, she slipped between my hands or pulled me to her so close that I could no longer see her clearly. Nothing that we did left a lasting trace, all my words dissolved into silence the moment they were spoken. Each afternoon, each night, was like a repetition of the same meeting, the same embrace, the same words. We were in continuous motion without going anywhere. It had no future, it was a wrong track, a track outside time, leading us astray.

But there were also times when she seemed to relent, rare moments when she let me believe I was not just another man in the string of men who passed through her life. Sometimes she stayed with me for several days. I cooked for her while she sat drawing, and when I came home in the morning she was still there. When we were satiated with lovemaking she curled up in my arms and told me disjointed stories of her rootless childhood, isolated jumbled pictures of London, Warsaw, and Cairo. One day in early spring, our only spring, it was raining as we lay in my bed leafing through a monograph on Vermeer. We listened to the rain and meditated on the quiet rooms with their soft, clear light, where Vermeer's women sat reading

letters or stood pouring milk from a clay pitcher. She said she
had never been to Amsterdam, and suddenly she smiled secretly and got out of bed. I could hear her talking on the phone
in the next room, and a little later she came in and pulled the
duvet off me. A train was leaving for Amsterdam in one hour,
she had already booked tickets. She laughed at my slow astonishment and said she was happy to pay. That was when I discovered that Inés always carried her passport around in her
pocket. She didn't even want to go home first, just to the bank
before we took a taxi to the train station. Her only luggage
was a plastic bag with the sundries she managed to buy at the
station before we boarded the train, euphoric as children on
their way to camp. I know quite well it is not so, but the way I
remember it the canals did not run in concentric circles but
in a spiral that we followed, Inés and I, as we coiled ourselves
into one of our philosophical escapades, interrupted by her
laughter among the houses with their high white-painted windows. I think we were both happy that rainy weekend in
Amsterdam. She seemed younger, which sounds silly, since she
was only in her mid-twenties, but from the beginning I had regarded her as someone much older. It was the men who made
the difference, of course, all the men she had known, but in
Amsterdam I had her to myself, and she really seemed to have
forgotten that she knew other men. As if she was on leave
from her life as the dark, dissolute, reprobate angel of love
who could make grown men howl at the moon. She even let
me put an arm around her shoulder as we walked, something
I was never permitted to do at home.

There were no curtains on the windows, in Amsterdam
you could look straight in, as if people had nothing to hide or
did not want there to be anything in their lives others must

not see, and for once I felt that was how it was with us too. She pressed close to me as we walked along the canals, and would suddenly stop and kiss me in the middle of the sidewalk. We sat in dark taverns drinking beer and smoking cigarettes, there were twenty-five in the Dutch packs, and we never tired of discussing whether that was the result of thrift or profligacy. We talked and laughed our way through the spirals of blue smoke and dark green, stagnant water, as if winding our way toward a destination that was always just out of range, but in reality we merely went in a circle. All the hotels were full and we ended up staying on an old passenger ship. Each night we lay in the narrow berth in our cabin, motionless with exhaustion from walking around all day, and I fantasized that we were far out at sea, between continents. I told her this and she smiled at me, softly indulgent, almost the way you would smile at a child, stroking my cheek with a slow, almost wistful tenderness that I could not recognize, and that made me happy and sad at the same time.

It was merely a stopping place on the way to the end, and I moved more and more headlong toward it the nearer we came. Soon she was again answering evasively or irritably when I asked where she had been or what she was going to do, and the less forthcoming she was the more I pressed her. Then I started circling her street again at night when she did not answer the phone, both hoping and fearing to catch a glimpse of her secret life. One evening I really did see her come out of her house and walk down the street, and I followed her in the car from a distance without her seeing me. It was as if I sat in the passenger seat observing myself as I spied on her, shaking my head with shame, but there was no way back. Clearly I had to abase myself completely before I could come out on the other side. She went into a twenty-four-hour kiosk and came out shortly after with a carton of milk and a bag of coffee. Deep in thought, with her eyes lowered, she walked back along her street. I had been watching her house since I left her earlier in the evening; for once I knew for certain that she was alone. All the same I parked a short distance from her entrance, far enough so that the car would not be visible from her windows. I don't know how long I sat there like a private detective, glowering stupidly at her entrance, when I suddenly saw a man stop in front of it. I could not see his face, but he looked a good deal older than me. He wore a camel-hair coat and shiny black shoes. I had not seen him coming, even though I had kept my eyes trained down the quiet side street. My concentration had put me into a kind of trance, and he must have crossed my field of vision while I was meditating on intercom buzzers or the basement shop's display of sinks, gas heaters, and faucets. Then he was let into the hall, and I barely managed to get out of the car and over to the front door before it slammed. I imagined he was a rich businessman visiting Inés while his wife was on a ski trip in Switzerland, and I pictured him pushing a wad of crisp thousand kroner notes under her pillow while she was in the bath. I could hear his steps on the stairs further up, then he stopped and a moment later a door closed. I ran up the stairs two at a time, perhaps so as not to give myself time for regret. I had already rung her bell, it was too late to turn back.

I could hear music coming from the apartment, and I recognized Astor Piazzolla's melancholy, rapt *bandoneón*, our favorite music after we had made love and were lying stretched out smoking and daydreaming to the tango's abrupt changes from sweet indulgence to murderous passion. I rang again and again before she finally opened the door, rosy with sleep, her hair loose over her kimono, which she held closed with her arms folded. What did I want? I hardly knew. I walked past her through the living room and into the bedroom. There was no one. I turned around, she stood behind me with her arms folded and her head tilted to one side and an expression of patronizing contempt. Then suddenly it all happened very fast. I grabbed her and threw her down on the bed and she let herself fall, quite limply, her arms outstretched so the kimono slid away from her naked body. She lay there as she had fallen, regarding me calmly like an observer waiting to see what would happen. She let me do what I liked, completely passive, abandoning herself to my desperate fury, and meanwhile I observed myself without emotion, disengaged from my blind, furious body. We both witnessed my degradation, as I crouched between her parted legs, nailed by her dark eyes. It must have hurt her, but her expression did not change as I penetrated her with a rage that sought to turn her inside out, as if I were punishing her for my own helplessness. She lay there lifeless, looking at the ceiling without covering herself as I zipped up my trousers and went into the next room. I sat by the window looking out at the churchyard wall in the moving violet gleam from the streetlight swinging in the wind above the empty street. I must have been sitting there a quarter of an hour when she came in wearing an elegant evening gown I had never seen her in before. Her face was pale and powdered, and she had put on lipstick and gathered her hair elaborately. She looked dazzlingly, devastatingly beautiful. She had her coat over her arm, she was going out, I offered to drive her. She shrugged her shoulders. Neither of us said anything as she sat in the back seat looking out at the streets like any

other passenger. I drove her to an address in the embassy district and followed her with my eyes as she went into a capa-
cious building with marble tiles and mahogany paneling. A
few days later she came to give me back a book of Dürer's en-
gravings that I had lent her. She kept her coat on. I said I was
sorry, she did not reply. When she left it had started to snow.
I stood at the window and watched her vanish among the
shining, whirling flakes.

Two months later I met Astrid, but there was no way I
could know I was nearing a turning point that evening when
we had eaten together for the first time and I was in the taxi
again with customers sending me in every direction through
the night. I wasn't going to meet anyone, I wasn't going anywhere. There were unexpected meetings and turning points
occurring all over the town, but to me they seemed as meaningless in their unpredictable geometry as the movements of
the balls on the billiard tables in the pubs where I sometimes
spent an hour or two when I was tired of sitting behind the
wheel. Heavy, shiny balls that collided with a little click and
were set rolling in new directions over the empty green desert
of felt, now in one direction, now in another, until one by one
they vanished down into a black hole, out of the game. I could
be anyone at all, and I might meet anyone. One meeting could
be just as decisive as another, and neither the mystery behind
a beautiful unknown face nor my own decision to solve it
would tip the scales. But perhaps I am anticipating the events
and my own interpretation of them. I probably still thought
that the story with Inés had been something special, different
from all my other stories, otherwise it would not have hurt so
much, and afterward I would have forgotten our confused, depressing affair. I still clung to my battered dreams as I sat be-

hind the wheel, sent back and forth between the suburbs and
the city center, passive and uncommunicative as a billiard ball.
She was still my great lost love, it was a sharper, more dramatic world I had found myself in when I was with Inés. There
had been moments when I felt I was no longer hiding anything, when everything in me was transparent, visible to her
gaze. But if it all had been nothing but my own delusions, it
was only logical that I had destroyed everything by pursuing
them so greedily. If the Inés I had loved was merely an image
I had held up before her unknown face, it was only a manifestation of cruel irony that I had violated the precious icon of my
passion.

I stopped eating and sleeping, I avoided other people as if
I were a leper, I sat in the car or lay on my sofa plunged in
gloom, watching the cigarette smoke curl in transient spirals
before the melancholy view from my window. It suited me to
drive at night through the deserted streets, past the facades
with lighted windows. I couldn't have endured the evenings
inside my own walls, nor did I feel like going out and risking
meeting someone I knew. It was better to be moving, circling
around the unknown worlds of other people, outside everything. In my pathetic desolation I was certain I would never
love anyone as I had loved Inés, and I was right in a way, in a
completely different way than I had imagined. With Astrid it
was a different kind of love, not so vehement and blinding. It
was gentler, slower, and I took longer to discover it. She liberated me from the hysterical melodrama that had devoured me
from within, turning me into a hollow, ludicrous vessel of unhappy love. She seduced me into betraying my own inflated,
self-consuming heart, without even knowing it herself. But I
do not think I saw it that way. At the start I did not think

about it much at all, I who had driven myself nearly crazy with thoughts in my self-chosen wounded solitude. With Astrid everything was very easy, very smooth, as if things happened on their own, in their own rhythm. Did I think about her that night, when we had said goodbye at my door as if we already lived together? Did I think of her as a sudden opening, an unexpected promise of reprieve? Or was she still only an attractive and obviously very sweet woman, who had gone off with her child and found refuge with a broken-hearted taxi driver on the night shift? I thought about Inés among the snowflakes, her dark remote expression on the bed as I raped her, raging with shame and self-hate. That night too I thought back to a summer afternoon among marble emperors or gods robbed of their arms and legs. I can see myself eighteen years younger, heading I didn't know where through the night, but I cannot repeat the small leaps, the imperceptible shift that leads from one face to another, from one story into the next.

I can't quite distinguish between what I thought then and what I think now, when I am thinking of Inés again because I am thinking of my first meeting with Astrid. The stories that events wove into the pattern I am trying to unravel became entangled and changed in the process. I'm searching for a place, a knot where I can begin to try to understand Astrid's disappearance, but I don't know whether I will succeed. I follow the strands back to find the pattern's logic, but the knots loosen between my fingers, and in the end I am left with nothing but loose ends. I knit them up again, hesitantly, because I know the story will only be one of many I could have told with the same strands. How could I know whether any one is more truthful than another? Perhaps it makes no difference which one I tell, perhaps they would all turn out to have stitches that are too loose, too slipshod and uneven to hold fast. Probably so, yet still I try, and the more I try the more I realize how little I know and how imperfectly I remember. It is sure to be unsuccessful, sure to be nothing but a fantasy of suppressions and omissions, rough approximations and vague sketches, but it is all I can do. I must discover everything afresh, knowing well that I risk covering up the pieces I might have been able to uncover as I worked. While I work my way forward, it occurs to me how much in a life remains unspoken, in shadow. How does it take shape? When did it take its decisive direction? Where could it have taken a different turn and become another quite divergent story? I stare into the darkness, but it closes around my eyes; I see something gleam briefly, but the gleam dazzles me and then immediately dies away, leaving only an indistinct fading afterimage on the retina. For it isn't there any more, it was all so long ago. Still, I go on, even though I know that the truth dwells in the pauses, in silent spaces between the words. In the end my narrative is merely an attempt to fill the gap where time has gone, hold it open, sometimes in the form of questions that cannot be answered, other times as a tentative answer to questions no one has yet asked.

It was a quiet night in town and I drove home earlier than usual. I took off my shoes in the hall and tiptoed in. She had found an extra sheet and made up the sofa, my duvet was there too, she obviously thought it was her turn to have the woolen blanket. I was quite touched. As I was brushing my teeth I heard the floorboards creak in the living room, and then she appeared in the bathroom mirror, standing in the doorway smiling apologetically. She couldn't sleep. I was not especially tired either. It struck me I must look like an oaf standing there with my mouth full of toothpaste, scrubbing away. I have never liked people to see me brushing my teeth, but of course she couldn't know that. I rinsed my mouth. She looked sweet leaning against the door frame in the sweater she had pulled over her nightgown, without makeup, her hair tousled and her narrow eyes tired. Most women are more attractive without makeup, but of course they don't believe that. Nor do they know they are most lovely when they are tired. Perhaps because they are too tired to think about their appearance or be concerned about what anyone thinks of them. I have always had a weakness for tired women. Their faces relax into the features that are theirs after all, they forget someone is looking at them, forget to take account of it, and a softness veils their gaze, as if their eyes are resting on something else, something inside themselves or far away, a different place. That was what it was like with Astrid as she stood waiting for me to finish, and slipped into a reverie over who knows what. It struck me for the first time that she was more than attractive. I suggested we finish off the half bottle of red wine from dinner. We sat in the living room without switching on the light, smoking in the dimness and the faint glow from the lamp in the hall, and I can remember thinking how unpleasant red wine tastes when you have just brushed your teeth. She spoke quietly in her brittle drawling voice, almost intimately, as if we knew each other. She told me no one knew where she was. It was a long time since she had had this feeling of being outside everything, in a secret hiding place, and at the moment, I must surely realize, at the moment it suited her rather well. I said she could stay for a few days if she liked. What would my girlfriend say about that? It surprised me that she assumed I had a girlfriend until I recalled the half-empty package of sanitary napkins Inés had left in the bathroom, which my guest had of course noticed at once. I had

left it there as a little nostalgic fetish. She must have read my
face through the half darkness and realized her mistake, for she
went on without waiting for a reply. I was surprised at her
frankness. She looked away with her tired dreamy eyes as she
spoke, and every so often she met my gaze to see the impression her words made on me, but not to appeal to my sympathy.
She merely registered me, as if watching me listen to her story
was a way of getting to know me.

She had met him when she was twenty-one and he was
forty-four, the gray-haired man who had stood shouting into
the evening cold. In the beginning she had been his mistress.
She was alone in the world. Her parents had died when she
was a child, and her only relative was an elderly aunt. He was
married and had a daughter her age. He was quite a well-
known film director, but I had not recognized him when he
was outside the taxi in flapping shirtsleeves. She had been an
assistant in the editing room on one of his films, that was how
it had started, with furtive kisses and feverish couplings in the
editing room and hotel rooms. She described how he had overwhelmed her with his insistent gaze, his assurance, his calm
deep voice. She had been fascinated by his mature desire and
by being the young woman this famous man desired. Everything was different with him, different from the other men and
boys she had played at romance with and run away from, but
still she was surprised. Talking about it now she couldn't understand why she had had a child with him and why she believed they would live together. But then she had also been
surprised, she remembered, at herself as well as at him. He had
once taken her with him to Stockholm, where he was to meet
a producer. She had lain in bed waiting for him one afternoon
at the Grand Hotel, wondering about being there. She could
remember the birds outlined in gold on the walls, blue tits and

robins and the like, with their trustworthy little heads askew,
looking down at her. She had been almost shocked at their innocence. She was the mistress of a married man. It rather
amused her to see herself in that light. A precious, awesome
secret, compelled to lie and wait among the little birds. She
had looked at her breasts in the mirror, certainly they were
pointed and industrious then, like the snouts on a pair of
Dutch clogs, and yet what could they be the answer to? She
described how she had once seen him with his wife on their
way to a film premiere. Astrid couldn't see what was wrong
with her, why she had to be replaced. Desire. The word made
her smile, and I can see her smiling the same way when she
stood at the rail of one of the small steamers in the Skerries,
dazzled by the sun's reflection on the water. While he was at
meetings she went to sea. When he came back he indulged
his desire, gray-haired and cleft-chinned, a real man, and she
yielded to him, wonderingly. Afterward she let him talk of the
future, until he got lost in it and lay crestfallen among the
twitterers at the Grand Hotel, looking at her as if waiting for
her to rescue him from drowning in his prospects. She was
frankly astonished when he came to her door with two suitcases one day, having "burned his bridges." He had obviously
meant what he said, and she yielded to him again. She forgot
her surprise and quickly became pregnant, and as she watched
the boy grow she began to believe that their future was more
than just words. The bigger he grew the more she believed it,
until the evening I met her, when she discovered by chance
that the film director's desire had found a new, sweet young secret with the future before her.

When I woke up she and Simon were gone. She had been
out to buy bread and left a thermos of coffee on the table. There

was a croissant waiting on a plate, and a napkin folded under the knife, hotel style. I wasn't in the habit of eating croissants. Unlike the previous day the apartment was full of signs of my visitors. Simon's toy soldiers were lined up along the windowsill ready to clash swords between a pile of paperbacks and the stack of telephone directories, their clothes were folded and heaped on a chair in the bedroom, there was even a dress hanging among my shirts, and on the shelf under the bathroom mirror stood an entire column of female bottles and tubes. It looked almost as if she had moved in. I continued spending the days and nights alone and saw them only in the evenings, when they came back before I had to leave. We took turns cooking and in general adjusted to each other adroitly and politely in the small apartment, and when our eyes met we couldn't help smiling at this unexpected, improvised cohabitation. I was surprised at how easy it was. Even the silence was easy, almost weightless, when we sat opposite each other like the two strangers we were, and sometimes couldn't find anything to say. She was the first person I had met with whom I could remain silent without feeling uneasy. It surprised me that she could repose so naturally in a strange man's apartment, how easily she became quiet when she had said what she wanted to say, not in the least affected by the silence between us. But we actually didn't have anything to talk about, we had nothing to do with each other, she was just a stranger staying with me. Nevertheless, my brooding was continually disturbed by Simon's chattering and her crooked smile. Now and then I could feel her watching me while I helped him fix his toys or read aloud from one of the books I had borrowed from the library for him one afternoon when I had nothing better to do. I paid no attention when I felt her inquiring gaze, and concentrated on the jolly little plastic men or the tales of animals in clothes. The boy seemed to have gotten used to me and behaved as if we had known each other for a long time. On Sunday we went to the zoo, she had asked if I would like to go with them. I hadn't been there for years and it seemed to me the shiny seals and grubby polar bears were the same as those I had seen when I was Simon's age. He was very disappointed that the bears were not whiter. As we walked on that gray day among the cages and grottoes with listless, melancholy animals, for the first time I couldn't hold the image of Inés in my mind. Hearing Astrid make Simon laugh, I wondered how she had managed to create a feeling of normality around him so quickly. How she soothed his terror over what had happened in simple little ways, by putting his drawings up on the wall or making him laugh in the middle of a crying bout by putting my tea cozy on her head and rushing around the apartment blowing like the kettle whistle. Afterward she blushed a little, still wearing the tea cozy, when she met my gaze. She must have been in a terrible state of mind, but she didn't show it, and perhaps she herself found it diverting and comforting to try to distract Simon with her clowning tricks and her lightness. But when he went on crying, inconsolably, I could see that the perplexity in her eyes concerned not only him, but also herself, and I thought of her resoluteness as she stormed down the front walk holding Simon's hand, with her husband at her heels, and got into my taxi, and of the strength in her voice when she shouted at me to drive, just drive.

One evening she told me the film director had been outside Simon's nursery school when she went to pick him up. He had been beside himself with remorse and self-pity, and I asked if she was thinking of going back to him. She said I should tell her if I was tired of having them live with me. I shook my head, that wasn't what I meant. She looked over at Simon sitting on the sofa hypnotized by a cartoon film. No, she had made her decision. She cleared the table as if to end the conversation and started washing up. I sat gazing absently at the screen, where the cartoon animals laid spiteful ambushes for each other to the accompaniment of crazy music that sounded like the spasms of a merry-go-round run amok. Simon had flopped down on the sofa, his eyelids about to close. I switched off the television and laid a throw over him. I sat watching him for a while, then went into the kitchen, after all I could always dry. She stood at the sink, quite still, as if looking out at something in the darkness. I went over to her, she turned around. I remember us standing opposite each other for a long time in the little kitchen, as her eyes grew even narrower and she looked at me expectantly, that's how I remember it, but it couldn't have been more than a few seconds at most.

Was she waiting for a move from me? Was the movement released by something in me or something in her, or did it simply occur by itself, independently of us, in the unexpected pause, the unexpected closeness in the space where our eyes met? I had not thought it would happen, I can't even say I had hoped for it. I cannot explain the sudden impulse, the vague but crucial inner shift that made me lift my hand and let the back of it slide down her cheek. She slowly moved her head sideways and leaned her cheek against my hand. I moved my hand around her neck beneath the soft ponytail, and she leaned her forehead against my shoulder. Her skin was dry and warm, and I stroked the light down on her neck while I tried in vain to imagine how my hand might feel on her vertebrae, and what she might be thinking as she felt it there. I

hadn't touched anyone since that afternoon a few months before, when Inés vanished in the snow. Astrid's neck and the
palm of my hand, her forehead and my shoulder, it was a connection beyond my imagining, unpremeditated and strange. It
happened to us without our help, my hand on her skin, my lips
against her head, her hair tickling my nose, her hair's unfamil-
iar scent. Unknown, separate worlds, whose boundaries suddenly impinged on each other. I felt her hands on my hips,
she lifted her head and looked at me again, and I had no idea
what she saw. She closed her eyes, maybe in amazement, and
we kissed each other, tentatively, as if we had to learn all over
again what we knew by heart. I could not help thinking of
Inés when I kissed Astrid for the first time, I saw her growing smaller and disappearing among the snowflakes, and I
thought I had already entered another time, that one time had
ended and another begun. Astrid's mouth was different, and I
myself, I thought, I myself was not quite the same, but on the
other hand I wasn't quite sure what the difference was. People
kiss each other because they don't know what else to do. You
have nothing other than your foolish lips, your foolish hands
that brave the same language while the world changes. Simon
was still asleep on the sofa when we went in. That night we let
him stay there.

No one knew where she was that first week we spent together in my apartment, and I myself knew infinitesimally
little about her. For that matter, I don't know where she is
now, whether she is still in Lisbon or has journeyed on. She
vanished the same way she turned up, without warning, into
the air one winter evening. I picture her alone, alone again, as
she was when she got into my taxi with her little son to leave
everything she knew. I imagine her sitting at a window look-

ing onto a strange street, where children shout in a language she doesn't understand and the trams rattle past the glazed tiles of the facades, thinking of the time she hid herself in the home of a man she had never seen before, and wondering why he should have been the one she would live with for so many years. I try to summon her before me, just as the gray-haired film director must have done, alone in his house, when he realized she had slipped through his hands, and thinking she must be somewhere in town, in some unknown, inaccessible place. Perhaps she walks over the Rossio at the end of the day between the battered trams and the smoking charcoal braziers of the hot chestnut vendors, through the crowd of leisurely strolling people, and perhaps she thinks how easy it is to change direction, how little it takes. Perhaps she walks along the river watching the small ferries blacken on the gleaming water in the low sun over the river mouth, behind the hair-thin cables of the bridge that look as if they are about to burn up, themselves only a silhouette among the silhouettes of people walking along the quay.

3

I left for New York five days after Astrid had gone. I couldn't know then that she was in Oporto. She had simply disappeared. I had almost decided not to go, and when the plane took off I regretted it. It was no use trying to reassure myself that she knew my travel plans and when I would be back. Sitting in the plane I realized that it was not only my anxiety and unanswered questions that had paralyzed me in the days since she had vanished down the stairway with her suitcase, her steps growing fainter as she descended. It was simply that I missed her, and the loss grew stronger, more crushing, as the days passed without any word. Previously, when for one reason or another she was away for a few days, we had joked and said it was good to have a little holiday from each other. I actually enjoyed having the apartment to myself in the evening, when Simon and Rosa had gone to bed, and besides I had plenty to do carrying on the domestic routine without her. I liked being alone with the children, I was closer to them when they were alone with me, whether I helped them do their homework or took them out to eat because I couldn't be bothered with shopping and cooking. I didn't have time to imagine what Astrid was doing. Now I had all too much time. I could not explain why, I had no tangible reason, but in the days after her departure I grew more and more convinced that I was about to lose her. Previously the notion that

a misfortune might occur, that she could fall ill or simply fall in
love with someone else, had only crossed my mind as a theoretical possibility, but it had been easy to brush my fears aside.
Her presence had erased them, and I had smiled as one smiles
at the overwrought warnings of insurance companies about
how dangerous it is to be alive. Just as one never really believes
anything will happen to oneself, I could not imagine anything
happening to her, or to the obvious, almost banal, fact that we
were together. She was that much a part of my notion of myself. I felt as if I had been woken out of a dream and was now
looking around at a world that only superficially resembled
the one I had been familiar with. When I woke in the morning
and saw her duvet lying smooth and immaculate beside me, it
seemed to me that my world had become a strange place, or
rather that there was no longer any clear boundary separating
our home from the rest of the world. And when I let myself
into the silent, empty apartment we had shared so long, it was
like visiting a place where you had once lived, and realizing
that the feeling that it is precisely this place and nowhere
else that is home lasts only for a time. I had last been in New
York seven years before, but the town looked familiar, rising
gray and vertical on the other side of the East River as the
taxi crossed the Queensboro Bridge. Once again I stood in
the strangely cross-illuminated shadow at the bottom of the
streets' deep shafts, confused and weightless with fatigue in
the restless, unceasing stream of cars and faces, the same stream
as always. When I arrived in my hotel room I went straight to
bed, but could not fall asleep. I lay looking out the window and
watched the sky darken above the top of the glass facade opposite. I dozed a little, and when I looked again the dark blue,
monotonous reflection of the sky was broken by brightly lit

squares in which men in white shirts sat bent over their bluish screens or walked around the floors like ghosts wearing ties in the dreamlike, shadowless light. In Europe it was already night.

I recalled the empty, aimless days after Astrid left. Each time the phone rang it might be her, and I would tense as I lifted the receiver and heard myself utter my name. One of our friends had called to invite us to dinner, and I strained to sound casual and credible as I said that Astrid was in Stockholm visiting a friend. I had no desire to socialize, but I sensed it would seem more unusual if I refused than if I went on my own. If I had a plausible reason for saying no I should have given it right away instead of explaining why Astrid was unable to come. I said I would look forward to it, and felt irritated with myself for the rest of the day. Incidentally, it surprised me that there were so few calls for her. Normally the phone rang constantly, more often for her than for me. She must have used the Stockholm pretext for cover with people who might call her, as she had done with Rosa. If that was the case she had obviously planned to travel for quite a time. But she must have realized that the Stockholm pretext would have gotten thin after a week had passed. Friends seldom visit each other indefinitely, and the credence given the story would soon be replaced by curious or worried inquiries. So I guessed that the motive for her white lies was to enable her to slip away as adroitly and inconspicuously as possible. Once she was gone, it wouldn't matter. That she had not told me the same tale was understandable, considering I would be likely to call her at Gunilla's, as in fact I did. Presumably she did not want me to worry, but on the other hand she must have realized the state I would be in over her mysterious departure. Perhaps it had surprised her that I did not insist on an explanation or try to hold her back. Perhaps she had been relieved. Perhaps she respected me for it, or perhaps it had merely confirmed her secret reasons for going away. This was the confusion my speculations reduced me to as I sat in my study poring over my notes on Cézanne. Having spent the rest of the day rewriting the same section over and over it was a great relief to take a taxi out into the northern suburbs and look forward to an evening of nicely balanced Italian wines and nicely balanced conversation.

It was a dinner party like so many others we went to over the years, with the same people. Now and again a couple divorce, one of them disappears from view, and after an interval the other introduces a new face, but otherwise it is the same more or less regular group that has stayed together, at a distance or as close friends. I have known some of them since I was young, among them the host, a well-known architect, and his wife, who was my girlfriend for a short while long before she met him, long before Inés and Astrid. She runs a shop selling humanistic artifacts from India and Bali, and when we talk she always puts a hand on my knee as a little painless memory of that long-ago summer when we were young together. We would have been eight with Astrid, but luckily no one was surprised at her absence, and after I had repeated the Stockholm story to the couple who arrived last she was mentioned only in passing. There I sat with my dry martini like any other grass widower, my back to the dusk in my friends' garden, concentrating on appearing relaxed. I looked around the stylish interior with its modern, fairly expensive furnishings, which carefully avoided any superficial flamboyance, and which were placed so harmoniously piece to piece that the room created an airy, almost severe impression. I would have created much the same atmosphere in my own home if Astrid hadn't had a weakness for mixing sedate antiques with eccentric kitsch. For the first time I felt like an outsider, a new arrival in the group. I participated in the conversation only when I was asked about something, and didn't really listen to what the others said. They chatted about the usual things. It struck me that even though there was something new to talk about each time we met, it was always the same kind of topic, not only because I could usually guess what one or another of them would say about this or that, but also because the way they expressed themselves neutralized the differences between the subjects. They were all treated with the same reflexive irony, the same casual, fastidious distancing, as if, sitting around the fire in the heavily atmospheric twilight of the villa, we belonged to a chosen, exclusive elite, who subtly, tilting their heads, observed and commented on the world's folly.

I looked around at the cluster of familiar faces. Each one of us is a constant bearing on the others' horizons, witness to their lives, and because we have known each other so long, we aren't aware of the passage of time. We belong to the same age group, our lives have more or less taken a definite shape, yet we are still not too old for the future to seem long, indeed almost remote, just as when you are out sailing the horizon doesn't seem to move. Most of us have had children, some early, some late, and most of us have done what we are doing for so long that we have nothing to prove to anyone, but with each goal we reach we have already started making new plans. We can't imagine how anything could be different, we still don't give weight to the fact that our story is getting longer than our future. And yet it is a long time since we took over our places from others. Here and there an old white elephant still trumpets away, but otherwise we are the ones in charge now. It's just that we haven't discovered that only for a while can we allow ourselves to smile benevolently or tolerantly at the youngsters fidgeting behind us. We can't really picture their hunger and self-assertive stridency giving way to smug, tolerant causeries, when they sit where we are sitting now. Of course we do not have an answer for everything, we still can ask questions. We refuse to believe we shall ever be as pompous and bloodshot with red wine and accomplishments as the old fools we have replaced. We still laugh at them when we see them clutching their reputations like anxious dotards raking through their drawers with trembling, liver-spotted hands, in terror that the help has stolen some of the silver. We are not without scruples, we have our ideals, and we can still manage to say something outrageous and amusing. We recall the amazing sensation of feeling the warmth of the seats when we finally sat down. We have not forgotten what it was like to be cold, and we still sometimes find it hard to believe that we really are sitting here. Nevertheless, we can't quite understand why it should be so hard for the new ones to stand outside waiting in the cold. It won't hurt them to wait a bit longer, as we ourselves had to wait. We can't fully understand what it is like to be them, there is far too much hate in their eyes. We can't imagine what it will be like for our successors to feel our warmth in the empty seats, even though the warmth is always much the same.

One of the men at the party, a museum curator, had launched into a long exposition. Something about an exhibition he had recently seen. He was as prolix as ever, his expression as intense. He bears a slight resemblance to Stravinsky, and he knows it. He has been bald from the time he and I studied art history together, and he speaks in the same insistent, almost inquisitorial tone as he did when we would spend whole nights discussing how subtle it was of Marcel Duchamp to drop art and devote himself to playing chess for the rest of his life. He hasn't changed, he has just grown older, but he interrupts himself more and more often with sudden raucous laughter, as if crumpling the edifice of his ideas before the eyes of his deferential listeners, leaving them with the embarrassed and offended feeling of having subjected themselves purely for the sake of his enjoyment and not, as they believed, out of respect for his deeper insight. Preoccupied as I was, it only gradually dawned on me that it was Rosa's boyfriend, the installation artist, who was the subject of the monologue. In the curator's opinion his casts of embryos and child pornography in slow motion were a parodic example of the avant-garde being stone-dead, for if tradition no longer had any authority for rebellion to attack, if the provocation itself was part of the endless disguises of tradition, then the term "avant-garde" was just a lazy excuse for not knowing the job, not having any ideas, a fig leaf over the bourgeois ambition to call oneself an artist. In the end Rosa's boyfriend was just another young opportunist disguising his grubby Oedipal tricks as art-historical patricide jumping straight out of the gutter into *Who's Who*. Everything my bald friend said I could have said myself, and actually it should have delighted me to hear him make the company snigger at the contemptuous young man in black who, possibly, to my secret chagrin, might become my son-in-law. Nevertheless, and without quite knowing why, I felt like coming to the defense of Rosa's hard-boiled, mulish beloved, and I had begun a long exegesis, the first of the evening, not knowing exactly where it would lead, when the curator looked at me derisively over his steel-rimmed glasses as I paused to take a drag of my cigarette. Incidentally, he had seen our indomitable iconoclast at a private showing with his tongue down my daughter's throat. His narrow steel-framed eyes searched my face for an involuntary twitch he could exploit in making his revelation, but I remained impassive as complete silence fell for an instant. He wouldn't have said that, I thought, or not in those words, if Astrid had been there. I might as well give up, the others had succumbed to the uproarious eager laughter that deafens the embarrassment when someone's bounds have been overstepped. But there was no danger, I could safely laugh at myself in their presence, it was only the small obligatory reenactment of the original initiation rite of friendship, in which you had to humble yourself once and for all in a kind of mutual pledge, as if you had to mortgage your self-respect before the others would respect you. After all, no one should think one member got more credit than the others.

Before we went in to dinner I went up to the bathroom to be alone for a few moments. I sat on the edge of the tub, staring stupidly at our hostess's perfume bottles and the dried cornflowers hanging in coy little bouquets tied with lavender blue bows, like a charming feminine touch amid all the white sanitation. The five-year-old "afterthought" of the house had left a yellow plastic duck with big blue eyes in the bathwater, and it rocked and smiled encouragingly at me, as if trying to infect me with its good humor. I felt like throttling it, as if its naïveté were a genuine, live innocent's blue-eyed frankness toward the world and not a contrived, molded plastic ingenuousness, and at the same time felt guilty at my impulse, as if it would have been a real wrongdoing to punish the plastic duck for its happy ignorance. Everything suddenly seemed impalpable and distorted, as if seen through water, in this house where I had so often been with Astrid, among these people who were supposedly my closest friends. Why had I come? What was I doing here? How had they become my "closest friends," this flock of lax, vain, self-congratulatory and intellectually constipated examples of the academic middle class, sitting there washing down their blasé remarks with Brunello, as if the cosmopolitan gestures they had acquired could mask their rapacious ambition? As if their culinary humanism and their car trips to Tuscany could make anyone forget that every one of them came from a suburban yellow-brick apartment building that smelled of blood sausage every afternoon at five o'clock. A futile godforsaken suburb where the weather was always gray, and where their mothers "who stayed at home" had vacuumed out of frugality and longed for something better. As if their worldly detachment and their muted, sure taste and all the slim volumes of verse on their bedside tables could hide the fact that they had been pushed out between the thighs of these worn gray pensioner mothers with bad backs, whom they visited seldom and reluctantly because they were slightly ashamed of their permed poodle curls and polyester pant suits, sitting there in the apartment building beside the oilcloth with glossy magazines, rolling their own cigarettes and reading about the "celebrities," and perhaps now and then even getting a glimpse of their own children in the glossy, glittering, and awe-inspiring world into which they had vanished.

How had I become one of them? How had I grown old enough to sit laughing at an angry young artist merely because he was as fanatical in his adolescent anger as we were lukewarm in our studied, well-heeled maturity? Did we mock his perverted, grandiose dreams of changing the world because we ourselves had made our perverted ambitions seem more adult by scaling them down, lowering our sights and aiming for what was within reach? Did we smile at his existential funk because we ourselves had long since gone down on all fours and reduced ourselves to social animals? Was the curator's cynical abandon in skewering the young avant-gardist other than a defensive mask of his own disillusioned shamelessness, a self-justification of all the times he had kissed the ass of a minister of culture, board chairman, or prominent artist in order to get where he was now? My own anger surprised me. Strictly speaking, neither the museum curator nor the others had done me any harm. Was I sitting here on the edge of the tub silently reviling them because I needed to unload my growing self-disgust? Or was I only now seeing them as they really were, now that nothing was as it used to be? I pictured the curator, his expression during the silent pause before the others broke out in laughter around me. He had looked at me as if he knew what I was trying to hide with all my strength. But I was sure that Astrid would have come to the defence of Rosa's installation artist. She was no more delighted with him than I was, but she accepted him because Rosa loved him, and she at least tried to hide her skepticism when our daughter was around. Even before the children started growing up she taught me that I might as well stop trying to influence them with my own preferences. The children's upbringing was one of the few things we quarreled about. Time after time I criticized her blind trust that all would be well if the children were only left in peace, and time after time she pointed out that I was trying to control them and mold them according to my own perfectionist criteria. She had been right, I had to admit that now, when in any event they were out of my reach. Simon and Rosa comported themselves with the same adroitness and self-assurance as their mother, and if I didn't care for Rosa's installation artist, that was my problem. It would become hers only if I was tactless enough to reveal my skepticism. As I sat scowling on the edge of my so-called friends' tub I wished Astrid had been there to defend her daughter's lover, now that I had failed. The evening would have gone differently if Astrid had been with me. They would not have laughed at her as they had at me. When Astrid entered a room the tone of the conversation changed. Her mere presence exerted a remarkable influence on those around her, probably without her knowing it. In others' eyes she represented something unattainable, because she had been born and brought up to take everything for granted that they themselves had dreamed of and struggled for and degraded themselves to gain. They were afraid of her because of the disregard she could allow herself, when they had to be constantly on watch to take care they held their glass properly or used the right cutlery. She was from what used to be called an "old family," and even though her parents had driven their Jaguar over a cliff on the Amalfi drive when she was only fifteen, they had imparted to her the naturalness you only find in people who have had centuries in which to become civilized. She was never embarrassed and knew nothing of the anxiety and scorn of snobbery, she could talk to anyone and everyone and behave naturally wherever she went. When she left boarding school she left her privileges behind her, and when I met her there was nothing the least bit worldly about her lifestyle, but she carried herself with the same invulnerable naturalness, and even if she had happened to pick her nose at the table, she would have done it in style.

Astrid was inviolable. The most intimidating comment, the most offensive idiocy met with her crooked smile and indolent narrowed eyes, and I couldn't count the times I had seen a puffed-up, self-aggrandizing stud or scheming little jade slink off with their tail between their legs after trying and failing to muscle in on her. She decided for herself when she would reduce the distance that surrounded her like an invisible defence, and when she did she could be both surprisingly generous and unexpectedly direct, but no one could ever guess what she was thinking, not even I. If she had been there that evening, she would have entertained me on the way home with her observations and interpreted them unmaliciously but with an almost merciless curiosity, because she simply never tired of marveling at people's little games, the invisible commerce of emotions and social status in which the prices swing from hour to hour. On the way home from one of the last dinner parties we had been to together, she had analyzed every couple there and pointed out every small gesture, every unguarded remark, every flickering side glance I had not noticed myself. Her experience in the editing room may have stood her in good stead here, her professional knowledge of how the studied mien and involuntary twitches in a face comment on each other and change meaning, all according to the story they appear in and their part in the story's sequence of scenes and dialogues. Once again I was amazed by her acuity, although I couldn't resist reminding her that our friends must certainly dissect us in the same way. Like her, all the others thought that their view alone was privileged because they all felt themselves to be at the center of their own universe, in which the rest of us were merely planets and moons, the direction and course of whose movements were determined by their good sense, fear, and desire. She shrugged her shoulders, but I persisted, saying you could never know whether you were unable to see through someone's unfathomable expression because it concealed some arcane knowledge. She smiled fleetingly, almost as if the idea amused her, keeping her eyes on the white lines streaming toward us in the headlights.

She was driving, I wasn't quite sober. She drove fast, she is actually quite a speed demon, but she drives with the same assurance with which she handles the sharpest kitchen knife. I contemplated her listening, secretly smiling profile and her eyes fixed on the road, while continuing my train of thought in a somewhat muddled and uncertain way. I asked if she had noticed that people always seem diminished when you talk about them. As if you had to make them smaller to fit them into your perspective. Shouldn't that in itself be enough to make you doubt your own judgment? And if everyone looked at everyone else from their limited but totally different viewpoint, who could designate himself as the one who saw accurately? If the many opposed and intersecting and overlapping views were each equally right, then each of us was no more than the infinite, but also incoherent and contradictory sum of distorted, truncated and incomplete reflections in each other's eyes. I mentioned the curator. We knew he slept with his students, but his wife didn't know. On the other hand, she may have known that he snored or suffered from hemorrhoids, which his trim little girlfriends at the academy of art didn't realize. We knew he had slandered a colleague in order to gain his present position, in which he regarded himself as the uncompromising and altruistic protector of art's absolute elite, whereas we could not know whether at that moment he was ridiculing my catalogue texts, although he had told me how excellent they were. On the other hand, we may have been the only ones who knew that

once, when we were on holiday with him in Greece long before
he was married, he had leapt into the sea off a sailboat far from
shore to rescue a puppy which Rosa had insisted on bringing
on board. Astrid's lips creased in an inscrutable smile as she
shifted gears to move into the passing lane. I continued, animated by her expectant smile. But it was one thing, I said, how
little we knew about each other. And another thing how much
we actually knew about ourselves. For if you were never really
able to evaluate yourself, if you always had a blind corner, a
white spot where you could not see yourself, then you could
never achieve self-knowledge, regardless of how hard you were
on yourself, perhaps precisely because you are always either
too hard or too easy where your own self is concerned, and
furthermore if there really was someone who saw you in the
round so to speak but uncommunicably, inscrutably, perhaps
even without your noticing it, would you then have to resign
yourself to the fact that your real, full, and true identity remained a secret behind this stranger's eyes. I stopped, my
mouth dry after the stream of words, and she laughed suddenly. I didn't know whether she was laughing at what I had
said or at something else that had struck her. She went on
laughing, not maliciously, almost heartily, keeping her eyes on
the road, as if it was there, among the cars' red taillights, that
she had spotted whatever was so amusing, while I sank back
exhausted in my seat as the lights of town came into view.

Perhaps she was only laughing at my words. It was Astrid
who taught me to laugh at myself. To her, words were useless
for getting close to reality, in her opinion they were rather an
impediment. She admired my rhetorical skills, but not so much
for what I said, more as one admires someone who is good at
waterskiing or flipping pancakes. To her words were a kind of

pendant, like speech balloons. When she listened to people she always took account of who they were, even when it was I myself who had spoken. For instance, if we were going out in the evening, and she had changed her clothes for the fifth time before the bedroom mirror, it didn't help if I said she looked lovely. That's what *you* think, she would say with a crooked smile, inspecting herself skeptically in the mirror. We were both equally conscious of the unpredictable gaps between reality and the descriptions of it in which people reflect themselves. But while my doubts have made me twist and turn the words endlessly, Astrid seemed to have drawn the opposite conclusion. She preferred to keep silent and let the words die away as if it was only through silence that truth became visible. If I said I loved her, and that she was the first woman I had been happy with for more than a few hours at a time, she just smiled and shyly stroked my hair away from my forehead, as if my words were an over-extravagant bouquet of flowers. Her modesty about words therefore made it seem all the more powerful when she would suddenly embrace me from behind and whisper that she loved me. I asked her why once, but she just smiled and said *because*. Because what? She looked at me as if surprised that I would ask. Because you're so stupid, she replied, and kissed me on the brow. To her there was no why or wherefore, and there was almost a touch of disappointment in her smile, as if I had revealed that I was not as sure as she was. But as resistant as she was to words, to the notion that everything can be explained, and as cool and reserved as she could seem to those around us when we were out, she found it equally easy to let herself go when we were alone together. She gave herself to me without hesitation, in her playful, light way. She was generous with her tenderness, almost careless, because her caresses were not little letters hungrily or fearfully waiting for an answer, but extensions of herself, without reservation. At times she almost dazed me with her love, as when she made herself invisible by kissing my eyelids with her warm soft lips. But when she laughed at me that night in the car on the way home from yet another dinner with our circle of friends, it may not have been only because I lost myself as usual in my own words. Perhaps she also thought I was making myself worry needlessly. Although it amused her to see through the cockfights and mating dances of the social game, when people saw their self-esteem reflected in each other's lust or envy, deep down she seemed unaffected by what others thought of her. And although she might spend a long time in front of the mirror before she was reasonably satisfied with her appearance, I think it was as much for herself, like a game, when she tried on one dress or blouse after the other, just as long ago she had passed the time dressing and undressing her dolls. That was the secret behind the unconscious assurance with which she carried herself when she associated with other people, and only I could see it, because only I knew she was as much at peace with herself when she was out as when she came out of the shower and walked through the apartment naked and dripping beneath her fluttering kimono.

I ran the cold water in the sink and lowered my face to the faucet. There was a cautious knock at the door. I felt the skin on my face contract and observed the small drops glinting like sweat in the bright glare from the light above the mirror. I was in the wrong place, everything was wrong, I shouldn't have come. It has been a mistake, I should have thought up an excuse, never mind what, or given no excuse at all, simply said

I could not come. I should have sat at my desk and thought about Cézanne or just looked out the window, into the darkness over the Lakes, over at the lighted windows along the row of houses on the other side, all the windows looking into others' unknown lives. At that moment all I wanted was to be home alone looking out front from the window in my study. Astrid might even have tried to phone, I couldn't know, perhaps everything was different from what I believed. But what did I believe? That everything was over? That she had gone off with someone else? That I would never see her again? That there had been an accident? That she had taken her own life? I was like a blind person reaching out into the empty air and finding nothing to grasp. But why did I imagine the worst? There was another knock, and I recognized my hostess's anxious voice through the door, the old girlfriend I had fooled around with one long-ago summer when we had nothing else to do. If fate had dealt the cards differently, I might have been the one she shared this bathroom with, but wouldn't I then have long since turned into someone else? Someone who couldn't stand her dried wildflowers and Balinese textiles? Someone who grew sick and tired of mauve silk ribbons and oriental designs? Someone who one day might pass a strange, unknown Inés or Astrid on the street, as she walked by herself smiling at some private thought, only to go on in the opposite direction, homeward, absorbed in vague, aimless daydreams. I looked at my face in the mirror, spotted with little drops as if I had a fever, and I pictured Astrid as she had stood in the doorway the morning she left, I saw her strangely detached and yet insistent, penetrating impenetrable gaze. I dried my face and opened the door and smiled as naturally as I could. No, there was nothing wrong, just a bit of an upset stomach,

no doubt it was all the black coffee I drank while I was working. The others had gone in to dinner. We went downstairs,
and on the way she turned and asked how long Astrid would
be away, still with a trace of worry on her face like a residue
she had forgotten to wipe off, and I wondered how much my
own face gave me away, and if she might have guessed everything was not well, as I replied that she was coming home in
a week.

I pretended not to notice the others' curious glances as I
sat down at the table. They were discussing a big Mondrian
exhibition that had just opened, and I pointed out that Mondrian did not, as one might think, plan out his compositions
before executing them, but on the contrary felt his way forward by intuition, as could be seen from his unfinished pictures, where you can make out how the charcoal guidelines
had been wiped away and drawn over each other until he had
found the correct complementary order. In other words, his
art was slightly reminiscent of the abstract expressionists,
who used to paint over the same picture many times before it
was completed, which merely pointed up how superficial it
was to differentiate between constructivism and expressionism. I could tell it was going well, my voice was calm and confident without sounding didactic, even the curator regarded
me benignly from behind his glasses, as if wanting to show he
had always known he could rely on me, and our hostess, my
old summer sweetheart, looked at me with something akin to
tenderness, as if I had returned after a long convalescence.
While I sat there expounding on Mondrian and thus made my
comeback into the circle, I met the eyes of one after another,
and asked myself who I might seem to be to them. To some I
was an established, sometimes even feared, art critic, to others

I was the man who had been able to conquer a woman like Astrid, to one or two of them I was an arrogant, aloof, and self-absorbed intellectual who smoked too much and probably didn't even know how to change a lightbulb without getting a shock, and to the curator and our hostess with the dried flowers I was someone transformed into all this from a passionate, awkward, and precocious young man, who had once wasted eighteen months of his youth getting torn to pieces over an exotic-looking bitch everyone would have told me I hadn't a chance in the world of holding on to.

There was a great deal they didn't, and couldn't, know. There was everything I hadn't known myself while it was going on, and everything I knew while it was happening but no longer knew, either because I had forgotten it or because I was no longer quite the same. For I'm not quite the same as when I met Astrid. I can see it in the few photographs where I am present. There aren't many, because I have always hated being photographed, I've always felt exposed, whether because I try too hard to look natural or because I stiffen at the thought of being reduced to a single grimace out of all the grimaces, a single moment out of all the hours and days. In any case, I always tense up and get self-conscious when someone points a camera at me, I suddenly feel it isn't me being photographed but someone trying to look like me. I can see my features become sharper in the pictures, but I can't decide whether it is my real face that gradually becomes recognizable through the soft indefiniteness of the young skin or my original face that is gradually distorted by the folds and furrows of the years. When I meet my own eyes in the photos of our life, with my normal, slightly skeptical expression, the man in the picture seems to look at me and ask himself: Is that really you?

Perhaps Astrid feels the same way, although of course it isn't something we think about every day. She too is different than she was when she sat in the back seat of my taxi one winter evening, humming to her little son as she left everything she had believed in. She must have wondered too, when she saw the old pictures of herself, whether those were the same eyes that met her gaze across time. The same eyes that had once answered the insistent gaze of the gray-haired film director, as if to read there the person she would become. We have changed side by side, staying in time together, and so we didn't notice that we were changing; only occasionally, as when the children, tall and gangling, rushed up to us across the beach, or when we saw them from the window going to school, did we feel surprised at how big they had suddenly grown. Each stage wiped out the previous one, in the children and in our-selves, so only the pictures and our own imprecise recollec-tions remain, and although we have gone on changing, only in rare moments have we thought about the change, and only as something that happened to us, not as something that bore us along with it and took us away.

I can hardly remember what it was like to be me before I became the man who was with Astrid. When I think of myself as young it is as you think of a pair of shoes you once had, a pair of worn-out shoes you threw away long ago. You think of them as your old shoes just as you talk of your old self, al-though the shoes were new once, and strictly speaking it is you who have grown older. I have hardly any pictures from that time. I have only a single picture of Inés, taken in Am-sterdam. I have never shown it to Astrid, there has never been an occasion to do so, and if she has in fact seen it she hasn't said anything about it, perhaps because if she did she would reveal that she had searched my study. The picture is between two pages of the monograph on Vermeer, beside a color print of the famous painting of a girl with pearl earrings and a blue turban, standing in a dark room, startled out of her solitude, her lips slightly parted and a timid, expectant look in her eyes as she turns toward the light to meet the strange, penetrating gaze. I am in the picture myself. I am sitting beside Inés, my arm around her shoulder among the Japanese and American tourists on board one of the boats that sail around the canals of Amsterdam. We are all looking up, and some of us wave to the photographer. It is the same picture he has taken thousands of times before, the unknown photographer. I can barely make us out among the other tourists on that spring day in Amsterdam long ago. A flock brought together by chance, who half an hour later will scatter to the winds, and some of whom must have died by now. We all look happy, perhaps because we are in Amsterdam, perhaps because the sun has come out at last and gleams on the green water and the still-wet raincoats and folded umbrellas. Our faces are so small that the features are almost invisible. I have to pore over them through a magnifying glass to bring us into focus, Inés with damp hair, her head leaning toward mine, looking so sweet, not at all like a bitch who makes men howl at the moon. Our eyes are small and indistinct, like black motes in the picture's fog of tiny particles that reproduce the colors of hair, skin, coats, boat, and water. Our eyes are no more than minute black holes in the suspended moment's field of colors, reflections, and shadows, insignificant perforations into all that went before, out to all that was to come, memory and uncertainty, limbo and flickering hope.

I can't remember what I saw, I can't remember anything about our boat trip through the canals of Amsterdam, and I

wonder if I would be able to remember something out of all I
have forgotten if I didn't have the picture of myself sitting beside Inés, looking up and smiling. I wonder whether it is the
picture of us that shadows everything I may have seen. Inés
leans toward me, tender and girlish, whether for the sake of
the photographer or because she wants after all to have a picture in which you can see how sweet she could be. I can remember her spicy scent, the Maja soap which always makes
me think of Spain even though we never went to Spain together and it is only her name that sounds Spanish. She has a
flat paper bag in her hand and I know there's a postcard in the
bag, she had just bought it in a museum and I can remember
the picture although I can't see it, a dead pheasant with blind
extinguished eyes, hanging head-down from a hook, painted
with meticulous invisible strokes. I can't remember what I was
thinking as Inés leaned her head against me, I only remember
what it meant, or what I hoped it would mean even though it
has long ceased to matter. My eyes look at me like small black
pinpricks in a remote faded second, but I cannot look inside,
they are too small, it is too dark in there behind my young face
in the pale spring sunlight above the canal. I know I loved her,
but I can't remember what it was like to know that, how it felt.
I know my love tore and dragged at me, but I can neither recall the pain nor the unexpected outbreaks of seeping happiness. I can tell myself that in reality it was not Inés who made
me suffer, that I merely flayed myself on her until I bled, that
it was not her I loved but my own intoxication, my own poi-
sonous chocolate-box picture of who she might be, and what I
longed to make her into. I can tell myself that my young, ravenous, and tempestuous love for Inés was a blind alley, a mirage, but I cannot know it. The memory of her soon lost
feeling, I could no longer sense anything, where before there

had been pain. The wound healed and became a shiny scar without nerve fibers.

I looked around at the others as I talked on about Mondrian, explaining that it was wrong to regard his primary colors and vertical and horizontal lines as emblems of the rationalism of an antimetaphysical century, and that his apparently extreme concrete abstractions should rather be understood in the light of his theosophical mysticism, an ancient oriental dream of cosmic harmony. I drew their attention to the richly painted landscapes of his youth, with their dim forest fringes and mirror-calm lakes at twilight, and argued that in reality Mondrian was an incurable romantic. They listened intently, almost reverently, and even the museum curator nodded his bald head encouragingly. Suddenly I thought he looked like a caricature of himself, and his shiny pate, flashing glasses, and almost satanically conspiratorial smile meant to signal that really nothing in this world could surprise him in the least, and that of course he was familiar with Mondrian's spiritual bent, as if we were speaking of his own uncle. I glanced at our hostess and she gave a kittenish smile. The thick makeup on her cheeks threatened to crack. Evidently she couldn't get enough of Mondrian, and she widened her eyes as if she listened with them and not her ears, which she had adorned with something resembling gilded pinecones. She, too, resembled a caricature of the crazy kid I had rolled around with in the dune grass, she didn't even refrain from bending forward slightly on her elbows, inviting me to peek down her scoop-neck blouse. She had pushed her breasts into a black bra that must have been at least one size too small, presumably to recall their once legendary abundance. But what about me? Was it really me sitting here showing off my knowledge of Mondrian? Wasn't I myself a caricature of the refined art expert who could say something well-chosen and witty about any painter, providing he was dead and famous? I smiled at my old girlfriend, no doubt absolutely charmingly, and thought of the time she had seduced me in a beach hut. I could almost recall the feeling of wet coconut matting against my buttocks and her cool, conical breasts as they slipped out of her bathing suit. I smiled at her in acknowledgment of her symbolic little flirtation over the table, and thought about how the earliest experiences we have with each other set the keynote of the music we later play together. She was a year or two older than I was, enough for her to be well embarked on her erotic career, whereas I was still a bit of an amateur. When I was young I felt I was different inside, someone other than the slightly clumsy, shy youth she had taken under her wing. I had imagined that one day I would shed my uncertainty and be myself at last, fearless and imperturbable. I longed to come into view and show who I really was. I was open to everything then, I concealed nothing and everything went through me. I was far too easily shaken, susceptible to the smallest vibration, and I saw my anxious reflection in every glance that fell upon me. Now I sat there giving her my best roguish smile, but was that really me, was that what I had become? A windy, slightly gray charlatan with a chiseled face, who could serve up Mondrian in paper-thin slices? Had I paid for my adult assurance, my firm views, my unswerving powers of judgment, by stiffening into this talking mask? Was there still someone behind the mask, did it still hide a secret difference?

I made them laugh with the story of how Mondrian had left the Stijl group, offended that Van Doesburg had betrayed the principle of strictly vertical and horizontal painting by

placing his squares aslant because he found diagonals more
"dynamic," and while they laughed at this example of almost
fanatically puritan and formalistic adherence to principle, I
thought it was precisely this genial, mature, and well-tempered
laughter that separated an artist like Mondrian from such a
band of complacent, conformist, and intellectually lazy culture
snobs. But actually I could not have cared less about Mondrian, just as I had not been able to work up any enthusiasm
about Cézanne in the days since Astrid left. For the first time,
I had lost all desire to write, any expectation of excitement
at seeing the sentences follow one another, seeing the words
pull themselves out of the chink at the end of my fountain pen
in long, vibrating wavy blue ribbons of wet signs that dried
into the paper. I had begun to write after meeting Astrid, and
I had begun to make a living from writing when Rosa was
small. If I had been prevented from writing I would have felt
suffocated by the accumulated triviality of the everyday, but on
the other hand I had only been able to breathe in the flat, silent,
and unmoving world of pictures. It offered shelter from the
real, noisy, moving world that drew me into its turmoil all the
time, speaking to me and demanding answers. One world had
called me when I was in the other one, and my adult life had
consisted of traveling back and forth between them every day.
While hunting for a can of anchovies in the pantry I could fall
into a reverie over the way the empty bottles reminded me of
one of Morandi's humble and crookedly melancholy still lifes.
Likewise, in the middle of my meditations on Brancusi's porous
marble eggs I could not help thinking of the pale down on
Astrid's buttocks when the morning sun touched them as it
slanted in beneath the blind. It had been a precarious, changing, and unpredictable balance I had maintained, and I had

never imagined being relegated to one of these worlds alone, cut off from the other, but when Astrid left the apartment became as still and silent as one of Hammershøi's deserted, gray rooms with white doors gaping onto emptiness, and I had nothing to add, nowhere to go.

I became the person I am living with Astrid. Everything people connect with my face and my name came into being while we were together, not only what I have written but also many of my quirks, reflexes and habits, all the things people find attractive or repellent in me. If it is true, as some say, that the first impression you get of others is also the one that lasts, and determines how light and shade are distributed in the more detailed picture that gradually forms, then with the years I have become the unknown taxi driver who one winter's evening long ago drove Astrid and Simon into town, and whose eyes a few days later she wonderingly, but actually not with surprise, looked into as he lifted his hand and stroked her cheek. Anyway, that's how I see the change which took me from the gloomy young man sitting beside Inés in the boat on a canal in Amsterdam. He and the taxi driver are actually almost the same age, but the taxi driver Astrid saw is someone else, someone unknown whom she and I have gotten to know simultaneously. It was she who saw him first, it was her glance that released me from the young man in Amsterdam and his flayed longing. She knew nothing about me, she did not know who I was, in her eyes I might have been someone different, not an unrequited young man who kept hitting his head against the same wall, frantic with jealousy, shame, and wounded vanity. Astrid freed me, and she didn't even know it. The world opened again, I no longer felt like an expelled monster skulking outside the gate, love was no longer a losing game, and I vowed never again to love in vain, never again to wear my heart on my sleeve like a war veteran displaying his medals from a war no one remembered. It happened very fast, but it was a slower, more casual, almost refined way of loving, not a feverish, insatiable hunger, not a white-knuckled pounding against a locked door. At the beginning I was dizzy with lightness. With Astrid everything seemed possible, I did not need to weigh my words, nor was it necessary to accompany each caress with pathetic declarations or anxious questionings. We still knew infinitesimally little about each other, and yet it felt very natural that Astrid and Simon simply stayed on in my small apartment. I began to drive in the daytime when I wasn't attending classes, and when I arrived home in the evening they were already there. It was a new and remarkable feeling to find someone there, to find light and voices when I got home. In the evening we put Simon to bed on the sofa before retiring to the bedroom, and soon began taking turns getting him to nursery school in the morning.

One morning as I was walking along the street with him, an elderly woman came running after us with something in her hand. Smiling, she said my son had dropped his glove and handed it to me. I hadn't seen him lose it, I hadn't even noticed Astrid putting gloves on him, and I smiled back slightly flustered, for a moment ashamed, as if I had lured the child away from his mother and was also irresponsible and inattentive. If the woman had children herself they would long since have left home. There was something motherly in her smile, which seemed directed not only at Simon but also at me. To her I was a sweet, slightly distrait young father who couldn't quite cope with everything I had become responsible for, and when I continued on with Simon's little hand in mine, and replying to his unpredictable questions, I secretly relished my false status. He asked about everything under the sun, and as I replied it struck me that to him I represented a limitless universe of knowledge, immense as the Alexandria library, so I was not only a fraud to passing elderly ladies, but in a way was also duping him with my cocksure answers about how far it is to the sun, and what happens to you when you die. Like the library in Alexandria, my own idea about the order and meaning of things had long since gone up in smoke, but this youngster took me at my word, trusting unshakeably in my powers of judgment. When he tired of walking I lifted him onto my shoulders and let him hold tightly to my hair. I was amazed how light he was and realized as we walked along in the thundering morning traffic that he was completely in my hands, a stranger who had kissed his mother without quite knowing what he was doing, simply because it had occurred to him. I also thought about the gray-haired film director who had stood in his shirtsleeves one cold night shouting at Astrid in the taxi. Once she must have believed that her life would take shape and become a story with him, I carried the proof of this on my shoulders. Simon pulled at my hair and my ears, to draw my attention to something, and while I answered at random I thought that the small snowsuited proof of love I was carrying with a firm grip on his winter boots was the only thing that remained when her dream fell apart. He had come toddling out of the story when it was a thing of the past, just as once he had struggled out of her body. He had gone with her out of one story into another none of us had foreseen or so much as dreamed of. I would never be Simon's father, I would always be another man in another story, and as I walked hand in hand with him in the wintry blue morning beside the roaring stream of cars, among the busy pedestrians with little puffs of cold air around their mouths, I thought that the time

of blue-eyed openness was past, the empty-handed innocence
in which nothing is written in advance, and you can be anyone
at all, anything can happen.

Astrid must have had similar thoughts those first times we
woke up in my bed and stretched out to each other with sleepy,
slightly cautious caresses. She too must have wondered how
much of herself had remained behind in the blind alley she had
left, and if she was the same person now that she was exchanging the same caresses with another. Our meeting was pure coincidence, and we both enjoyed the feeling of fooling the rest of
the world in those first weeks together in my cramped apartment, where no one knew she was, and when no one knew yet
that I no longer lay alone there pining away. I felt a lightness,
at last I was free again, and I could laugh again for the first time
in ages. Months passed and we started to go out together and
meet each other's friends. Astrid divorced the film director, and
when spring came we found a larger apartment. Our story had
begun, had already found its tone and style, and the more often
one of us talked about our meeting one winter night in a taxi,
the more it sounded like the creation myth of our love. Gradually, as the anecdote was repeated, our chance meeting came to
resemble an hour of destiny, and in time the years before our
meeting were reduced to a prehistoric wilderness of overgrown paths, failed experiments and unfinished sketches. But
sometimes when I heard myself telling the story yet again, it
only intensified my memory of the accidental nature of our
meeting. I recalled the weightless, dreamlike feeling of suddenly having stepped off my course into another world, where
I too was someone different from the man who had lost his
bearings in his immature obsession with Inés. In brief fleeting
moments before I fell asleep, on the threshold between thought

and dream, I wondered if it was so easy to love Astrid because I had finally learned to love, or because I had learned to love less. It was only a passing notion, and I forgot it when I was in her company again. For example, when we would go into town together on one of the evenings Simon was with his father. She liked to dance, and when she stood with her eyes closed, twisting and turning in the throbbing music and the whirling lights, she was like an island amid the din and morass of flickering silhouettes, an island I let myself be washed up on as I embraced her. She had not danced much when she was married to the film director, it hadn't been his style, and so it had stopped being hers. He had made her feel much older than she was, and when she met me it felt like regaining her youth. That's how she described it, as if she had taken a wrong turn in time and had found her way back to the starting point, a bit nonplussed that she had become a mother in the meantime. And she really was very young when she rolled around in bed playing tickling games with Simon, she was more like a big sister romping around again. It felt strange to stand embracing her in the swarm of dancers, as I had stood so often with an unknown girl on one of my nights in town. It felt strange to stand like such a young and unruffled pair, two people who have just bumped into each other, but at the same time already belonged together.

I shared a taxi into town with the curator and his wife. They had already called one when I decided to leave, so I could hardly decline. I kissed our hostess goodbye, she looked intimately into my eyes and laid her palm on my chest, her fingertips lightly touching my skin between two buttons, and said I must take care of myself. I smiled this time, a little fatuously, and said of course I would. What did she actually have in mind? A flirtation for old time's sake in Astrid's absence, while her husband stood watching for the taxi? Should I with a flicker of lust assure her she was as attractive as she used to be? Did she just want to remind me that in her way of thinking she had a kind of claim to my cock because she had had her hands on it before Astrid? And what was I actually to take care about? That she didn't come at me with her long red nails? What had she seen? Was it written on my face? Had she alone out of the whole party observed me and seen what was hidden from myself with a secret, inaccessible knowledge? The thought was as irritating as it was disquieting. It had started to rain, and we ran out to the waiting taxi, a little ridiculously, as if we could avoid the drops if we ran fast enough. The curator sat in front, I was in the back with his wife, a well-padded but quite attractive woman with short, sensible hair. He, who had cruised the parties and bars of our youth like a Dionysiac centaur and been in the pants of every beauty he felt like seducing, in the end had married this mild, retiring, and unremarkable woman, and I was not the only one surprised at his choice. To begin with I thought it was some kind of moral reform, and he did talk about having children with an unctuous piety I would never have ascribed to him, but they didn't have any, and soon he was on the rampage again like a fox in the henhouse. An old fox eventually, but one who hadn't lost his taste for young flesh. I wondered why the new generation of beauties, like their by now mature and eternally pregnant predecessors, kept falling for his bald, skinny, and not especially virile physique. I learned the explanation from a mutual acquaintance, a poet who himself continued to look not a day over twenty-five. I had to remember, he said, that young women always fuck upward. The curator may have become flabby, but his steel-rimmed glasses radiated the irresistible charm of power.

He did nothing to hide his rampant unfaithfulness from others, apart from his mild and totally unsuspecting wife; apparently he relied on his friends to shield her from the bitter, salacious truth. I was pretty piqued and didn't refrain from telling him so, whereas Astrid was remarkably unaffected by his grotesque deceptions. When I asked her what she would say if I romped around as freely as our friend, she merely kissed me on the forehead and said I would never have the nerve. She observed his aberrations without condemning or excusing him, from a distance, as if they were neutral, arbitrary events not worth having an opinion on. That was probably true, and in fact I admired her ability to distinguish between the sides of him she found unpleasant and those she admired. She had a weakness for cynics, for their ruthless, blasphemous humor, and the curator could make her laugh till tears came to her eyes. I'd been seated some way from his wife at dinner and we had not had much chance to talk. Now she obviously was trying to be friendly, because she asked innocently how Astrid was, and what sort of film she was editing. I answered her questions, and we kept up quite a lively little conversation on the ride into town. I have always had a calming effect on shy people, they feel safe with me and soon loosen up, which can be a bit of a burden, but also a real advantage when you're stuck together, as in the back of a taxi. In the end she grew mawkish and begged my pardon for her husband's disparaging remarks about my daughter. I brushed it off and said strictly speaking it was her boyfriend and not Rosa who had been mentioned disparagingly, and the curator took immediate advantage of my evasive tactics. That's right, it wasn't at all about Rosa, and why was she getting mixed up in it? Surely you can say what you like among old friends? His wife said there had to be some limits, they were young after all, and what if I happened to think Rosa's boyfriend was a nice fellow? The curator sneered at her "nice fellow" and repeated his scathing description of the artist's ludicrous and pathetic avantgarde posing. I tried to referee and soon found myself standing up for his wife.

Their arguing continued until she asked the driver to stop at a kiosk and went in to buy cigarettes. While we waited, silent and rather uncomfortable in the presence of the expressionless driver, he suddenly turned in his seat and looked at me in a way I would almost call desperate. He said I was lucky. What did he mean? Yes, I was lucky because I had Astrid. I didn't know what to say and concentrated on keeping my face calm as I met his distraught glance in the half-light. I could smell his vinous breath in the corner where I sat. There was something he wanted to talk to me about. Had Astrid ever told me that he had tried to sleep with her once when I was out of the country? Apparently he was not concerned about the driver, who sat there with his blank face swallowing every word we uttered, while he stared listlessly at the long glittering tracks of raindrops on the windshield. I mustn't worry, it was a long time ago, at least five years. Anyway, she had rejected him, could I imagine otherwise? His eyes blinked behind the neon reflections of his glasses with a flash of demonic joviality that distorted his solemn, almost humble face into a two-faced theatrical mask, as he went on with his confession. It was after a dinner like tonight's, his wife had been ill so he had gone alone. He had driven Astrid home, the two of them were alone in his car. He felt they'd enjoyed themselves so much together, there seemed to be a special connection that evening, and you never know, he couldn't know, could he, how she and I got along. They had talked about everything, the way you can with Astrid. I wondered if anyone knew about what he was telling me, and that when, as they drove, he laid a hand on her knee as if by chance, she left it there. I looked out through the ephemeral transparent fans the wipers made on the windscreen. I could see his wife standing in the kiosk, leaning on one leg in the queue and apparently engrossed in the pictures of hamburgers and hot dogs above the counter. Her face was quite pallid in the neon light and her gaze faraway. He didn't know if Astrid even noticed the hand, she wasn't entirely sober, but she did not push it away, and there really had been, what should he call it, this connection, so he left his hand on her knee. When he stopped at our entrance he tried to kiss her, but she just turned her face away smiling, and before he could say anything she had said goodnight and slammed the car door after her. Neither of them had ever spoken about the episode. Had she really never told me about it? I followed his wife with my eyes as she stepped out of the illuminated sphere of the kiosk, suddenly just a dark silhouette approaching. The curator smiled in a conciliatory way. Now at least I knew what kind of a shit my friend was.

I couldn't compose myself and go to bed, although it was past two in the morning. Again I sat in the dark in my study looking out over the deeper, more limitless darkness of the Lakes. So far as I could see it had stopped raining. The glow from my cigarette was reflected in the windowpane, its slightly redder intensity when I inhaled was the only sign of life. The lights were off in the windows on the other side, only the streetlights shone and the faint orange cast in the sky from the city's lights, which has always reminded me of the firelight over Hieronymus Bosch's creepy fantasies of judgment day. The lamplight reached only partway up the row of

facades over there, in insufficient fans on the brickwork between the dark windows. The rest of the walls faded into the
darkness, the same darkness as over the lake, so that the shining wet asphalt of the street on the opposite bank seemed re-
moved from its surroundings, an outstretched ribbon of light
beneath the blurred and sketchy ghosts of the houses, stretch-
ing out into black nothingness. The view made me think of the
famous picture by Magritte, *L'empire des lumières*, depicting a
gloomy house beside a nocturnal lake surrounded by dark
trees, illuminated only by a single mysterious and ominous
lamp, paradoxically and subtly placed beneath a pale blue sky
with white clouds. At any other time I would have tried to
discover precisely what it was about the view that made me
think of the picture, as a picture had often sent me hunting for
an early sensory perception, the particular light in a half-
forgotten doorway or side street, which for a moment brushed
the edge of my mind only to fade and grow dim the next moment. With time my recollections had transformed themselves
into pictures and merged with the recollections of all the pictures I had seen, until I was no longer sure of the difference
and had difficulty distinguishing one kind of memory from the
other, because both were equally diffuse anyway, equally distorted, bound to the impulses, preoccupations and anxieties of
the moment. Now I no longer cared about Magritte or *L'empire des lumières*, I merely sat staring stupidly out into the darkness because I knew I could not fall asleep. Besides, I had
always thought Magritte was an unusually facile and inferior
painter.

I asked myself what I would have said to the curator if his
wife had not sat down beside me on the back seat just as he
had finished his confession. I was afraid it would not have

made any difference if she had come at that moment or two minutes later. He had paralyzed me, forced me into my corner in the back seat of the taxi, and he must have known that I was defenseless, disarmed. But why had he told me that story, and why this evening? Why had Astrid never told me about it? Was it because he had lied? But why should he lie and show himself in such a bad light, even risk losing my friendship? And why had Astrid kept silent about an episode that with a little goodwill and a light edit would only have demonstrated her faithfulness and constancy? Perhaps because otherwise, if with an ironic and soothing smile she had told me about the little episode, I might have gone and confronted the curator with it and thereby in fact heard his version, the one in which she had let his hand stay on her knee, whether out of forgetfulness or misplaced tact. Perhaps because in reality, whether for only a short distance or for an hour during dinner, she had contemplated or at least played with the idea of what it would be like to sleep with the museum curator, and because the mere thought, although it had never been put into action, seemed shameful and half-criminal to her. I thought of Astrid's surprising tolerance for his affairs with his female students. Was she so tolerant only because she wanted to excuse herself for her own small tête-à-tête with him? I thought of how she had laughed in the car on the way home from a dinner party like tonight's, when I had philosophized over what people really know about each other, and used the curator as a grotesque example. Was it him she was laughing at? Was it me? Was it herself? Was it quite a different story I would never hear?

Perhaps it didn't matter whether the story was true or not. In any case, if it was true nothing had happened. A hand

resting a few minutes on my wife's knee could easily be relegated to the scrap heap of chance mishaps and misapprehen-
sions. After all, so much happens *en passant.* If, on the other
hand, this fully innocent story was pure invention, it merely
strengthened my sneaking feeling that the curator had not
told it to me to exult in the fact that even Astrid, the uncon-
querable, impregnable Astrid, had wavered for a moment
under the influence of his fabled talent as a seducer. That he
had instead told it to me in order to verify that he had seen
correctly when he glimpsed a crack in my relaxed grass widower's facade earlier in the evening as he described how the installation artist had made free with my daughter in public.
Perhaps he had merely invented his piquant little story to let
me know he had understood or anyway sensed, ferreted out,
sniffed his way to discovering there was "something in the
wind" or that "the knives were out" or there was "a rift within
the lute" or whatever it was my mother had hinted at on the
phone. But why should he care about what went on between
Astrid and me? Perhaps he had been speaking from the heart
when his dull wife had gone to buy cigarettes and he told me
how lucky I was. Perhaps because all his little student doves,
however smooth and supple they might be, were only a form
of extremely sensual but nevertheless despairing sublimation.
Perhaps because like so many others he had secretly lusted
after Astrid and so was relishing the knowledge that I was
about to lose what he himself had never come close to pos-
sessing. I tried to remember what had actually happened on
that trip to Greece many years ago when he had so heroically
rescued Rosa's puppy from drowning. But I couldn't find even
a scintilla of one alarming picture to illustrate my suspicions.
That holiday dissolved into a cracked film of quivering heat

haze and fleeting shadows, gleams of light in a bottle of retsina beneath an awning of plaited bamboo, crimson lobsters, the children's sunburned shoulders and bleached hair full of sand, the turquoise blue finger of sea behind the shutters, and Astrid's shadowy body waiting for me in the afternoons in the semi-darkness of our room.

When I awoke I did not know where I was. It was dark around me, and the darkness was parted by a vertical, frayed strand of yellowish light, falling from the ceiling and almost down to the floor, as if a crack had opened in the wall and light was coming through it, a strange, unrecognizable light from another place, another day. I turned on my other side and saw the narrow strip of lighted windows through the curtains I had not completely drawn before I fell asleep. I sat for a long time on the edge of the bed, dazed and confused, before getting up and going over to the window. The white shirts had stopped circling around each other in the buildings opposite, the offices were empty but still fully lit, shadowless. I stood at the window watching the night traffic down on Lexington Avenue, the chain of the cars' red and white lights between the formless, shifting, undifferentiated shoals of bodies passing opposite each other on the sidewalks. In a short while, when I had taken a bath and changed my shirt, I would go down in the elevator and mix with the crowd at the bottom of the shaft among the columns of shining glass. I would reduce myself to a particle among the particles fluctuating beneath me, each with its own direction and yet swallowed up in the same stream of continual, unstoppable, directionless movement.

4

The sun had reached the other side of the block when I awoke, already throwing its afternoon light onto the facades on the opposite side of the Lakes. It occurred to me that for the first time since Astrid had gone I felt no surprise at her absence. For the first time I did not expect, in a moment's forgetfulness, to hear her sounds in the bathroom or the kitchen, the trickle of water on the tiles, the clink of a teaspoon on a saucer. I had begun to accustom myself to solitude and spread myself out in it, now that I did not need to show consideration for her. I had fallen asleep in the middle of the double bed instead of keeping to the half which usually constituted my nightly territory. I threw my cigarette stubs into the toilet bowl, a habit Astrid had cured me of many years ago. I played all the jazz I hadn't listened to for years because she couldn't stand it, and I made do with a sandwich in the evening, when for eighteen years we had cooked a hot dinner every evening, regardless of how tired we were. Within a week part of me had grown used to being alone, completely unaffected by my thoughts constantly circling around her disappearance. I could see the details of a life without her even though I still did not have the remotest idea of their perspective. As I wandered barefoot around the apartment or sat passively at my desk watching the shadows growing under the trees along the lakeshore, it occurred to me how quickly even

an exceptional state acquires a dull tinge of the mundane.
When I decided to go to New York as planned it had been almost in spite of this state and probably also in spite of Astrid,
who had given herself this mysterious advantage in a process
of which I had only vague and anxious notions. The only thing
I knew was that a change had taken place, in her, in us. I did
not know to what. There were times when I felt violently
wronged, but soon after I collapsed again into inertia and self-
reproach because I had allowed her to leave and because I could
not imagine why she had gone. I was convinced it was my own
fault, but at the same time I had to ask myself if I really believed that I alone was responsible. If this too was not yet
another manifestation of my usual self-obsession, my all-too-
frequent fruitless speculations that circled irremediably around
my own frozen ego like moons around a barren planet. Perhaps it was meaningless to ask why. Perhaps even she herself
wouldn't have been able to give an answer.

Hunched over my notes on Cézanne again that afternoon
I realized that I might as well give up. As far as I was concerned Cézanne's apples could rot in peace. If my former life
was about to fall apart I would at least concentrate on seeing
it happen without being distracted by ambitions or promises
that had lost their power over me. I called the editor who had
commissioned the article, and to my surprise he was full of
understanding even though I made no attempt to explain. Afterward I felt how stupid I had been in my fruitless efforts
during the last few days. Obviously Cézanne did not matter,
unless it had been my blunt tone on the telephone that had
made the editor so amenable. I was usually very polite and was
surprised to hear how brusque, indeed almost unfriendly, I was
to him. I felt quite cheerful when I put down the receiver, but

that could have been because the sun was shining and filling
the apartment with a warm, living glow. I decided to go for a
walk, now that I had extricated myself from my duties. It was
a long time since I had strolled along without having to go
anywhere, without anyone waiting for me. During the years
with Astrid and the children, the town had gradually become
a mere backdrop to my purposeful and planned activities in
one sphere or another. There were streets I used every day,
but also areas where I hadn't been for years because I had no
reason to visit them. The town had long since ceased to be the
beckoning, strange and promising world of opportunities and
potential, of intersecting paths and glances, which I had once
explored curiously, full of youthful expectations. It had become ours, Astrid's, the children's and mine, almost as familiar
as the rooms of our apartment and their furnishings, and I
moved around it like a sleepwalker although I knew our town
was only one in the millions of parallel towns, each formed by
their inhabitants according to their own memories, routines
and disappointed or fulfilled hopes. That afternoon, while I
walked around aimlessly, the town was once more an unknown
labyrinth, and although I knew every crossing in the net of
streets, I felt as if I was getting lost. It was Friday, people
crowded the downtown and there was the usual mood of
hectic expectancy when the weekend is approaching with its
measured hours of leisure and indulgence, adventures and at-
tempted escapes. Now and then I would glimpse myself in
bus windows or the dark glass of display windows when I
walked through a ray of sunlight between buildings, and ask
myself, as I had done at dinner the night before, if it was
really me, that man slipping by his own transparent reflection
among the pedestrians and bus passengers and the motionless

wax mannequins in the windows. At other times I searched in vain for myself among the broken-up, momentary reflections of window panes, but saw only other pedestrians' insignificant bodies and faces, as if I was merely a random pair of eyes that were not in the film playing between the light and my retinas.

I went into a café to read a newspaper, but could not even concentrate on the headlines. The great events of the world were too small and indistinct in my field of vision, dominated as it was by Astrid's absence, a sudden, enormous vacancy that the crowd of humanity in the afternoon penetrated and frequented. I could only sit in my corner and watch the passersby with the same apathetic homeless feeling you can have when you sit in a café in a strange town, watching people whose language you can't understand. Although the air was cool they had set tables and chairs out in the sun, and there were as many people outside as in. A girl sat alone at one of the tables furthest out, she must have been about Rosa's age and was dressed like Rosa, in the same casually inventive way, in a big loose-knit roll-neck sweater and a pair of shabby, Prince of Wales tartan men's trousers she must have found at the Salvation Army. Like the sweater the trousers were several sizes too big, and there would have been something comical about her figure were she not sitting so elegantly with her legs crossed and her cigarette raised in an abstract, world-weary gesture as she slowly surveyed the square through her narrow sunglasses, back and forth past the fountain's plumes of pulsing foam and pigeons periodically scattering in fluttering explosions. Her copper hair was gathered at her neck and held in place with a pencil pushed through the loose knot, her thin face was freckled, and I suddenly felt keenly interested in knowing who she was waiting for, what kind of young man she might have fallen for, arrogant and unapproachable as she looked. I ordered another cup of coffee, waiting along with her as she gracefully sipped her tea. Then she straightened and directed her gaze on a point at the end of the square, expectantly, until the person she had caught sight of had seen her too, whereupon she lifted her slim hand and smiled. I looked in the same direction and tried to get a glimpse of the young man she was waving to, until I saw a girl detach herself from the crowd and a moment later recognized Rosa, as she stepped over to the table and embraced the red-haired girl.

I quickly unfolded the newspaper as if in an instant I had become absorbed in an article about economic growth in southern China, and immediately felt annoyed at myself for the abrupt manner in which I had concealed my presence, as if I had a bad conscience. Abashed, I asked myself if I had really been sitting there spying on the red-haired girl like some old lecher who doesn't want to acknowledge his own covert and futile lasciviousness. I who was still far from old, and had been no older than Rosa's young-rebel installation artist when I became her father. Why hadn't I just waited until she happened to see me, waved cheerfully, and let her decide whether she felt like coming over to say hello? Why hadn't I just drunk my coffee and on the way out feigned surprise, kissed her on the cheek, and exchanged a word or two before leaving them to themselves? The longer I sat hiding behind the business pages, the more inept I would seem if Rosa discovered me. But I couldn't bear the thought of looking her in the eyes, I couldn't endure Gunilla in Stockholm hearing yet again the feeble lie that made Astrid's absence into something normal and credible, and I was far from sure I could keep up my guard and conceal the inner turmoil of disquiet and unanswered questions. All the same, I couldn't help peering over the newspaper now and then. There was absolutely nothing in the least arrogant or world-weary about the red-haired girl now. She had pushed her sunglasses up on her forehead, no longer masking herself as an exclusive and unapproachable Bohemian, and she nodded approvingly and laughed aloud at what Rosa was telling her. Hearing their laughter I remembered the countless times I had heard that sound through the closed door of Rosa's room when she had girlfriends visiting. The muffled giggles from a secret and inaccessible world of dreams and intrigues. When she began to grow up Rosa had gradually pulled back from our old intimacy and confided solely in Astrid, and I was completely unqualified to guess what it could be that made the two girls alternately draw their heads close together and then laugh uproariously. We were still affectionate with each other, but at the end of her visit I could sense from her light, somehow evasive way of kissing me goodbye that apart from the increasingly rare conversations with Astrid it was only our washing machine and a few practical pieces of fatherly advice, or perhaps even a few fatherly thousand-kroner notes, that she still had any use for. The rest she found elsewhere, some of it with the red-haired girl with the pencil in her hair, some with the close-shaven installation artist, and some with others I had yet to meet.

When at one point the red-haired girl came into the café and went downstairs to the toilets, Rosa sat gazing pensively across the sunny square, where throngs of people gathered and scattered at random. I could have got up and gone out to her, I could still pretend I had just noticed her, but I just sat there. It occurred to me that I wouldn't know what to say to

her. Here, sitting each on our own side of the big glass pane
looking onto the square, I suddenly saw that the years when
we could find hidden channels into each other's innermost
selves, channels sometimes unknown even to ourselves, were
behind us. It would not have taken much, I could simply have
asked how she was, knowing that she would smile and say she
was fine, but it was precisely that balance between distance
and intimacy, between tenderness and politeness, that I was
not sure I could maintain. I was actually quite happy that she
had no use for me anymore, even though I allowed myself an
occasional bout of wistfulness. But I would not let her see that
for once I was the one who might need her, because I was at
a loss and felt the ground moving beneath me. I wanted to
shield her from the sight and shield myself from her seeing
me like this. I had a strong feeling that she moved so self-
assuredly in her new world only because she knew where she
had me, and because she reckoned I was always so unshakable
and at ease with myself, whether she needed me or not. And I
sensed that I could not bear to see her surprise, or perhaps
even fear, when she saw that I knew even less and was even
more vulnerable and confused than she was. She enjoyed teasing me, but she did so only because she could not imagine it
really hurting me, and in fact that was why she teased me, to
play at shaking my equilibrium, secure in the knowledge that
she would never succeed. If she had just turned her head
halfway around to see what had become of her friend, she
would have seen me, but she kept looking in front of her, smoking her cigarette, thinking her unknown thoughts. She looked
very lovely and mature as she sat in profile with half-closed eyes
and the cigarette between her soft lips. She resembles Astrid
more and more, when Astrid was young, she has the same thick

brown hair, the same narrow green eyes and broad cheekbones, but as I sat observing her that afternoon I could also glimpse in her face the last, blurred traces of the child she had been not so long ago. I walked again along the Lakes with her plump little hand in mine, answering her impossible questions, again I paced the floor with her at night as she screamed as if possessed and vomited down my back. Again I stood in the hospital one night and saw her come into sight between Astrid's thighs, violet blue, covered in blood, with her blind prune face that made me think of the dark, constricted faces uncovered at the bottom of a peat bog, but alive, indomitable and terrified, roaring, head hanging downward, boxing with clenched fists in empty space. It was not so very long ago, and now she sat in the sun smoking with her eyes screwed up.

Astrid, Simon, and I had spent our first summer by the sea in a house she had rented from some acquaintances. She had just divorced the film director and had refrained from making any financial demands, not only out of pride, I think, but also to get it all over with as quickly as possible. Her decision had floored him, since she was the injured party, but it only made things worse that she didn't try to fleece him. He had been un-faithful and yet he was allowed to keep his house and his money, so he played the cad all around. In the long run Astrid could not keep him in the dark about where she had moved, but she always asked me to leave her alone when he came to get Simon. Naturally he would comment on the humble sur-roundings she apparently preferred to the stylish villa in the northern district, but the next moment he might burst into tears in front of his son and ex-wife, shattered with remorse and pleading abjectly for one more chance, despite everything, and referring to "all they had had together." Simon was quite

impossible when his father was expected, he didn't want to go
to Tivoli or the cinema, more than once Astrid had to tear herself away to get him out the door, and when finally he had
gone with his contrite, gray-haired father, she would furiously
batter the apartment with the vacuum cleaner or clean the
windows. When she mentioned the film director it was as if
she was talking about a mistake, an aberration, a blunder, which
she could come to terms with only by standing at a wondering
and ironic remove from the girl who had succumbed to an
older man's formidable passion six years before. In her account of their years together, her love for him became a youthful infatuation, a delusion that had gone on much too long and
too far. I never told her what I thought when she described her
first marriage like that; that perhaps she only reduced her own
and the film director's feelings to lightweight erotic grimaces
in order to be able to convince herself that our emotions were
as dependable and inevitable as gravity itself. Because she
needed to reassure us both that I was the man in her life and
not just a taxi driver, the first one who happened by chance to
come along. We were still young, and perhaps we were both
afraid of our own youth, of the haste with which love had
changed face. It may also have occurred to her in unguarded
moments that her love's new face might turn out to have been
only another mask. We still had so little life behind us, we
couldn't yet know that history is just as uncertain and ambivalent as the future. We still believed that the past could be
exorcised with occult gestures, we still believed that our warm
breath alone was enough to blow life into our hopes.

It was unplanned, but we did not view it as misfortune
when Astrid found herself pregnant in the spring. It was just
another accidental occurrence that changed our life. She did

not say anything to me about her suspicions until she had been to the doctor and had them confirmed. When she did tell me it was in the same offhand manner as when she said she was fond of me, with the same reticence toward the words, as if she had to weigh them in her hands, surprised at their gravity and significance. When she had managed to say it, one night when we lay side by side, while she absentmindedly played with my hair, I had the same feeling about her as some months before, when I'd seen her standing at my kitchen sink and gone over and touched her for the first time. It was with the same recklessness, the same dizzy feeling of life opening out to me, and once again I sensed the reply the moment the question was posed. Why not? She looked away after she had spoken, waiting, and I took her face in my hands and smiled as I met her questioning gaze. Why shouldn't I have a child with her? If my life didn't take form now, when would it? What was I waiting for? What was I afraid of? It was my calm smile that convinced Astrid that it could be the two of us, that it was no longer only an idea, a hope in the sequence of hopes that sets one in motion when one is young, sets one wandering. I had no idea what I was doing, but I did it nonetheless, and the breathless feeling of leaping without hesitation into the unknown, the liberating weightlessness of the leap itself, filled me with a remarkable certainty, one I had never known before. She was in the third month when summer came and we settled into the house by the sea. We didn't tell anyone where we were. It had been impossible to keep the divorce secret, the papers had printed front-page photos of the noted film director who had been deserted by his beautiful young wife, and I had to disconnect the phone for days when Astrid's whereabouts were revealed. The house by the sea was our hiding place while we waited for new divorces and deaths to attract the interest of the vulgar world of shouting headlines and predatory grins, the limelight Astrid had taken her leave of. It was early summer, the beach was still empty, only Astrid, Simon, and I were in the house, and the weeks flowed together as the colors of the sea do in the course of the day. In the end we couldn't distinguish the days from each other, just as you don't notice the sea changing color, pale gray in the morning, dark green in the afternoon, violet blue in the evening, flecked with the dazzling reflections of the low sun.

The sun had just disappeared beyond the horizon. Simon and I were kneeling in the cool damp sand, digging a trench near the water so the waves could fill the moat around the sand castle we had spent the afternoon building, a somber gray medieval fortress with conical towers made with his little bucket. We forgot to talk to each other, absorbed in our laborious engineering, and we hadn't noticed the sea growing dark beneath the orange and green sky. The wind blew off the land and the little waves collapsed onto the wet sand. We slowly succeeded in routing the water into the moat, but only for a moment at a time, then it sank down through the grains of sand, leaving only a feeble scrap of foam. I heard Astrid calling me. Obviously it was time to eat already, but Simon seemed not to hear her, and I went on digging although I had begun to doubt whether it was any use. Astrid called again and I looked up. She stood at the top of the steps leading up to the house behind the small dune where rosebushes grew. She called my name again, and then once more, louder, only my name, her voice was shrill, almost hysterical. Only when she called again did it strike me that something might be wrong. I threw down the little plastic shovel and ran as fast as I could.

She was pale and she began to weep when I reached her and saw the trickles of blood running down her bare legs beneath the thin summer dress. I carried her inside and laid her on a sofa, then called for an ambulance. Simon started to cry too when he saw the blood on her legs, and she tried to comfort him, darting glances over at me by the telephone. I sat I don't know how long holding her hand and stroking her hair without finding anything to say except the same few inadequate and banal sentences, before at last the ambulance came. She wanted me to stay in the house with Simon, who had crept into an armchair, mute with terror, and so I stood beside him watching the ambulance vanish along the quiet road in the twilight. I went on talking to him while cooking, in part to soothe my own anxiety. I talked about everything that occurred to me, about the moat we had dug around our baronial sand castle, about the deserted medieval castles where the knights had once sat in boredom while they waited for a dragon to come along. Later I settled him under his duvet on the sofa in the living room and stayed with him until he fell asleep. I went outside and sat down at the top of the steps from where she had called me. I sat and looked at the glasslike, transparent reflection of the water beneath the pale evening sky. There was nothing to see and yet I stared into the empty, unmoving surface of the sea as you can stare into a wall because you don't know where else to look. I could see the little outline of the sand castle against the sea, which had risen in the meantime so the waves beat the foot of the walls that rose like a dark, fragile island in the shining foam. Just as we had begun to believe it could be reality, what had begun in a chance meeting, a chance impulse, a show of hope, now threatened to leave us. Just when it was beginning to take shape, its own as yet incomplete and half-formed body, no longer dependent only on our ideas, our feelings, embraces, and words. For the first time in my life I spoke to someone who was not there. I spoke to Astrid, alone on the steps in the twilight I begged her to hold on, not to give up, as if my saying it would make any difference. I went on sitting there as it grew darker, smoking in the evening chill amid the bank of rosebushes, and peered at the first stars emerging in the cold gaping vault of the sky. I realized in a different way, more exposed and naked than before, that I was not the only one who was alone as I sat there getting a stiff neck from gazing up at the stars' dead light, that we were alone together, Astrid and I.

In the morning we went to visit her. They had told us she would have to stay in the hospital for a few days. They wouldn't promise anything. She was exhausted with worry, and Simon was terrified at the sight of his pale mother in the white bed. She spoke to him calmly, explained what had happened and asked him about our sand castle. It was still standing, he told her, the waves had not covered it. He smiled as if that was quite a miracle and totally forgot his anxiety. I thought of how she had hummed to him in the taxi that evening the winter their world had fallen apart. She had emanated the same calmness then, even though she had been in turmoil inside. She had made him stop crying by humming the same silly tune over and over as I drove them through town. She had no idea where she was going and still she had been able to hum to him, calmly and gently, as if he did not need to worry about where they were and what was happening around them as long as he could nestle in her arms. We went to see her in the hospital every day. Evidently it was just a question of lying quite still, the crisis was over, she had held on. Up to then I had not been alone with Simon for more than a few hours at a time, but he had already grown accustomed to regarding me as the man in his life. All the same, I wondered at myself when I kissed him goodnight and later in the evening crept up and opened his door a crack to see whether he was asleep. It was the first time anyone had need of me, needed me just to be there. He corrected me sweetly when I forgot to put a pat of butter on his oatmeal or brush his back teeth, and he helped me write shopping lists to make sure I included everything. We spent most of our time on the beach. I taught him to swim, and after a few days he let go of my hands and swam his first strokes quite fearlessly. A fortnight after Astrid came home from the hospital he swam with us right out to the sandbar. He laughed when he saw her admiring face and said as we were swimming that now we were actually four, three in the water and one in her stomach.

I did not forget my wakeful night on the slope by the sea. In my memory it is on those steps of black-stained wood that our story becomes one, a story which began inadvertently one winter night in a coincidence of circumstance. As far back as I could remember my thoughts and feelings had been like a distance between the person I was inside and the world flowing around me, its days, places, and faces. It was as if I was always somewhere else, and I longed to wipe out that distance, I wanted so much to open myself up, let the light of places and the eyes of other people fall upon the unknown one hiding there in the darkness, but the light and the eyes never penetrated far enough, there was always a last shadowy corner where he hid himself, the person I ought to be. When Inés turned toward me one summer day in the semidarkness among the indistinct Roman heads I thought at last that someone had seen him, and

I tried to hold her fast, as if I could see in her eyes what I
hoped she saw. When I met Astrid I had given up on being different from any other figure moving between days and places,
just a face among the other faces in the city's mesh of hurrying changing reflections. But that night when I sat staring out
at the disappearing, almost invisible transition between the
darkness of sky and sea, everything that I was concentrated
into the two little words I kept repeating in a low voice among
the rosebushes, until the words no longer meant anything in
particular because they contained everything: *Hold on, hold on.*
And the evening the following winter when I stood watching
Rosa come into the light, covered in Astrid's blood, it seemed
as if at long last I too came into sight. While Astrid screamed
with pain and emptied herself of the child that had taken shape
inside her, I felt that the distance had finally been covered, that
my love was no longer merely a feeling, a question, a gesture
in thin air, that it had become something that definitively existed between us, someone who filled her lungs for the first
time and emptied them again with a roar.

Our first years are a bright mist of fatigue and happiness,
of days and months that lost their firm outlines in the mo-
mentum, dissolved in the dizzy whirl in which everything
took place. I recall them not as stationary, fixed moments, I recall them as movements on the spot, the same spot. Our first
years are a glade in time, and I remember the feeling of having
arrived, as if I had been lost among the tree trunks in a dense
forest, on blind, overgrown paths, until I finally came out into
the light and saw the sky again. I really came to believe that it
was Astrid I had been waiting for without knowing it. I believed I had arrived at the place where I ought to be. The days
flowed together as if they were one day, one night revolving

gently, and I was no longer impatient for the time to pass, I no
longer dreamed it would take me somewhere else. The days
resembled each other and I had masses of time, and with each
passing year I marveled again that the changes were fruits of
repetition, of the repeated cycle of daily events. We did the
same things day after day, and meanwhile Rosa and Simon
grew between us with the permanent features of their faces
emerging from their soft skin. We exchanged the same words
and caresses, and meanwhile their register of tones and nu-
ances grew, until a quick glance, a fleeting touch or a half-
expressed sentence took on a special meaning depending on
the context, which we alone understood how to interpret.
Each meal we had with the children, each time we made love,
our words and smiles and movements held all the previous
evenings and nights in their repetition, in the repetition's an-
nulment of the flight of time. The days did not obliterate each
other, they no longer devoured each other, but were united in
the same peaceful rhythm of parting and reunion, of business
and sleep, as if we had pitched camp in the midst of time.
Sometimes I was bored, but unlike before the boredom was
not a pain caused by the repeated undermining of my gaze and
my thoughts. When I was bored it was rather a kind of meditation on the unheeded physiognomy of trivial details, the pale
reflection of the winter sun on the wall beneath the kitchen
window, the dry, crisp, ribbed peel that crackled when I picked
up an onion, the drop of water that slowly swelled below the
tap and gathered the light before giving way and falling like
a silvery comet into the gray steel of the sink. When I was
bored it was actually not boredom, but rather a long moment
of unthinking rest in the center of gravity I passed through
repeatedly in the course of the day, in which all fluctuations, all

movements, took their strength. I might forget myself for hours at a time, whether I was changing Rosa's diaper or reading aloud to Simon, whether I sat at my desk watching the words come into view on the paper, or was in bed with Astrid feeling her desire awaken beneath my hands. The whole time there was something around me that grasped me and pulled me with it out of solitude, out of myself and into the profusion of events. Even when I was alone in my study I was only a pair of eyes and a pen, one with what I saw and what I was trying to say. Those were the years in which I couldn't distinguish between duties and freedom, it had come to me as a liberation that every day, every hour of the day there was something I had to do, and I was all the more engrossed in my work because of the knowledge that I did not have the whole day to myself.

I often had to travel for my work, and once again when I found myself early one evening in an ugly hotel room looking out the window at a strange town, I could see them clearly before me. Simon in his room painting tin soldiers, absorbed in the dark blue color of the Northern States' uniforms. Rosa in her little plastic bathtub, singing to herself as she washed the hair of a doll with a film-star smile. Astrid in the kitchen washing spinach with red fingers under the cold tap, and for a moment contemplating the wrinkled folds of the spinach leaves that looked like the folded skin on her swollen fingertips. When I phoned home I sometimes didn't really know what to say. I asked them to tell me what had happened during the day, but I didn't feel I had anything much to talk about, and the little everyday words that would overflow with meaning when their faces were before me grew thin and inadequate, incapable of reaching across the sudden distance. As a rule I looked forward to an interruption of the repetitive pattern of daily life, but as soon as I had left I almost always started to miss them, and roaming the streets of a strange town, left to my own devices, I could feel quite desolate. Whole days could go by when I spoke to no one but waiters and hotel receptionists, exchanging only the most vapid, expedient comments, and if now and then I met an art dealer, a curator, or a critic I warmed myself on the conversation ingratiatingly as if I were a homeless person who had been invited in out of sheer compassion. I felt more exposed when I was traveling than I had before, and it often struck me that in the streets of a foreign town, where no one knew me, I was merely a John Doe who spoke with a comical accent and carried himself rather hesitantly, without the self-contained naturalness of a person on the way to a place where he is expected. Astrid often laughed at me when I phoned home for the second time in a day to ask how things were going, as if something special was going on in my absence.

In the winter of Rosa's seventh birthday I went to Paris for a few days to see a big Giacometti exhibition at the Musée d'Art Moderne. I spent an entire afternoon walking up and down among the tall bronze people on their gigantic feet, thin and bony, their arms at their sides and their expressionless, narrow, loosely modeled faces slightly raised, as if they were listening for something. I had written about them before without managing to pinpoint what it was that made the air vibrate imperceptibly around them each time I saw them again. It was not only because they themselves were almost nothing but lines in the air, almost without dimensions, as if the air were a piece of thin paper on which Giacometti with quick strokes had produced their contours like rents in the light into an unknown darkness. There was also a quality in the space around them, the invisible, transparent space between their reduced forms and my gaze, which reached out to them and fumbled in the void into which they threatened to vanish. While I circled around the fragile, expressionless and introverted men and women in the white gallery, it dawned on me that it was the air itself they made me see, as they tottered on the edge of invisibility and absence. Not only did they withdraw while I looked at them, in toward the innermost limit of spatiality. It was as if my eyes pressed against their bronze bodies and stumbled forward in a free fall as they squeezed themselves in. As if the thin lonely figures, if I looked at them too long, would vanish completely. Perhaps the reason for their indomitable impression on me was the resistance my eyes met when they gazed at the figures so greedily. This last, impassable limit that separated us and prevented them from becoming one with the air before my eyes, this was the limit that Giacometti had apparently continued to search for. After the experiments of the earlier years his work was no longer a matter of renewal, of the continuing extension of the field of experiences. From then on he had stayed in the same place, concerned only with the final hesitation before the point at which presence and disappearance open to each other. And perhaps I am thinking of Giacometti again because it is the same boundary I myself keep approaching, and which I cannot cross when I visualize Astrid again, standing in her overcoat in the bedroom doorway, unmoving, as she waits for me to wake up. I rise, go to her, I stand face to face with her and meet her eyes, and she has already vanished. She stands before me, but she isn't there anymore, she looks at me and it is as if she looks through me, as if she were alone and I were merely a thought.

But there is another reason too for me to be thinking of that winter day in the Palais de Tokyo. As I walked up and down in the quiet gallery among Giacometti's bronze silhouettes, I suddenly felt a hand on my shoulder. When I turned around I saw Inés, standing there smiling at me. I hadn't seen her since my eyes followed her into the snowflakes, after we had said goodbye. There were one or two gray threads in her inky black hair, and she was wearing glasses, but they only brought out the Persian beauty of her eyes, and the slightly sharper, slightly deeper lines around her arrogant nose only accentuated the features I remembered so well, and which had once been the watermark of my sleepless nights. It was almost eight years ago. We asked politely about each other's life, and I told her about Astrid and the children, rather cursorily I felt, as we walked under the plane trees beside the river. She walked as quickly as ever, with the same mercurial nervous gestures while she talked. When I turned toward her I could see the steel girders of the Eiffel Tower weaving themselves in and out of the bare treetops behind her swift, registering glances. She said I looked older, and it suited me. I smiled, unsure of how to reply. We went into a café on the Place de l'Alma. We sat side by side on a long upholstered bench from where you could look at the square. She had lived in Paris for a year or two, she might stay on. She told me she lived alone although I had not asked. She did not make clear what it was she did, a bit of everything it seemed, just as before, money was still obviously not something she needed to worry about. It sounded a little lonely, a little aimless, although she took pains to sound like the anarchic, dissolute woman I had once known. I told her I wrote about art and she listened as if really interested. Emboldened, I spoke of the difference it had made to have children, and she smiled at this, a smile that seemed both sincere and sympathetic in a slightly condescending way, I could interpret it either way, as if to demonstrate that it was still the fêted, fluttering demimondaine who was now amusing herself with my new bourgeois status as happy paterfamilias. Gradually we ran out of news, and in the increasingly long pauses I sat watching the waiters' mechanical, almost hysterically punctilious and competent movements, feeling her gaze on my face. She already knew I was a father. I looked at her. She was calmer than I remembered, no longer afraid to hold a gaze, but her nostrils still flared a little when she smiled, and her teeth were as dazzling as before in her honey-colored face. I couldn't really decide what it did to me to see her again, how deep the sight of her went. She had once seen me on the street with Rosa in the stroller. She asked what my wife did, and I told her a little abruptly. Now she was the one watching the waiters rush around officiously. She would like to have a child too. I looked at her in astonishment, and she read my expression and smiled at herself. Was that so strange? I didn't reply. I lit a cigarette and watched the silhouettes passing on the Place de l'Alma beneath the gray sky. Then I felt her hand rest on mine, at first quite lightly and as if by chance, the dry warmth of her palm.

She had been about to call me several times the winter we parted, and later, the next year, when she guessed I must have given up. Of course she couldn't have known I had found someone else. Over the years she had realized what she had thrown away. Despite the passage of time, she couldn't help thinking that the two of us might have come to something. She probably hadn't been very nice to me. I shrugged my shoulders, I expected I was as much to blame. She asked if I was happy. Yes, I said, answering her gaze, yes, I was happy. But I said it after a pause, as if I had had to think about it. The word sounded wrong in my mouth, "happy." That word was both too big and too small, at once quiveringly ecstatic and too flat and pastel-colored to describe my life. She stroked the back of my hand slowly, took it in hers and turned it palm upward, as if she were a gypsy who could tell my fortune. I let her hold it and regarded it as it lay in hers on the seat beside her knee, which shone faintly through the black tights beneath the hem of her skirt. She too had met someone else, a year or two after we parted. They had been together a long time, and there had not been anyone else during that time. She smiled again, now slightly tentatively. She had really tried. They were still together the afternoon she saw me in the street with Rosa, but it didn't work out after all, and since then she had sometimes thought of me, and not only because she had seen me with my little daughter. She had thought of that time. I had been very young, I had loved her so, what should she say, so excessively. We both laughed at the word. She had almost been forced to guard herself, defend herself against my young, ravenous love. I pressed her hand kindly, and it made me feel old for a moment. But no one else had loved her like that before, and certainly not since. So fearlessly. I took back my hand and lit a fresh cigarette. She asked if I was busy. We could have dinner together, she would be glad to cook. I looked at her again and hesitated, until I came out with an excuse that was not too feeble for us both to live with. We talked about Giacometti for a while, about the ambiguous balance of the bronze figures on the edge of absence. It sounded far-fetched. She wrote her phone number on a napkin before we left, and when we were out in the noise and gray weather on the Place de l'Alma she kissed me quickly and told me to call if I had time. I watched her as she ran down the steps to the metro with her long black coat flapping, thinking that she had not kissed me on the cheek, as one might have expected, and of the feeling of her lips on mine, which I had almost forgotten.

On the way back to my hotel I congratulated myself on having refused Inés's invitation so resolutely, but I did not throw away the napkin, as I had thought of doing. I left it on the bedside table among the day's receipts and loose change. Not until after we had parted had I understood that she had been fishing in a fairly blatant way, which was all the more amazing considering how we had not seen each other for eight years, and only by an absurd coincidence had visited the Palais de Tokyo on the same afternoon. I had not even known she had moved to Paris. If I was piqued afterward over her advances, it was as much because I had allowed myself to be swayed by them. But was there actually anything wrong with talking of the past or admitting that she looked back on it with regret or at least a touch of nostalgia? Wasn't it I who had immediately misinterpreted her hand, which she had rested on mine in mere friendship, her eyes, which had examined the changes in my face with wondering familiarity? Could she be blamed for the sudden return of memories of her knee and her lips? Perhaps not. But still, she must have known what she was doing. She could not but know that her words illuminated my version of the story from an unexpected, unforeseen angle. And she had not merely asked whether we could eat together, she had suggested dinner at her place. I could see it all too easily. Had she really thought about me? Had I not been the only loser in the game? Was it in reality I who had "drawn the longer straw"? It was a wan triumph, it had come too late.

When she left me I felt only sorrow and self-disgust, and since then Astrid had made me forget her, surprisingly quickly it seemed to me now. But what if I had not met Astrid? What if the gray-haired film director had not followed the taxi that evening I drove her and Simon to her friend in town? Then she would have been just another passenger who paid and disappeared into a doorway. And what if Inés had come to me in my sentimental solitude? Ought I to have been more stubborn then, more persevering, since I loved her so immoderately? Could it have been our child I was pushing in a stroller a few years later, passing an unknown Astrid in the street without our giving each other a glance? The thought was too perverse for me to sustain for more than a second or two. Once again I felt confused to think how little it would have taken for my life to have turned out another way. The actual, randomly coincidental, mutually trivial circumstances would merely have fallen into place in a slightly different way. The subtle displacements between my thoughts, feelings, and impulses need only have undergone slightly other displacements and influences at a slightly different time. What if one winter evening I had not left the table without knowing precisely what I was doing, to walk into my kitchen where Astrid stood with her back to me, still only an unknown young woman whom I had helped out of a jam? What if I had never put my hand on her cheek? What if she had flinched at my touch?

The cherished life that had been mine, in which I had finally become myself, finally at home in the world, settled in my love for Astrid and the children, was no more than a blind, tentative shoot in time's desultory branching of possibilities. Neither more nor less in tune with my innermost self than all the failed shoots that had withered and fallen along the way.

One branch had grown strong and put out new shoots, because we wanted it, and because circumstances made it possible. Minuscule deviations in the blind growth of chance
could have prevented it from ever coming to fruition. Yet perhaps there had been a hidden, frightening connection between
the withered and the surviving shoots. When I stood in my
kitchen one winter evening and brought my hand to Astrid's
cheek, it was also a rebellion against Inés, against the grievous
state in which she had left me, and it was a betrayal of myself,
of the passion I had been one with and which threatened to de-
vour me from within. I saved myself, but only by betraying
myself. I could only cross the imperceptible threshold of a new
life by turning my back on the old one. I could only transform
this in itself coincidental and random step into the crossing of
a threshold by convincing myself that there was a world of difference. Thus I could not really know who it was that caressed
Astrid's cheek and held her face in his hands. If it was the person who loved Inés so hopelessly and uncontrollably, his caress in the kitchen could not be totally sincere. And if it was a
new and still unknown version of myself, who a few months
later smiled calmly when Astrid told him he could be a father,
shouldn't he perhaps have hesitated with his reckless *Why
not?* He should instead have considered why, but he still knew
neither her nor himself well enough to know the answer. He
surprised me. Before I could look around they had become a
family, he and the girl I had picked up in my taxi. It had come
to me like an unexpected gift, and he accepted it before I had
time to feel whether it was what I wanted. He had obviously
settled into me for good, and I grew used to his speaking and
acting in my place, until it was impossible to tell us apart.
Eight years later as I sat in my hotel room in Paris thinking of

when I loved Inés, it was like thinking of someone else's love, and yet I had to ask, uneasily, holding in my breath, if it was only myself I had betrayed. Or if I had not also betrayed Astrid.

I see her standing before me in our bedroom doorway, with an expression that seems to see something I do not know, from inside a place I do not recognize. I see Rosa sitting on the other side of the café window, out in the sunshine, looking away across the square, I have no idea at what. Her hair and her skin and her laughter were the living, material proof of my love. It was her child's eyes that had made me into a father when I walked back and forth holding her in my arms, her little, weightless body entirely in my care. Her trusting look later, when I walked beside the Lakes with her, holding her hand, and she suddenly stopped and asked me anxiously when time would come to an end, at the mercy of my reply. Now she was sitting in a café smoking, aloof and alone. When I saw her sitting there with her coffee and cigarette on the other side of childhood, I had long since stopped comparing my brief young love for Inés with my love for Astrid. Time itself made the difference. Sitting behind my newspaper observing Rosa's profile in the sun, I recalled the story the museum curator had told me in the taxi the night before. Now as I thought about it in daylight it seemed grotesque and incredible. I simply could not imagine Astrid having a fling with some bald old student friend of mine, not with him anyway. There was something tasteless and tacky about his confiding in me, which made me want to clean my teeth. I would never be able to accept his offer of a little chewed-over clot of knowledge, dripping with saliva and vindictive vanity. I had to stay inside the boundary of what I knew, on the threshold of the bedroom, face to face with Astrid and everything I could not know. She looks at me, in her coat, with her packed suitcase, and I cannot imagine what she sees, through what she is seeing me. Perhaps she too has faltered between one step and the next, perhaps she too, in the imperceptible transitions from one thing to another, has asked herself whether she was moving in the right direction or had lost her way without realizing it. And yet she did in fact go on, with only a faint shadow of doubt behind her eyes, as one day gave way to the next. Until she lay awake again in the darkness between the days, pushed a thought ajar and let the cold air waft in from the unknown, not quite sure if it really was she herself lying beside me or someone who just resembled her. Perhaps she also thought of the whirling fortuitousness of it all, and perhaps with the years she thought that it is not the paths and the faces that make a difference, the paths that open out all the time in all directions, the faces that approach you all the time and pass by. Perhaps with time she also came to think that it is only she herself who, step by step through the days and years, goes forward to meet a difference. A difference that has never been written in her heart because it can only be written in footprints. Because her love doesn't care whom she loves and why.

Some years ago, when we were leaving a cinema together and I greeted Inés across the crowd, she had long since become merely an old flame I burned myself on in my misguided youth. But perhaps I had taken too long to realize it, perhaps I had realized it too late. Astrid noticed the beautiful, exotic-looking woman who nodded and smiled briefly at me from across the lobby before disappearing onto the street, and she asked me who it was with casual curiosity, as if she was not really interested. I told her it was an old acquaintance, but I didn't say it was Inés. She may have guessed, but it may also have been that she didn't bother to wonder who the unknown woman might be. It was already a long time since I had told her about the lost love of my youth, a long time since we had stopped telling each other stories of our past, perhaps because it gradually took up so little space in comparison to our own story, perhaps because we really believed everything had been told. Why didn't I just say it was Inés? My lack of candor made me dwell on this fleeting encounter much more than I might have if I had told her the woman in the cinema lobby with the hawk's nose and gray threads in her black hair was identical with the young woman who had once been the object of my desperate longings. I had told Astrid about her the summer after we met, when she was pregnant with Rosa, while we were still interrogating each other about everything that came before that winter evening when our lives took their decisive turn. We were in bed in our room in the house by the sea, Simon was asleep in the next room. Her face shone indistinctly in the blue half-light of the summer night, and I caressed her forehead and cheeks as if I could brush away the fine dust grains of twilight from them, just as I brushed the sand from her calves and feet. I described, hesitantly at first, how I had abased myself, eaten up with jealousy, and how I had spied on Inés and hounded her until she could no longer breathe in my presence. I did it in such an ironic and detached manner that the very tone of my voice told her that it was not only a closed chapter but also a delusion, an infatuated dream, out of which she, Astrid, had woken me. She listened to me with her thoughtful, crooked smile, as if wondering that I could really have been so deranged. She seemed almost fascinated by my account, questioning me on apparently irrelevant details, and I allowed myself to be swept along. I depicted and exaggerated the portrait of the passionate madman I had been until I noticed a flicker in her eyes as if she was forcing herself to keep looking at me. I kissed her and said I loved her, that it was not until I started living with her that I had learned to love, because she had released me from my self-absorbed phantoms. She moved close to me and whispered in my ear not to say any more, it wasn't necessary. She cupped my face in her hands and looked at me with tender, veiled eyes in the twilight. "We are here, you know," she whispered. "Isn't that enough?" I caressed her warm body till I could feel she was ready, and then entered her, carefully at first, because I recalled the evening when she had stood at the top of the steps calling me, with the blood trickling down her legs, but she merely smiled and told me not to be afraid. It wasn't a disease, after all. Afterward we lay there quietly, still entwined, listening to the waves breaking under the window, their abrupt fall and the sucking, purling sound when they withdrew.

On that winter evening in Paris when I sat watching the light fall behind the shutters until it was only a dark blue lining behind the darkness of the room, I regretted having let Inés kiss me goodbye and disappear into the metro below the Place de l'Alma. I had been alarmed at the thought that I might succumb to her nostalgic allure as a kind of delayed revenge, as if in spite of everything I could pick apples from a branch I myself had lopped off. As I sat there in the growing darkness, remembering Inés's eyes behind her strange new glasses seconds before we parted in the gray winter light, I felt a desire to step off course, to draw her to me and inhale the scent of what had never come to anything. I felt like spending one night in a world that was no longer there, sinking away into her for one night, locked between her arms and legs in an old fury, until she would finally let go and I would finally feel that my old anger had left me. Perhaps I really believed that I would be able to lay the old ghost to rest by embracing it. Perhaps it was only the dormant nameless desire persisting in my imagination because she had so unexpectedly offered herself to me. My shortsighted, insatiable, and unscrupulous lust, which was perhaps the banal truth behind the masks of sensitivity. Her answering machine was switched on. I listened to her melodious, sensual voice speaking French, and only when the beep was followed by silence, my own silence, did I discover I had walked into a trap. Whatever I said, and however casually I said it, she would realize why I called. A single sentence, even the most banal and offhand, would be enough to betray me, betray Astrid, betray my new life, the new, cherished self-assurance that had given me the courage to pick up the receiver and dial the number on the napkin, which I should have crumpled up and thrown away while there was still time. Even if I let her understand, in the most neutral and undemonstrative manner, that I wasn't averse to the idea of seeing her again, I would risk letting my desire shine through. With a few apparently innocent sentences on her answering machine I would have given her proof that I too had lost my way in the tangled wilderness of chance, that my life with Astrid and the children was after all merely a resigned capitulation to whatever had been possible, whatever had panned out after she left me. It would have been Inés who had remained faithful to our genuine, young love, and I who had forsaken it because I had lacked the courage to suffer and wait, and who now, when she stretched out a hand, seized it immediately, wet with tears of gratitude and churning with pent-up passion.

I had just put down the receiver when the telephone rang. I let it ring once or twice before picking it up. It was Astrid. She wanted to know what time I would be landing the following day, and if I wanted to be met at the airport. She asked if anything was wrong. I thought my voice sounded completely normal. I said I had been asleep when she called. I told her about the exhibition I had seen and she told me an amusing comment Rosa had made that morning. Suddenly I missed all three of them terribly, and she laughed at how fond I could be on the phone, just because we hadn't seen each other for a couple of days. I soon forgot about my meeting with Inés, and afterward, when I would occasionally remember it, I felt surprised to have forgotten it as quickly as I had let myself be overwhelmed with doubt and second-guessing at the sight of her. If occasionally I lay sleepless at night listening to Astrid's peaceful breathing beside me in the dark, it was not because I was haunted by Inés and her eyes and lips one afternoon in the Place de l'Alma. Nor was it because I imagined Inés lying beside me in the dark, in a different apartment somewhere else in town, in another life. It was not the reunion that had shaken me, it was its aftereffects, not the spasm of desire in my Paris hotel room when I dialed her telephone number, but the unexpectedly chill light that had been thrown onto my present life, my sudden irresolution in the dull gray light of the Place de l'Alma. It was these sudden dizzy attacks of weightlessness that kept me awake and made me turn toward Astrid's invisible face and put my arm around her sleeping body, as if I was afraid of levitating from the bed and drifting away into the bottomless night.

I haven't been alone since she turned up one winter evening holding a little boy by the hand and got into the back seat of my taxi, and it is even longer since she herself was last alone. She was young when she had Simon, and younger still when she met a gray-haired man with sure hands and an in-

sistent gaze that seemed to mold her when he looked at her
and embraced her. She had smiled, the young woman, at his
adult desire, but in the end she had given in, perhaps weary of
playing hide and seek, perhaps because she longed to be seen.
She had been almost invisible when he noticed her. She had
still been a child when an aunt with whom she spent the
summer holidays told her one morning that her parents had
driven over the edge of a cliff in Italy. The rest of her childhood had been spent at boarding school, until at last she was
free to do what she wanted, but she was at a loss for what to
do with all that freedom. She was alone in the world, confused
by the thought of everything that was possible, bewildered at
the countless paths opening up to her, the crowd of faces coming toward her, and she had not yet decided on anything when
the gray-haired film director set his eyes on her. No one could
tell her who she was, no one was going to come and tell her
that. In the beginning it had amused her that she could drive
a grown man that crazy, and later it had fascinated her to be
the secret in his life, invisible to others and sometimes also to
him when she closed her eyes as he clasped her, beside himself
with passion. Until, that is, she decided she wanted to come
into view, perhaps because she was afraid of disappearing
completely if she kept giving him the slip, she, the precious secret he was so clever at keeping hidden from his wife and his
daughter. She could have been his daughter herself, and yet
she gave in when he grew tired of the intrigues and one day
appeared at her door with his suitcases and his dramatic gaze.
She thought that after all it might be love, what had begun as
a secret chase where the young prey roused the old hunter
with her musing or preoccupied smile. She convinced herself it
must be love, and she stood by her decision once she had made

it. She adapted to it, as she adapted to being with the little boy and his father in the white house in the northern part of town, and she let time pass. At first she thought nothing of it when her gray-haired husband came home later and later, and when one evening she discovered why, there was a long moment when she just fell and fell, in a bottomless and endless descent. When she felt the floor under her feet again she was not in the same world as before. They had not lived in the same world, she and the gray-haired film director. This was not her, it couldn't be her, this young woman who had borne their child and cared for it while he was in another part of town with another, even younger woman, and all she knew was that she could not stay an hour more in a house suddenly grown so alien.

She didn't belong anywhere when she sat in the back seat of the taxi with her little son, but she had already tried that before. Perhaps that was why she hesitated only a moment when the taxi driver offered her a few days' refuge in his apartment. He seemed nice enough, and they were even about the same age. So she had stayed on there. She must have asked herself later how it had happened, what about him had caught her attention, why he was suddenly not merely a helpful taxi driver with an apartment that happened to be empty at night. Did such things happen, just like that? In the beginning it did not mean anything, and that may have been why she gave herself to him, because it did not have to mean anything. He was only a random taxi driver, to him she could be anyone at all. He was in no hurry to tell her who she was, he let her think what she pleased while he embraced her. He wasn't trying to take her somewhere, he was not going anywhere in particular, the man who drove all over town every night. When she discovered she was pregnant she may have wondered about the risk she was running, but she couldn't help smiling when she told him and he looked back at her calmly and said *Why not?* Yes, she may have thought, why not indeed? It was his calmness, she told him later, that had convinced her, when instead of being seized with panic he merely looked at her like someone who knew what he was doing. She had to love a man who could look at her so calmly, a completely strange woman who confided to him that she could make him a father if he wanted it. His astonishing *Why not* made her forget to ask herself why exactly it should be him. She had to love a man who dared to take the chance when it came along because he knew that in any case it was coincidental who you met and when, and because he dared to believe it might be now that his life would take shape, and not next year or the year after. Not until after it happened, after the decisive step had been taken, blindly, did her love discover its reasons. To begin with she just liked his eyes, his eyes and his calm voice, such an arbitrary thing. She told him once, and he smiled. "Yes," he said, "it doesn't matter why one loves." She had awoken one morning when he spoke her name in his soft, calm voice, and had opened her eyes and discovered that it was here she belonged, in his calm gaze that seemed to completely enclose her. His affectionate, slightly melancholy eyes seemed to open a great space around her in which she could be herself, in which she could run as hard, as far, as she wanted without disappearing. But she no longer had any desire to run as she had run when she was young, when some lovestruck puppy or desperate grown man tried to tell her who she was and mold her with their lusting hands. When she was young she had believed she was someone else inside, a stranger that only a strange, unknown man would be able to recognize. She had deserted men, young or mature, one after another, when they turned out not to be the one who could lure her into the light. Who should it have been? She laughed at herself as she described her youthful restlessness. As time passed she could not think of herself apart from the life that had become hers that winter evening when she left the gray-haired film director because she had found out she no longer lived in the world she thought she lived in. Everything before that evening gradually seemed to her like rough, obliterated, rejected sketches for what was to come. But it is many years since she talked to me in that way about herself. It became unnecessary to talk so much. After all, it was enough that we were there.

I cannot unravel our first years, I cannot distinguish between them. Even when I unwind the long thread of the narrative, and no matter how much my story twists backward and forward between then and now, there is a difference between the thread and the ball of yarn. Even if the ball is made up of the same thread, it is not in itself a story. It is merely a globe of compressed days and places that succeed one another, so the innermost ones have long since disappeared into the soft darkness of the ball. As I unwind the thread into the light the ball grows smaller and smaller, and it loses its weight until only the weightless line of the narrative is left, the line's long series of continuous points, with its twists and turns marking my attempts to interpret the years' convolutions and entanglements, the years revolving in time with the earth's perpetual spinning rotation of repetition and change. It's funny how you always talk about time as if it is a place in which you move back and forth. Perhaps it really is a place, the place where all days and hours coexist, perhaps you tell your story in order to find a way through memory's labyrinth of moments separated by oblivion. But there are different ways through its crooked paths, and if you go one way you cut yourself off from all the others. You make your way into the labyrinth while unrolling your ball of wool, and when it runs out you have only a loose end to hold on to. Slowly you return, tracking yourself down. Now and then you hear voices behind the thin walls, now and then you see a gleam of light where you thought there was only a wall, but you keep to the track, afraid of dropping the thread and getting lost. In my memory I am everywhere at the same time, but not quite the same from place to place. In my story I can only be in one place at each single moment if I am to find the way between the places and discover how I went from one to another.

Rosa leaned her head back and closed her eyes in the sunshine, so her long hair fell softly over the back of her chair. I imagined her sensing the light like an orange fog through her eyelids, listening to the clicking footsteps of the passersby and the voices around her at other tables. When you close your eyes you are in the midst of everything. The sounds of the world and your own thoughts blend with each other in the same invisible space. There was the hint of a smile at the corners of her mouth, elicited either by the warmth on her face or by something she was thinking. She raised a hand and stroked her neck, caressing slowly. I recognized the motion, as Astrid did that too when she was thinking, at once self-forgetful and yet drawn into herself. I too closed my eyes for a moment, and it seemed to bring us closer together. Why couldn't I just get up and go out to her, why were we each sitting on our own side of the wide café windows, my daughter and her father? I was ashamed of hiding from her, but I knew I would also feel somehow ashamed to go outside and meet her gaze. I was

ashamed of Astrid leaving me. If sometimes, when the darkness
was too dense or too bottomless, I had needed to embrace
Astrid as she slept, afraid of slipping away from her, one look
from Rosa had always been enough to confirm I was where I
belonged, that this was my home, not merely some random
point on the globe. Her gaze had held me like the invisible
cord of a kite, and she didn't even know it, in her eyes it was I
who held the cord, so she could safely launch into the air and
explore the heavens. When I was in the delivery room with
her light, newborn body wrapped in a blanket, I was overcome
by a panicked fear of dropping her, and I mumbled the same
words in my head as I had spoken into the summer night, sitting between the rosebushes on the steps to the beach, *Hold on.*
When I opened my eyes again she was looking at the fountain's glittering jets, the wind whipping the water sideways in
a snow of shining drops and foam, constantly renewed and
vanishing in the same pulsing movement. I had held on. Now
it was time to let go.

I saw her red-haired friend come up the stairs. She had put
on lipstick and her red mouth resembled a sharp, mobile sign
in her pale freckled face. She caught sight of me and smiled
faintly. I smiled back and held her gaze as she drew nearer and
passed, and I could see a faint blush under her freckles before
she glided out of my field of vision. If I had looked away when
she saw me, my embarrassment would have revealed that my
gaze was not by chance. Now it was her turn to be embarrassed, because I had reciprocated her fleeting, cheerful smile
with eyes that read her face with interest. Perhaps she had
smiled because it had occurred to her in passing that the man
reading the paper in the corner actually looked rather good.
Perhaps she had basked for a second in my attentive gaze and

at the edge of her consciousness flirted with the thought that I was a man and not just a man who could be her father, and then immediately pulled in her antennae, afraid I might have interpreted her smile as encouragement. Perhaps, and now it was my turn to blush, perhaps she knew I was Rosa's father, perhaps she had blushed because my glance was a disconcerting transgression of our roles. I resorted to the newspaper again and stole a glance like an observant cat past the headlines at the two girls in the sun. If the red-haired one knew who I was she gave no sign of it to Rosa. Again they took turns speaking and nodding or smiling at what the other said, and at one point, when I had become reasonably comfortable with the situation again, she suddenly looked past Rosa and in through the window, and briefly caught my eye. She did this once or twice more, as if she wanted to assure herself I was still there, keeping an eye on her. My eyes darted among the headlines and I was conscious of every twitch in my face. When I looked up from the paper again a little later they had gone, and I sat looking out at their empty cups, Rosa's friend's with a faint red lipstick mark on the edge, like a greeting to my forty-four-year-old confusion.

I walked along Stróget, the pedestrian mall, into the evening sunshine, in which the crowd merged and branched out again in a black forest of strolling silhouettes, their long shadows plaited on the dazzling flagstones. The low sunlight shining between the facades ate into the silhouettes, frail and tenuous as Giacometti's bronze figures. The light dazzled me so I could not see the faces in the black stream of figures before they stepped out of their dark outline with a look that brushed mine, the second before we passed each other. I felt that at each step I passed through another's gaze, to be followed a moment later by the one walking behind me, just as the strange faces were transformed before my eyes when they came out of the shadows and up to me. It was as if they not only passed me, but also passed through me, even as I in the same movement passed through their gaze into the light, the same rhythm of footsteps and rocking faces, in which I constantly caught sight of another, and was myself ceaselessly seen by another and then again another, as if I too could not remain the same for more than a glance, a second at a time.

5

I left the hotel and wandered the streets between Fifth Avenue and Times Square, in a crowd of pedestrians between buildings with vertical slabs of lit windows and the horizontal stream of car lights. I observed the faces passing through the islands of light in the darkness, new faces unceasingly, strangers as I was in this city where everyone comes from somewhere else. It is the only foreign city where I am not reminded that I am a foreigner with each step I take, where my accent and my appearance are merely yet another difference among all the differences that counter-balance each other. If the taxi drivers and bartenders and wait-resses get impatient with me it is not because they see me as a foreigner, but because they consider me a New Yorker who is merely intolerably slow or indecisive or awkward. In New York I can be whoever I wish, as long as I remember to give a tip. That evening I steadied myself by drifting along with one, then another stream of pedestrians in the grid of streets. Fatigue numbed me, only my sight and hearing were exempt from the pleasant feeling of lethargy, and everything I saw and heard was a repetition of something I had seen and heard before, the car horns, the disconnected words, the shining buildings and the river of faces. It was like walking into a film I had seen hundreds of times, the same street scene that ap-pears in every film set in New York, but without going on to the next scene, as if the film ran in a continuous loop and I were just moving in place. As I walked on without stopping I saw the city twist and turn around me, it was the city that moved and I observed it, passive and unmoving, from a far distant place in myself.

I thought of all the people who had come here, driven by flight from something or by a vague hope of something different, who had walked the same streets I walked now, in the same deep chasms that opened up at right angles between the oblong, unapproachable buildings. Again it struck me that this city, which has attracted so many people from every corner of the world, itself has no visible, noticeable center like European cities, in which the streets, if you walk through them long enough, always come together at the one point. Old, sooty, mysterious cities, where you arrive one evening by train and soon after leaving the station come face to face with the apostles and saints illuminated on the facade of the cathedral. Here all the railways are underground. When you first arrive you can just float around the streets crisscrossing each other at regular intervals. In itself the city does not give you the feeling of having arrived at the enchanted vanishing point of dreams and hopes. In reality it is an invisible city, its streets no more than the invisible netted screen of the travelers' inner images of the places they have left and may have lost forever. New York is visible only to those who observe it through the faded transparent memory of the wheat plains of Ukraine or the mountains of Armenia, a slum district of corrugated iron in Puerto Rico or the inundated rice fields of Guangdong. It is so easy to find your way here, yet in a subtle way also easy to get lost, because the square monotony of the city plan does not help you trace what it was you were really looking for. But that evening it suited me perfectly, I was not doing anything that evening. I ate at a diner on Fifty-second Street, one of those merciful, functional places where you can eat on a bar stool at a long counter without feeling embarrassed to be alone. I sat looking out at the traffic behind the mirror-imaged red neon beer ads in the window, behind the pane's blurred reproduction of my silhouette, bent over on the bar stool, transparent, so the passersby on the sidewalk seemed to walk right through me, homeless beggars with outstretched paper cups, beautiful busy women of all races. I looked at my watch, added six hours, and tried to recall precisely what I had been doing at the same time the previous evening.

I had been standing in a corner of the stage with my back to the empty seats in the auditorium, watching my mother's rubbery, red-painted lips and the sparkling white crowns revealed in her predatory smile each time someone came up to kiss her cheek during the little *Nachspiel* after her premiere, which she had called to remind me of the evening I had had Rosa and her installation artist to dinner. She had been as self-conscious and histrionic on stage as usual, and as usual the tittering, maniacally affected gays and preening prima donnas with roving eyes flocked around her to swear how absolutely wonderfully and superbly she had once again surpassed herself with her sophisticated, expressive insight. If she had ever had even mediocre talent it had long since been lost through her insatiable hunger to be loved by her audience, who had gratefully and emotionally laughed and wept down there in the dark for years, thankful that with her vulgar and irrelevant grimaces she sanctioned their coarse, lowbrow sense of humor, and moved that with her crocodile tears and her heaving, ample bosom she raised their shallow and sentimental passions to fateful and universal stories of Great Love. At one time her wasp waist and deep cleavage had ensured her role upon role as a weak, enchanting woman at the mercy of her emotions, and on the whole she exemplified perfectly the maxim that what you lack between your ears you must have between your legs, which one theater director after another had in fact had the opportunity to confirm. In the end age had forced her to take "mature roles," but this had merely induced the critics to discover new and subtle sides of her talent, purified now by the wisdom of experience. The thought of growing old filled her with terror, and she was still too vacuous to comprehend a word of the dialogue she sobbed and wailed her way through, but when her nearest rival on the boards was disabled by thrombosis, the role of grande dame became vacant, and there being no other suitable candidates, it fell to her.

As I sat in the dark watching her sloppy gestures in the bright footlights, my reasons for never going to the theater were confirmed once more, and I regretted not having stayed home. But after I had seen Rosa and her red-haired friend vanish into the crowd and finally returned home from my walk, the evening opened up before me in the silent apartment, empty and dull, and I had seized on my mother's premiere as a feeble excuse for pretending everything was normal for an hour or two. Now I wished I was back at my desk, staring blindly at the lighted windows on the other side of the lake. My father sat a little further down the row, he had fallen asleep five minutes into the first act. He had been in the lobby, solitary among the high-spirited first-night crowd of sweating men, obviously uncomfortable in their freshly pressed funeral garb, and their wives, who looked as if they were about to trip any moment even though their long Thai silk dresses were uniformly ten centimeters too short. My father was as elegant as ever, scanning the lobby with his customary nervous gaze, more suited to an insecure teenager than a distinguished septuagenarian. I felt sorry for him when I saw how relieved he was to catch sight of me, and at the same time ashamed of my own sympathy. Not until we had stood chatting for some minutes did I notice that he had forgotten to ask why Astrid was not with me. Perhaps he had spoken to my mother, perhaps he was glad that for once there were only the two of us, or else he was merely distrait. No one would have been surprised that he was on his own. My mother despised his new wife, she had made no secret of that on the few occasions she had met her, and her contempt for her ex-husband was all the greater because he was satisfied with such an inferior substitute when she herself had ditched him. She couldn't care less whether he came to her premieres or not, but even though it was almost thirty years since she had left him he kept turning up, furtive and conscientious, "to make her happy," as he put it.

I seldom saw him. He had moved to the other end of Denmark a few years before I met Astrid, and the distance had made it easier to refuse his invitations. I visited him several summers in a row with Astrid and the children, and each spring he called again and asked if we would be coming that summer, but after each visit I had found it hard to be friendly toward his new wife, a potter who was twenty years younger than him and interested in astrology and organic vegetables. When we went to visit them in their little thatched bungalow she fell upon me as if she hadn't spoken to a civilized person in months, and excitedly insisted that I must justify why, many years ago, I had written in an article that craft could not be on the same footing as art. Out of consideration for my father I had refrained from telling her what I thought of her clumsy pots and bowls, a reticence that only made her persist further and triumphantly explain my cold and distant arrogance by saying I was a typical Scorpio. But I might have stood her aggressive inferiority complexes and her musk-plant scented, esoteric provincialism had I not had to put up with being a passive witness to my distinguished father's subjecting himself like a whipped dog to her wayward, neurotic mood swings, whether she attributed them to the moon's phases or his masculine lack of feeling for her biorhythms. My father had been an engineer before retiring, he had built bridges and dams in Africa and the Middle East, and now he spent his time lighting incense candles and serving herbal tea for his holistic partner and giving her Tibetan foot massages and fondling her astral body while allowing her to instruct him with her twaddle about the emotional life of plants. I was not resigned to his choice until Astrid once made me aware with a crooked smile that in my rage I had quite overlooked the fact that he was apparently happy. I think she was right, and perhaps the leap was not after all so great from his old blind faith in mathematics to his new ecological piety, both were sustained by the same resolutely radical consistency, the same fear of life's irony and unanswered questions. In my view his new marriage was a parody of his marriage to my mother, the only difference being that the degradation was no longer painful, merely ludicrous. Behind the concrete engineer's masculine exterior beat a kind but nervous heart, in its loneliness pleading to be loved, believing naively that it was something he could deserve. When I was a child he sent me postcards from towns with strange names, and I kept the cards with African or Arabic themes in a box under my bed. He was always building a bridge or a dam or a power station somewhere or other in a tropical country, he was often away for months at a time, and every morning I sat feeling the oatmeal swelling in my mouth while waiting for the clatter of the mail slot and the soft thud on the hall floor. I have kept one of his cards, which I find particularly moving today. It is not the aerial photograph in itself that moves me, the sunny view over a tongue of land densely built up with white high-rises surrounded by the improbably blue sea. Nor is it his laconic note on the back about the temperature and his own well-being, dated 9th October 1965. It is the printed text, in small type above his faded handwriting: *Beirouth Moderne, Vue générale et les grands Hôtels de la Riviera Libanaise.*

I learned early on to look after myself, my mother always slept late, and when I came home from school she had usually gone to a rehearsal or was "on the air," if she was not resting behind the closed door of their bedroom with the curtains drawn. My friends' mothers were always in their suburban homes wearing their aprons, ready with hot cocoa in the pan, but she lolled on the unmade bed, reading the paper with a cigarette hanging from her mouth, unapproachable and blowsy in a dissolute way that offended my puritanical boyish mind. We did not meet until the evening, when at long last she emerged from her boudoir, heavy with sleep and provocatively voluptuous in her open kimono, to heat up a can of soup or a thawed frozen dinner for us before vanishing again to "get ready" before she left me to myself and took a taxi to the theater. Only when she gave interviews to "the magazines" did she tidy the house in a rush so it looked like a home in case we were to be photographed together, she bending over slightly, her chin pressed into my hair so the photographer had the benefit of both my plump childish cheeks and her bulging bosom. Even I have to admit she was beautiful then, unnervingly beautiful when she leaned over me, powdered and with her hair piled up, to kiss me goodbye before she walked down the front path to the waiting taxi, her high heels clicking, her hips rocking in her narrow skirt. Her beauty had the effect of a vague and incalculable threat, it alienated her from me because it was so clearly meant for others, and when she bent to kiss me on the cheek with her soft full lips, her perfume and her white conical breasts in the low-necked dress made me feel like an ugly little manikin who, undeservedly and as a special divine dispensation, was brushed for a moment by the murderously gentle light of a world in which I would never succeed. We seldom talked for very long, and if we did, it was usually in the form of a continuing monologue, as if she was thinking aloud just because I happened to be there, when she sighed and said how hard it was, how everyone harassed her so much, and how sometimes she felt like "running away screaming." I imagined her running down the suburban road, screaming, in her slip and with her hair flying. I am not exaggerating when I say that in extent and depth of content my mother's communicativeness toward me more or less matched what my father found room for on the backs of his postcards with camels, Bedouin tents, minarets, elephants, and African villages. Terse, brief messages, which apart from observations about the weather merely stated that he was well and hoped I was well too, and that he was looking forward to seeing me again. Only rarely did he go any deeper and then merely with the vague assurance that he was "thinking of me." I never knew what he thought when he was thinking of me. But it never occurred to me to reproach him for his timid brevity. I took it as proof of his indisputable and sovereign masculinity, involved as he was with his bridges and dams and power stations, which in my eyes he constructed almost with his own bare hands, with his chin stubbled and a tropical helmet performing feats of inhuman strength as, dogged and unswerving, he defied the baking sun and wild animals and the natives' incorrigible laziness. In the evening I lay in bed imagining that one day he would take me with him, how we would leave my slut of a mother to her afternoon sleep and her theater, how I would stand on the desert sand and pass him the monkey wrench, and how, dripping with sweat and without glancing at me he would take it and, his muscles flexing, tighten the last nut in a steel bridge across a godforsaken wadi in the white heat of the Sahara.

The day before he returned from his engineering exploits there would be a dramatic change. Instead of spending the afternoon in bed my mother would be seized by sudden energy, she would storm around the house straightening things and vacuuming, beating sofa cushions and airing the rooms, and what had come in the past weeks to resemble a brothel after closing time was transformed in a couple of hours into a solid bourgeois home like those of my schoolmates. For the first time in weeks she went shopping and exhibited a hitherto unsuspected gastronomic potential, and when my father finally stood in the doorway, suntanned and mythical, she flew to him and flung her arms around him, clasping him so hard that in the end he had to laughingly pry himself loose from her amorous embrace. For one single evening I was in heaven, the calm cloudless heaven of bourgeois life, and my mother and I sat at the table listening with smiles and amazement to his stories of exotic lands. For once my mother's dazzling beauty was not a threat, and I did not find it at all painful when I saw her kissing my father, putting her arm around his waist and seductively stroking his behind. She played that role too, so not an eye was dry, but as early as the next day she began to be irritable, and I saw how my father, the bridge-builder, turbine constructor, and imperturbable concrete expert, had to exert himself to please her and win even a single casual caress. Again she retreated to her bedroom in the afternoons. When he came home she produced dinner sullenly and grudgingly from what was in the fridge, and his gentle voice and entreating eyes only made her still more distant and short-tempered. When she had gone off to the theater we took refuge on the sofa, in Kipling's, Cooper's, and Stevenson's worlds of palpable dangers and simple virtues, but more than once I saw him, through the half-open door of my room, after he had said goodnight, sitting with his whiskey in the living room gazing vacantly, lonely in his own home, and I listened to the ice cubes chinking in his glass and how they hit his teeth as he downed his drink. Sometimes I woke in the night to hear them quarreling on the other side of the wall. I must have been about thirteen when it dawned on me what went on. To begin with there were only forebodings I could barely put into words, when he had gone away again and I heard her behind the door of their bedroom, whispering on the telephone in a strange, ingratiating voice, or when it was not a taxi but a private car waiting for her in front of the terraced house. On several occasions she called home in the evening, suddenly very affectionate, and asked if it would matter if she stayed in town with a friend, after all I was "so big now," and anyway I was used to getting up alone in the morning. One evening I had told her that I was staying overnight with a friend I often visited not only to play, but also to be surrounded for at least an

hour or two by a little homely everyday life. But during dinner
my chum suddenly got a stomachache, and I was sent home.
In the night I was woken by the sound of my mother's low
laughter on the other side of the wall. At first I thought she
was laughing in her sleep, or that I had dreamed it, but when
I heard her sighing continuously and rhythmically, I was
about to go in to her, convinced that she must have fallen ill
like my friend, an epidemic might have broken out, but I
stayed in my bed when I heard a deeper groan blending with
her half-stifled, intermittent sighing. In the morning, I cautiously opened the door of her room. She was asleep alone in
the wide bed, and on my way to school I was almost sure that
it had been only a dream.

As time went on she did less and less to hide her infideli-
ties, or else I learned to interpret her maneuvers, because inadvertently she had lifted a corner of the veil that covered her
secret, profligate life. Just as she had left me to my own company, now I began to leave her to hers, and when I was not
with a friend I went into town and wandered around. It was
thus, by chance and almost out of boredom, one winter when
it was too cold in the streets and the parks, that I began to
visit the museums and gradually became aware of the motionless and mute universe of pictures, where my gaze could release itself from my nagging thoughts and give itself up to the
forms of light and shade, the presence of faces and places. In
the museums I could be at peace, no one spoke to me, no one
turned their back on me, and there were days when I played
truant to sit in the quiet galleries and allow my gaze to lose itself in the hermetic landscapes and arrested events, the unchanging and timeless moments of portraits and still lifes. I
sat for hours at a time, until there was no longer any distance

between my eyes and the mythological gestures of naked figures surrounded by clouds and flowing cloaks, no marked
boundary between my thoughts and the azure blue sea behind
the closed shutters in a dark room where someone had left a
violin. Although the pictures had been painted at greatly varying dates, and although they opened their frames onto widely
different sceneries, they always left me with the same idea, as
evident as it was surprising, that the world did not consist of
different, mutually separated places, that the world was one
single connected place, which was merely very large. It was
then that I began to see things as they are, literally as it were,
precisely as if the world was syllabic, as if it consisted of syl-
lables, of the light's vowels and the shadows' consonants. I
observed inanimate things and forgot the time. I stopped listening to what people said. I could see that my indifference to
their disconcerted expressions worried them. I didn't care
whether they understood me or not, and I stopped attempting
to make myself understandable. I stopped doing my homework, but could still answer randomly and not completely fail.
They wanted answers to everything, and I tried half-heartedly
out of politeness, until I began to answer by coming out with
the same sentence: "I don't want to answer." Giggles sounded
around me. "You don't want to answer?" The teachers' injured
feelings and anger took me by surprise. The simpler I made
things for myself, the more complicated everything became.
One morning one of them stopped me in the corridor and,
leaning against the row of hooks holding damp coats, looked
at me doubtfully. Did I intend to go to seed at the age of thirteen? I couldn't help liking him for the expression, and smiled
pleasantly as I informed him that I was only twelve. He rolled
his eyes and said he was going to cry, but he didn't.

I sat at my desk in the classroom, reading the names of those who had sat there before me and carved their runes through the varnish. I gazed at the waxed canvas map of the world unrolled in front of the clouds of chalk and the sloping rows of meaningless numbers and signs. Africa resembled a buggy that was tipped forward, and my own country looked like a pixie with a cold, speaking admonishingly to his children while the wind blows down his neck. I did not think of my father anymore, he was far away beneath the cruel sun, among concrete mixers and building cranes, while his wife opened her legs for her unknown lovers. I imagined sandstorms, the monsoon that whipped the palm leaves, the deltas, the lake villages, the deep clefts in the mountain ranges, the long-drawn-out wailing from the minarets in towns where you slept on the roof. I no longer took part, I had quite simply forgotten the necessary words, the ordinary exchange of information about family circumstances and holiday plans that make people trust each other. Even love slowly released its hold on me. There was a girl in my class who had breasts, pointed and very obvious beneath the tight cotton blouses she wore. She sat in the row in front of mine, sway-backed, with her elbows on the desk. Her fair ponytail brushed the skin of her neck, and her shoulder blades were outlined under the white cotton like folded wings around the dotted line of her vertebrae, which disappeared into her trousers, the waist pulled tight with a belt over the reversed heart shape of her pelvis and bottom, a swelling, pale blue, washed-out heart. Her eyes were blue and her earnest beauty made me think she would be able to understand me better than anyone else, if I could only find the right words. I imagined her blue eyes would be able to see things just as I saw them, things as they were. I had been to her home with some of the others, we had sat on the floor drinking tea and listening to music. There was always a bright lad who could say something funny, and I watched her as she laughed prettily at the brainless cracks. I was the last to leave, we sat opposite each other while the empty turntable rotated and the candles burned down. Words were a barrier between us, a gigantic building with empty rooms where we would never be able to find each other. I had danced with her once at a party. We danced standing still in the half darkness, as you dance to slow numbers, close, and I could feel her through her clothes and breathe in the perfume of her newly washed hair, but I did not know how my hands should advance from their prescribed places on her hips, she was so near and yet so far. One afternoon, after I had begun to be eccentric, she caught me on the way home from school. We stood by the mesh fencing of the school sports field. She asked what the matter was, why I avoided them. Behind her the grass spread out like a steppe between the empty goalposts. She was an envoy, she had not come of her own accord. "They" had sent her because they had noticed what her blue eyes did to me. Her breasts pointed scornfully at me in their clean, soft cotton whiteness. The conversation was a gift of charity, her blue eyes gazing at me, a conspiracy. I looked at the grass. I was always surprised by the enormous distances on the field when we went out there in our shorts and the others spread out and grew small around me on the green space. I avoided the ball as much as possible, and when on rare occasions it landed where I was, I left it willingly to my nearest opponent. I stood there watching her vanish on her bicycle between the horse chestnut trees down the suburban avenue, I watched the signal light treacherously flashing at regular intervals on her white back.

I don't know if I had really expected my father to inter-
vene in my mother's flagrant unfaithfulness, or what I had
imagined he might do. Throw the china around? Beat her? Cut
her throat with the Arabian dagger he had brought home for
me, and then stab himself in the stomach? She grew ever more
careless with her subterfuges and digressions, even when he
was at home, but he took no notice of anything except at
night, when he thought I was asleep, and he waited up for her.
I heard him through my door when she had at last come home
and he voiced his pathetic, humiliating questions. If she answered him at all it was with anger or jibes. Once I heard her
say that if he kept up his ludicrous jealousy she would have to
take a lover to satisfy him. As a rule the nightly scenes ended
with her going into their bedroom and slamming the door
behind her, and shortly afterward I heard him in there, presumably sitting on the edge of the bed, if he wasn't actually
kneeling, despondently begging forgiveness and assuring her
of his deep love. At other times she left the house and he
again sat in the living room with his whiskey and cigarettes,
until it grew light outside and the blackbirds began to sing
along the deserted road. More and more often she did not
come home from the theater at all, and it might be several days
before we saw her. My father revealed new sides of himself
when we were alone, he cooked and cleaned and asked me how
things had gone at school, and I lied because I thought he de-
served some good news in the midst of all the misery. But
I couldn't return his affectionate solicitousness in the afternoons, when I got home and he was already going around the
house in an apron. I entrenched myself in my room and replied
reluctantly when he knocked cautiously and came in and sat
on my bed. I knew my distance wounded him, as if he wasn't

suffering enough as it was, but his unhappy eyes and gentle, dispirited smile made me even more taciturn and withdrawn, and in the end, before he went away, he stroked my hair tenderly, making me turn quite black inside. One afternoon in early summer when I got home she had come back after several days. She stood at the living-room window looking out at the road, he lay on the floor with his face to the wall, crumpled up and shaking as if with cold. He didn't see me and she only turned around after a long moment in which I stood listening to the incredible, shocking sound of my father weeping. Her face was completely expressionless, slack and white with exhaustion, and she looked at me as if I were a stranger who had strayed onto the scene. I made my decision instantly and went to my room to fill my backpack. They didn't notice me leaving the house, totally wrapped up as they were in their own drama.

The ruin was barely discernible behind the trees and overgrown shrubs in the front garden. In one place it had caved in from the roof through the ground floor, making an opening in which pieces of beams, broken bricks, and crushed tiles were piled up beneath a jagged hole open to the sky. I had often explored the wrecked house on my way home from school, or on Sundays when I cycled around the quiet roads. I could spend hours at a time sitting on an old mildewed sofa, sunning myself or watching the rain fall unhindered through the hole in the roof, hitting the dust in dark patches among broken glass, remnants of wallpaper and shattered window frames. The place was at the end of a cul de sac at the edge of a forest. The forest had started to spread into the wild garden and the wind had blown seeds in through the windows and roof, so the cracks in the cement of the basement floor had opened wider beneath the slow steady pressure from the plants' growing network of roots. The green stems pushed their way right up through the fallen floorboards, and the fresh shoots brushed against the torn wallpaper in what had once been the living room. In a few summers they would reach the crumbling stucco in the remains of the ceiling.

The first time I placed my bicycle against the tumbledown wooden fence and approached the house through the tall grass, I had the sensation of being watched. It was completely still on the road and in the wilderness inside the fence, where the ruin came into view behind the thick foliage, its black window openings staring like a skull. I crawled in through one of the empty eye sockets, ducked under the fallen rafters, and balanced along the edge of the wide crater in the floor, alternately dazzled by the sun and fumbling in the half darkness. The staircase to the upper floor was almost intact, and I proceeded down a passage with doors, which on one side led into the open air, where a section of the house had finally disappeared. At the end of the passage there was a room which apart from the hole in the roof was more or less preserved. It was here the sofa stood, surrounded by walls covered with bookshelves in which a few books had been left behind, bound in leather, with yellowing worm-eaten and mildewed pages. On the floor I found a rotting gold frame with an old photograph of a now yellowed steamship with a tall funnel sloping backward. The ship lay at anchor on the grayish sea off a coast with gray palms that framed the view with their curved trunks and ragged leaves. I also found water. A moldering cracked rubber hose, rolled up under the house wall, turned out to be fastened to a tap hidden behind the thick growth of ivy. Remarkably enough it was not rusted out, and I was quite euphoric when I saw the spluttering, red-brown stream change color and become transparent, glinting in the sunlight like newly polished silver.

At first I had merely toyed with the idea of having a place I could retreat to, a place no one else knew about. In the preceding weeks I had secretly smuggled various useful things from my parents' house, books, preserves, packets of crackers, assorted kitchen utensils, blankets, a sleeping bag, a camp stove, a transistor radio, and a hurricane lamp. I had discovered I could just fit on the moldy sofa if I lay on my side with my legs bent. It was to be my bed. I made use of the daylight hours to organize things, and when dusk fell the former library almost resembled a home. I talked to myself encouragingly as I listened to Brahms's violin concerto on the transistor and heated a can of tomato soup on the stove. I had done it, I had left home, it was no longer merely an idea. All the same, I had trouble falling asleep the first night, and I lay awake a long time listening to the distant cars on the road and the mice rustling below, while trying to distinguish the constellations of stars. Despite my careful preparations there were things I had forgotten to think of, toilet paper for instance. That did not become material until morning, when I was woken up by a bright ray of sunshine, which made the dew glisten on my sleeping bag. I trained myself to use the grass, which reached up to my knees, and each day following I chose a new place. After almost a week had passed I had gone all the way around the house, and when I returned to my starting point my leavings were already so hardened that they no longer smelled, and the earth took care of the rest. My pants were soaked with dew when I made a path through the wilderness of stalks and stems the first time, holding my arms above my head to avoid nettles and thorns. As I squatted at the bot-

tom of the garden and looked up at the house, I imagined the
window of my new room was a square pupil looking at me
unblinking. I hadn't brought my schoolbag with me, and this
omission made me take the final decision to stop going to
school. In the morning I roamed around the roads and stole
food from the back entrances of supermarkets where the
trucks unloaded. In the afternoon I lay on my sofa and read or
watched the birds that flew through my room.

I soon got used to the inconvenient details and laborious
routines of my new life, I even grew used to the mice, and
went so far as to take them into my care. The ruin was the natural meeting place for the wild cats of the district, and in my
forays to the supermarkets I got some cans of cat food, but at
night I could hear that the cats still preferred the real thing. I
even kept up my personal hygiene to a certain extent. Every
morning I washed at the cold tap behind the house, and I
washed my underpants by beating them on a stone as I had
seen African women do on television. I felt like a Robinson
Crusoe gone of his own accord on a journey of discovery
around this desert island amid the suburb's almost cosmic
tedium of interminable well-groomed gardens. Listening to
the radio seemed like receiving signals from a distant planet,
and one afternoon, when I heard the announcer reading a description of a missing boy with my name and appearance, my
first reaction was that it must be a funny coincidence, an unknown boy who was my double. Naturally I had realized my
parents would probably be worried, although they clearly had
enough to deal with, but I didn't dream of telling them where
I was. It fascinated me to be one of the missing persons you
hear about now and then, for whom marl pits and lakes are
dragged, and I thought of Leslie Howard's cheeky jingle in

The Scarlet Pimpernel: They seek him here, they seek him there, those Frenchies seek him everywhere. Is he in heaven, is he in hell, that damned elusive Pimpernel? Sometimes when my mother isolated herself in her bedroom she had half apologetically, half self-deprecatingly said she needed "to be herself." Now I under-stood what she meant, now I could finally "be myself," far from the others' words and eyes, all their irrelevant stories and fruitless plans. But I was only "myself" because I forgot myself in my ruin, lost in books or in the endless play of sunbeams, linked shadows and jagged leaves in my room. When I as seemingly lost in daydreams and deep inside "myself" I was all the more present and aware of the visible world's unheeded and wonderful details. I forgot about time and all I knew. In the evening when I walked in the garden my eyes fell again on everything as if awakened from the stupor induced by thoughts and words, and I watched the light extinguished in the grass, blade by blade, as my broken house was slowly shrouded in blue. When I sat among the blades of grass and closed my eyes and felt the last rays of sunlight leave my face, I repeated, as a private liturgy, a pagan evening prayer, some lines from a poem we had read in English. I couldn't recall the poet's name, but the first lines were engraved in my memory like a mantra which, even better than Leslie Howard's rhyme, interpreted what I was feeling: *I'm nobody, who are you? Are you nobody, too? Then there's a pair of us—don't tell! They'd advertise, you know. How dreary to be somebody, how public, like a frog...* I don't remember the rest, only the image of public frogs came back each time I listened to the voices on the radio croaking their news and views, their details of missing persons and lot-tery results and shipping forecasts into my dripping, rustling, rattling, soughing silence.

I remember it as an entire summer, but in reality it lasted
only a week or two. I forget how my father found me, but one
day he was standing inside the fence calling me, gently and
cautiously as always, as if I were a runaway cat. I showed him
around the ruin and pointed out the places where the footing
was secure, and after I had sat him on the sofa I asked in a
well-brought-up way if he would like a glass of water. He held
the glass up to the light before drinking, as if he couldn't quite
rely on me. So this was where I had been hiding. I said I hadn't
been hiding, I had just moved, and he looked at me mildly. He
had moved too. I expressed surprise that it wasn't my mother
who had left. It was best that way, he said. After all, he traveled so much. He had found a place in town. He said my
mother missed me, and he looked as if he believed it. I asked
if it was painful. "Yes," he said, smiling almost apologetically.
He complimented me on the way I had made myself comfortable, and laughed when I told him how I obtained food. When
he rose to leave he gave me a handful of hundred-kroner notes,
so I could "provision myself in a more organized manner." He
didn't try to persuade me to give up my hermit's existence,
he knew well enough that it would be superfluous now that I
had been discovered. He stood there for a little while after saying goodbye and I hugged him. He looked quite surprised.
When I think of my father I like to visualize him turning one
last time to wave to me among the broken beams and crushed
roof tiles. The next day I went home. My mother told me he
had gone to Yemen, he would be there for several months
supervising the construction of a turbine plant. For a while
she did her best to play the role of single, caring mother, especially in the week when my parents' divorce filled the front
pages of the tabloids. She even baked cookies one Sunday, but

soon she resumed her afternoons behind the closed door of her bedroom, and frequently she did not come home until morning. One evening, standing in front of the mirror in the hall putting on mascara while waiting for a taxi, she suddenly looked at me and said, as if it had just occurred to her, that my father was a poor sap. I felt like answering, coming to his defense, but I didn't, and was angry with myself for leaving the words hanging in the air when she went out to the taxi with a quick kiss of her fingers. We left each other in peace. Sometimes she slept at her successive lovers' places, sometimes they spent the night at our house. They always treated me politely, as if I were an adult, and I grew used to the varying faces appearing in the bedroom doorway when I was getting ready for school in the morning. Although I resumed my old existence, my stay in the ruin had marked a turning point. The tale of my escapade spread through school, it invested me with something fabulous, and I went from being class eccentric to being almost sought after. Besides, in the long run the house was more comfortable to live in than the ruined villa, and when some years later I started going to bed with girls I even came to appreciate my mother's egocentric way of life. She couldn't care less who spent the night in my room, and it merely amused her that it was seldom the same one. At least her son wasn't a poor sap.

I learned to get along. I taught myself the rules of the game, the sweet innocent game that means nothing because it can mean anything. But when on yet another light Nordic night I lay in my room or on the beach in the sand dunes with my hand buried in yet another bold or timid girl's underpants, there was always the same gap between the hand and my head, between the person I was inside and the probably quite sweet but undoubtedly chance guy into whose eyes she stared while he fumbled with the condom. I would contemplate the tender scene from some far-off place, deep inside, and think again of the happy weeks in the ruin where I lay looking at the stars beneath the gap in the roof, at peace with myself on my moldy sofa, beheld only by the feral cats and trembling mice. The hermit regarded me coldly from his dilapidated, dry-rotted kingdom, and I felt the coldness of his eyes, but I couldn't see him, I saw only the dull snowflake stars framed by broken rafters. When yet another girl whispered sweet nothings in my ear, and when I answered her the way you answer, I thought it was only words, only a barter in the dark, one word in exchange for another, a caress for a kiss, a romantic glance for a dizzy little fall between her charming thighs. The difference was still too great, the difference between inside and outside, which I had been able to forget for a while in the house where the birds flew around the rooms and trees grew up out of the basement floor. When I saw my mother making up her face before going off to her lovers, I wondered why she had ever lived with my father. But they had been so young, only slightly older than I was, mere children who lost themselves in the light nights. Perhaps it was a chance night in the sand dunes or in a rented room that had tipped the scales, an accidental encounter, a sweet minor dizziness to which they had attributed far too much significance. Perhaps they had only given themselves to each other because they were tired of all the running around. The way things had turned out, I'd been forced to wonder if my being born hadn't been a slight misunderstanding, if in her eyes I should have been someone else, some other time. But as I gradually turned into an attractive young man, she began to take more interest in me. She pumped me teasingly about my adventures and took me into her confidence, as if I could really want to hear who she slept with and where. We were "pals" now, I was the only one who "understood her." When my father was in Denmark I went to see him in his apartment in town. He talked about his bridges and dams as before, but I just listened absently to his stories and replied evasively to his guarded questions about how things were at home. Suddenly it seemed ages since I had dreamed of standing next to him on the tropical building sites, and when I received his always laconic and insubstantial postcards they seemed to me as childish as I had been when I kept them in a box under my bed to take out when I couldn't sleep.

He didn't wake up before the curtain calls, but he was the first to stand up, and he applauded with great enthusiasm, as if wanting to compensate for his snooze during the performance, when my mother stepped out onto the stage alone, received the bouquet presented to her by a blushing ticket-seller, and bowed with studied humility to the enthusiastic audience. "Enthusiastic" was hardly the word, people were practically delirious, their eyes shone like born-again Christians', they stamped and clapped so hard their palms must have been raw. My mother had done it again, once more her limited but routine, and even overplayed, repertory of pretentious and vulgar mugging had coerced the audience into feeling that here before them was life in its essence, genuine, deep, amazing life, and not the cheap, colorless, and insidiously shabby counterfeit they had taken a break from for one night and would soon, when the lights came on, return home to again, blissful and crestfallen at the same time. After the last curtain call I accompanied my father and the other special guests backstage for "the little festivity" she had so zealously phoned to remind me of. I stayed in the background as she screwed on her smile and offered her cheek for him humbly to kiss. I could see how still, even thirty years later, he tried to combine a certain intimate, familiar closeness in his expression with the survivor's light, sociable, and unscathed tone. This was the moment he had come for, the one he had been seeking through the years, as if he could never finish proving to her and to himself that the old wounds were healed. But before he had been rewarded with even one warm and acknowledging glance, she had offered her cheek to the next admirer. To her he was only one familiar face among the many flocking around her like the seven dwarves around Snow White, equally as innocent and touchingly naive in their devotion. To him she represented an old injury, a slight but disfiguring limp from which one tries to divert attention by keeping well-groomed and always smiling obligingly at the world. He looked around him at a loss, alone again, his mission suddenly brought to an end, and I hid behind a group of board directors' wives who were standing in a cloud of perfume listening raptly to the art director describing with dangling wrists and voiced *s*'s the artistic crises he had been through during his work on the performance. When I looked in my father's direction again he had gone.

I was about to seize my chance to sneak out into the wings when my mother caught sight of me and steered her way through the gauntlet of champagne glasses and waving cigarettes, intent as a heat-seeking missile, loudly voicing her maternal joy at our reunion so that everyone turned to look at me. Had she been terrible? I had to smile at her anxious little-girl's face. She knew what I thought of her dramatic efforts,

although I had always confined myself to equivocal ironic
comments, but before I could answer she had put on a quite
different, falsely aggrieved and sorrowful mask. Where was
my delightful wife? She had been looking forward *so* much to
seeing her. I mumbled something about Stockholm, but she
saw through me. She is not just stupid, I thought, she's also
cunning, which in her case has never been a contradiction, and
her intuition is all the sharper because it is the only thing
about her that can't be bribed. What was the matter with us?
From the way she said it you would think Astrid and I were
two children who had quarreled over a toy. I pretended not to
understand what she was talking about, hoping that would
make her reveal how much she knew and where she had got it
from, but again I had miscalculated, for she contented herself
with patting me on the cheek and twittering that it would be
all right, and with a sparkling smile she turned to the photographer, who had been standing around itching to get a picture
of the diva arm-in-arm with her faithful son. The green and
red afterimages of the flash had barely faded before I was left
to myself again in my corner of the stage. It was I who had to
give up on getting her to reveal herself, she had merely let up
when she realized I did not intend to satisfy her inquisitiveness and pour out my heart on the spot, in that jungle of car-
nivorous eyes.

My eyes followed her as she embraced a pretty woman in
her mid-thirties I have seen somewhere before. She looked almost alarmed by my mother's overpowering welcome and
leaned against the man at her side, who was now allotted the
obligatory kiss on the cheek. He was an elderly sun-tanned
man, lean and furrowed, but still upright, with wavy white
hair and a hard, insistent gaze. A few seconds passed before I

recognized him. Of course he had been invited, my mother had acted in several of his films, and if I wasn't mistaken she had also had an affair with him once, long before he had met Astrid, when Astrid and I were still toddlers. As I saw him put a brown, wrinkled, and liver-spotted hand on my mother's back, I asked myself if I had never considered that he was the same age as my father, the film director who had stood out in the winter cold long ago, in shirtsleeves, already gray-haired, and called to Astrid in the taxi, less than a minute after I saw her for the first time. Now he was here, with the young girl from that time, the next new object of his restless desire, whom he had been unable to keep his hands off, even though he could be his own son's grandfather, and even though at that point Astrid was still quite young and slender. When he had realized Astrid was not coming back, he had stayed with her successor after all, he had even had a child with her to stop her from running away, and now he had to face it, his time of conquests would soon be past. She too could almost be his grandchild, but no one thought of that when they saw them together. He had aged very well, and although her stomach wasn't quite as flat as it had been before she had a child, all in all he still looked like a man who had hit the jackpot, so to speak, as he stood there discreetly supporting himself by lean-ing on his young wife. If he was really nice to her, she might stay with him until he died. It was almost ten years since I had last seen him. When Simon was thirteen he had asked us if he could be excused from visiting his father. It had become more and more painful for him to go out to the villa where he had once lived, and where the film director was now so absorbed with his new family. I don't think it was just because he felt like a rejected child, I also think he was old enough to see the real reason for the visits. His father wanted him only because his son's visits confirmed that his betrayal had been forgiven, and that therefore it had been forgivable.

Astrid accepted, reluctantly and out of regard for Simon, that she had to deal with him. He only phoned every few months and if she answered she always looked agitated when she went to call Simon. She never spoke of him other than as "your father." She never said just "Father." She never forgave him, but neither apparently could she forgive herself for once having played the role that her successor did later, the role of his cock's sweet little secret. But in spite of everything she wasn't unbending enough to skip his sixtieth birthday. I have often been amazed by how strong a grip these conventional family occasions have on us, regardless of how we get along with our family. No Christmas Eve passed without my mother joining us for dinner, despite the fact that I would happily go several weeks at a time without calling her. How can we be so sentimental about dates set not by our feelings but by the calendar's completely inane highlights? In Astrid's case it was all the more remarkable because her parents had died when she was still a child. She had no siblings. Simon, Rosa, and I were her only family, and she had chosen us herself, whereas she had long ago rejected any familial relationship with the film director. It can't even have been for Simon's sake that she turned up at the soiree, for he merely shrugged his shoulders at the invitation that slipped through the mail slot one day, illustrated with a pretty tactless picture of the film director in bathing trunks, his arm around the new wife and his new child on his shoulders, taken in front of the politically correct peasant's house in Provence of course. There he stood, the charmer, with his hard eyes and a hand on his new wife's firm buttocks, bluff and virile like one more Picasso look-alike. He would be pleased to see us. Yes, naturally he would be pleased to gather his harem for a day and act the kindly pasha, stroking his chin as he admired the fruits in his perfumed garden. When we arrived at the residence where I had once waited in my taxi as Astrid came storming down the front path holding Simon by the hand, the birthday boy stood ready with his new family in an exact replica of the invitation, greeting his guests, although not in bathing trunks, but in a pink shirt and summer whites, as if it was not Picasso after all but rather Visconti he was trying to imitate. I could see that his smart new wife was ready to swoon in terror at the sight of her predecessor, but Astrid reassured her with a conciliatory sparkle in her eye, while the film director shook my hand in a long, patronizing pincer maneuver. Everything was ready for the great peace treaty on this summer Sunday in his imposing white villa with its palatial windows and black glazed tiles.

So now he was sixty, Astrid and I were in our mid-thirties, Simon was thirteen and his new wife was twenty-something. His first wife was in her late fifties, and his daughter from the first marriage was our age, while his little "afterthought" was three. I don't mention it out of pedantry, I am simply trying to maintain perspective in this convoluted account with its spiraling shifts of time and place. But I couldn't help thinking of it when I discovered I was seated next to his first daughter in the big tent set up in the garden for the numerous guests, "in case the weather did not smile on us." This precaution had been unnecessary. The sun was baking the canvas, the air was heavy and smelled of rubber, and before we had finished our appetizers it was like sitting in a sauna. Imagine sitting in a sauna in jacket and tie. The sweat dripped from my eyebrows as I tried to converse with the daughter, a gray bony woman with thin lips and a sensible hairdo, who looked ten years older even though, as I mentioned, we are the same age. She was a nurse in a cancer ward, and when I had managed to warm her up she entertained me through the whole dinner with the ethical problems concerning the analgesic use of morphine in the terminal stage. Should the pain be eased when there was no hope left even though morphine itself would kill the patient in a short time? Wasn't it a *slide* in the direction of euthanasia? I visualized the emaciated patients in their oversized hospital gowns, clutching the IV stands holding their death-inducing drops, staggering in the middle of a frozen lake. While considering what I myself would prefer I secretly observed the nurse's mother, the film director's first wife, a stout woman in a gaudy loose-fitting smocked dress, who laughed loud and long at her own jokes. She had obviously determined to be Junoesque instead of just fat, and instead of harboring a grudge she had decided on a life-affirming, almost jovial attitude at this great reconciliation feast despite the fact that she had lived alone ever since the film director deserted her for Astrid. The corners of the cobalt blue silk scarf that hid her double chins settled among the lettuce leaves on her plate as she bent forward across the table to advise her ex's new wife on child rearing, and the shy girl nodded compliantly at the maternal exhortations out of sheer happiness in the heavy, rejected woman's demonstrativeness. But all the same, now and then, when the fat woman raised her glass, I saw her glancing nervously at Astrid, who had naturally been given the place of honor on the host's right. As usual Astrid rose to the occasion and smiled politely, as one smiles at strangers, at the harmless

little anecdotes from their mutual past that the film director es-
sayed, glistening with sweat in the damp tent. Sometimes he
put out a hand and rumpled Simon's hair, and I saw Astrid's
eyes grow distant and the boy shrink away each time, although
he smiled dutifully. We got to talking about children, the bony
nurse and I. She had never had any herself, she lived alone like
her mother, but she traveled a lot, she told me bravely, on her
own in Mexico and India. She almost succeeded in making her
exotic journeys sound like dreams come true. The film director himself was the first to speak, unconventional through and
through as he was after all, and in the speech he had composed
he thanked one after another, his eyes shining, the women who
had meant so much to him and "enriched his life," if he might
so humbly express it, "although it had not always been so easy
for them." His new wife sat like a girl on the edge of her chair,
playing timidly with the bread crumbs on the tablecloth. His
plump ex-wife tilted her head sideways with a heartfelt smile as
a tear rolled down her powdered cheek. His youngest daughter
sat under the table pulling blades of grass from the lawn. The
eldest stared down at her empty plate, absorbed perhaps in
thoughts of euthanasia or her last walking tour in Nepal. Simon
had left the table, I didn't see him anywhere. Astrid turned
away from the speaker and fixed her eyes on me, raising her
eyebrows slightly and curling her lips.

   I left the theater without saying goodbye to my mother. It
was a long time since I had last strolled alone through town
late in the evening. I enjoyed the cold air on my face and the
sound of dry leaves crunching beneath my feet as I walked
under the trees of Kongens Nytorv, and I was cheered at the
sight of the white illuminated facade of Hotel d'Angleterre

flickering promisingly behind the crooked trelliswork of the
treetops. As always on a Friday, the town was full of people
flocking in front of the cafés, the same cafés where I had once
stood swaying in the throng, happily intoxicated and buoyed
by my vague expectations. As I passed the queues of young
people pushing at each other, impatient as moths to get into
the light inside, I suddenly felt old and tired. It was their
town, at least in the evening, not mine. I remembered what
one of my friends had said a few years ago. "When we're
standing at a bar like that," he said, glancing at a crowd of
noisy kids, "and one of them suddenly turns and shouts Hi,
Dad, then it's time to go home." Was I about to catch sight of
Rosa for the second time that day, I wondered? I looked at the
girls made up and dressed like hardened, lost women, much
older-looking than the red-cheeked boys in baseball caps,
whose loutish, sheepish jokes only made them smile like bored
fashion models. Behind their immobile faultless masks another
film was running, in which the light was sharper and the shadows deeper, in which adult men with calm, gray eyes and grav-
elly voices and dark, painful pasts carried them away in black
sports cars out to the big white hotels by the sea. A slow film
orchestrated with slow, sad strings, in which the wind lifted
the light curtains between the half-open shutters of deep,
shadowy rooms, so they could feel its coolness on their skin
like a strange, unknown glance as they lay waiting with closed
eyes. I had a hot dog at a sausage-stand in front of Nórreport
Station. It was many years since I had tasted one, but I had not
eaten all day, I'd forgotten to eat although I had masses of
time. I went home slowly. The neon signs along the Lakes
were reflected on the surface of the water in a vibrating colored haze, and I stood a while watching the neon hen laying

her neon eggs, as I had done so often with Simon and Rosa. The last neon sign of the row on the roofs was a leaf from a calendar. The date shone red against the black sky, the 17th of October, it would soon be a week since Astrid had left. I was tired. In the past few days I had summoned all my energy to maintain an illusion of normality, to Rosa, to the curator and the other dinner guests, and to my parents, all while constantly turning over in my mind the same questions I feared the others would ask. Where had Astrid gone? Why had she left? Tomorrow I would be on a plane, out of their reach, alone at last with my unanswered questions. Somewhere behind me a man sat on a bench in a shiny worn parka with a cord around his waist, spewing a torrent of abuse at all and sundry, surrounded by his bulging, moldy plastic bags. I had often wondered what was in those bags. As usual the light on the staircase went out before I was at the top. When I reached the last landing I saw the glow of a cigarette faintly smoldering in front of our door. The glow rose into the air with a sudden movement, and a moment later the light came on again.

Rosa's boyfriend had been shaved since I last saw him. Only a dark shadow of growth remained on his bony crown, but it didn't make him look in the least formidable, he rather resembled one of those Moroccan street boys whose heads are shaved when they have lice, looking neglected with their filthy little outstretched hands. The installation artist stretched out his hand too, not to beg for alms but to shake mine, a manifestation of civility I had not expected him to stoop to. Did I know where Rosa was? He came straight to the point, but in a voice that was so low and subdued that I couldn't understand how I could ever have felt intimidated by this polite and serious young man. I replied that I had no idea, as I decided to keep silent about Rosa's presence in the café in the afternoon. Anyway, that was some hours ago. Did I have any idea where he could find her? It occurred to me she might be with her red-haired friend, but I shook my head and suddenly had a gratifying feeling of solidarity with my daughter. He stood there looking down at his cigarette stub in a lost way, it had burned down almost to his nail, but he obviously didn't want to throw it on the staircase floor while I was watching. I asked if he would like to come in to put out his cigarette. He threw it into the guest toilet, it seemed we had the same habit. It was a good thing Astrid didn't see. He walked around the living room, I was obviously not going to get rid of him easily. I said I was going to New York the next day and had some shirts to iron, but he just looked at me without getting the hint, amazed at what that could have to do with Rosa. He had not seen her in twenty-four hours. Good Lord, he should only know. Had they quarreled? He looked at me again, this time searchingly, then shrugged his shoulders. He didn't understand it, she had just gone, suddenly. At first he thought she had gone out for some cigarettes. He had been looking for her all over town. Classic, I thought, she went out for cigarettes and never came back. At least Astrid hadn't made use of such a hoary old pretense. I didn't know what to say and asked instead if he would like a beer. Now I was really stuck with him, and on the way through the apartment I thought disconcertedly that we were developing a mutual fate, two abandoned men.

He sat at the kitchen table looking at me while I got out the ironing board. He said he had read my essay on Jackson Pollock. I smiled at him and began ironing the collar of one of the damp shirts rolled up beside him on the table. What did he think of it? In reality I was not interested in what he thought of my essay, I could almost guess. He lingered, as if reflecting in order to discover what he did think. It had an interesting point. That way he had not said too much. I always start with the collar, I said, and then I do the sleeves, the sleeves are the hardest. He gaped at me as if not sure he had heard right. I looked down at the flat shirt sleeve and pressed the iron along the edge to make a sharp crease. It was not that he was usually jealous, he said, lighting a fresh cigarette. It's really pointless, I said, they get wrinkled anyway on the flight, no matter how carefully I pack them. Did I have any suspicion that she was seeing anyone else? I met his eyes. Someone else? He looked away. His eyes were shining brightly, and I was afraid he might start to cry, this tonsured young man in a worn leather jacket. If she was, she probably wouldn't tell me. He smiled bitterly and took a swig from the bottle. A few weeks ago he had seen her on the way into Kongens Have with an older man, well, not really old, about my age. He had caught sight of them by chance, from the bus. Had he asked her who it was? He blew air from his nose, but it sounded more like a snicker than a snort. Would *I* have asked? I shrugged. He had asked if there was "someone else." He had asked several times, but they had always ended up fighting. She felt she was being watched. She said she had never promised him anything. I looked at him again, he was looking down at the floor. I wanted to say something friendly but I couldn't think of anything, although I knew every thought tumbling through his bald head. Then he rose quickly and thanked me for the beer. I didn't need to see him out.

Now he was going out into the dark again to shamble around, alone and rejected. I understood his position but I had forgotten what it felt like. I could only smile at myself, at my young, bleeding heart when I once stood at a window and watched Inés leaving me in the whirling snowflakes. My wounded self-esteem barking despairingly in my head as I drove around town with the night's passengers, like a mangy starving cur running in circles and snapping at its own tail. I smiled at the installation artist too after he had gone, but it was not a malicious smile. I thought of everything he was about to suffer and how really the worst thing was his being so sorry for himself. It was rather ironic that my own daughter should have occasioned this opportunity to confront my youthful self. I remembered her sitting in the afternoon sun in front of the café, thoughtful, introspective Rosa contemplating the fountain and the pigeons, unaware that I was observing her. I could not have reached her even if I had knocked on the window and waved. She resembled Astrid more than ever with her mass of brown hair and wide cheekbones and her narrow eyes that saw everything without revealing anything. A young Astrid, so young that she had not yet met me. A young woman who had just grown up, alone in the world. Perhaps she really had been on her way to meet an older man, not old, just older than herself, someone like me, just as the young Astrid had once walked through town with quick, furtive strides, as if she were a secret agent in the adult world, on her way to meet a married man with gray hair and strong hands. Perhaps that was how Rosa had walked through town when she had said goodbye to her red-haired friend with a conspiratorial smile, on her way to a grown man with furrowed cheeks and a calm, confident gaze that seemed to enclose her on all sides, as if she could sink into that gaze and disappear into it, let it take her, unresisting, to an unknown destination.

Perhaps Rosa walked through town with the same determination I picture in Astrid when she walked beside the gray-haired film director along a corridor of the Grand Hotel in Stockholm and let him open the door of the anonymous room where in a little while she would be lying, unbeknown to the world, with this married man between her girlish knees. The same undeviating sleepwalker's stride that in its time had carried Inés through the streets from one man to another. Secretive, treacherous strides toward something unknown and menacing. Perhaps Rosa too smiled at the helplessness of this mature man's desire. Perhaps she already suspected she was merely his little gesture of defiance against boredom and the weight of time, perhaps she laughed at him when he clutched her young body with his adult, breathless lust, as she closed her eyes and vanished in his hands into the free fall of a blind moment. Rosa, Astrid, Inés, perhaps it was the same urge to disappear from the gaze of these helpless, grown men, to surrender and escape in the same movement, as they bent over their young bodies to possess them; the same secretive smile when they vanished through an invisible door in the wallpaper, between the pictures of little colored birds at the Grand Hotel. It may have been with the same weightless feeling of being strange and unknown to themselves each time they rose from another strange bed, as if their faces were painted shells which those poor married wretches had crumbled between their lustful hands. Each time they left another man and walked alone through town in the evening the cool air on their skin felt again as if there was nothing but a thin porous membrane where their faces had been. No one had better tell them who they were as they walked along in the streets, Inés, Astrid, and Rosa. It is the same young woman who walks like this through the night with quick strides and wide-open eyes, so the strange faces float past her one after another, like fleeting reflections in the whirling stream of darkness. Unknown faces with unknown eyes that open to her and close behind her again, as if she is constantly crossing yet another threshold without ever going forward. She always wants to be somewhere else, but she does not know where, she only knows that every room and every town will be a trap. Thus she continues, as if she were a letter without a sender and without an address, a letter to everyone and no one, forever being torn open and forever being sealed up anew before anyone can read what it says.

6

It was cold and windy the day after my arrival. The air was clear between the square gray buildings that cut into the uniform blue surface of the sky, themselves cut through by the shadows of other buildings and the water tanks on the flat roofs. In the afternoon I went for a walk in the side streets of old warehouses between Greenwich Street and the Hudson. There was nobody to be seen, only the endless stream of cars on the West Side Highway, beside the river. The neglected industrial facades reminded me of Edward Hopper's towns. A few hours earlier I had been in the Whitney Museum in front of one of his solitary women. She sits in a room with pale green walls, on the edge of the bed. She looks out the window at the water tanks of sooty wood similar to those on the roofs above my head, between the gray and dark red walls' faded, peeling names painted in capital letters. She is blonde, still young, and she sits looking out of the open window, the pale sunlight falling in on her equally pale face, torso and thighs. Her face is expressionless, and her body is presented without the slightest suspicion of desire, almost a little clumsy, as Hopper painted them, a little stiff in the joints, which only serves to strengthen the immobility of the picture, the impression of a long moment suspended in the flight of minutes and hours. I could say her gaze is absent, but at the same time it is fully and completely there, resting on the edged

outline of the buildings and the conical zinc roofs of the round
water tanks, or perhaps on a distant point between them, outside the picture, at the end of the view from the window, where
an invisible barrier prevents her calm gaze from reaching further. There it stops while she sits, perfectly still, halted in a
pause on her way through the day, where nothing will happen,
where she is alone, where there is nothing to say nor anyone
to say anything to. Perhaps she is listening to the deep notes
of the distant traffic, perhaps she hears neither the muffled
noise of the cars nor the horns and occasional shouts that
probably reach her through the open window. She looks neither particularly unhappy nor the opposite, she just sits on the
bed in the silent, pale green room, in the transilluminated silence of the picture which is also her silence, the silence of her
body and her thoughts. She may have fallen into a reverie, as if
she has fallen out of time, alone with herself, but no longer
than is quite ordinary and unremarkable. In a little while she
will get up from the bed and dress and go out into the day, out
into town and on through life, but not yet, not just now. She
will sit for a little while and allow her thoughts to open out
and widen and extend, until they can no longer be thought. It
is not that the world is empty. The world is full of houses and
things, and emptiness is just the arbitrary yet necessary distance between houses and things. The special thing in such a
pause in the day's course is not emptiness. What makes her
continue sitting, what makes me stay in front of her, is not that
the pause is empty, nor are the pale green walls empty, nor the
sky in the window above the roofs. They are there, we know,
the walls and the sky, they just happen to be there. What for a
moment makes us hold our breath, she on her bed, I in a gallery
at the Whitney Museum, is rather the totally banal, though

still only in the pauses and only slowly dawning, observation that the houses and the things and the bodies and the light and shadows look as they do. That the world is what is present at any time, at any place. That there is nothing more to it.

I walked along the wide sidewalk beside the Hudson toward the World Trade Center. Runners in jogging gear passed me at regular intervals from either direction, breathing hard and red in the face. On the left cars streamed toward me on their way up to the Holland Tunnel, a ceaseless river of coated sheet metal, like a noisy, moving reflection of the river on my right side, peaceful, gray blue and very wide at this point. Across the river I could see the Colgate clock, an enormous white face that seemed to float on the water, quite small at a distance, about the size of a watch face. It was around four o'clock, so it was ten at night in Copenhagen and nine in Portugal. I did not know then that at that point Astrid had arrived in Oporto, she might have been in her room at the Infante de Sagres or walking beside the dark river and under the steel bridge to the Cais da Ribeira, as I went on down Chambers Street and turned up West Broadway back to SoHo. The bank statement showed she paid her hotel bill with her Mastercard the next day and continued south. It was not like her to choose the most expensive hotel in town, but we had stayed there together seven years before. Perhaps that was why, perhaps it was because she had driven from Santiago de Compostela to Oporto in one stretch and needed a comfortable night. The statement helps me not only to reconstruct her movements, but also to remember what I was doing myself at the same time, constantly subtracting or adding five hours. We were displaced in our relative movements, each in our own time zone, our own continent, both of us far from the town where we had lived together. Later that afternoon I was in the cinema on the corner of Houston and Mercer Street, for some reason I still have the ticket stub. I did not pay attention to the film, but I liked sitting in the dark and watching the faces and places succeed each other. As long as the film lasted I did not need to walk restlessly down street after street, not knowing what to do with myself. As I sat in the darkness of the cinema she may have been sitting on her five-star bed looking out the open window, out into the treetops of Filipa de Lencastre. I can't remember if they were planes or fig trees. I suppose she had a bath before going out to eat. She came out of the bathroom in the hotel bathrobe with a towel tied like a turban around her wet hair. She opened the window and lit a cigarette and sat on the edge of the bed before the view of the square, motionless with fatigue. She listened to the invisible cars and the voices of the invisible people down in the square, while her gaze sank into the darkness among the dark green, dry leaves of the trees, faintly illuminated from below by the street lamps. She sat there for a while, her arms stretched out behind her and her palms resting on the bedspread, as the glow ate its way down the cigarette between her lips. Perhaps. It is just something I imagine, but perhaps she knew I would try to visualize her in the places we once visited together. Perhaps it was on purpose and not only for convenience that she used her Mastercard all the way to Lisbon instead of cashing money on the way. Perhaps she did not merely want to show me she was taking the same route we had followed seven years before. Perhaps she also wanted me to see those places again and picture her alone in those places, where we had been together. As if something particular had happened on that journey, something decisive. As if en route, without noticing, we had passed a turning point.

It had rained the whole way to Santiago de Compostela. I have a picture of Astrid standing on the square in front of the cathedral lifting her face to the drizzle. The Gothic lace of the granite facade seemed to dissolve in the fine rain, flickering like a distorted vision in the white light, and in my memory it is as if the denticulation and her features touch through the rain. I put her wet shoes on the radiator in the hotel room and held her chilly feet in my hands until she fell asleep. The next day we crossed the Rio Minho on a small ferry rather like a barge, and continued southward through the desolate mountains. We could drive for a long time without saying anything. Sometimes she would point through the side window at an eagle she had glimpsed high above or a distant house washed the same pale blue as the sky. Now and then one of us switched on the radio and flipped back and forth between channels, but the signal was poor because of the mountains and the music constantly faded into static. There was hardly any traffic on the mountain roads. We were far away. At home we were not used to spending so many hours together at a time. We parted in the morning and met again in the evening, and when we were together the children were generally around. It was an unaccustomed feeling to sit motionless beside each other for hours as the mountain slopes opened and closed before us in time with the bends of the road. At home we always had something or other to do, trivial or interesting, in the car there was nothing to do except to go on, all the time on the way to the next town. As we drove through Trás-os-Montes, I thought once more how quickly the years had gone since the winter she moved into my apartment and broke my solitude. The years were like a train in the night that moves at such speed that the lighted windows flow together and you see nothing. I thought about how much of our time had been taken up with doing the same things every day, as the months passed and the children grew and we talked about all that happened. In the evening, when everything had been done and the apartment was quiet and we lay down beside each other, it was sometimes like meeting again after a long separation. Slightly hesitant, slightly fumbling, like seeing each other again after a while and having to search a little before you can find the thread. Had she been happy? Like me, she must have been too busy to even ask, happily occupied with everything but herself. Like me, she was immersed in her work, like me she let herself be whirled around on the merry-go-round of family life, so the background faded into a swarm of lights and colors.

The distances grew longer between the villages in Trás-os-Montes, and the pauses when neither of us said anything grew longer, until she would look at me again and smile with her narrow eyes, as if everything was as it had always been. I can remember pulling over to the side because she had to pee, at a place where the road made a curve through the round, grass-covered mountains. I stayed in the car while she walked in among the mossy rocks and withered grass and the prickly evergreen bushes. She vanished from sight when she squatted down, as if she had been swallowed by the naked, knobbly landscape, with its meager growth of brown, gray, gray green, and rust red under the pale sky. It was perfectly still. There was only the sound of my seat creaking slightly under me, the wind in the grass and the distant trickling sound from the place where she had disappeared. Perhaps it didn't matter, my being unable to think of anything to say to her. Words had never been what bound us together. They had merely been the sound of our story when we talked of everything under the sun on our way through the years. We hadn't needed so many words, we seemed to understand each other without them. A look, a gesture, a sigh or a smile was enough. The story told itself. But at some point I must have lost sight of her, even though she was there the whole time. Because she was always there, and because she was so close. As when she kissed me and her face widened so I could not make out its outline or proportions and saw only her blurred skin and huge eyes. I had not seen her in a long time. That's how I was thinking when half a minute later she appeared in the landscape again, as if out of nowhere, and came toward the car through the dry grass. She screwed up her eyes against the sun as she looked down into the valley shadowed in thin transparent mist. Her shadow went winding, long and without joints, across the shining blades of grass as she walked, as if it lived its own life beside hers. It was an interval in the story, this journey, not a continuation, and we moved through that interval, among the bare, monotonous mountains, without having the story to tell us where we were going. That's what I was thinking as she approached the car, looking around her one last time, still alone for a moment in the unmoving landscape.

When I came home from New York the second time and was waiting to claim my suitcase among the other passengers, I caught sight of her behind the glass in the arrival area. She had not seen me yet. She stood waiting there, craning her neck, with her arms folded, fingering the car keys as if they were rosary beads, a bit impatiently, a bit anxiously, as if doubting for a moment whether I had been on the plane. For another few seconds I was only a passenger among others who stood waiting for their suitcase to come into view on the conveyor belt. Then she smiled and waved, and I waved back, in one moment her husband again, hers among all the men in the world.

In the seconds when she stood peering through the glass wall, not knowing I was observing her, she was still the woman I had left. The next moment, when her expressionless face broke into a smile, she became the woman I had returned to in order to continue where we had left off, where I had let go of her. A week or so earlier, in the middle of September, I had been on a plane again on the way to New York. I sat looking out at the empty sky above the clouds, wondering as usual what Astrid and the children were doing. No doubt they had already eaten, Rosa would be putting plates in the dishwasher, Simon would be in the living room, lost in an opium den in Shanghai with red dragons on the walls where at that moment Tintin stuck his head out of a Chinese vase as tall as a man. Later on Astrid would read another chapter aloud from *Huckleberry Finn,* maybe one of the chapters about the nights on the great river, about the flickering lights on the shore and the voices rolling across the water to Huck and Jim on the timber raft, smoking a pipe as they drift with the current. She would kiss them goodnight, put out the lights in their rooms and sit down in front of the television's brief, leaping flakes of everything that was happening at the same time in another place, and if she had not drawn the curtains, she would be able to see herself, in one of the window panes, far away in the darkness, a diffuse, blurred and transparent figure on the sofa, her face a yellow patch in the lamplight, with dark shadows where her eyes were. She might light a cigarette and look through the blue-gray swirls of smoke past the screen's changing, synthetic color combinations into the darkness behind her reflection, knowing nothing of the cat that rose at the same moment and stretched in the ray of sunlight on the floor beneath a window in the East Village, before running out into the corridor where a tall young woman in her late twenties was coming in through the front door with a brown paper bag full of groceries and, with the cat at her heels, walking through the apartment, switching on the answering machine and listening to my voice announce that I would land that evening soon after eleven.

In the spring I had spent a month and a half in New York to work on my collection of essays on postwar American painters. I had stayed in Brooklyn Heights with an acquaintance of my father's, a Lebanese cardiac surgeon whose wife had died the previous year. He was at the hospital or with a woman on Long Island most of the time, and I had the house pretty much to myself. When I was not in my room watching the gray squirrels in the trees in front of the somber and very elegant town house, I took a train from the station on Clark Street into Manhattan to spend the morning in the archives of the museums and university libraries. They were tranquil, monotonous days, and I was content in my solitude, completely absorbed in my book, which slowly but surely began to take shape. Of course I missed Astrid and the children when I sat eating my lonely pizza in the evenings, surrounded by the oak panels of the cardiac surgeon's opulent dining room, but not as much as I had expected. The artists of the New York School filled my horizon and pushed Astrid, Simon, and Rosa from my field of vision. There was an ocean between us, and in their absence ideas came to me and arranged themselves continuously in one undisturbed, unbroken movement, as ideas do when one begins at the right moment. My friend the museum curator had given me the telephone numbers of various people he thought I might like to meet, among them an art dealer who had known both Rothko and Pollock, a distinguished critic, and a young Danish artist who had moved to New York after she finished at the academy. Very talented, he had said with a little smile and a sly glance behind his steel-rimmed glasses. But I felt like contacting neither the art dealer nor the critic, either because of my normal shyness and fear of seeming pushy, or because I was doing so well in pursuing my own ideas that the interpretations and views of others would only have been a disturbance. And as for his talented young painter, his sly recommendation left me only with a vaguely insulted feeling that he was trying to lure me out onto thin ice with one of his discarded conquests from the academy, one of those ambitious and well-equipped fallow deer in overalls adorned with decorative paint spots he romped around with behind his wife's back. As if he wanted to put me to the test in the hope of proving I was no better than he was. Besides, it was of course American and not Danish art I had flown across the Atlantic to write about, and moreover I had come precisely to write, so altogether I saw no reason to seek diversion from my comfortable hermit's existence in Brooklyn Heights.

One afternoon I was sitting smoking in the sculpture garden behind the Museum of Modern Art, contemplating the drifting clouds and skyscrapers in the low ornamental pools. I had spent several hours among the collections, guided through the storerooms by an assistant who stood looking on at a respectful distance as I made notes about some of the pictures I wanted to refer to in my book. As I sat glancing at people and listening to snatches of their conversation, I asked myself what exactly it was in the New York School of painters that was so important to discuss, so many years after their lucent painting had in turn been succeeded by pop art, minimalism, and conceptual art in every possible aspect. Wasn't there something naive and unfashionably romantic in their pathos, their existential notion of the intensity of brush strokes, the strictly personal expression? Hadn't the world become too self-conscious and ironic in the meantime? Was there any sense any longer in tending the individual and authentic that could not be exchanged or reduced, in a world where everyone drove the same Japanese cars as they played merrily and without commitment with the cultural masks of identity, as if it were a masquerade all year round? I could easily find reasons for smiling wryly at the puritanical conceit of the American painters of the forties and fifties, when they listened to Charlie Parker with the same gravity as to Stockhausen, and strutted around Greenwich Village in black polo-neck sweaters with a dog-eared paperback edition of Camus or Sartre in their back pocket. But I had kept returning to their pictures when I grew tired of the ironic airs or dry theorizing of more current art. Where Andy Warhol's sham anonymous cans of soup already seemed outmoded, long past their expiration date, Jackson Pollock's and Mark Rothko's, Franz Kline's and Clyfford Still's canvases were still the same. They were the same kind of hermetic fields of paint unfolding themselves in a mediation between the hand and the eye, without the intervention of language or interpretation, a pure and autonomous presence of colors and contours. These canvases were what they were with an integrity that could still move me. You did not need to know anything to look at them, they could hang anywhere because they did not require an art institution or tradition as a background for ironic or theoretical games of meaning and meaninglessness. I loved looking at them. When I stood before

them again I felt that their absolute presence, devoid of refer-
ences, demanded my own presence, a concentration without
thought, resting in the center of the eye's gravity, precisely
here, exactly now.

I enjoyed sitting listlessly in the garden's niche of purling
water and lowered voices between the enormous buildings and
the restless, crosswise humming of the right-angled streets. I
felt a desire to stay as long as possible before getting swallowed up again in the traffic outside, but perhaps too, for the
first time in days, I felt like being surrounded by people without having to keep moving the whole time. I enjoyed sitting
there, a stranger among strangers, at rest among the skyscrapers for a quarter or half hour in scaled-down alertness. It
seemed almost like relaxing one's guard to sit like that, like
slackening the rope of one's watchfulness to close one's eyes
in the middle of Manhattan. At one point, when I opened my
eyes after nodding off I caught sight of a woman who had sat
down opposite me on the other side of the pool. She might
have been in her mid-twenties, perhaps thirty, she had fair,
short hair with a side part, and she was wearing a black tailored suit and dark sunglasses that made her face and the tri-
angle of bare skin in the neck of the jacket seem even paler.
Sunglasses were in fact not strictly necessary, since the sun
did not reach down into this crevice between the tall buildings,
and the dark glasses would only make it harder for her to read
the book she held up in front of her as she sat, unmoving, with
crossed legs. Pale and interesting, I thought, and I couldn't
help looking at her, especially not after I had managed to make
out the letters on the book jacket. It was *The Fall of the King*
by Johannes V. Jensen, in Danish. I hadn't read it since school,
and the only thing I remembered clearly was the scene where

a horse is slaughtered on a snow-covered field, in which the author, with graphic precision, describes the red, violet, and brownish entrails twisted about in the snow. As I looked at her, my mind's eye pictured a strange, both beautiful and cruel correspondence between the sobriety of the brutal image and her discreet, androgynous elegance. I smiled at myself, but all the same I went on playing with the idea that this might be one of those absurd coincidences you are always hearing about, and that the elegant young woman might be identical to the talented artist whose name and telephone number the curator had jotted down with a sly glance. In which case his slyness had been justified, considering how uninhibitedly I was devouring her with my eyes. Ashamed, I buried myself in my notes on Jackson Pollock and Barnett Newman, wrote down a couple of supplementary comments with steely earnestness, and when I looked up again, a Hassidic Jew sat smoking a cigar on the chair where the reading beauty had been.

I forgot her on the train back to Brooklyn, engaged in observing the groups of motionless exhausted faces carefully avoiding each other's eyes in the overfilled car, each on their separate way somewhere, and when I happened to look anyone in the eye by mistake I immediately redirected my gaze to a fictive point outside the window, where the gray walls of the tunnel rushed past. I did not think of her again until I had written out the day's notes and sat looking at the squirrels in the trees in front of the Lebanese heart surgeon's house. They moved at the same speed and with the same jumping wavelike movements as the green curves on a screen registering heartbeats. The image of the beautiful stranger was very clear to me, her regular features made even more expressionless and motionless by the sunglasses, her bare skin in the otherwise modest V-neck of her jacket. However naive it might be I could not relinquish the idea of the totally improbable fluke, that I might have been sitting opposite the curator's talented lady friend that afternoon in the sculpture garden. As if in this city of all cities it would be so unusual to come across a young woman who understood Danish, for instance, because she was a Dane. It annoyed me to be wasting time on such a fanciful notion, and I told myself it was another example of the rubbish that clogs your mind as you go through the day. Of course I had noticed her only because I was alone in a strange city. Could it really be anything else? I looked at my watch, it was six o'clock. At home it was midnight, Astrid must have gone to bed by now. Perhaps she was lying there thinking of what I might be doing, perhaps she had already fallen asleep. Our lack of synchronism suddenly made me sad, as if it was not only the ocean and the time zones that separated us. I had never been unfaithful to her, and though the idea had tempted me now and then, when a beautiful unknown woman looked at me appreciatively, it had only been in the form of diffuse and fleeting fantasies. The idea of making a pass at a strange woman seemed humiliating. Should I stand with my hat or my cock in my hand soliciting a little adventure? Besides, I would never be able to manage the smoke screen of pretences, white lies, and strategic omissions that I would be obliged to spread around me in order to meet my fairy-tale princess in secret. But the practical problems of infidelity were not all that terrified me. If I deceived Astrid and lied to her, if there was something in my life that she must not know, I would not only reduce her to less than she was, I would also diminish myself until I was nothing but a miserable calculating midget. That was my reasoning on the rare occasions when I was distracted by a woman's luxurious legs or dreamy eyes, but months might pass when the thought of straying did not so much as cross my mind. If Astrid mentioned teasingly that some woman or other had looked at me with interest, as a rule I had not myself noticed. I didn't really believe her and took it as a good sign that she actually had to tell me about my inadvertent success with the ladies. That she would bring up something like this in the first place must mean she couldn't dream of being jealous, and of course that was because she had no reason to be.

Was I perhaps not happy? As I watched the nervous gray squirrels cavorting in the treetops out on Orange Street, I recalled the afternoon in Paris some years earlier when Inés had put the same question to me. The word had seemed so inadequate and at the same time so inquisitorial. "Happy." As if by taking the form of a question it already held a silent accusation, because I was not sitting there in the café on the Place de l'Alma, overflowing with happiness like an ecstatic porker. It was the kind of question you asked when you were young, because you still had only the words to brace yourself, all those words with which you adjured yourself and the world because you hadn't yet formed the world and it hadn't marked your shining, hopeful mug. The fact that Inés had felt compelled to ask that question at all must have been because she had neglected to leave her youth behind and stop hanging onto herself. The years had gone by for her just as they had gone by for me, but she obviously still clung to the idea that every possibility was open, even those she had rejected. If she really believed, even for a moment, that she could make me forget my wife and children and jump into her arms because she happened to turn up one afternoon in the Palais de Tokyo, out of the blue, it meant that she had learned nothing. I had sensed the futility underlying the offhand account of her improvised and uncommitted Parisian life, free as a bird and insidiously lonely. She was still responsible only for her own pretty ass, and even the most passing fluctuations of her mood shadowed, as they always had done, events in the world outside her closed blinds. She was just as intense and quivering as in the past, but the intensity had acquired a slightly mannered quality. She still subscribed to the overworked idea of "living in the present" and so she had come to a halt. She clung to her precious freedom like a penny-pincher studying his savings account passbook, shiny with age, every evening. As she grew older she would change into one of the gray subscribers to great and passionate love, sitting on a bench in the shade in a straw hat with her summer coat buttoned up to her chin, gazing after the young couples in love and envying them their enamored ignorance.

I knew very well I was being unfair. Hadn't Inés said she would like to have a child? Hadn't she simply been unlucky? Why couldn't I just accept that I had escaped unharmed from the most painful disappointment of my youth, whereas she regretted, when it was too late, what she had thrown away? Was I nursing an old grievance? Would it have been too ironic if it should suddenly turn out that it was she who had suffered most? Was I afraid that my old feelings for Inés had merely been in hibernation when I turned my hopes to Astrid's new, unknown face? Probably it was all of no consequence now. The only thing my reunion with Inés had left me with was her simple and at the same time all-encompassing question in the café on the Place de l'Alma. It was not the remembrance of Inés that reminded me of her question, but something much worse. It was the recollection of a totally strange blonde in a black suit, with whom I had exchanged not a single word and at whom I had gazed for a total of less than a minute. She looked like one of the indolent beauties in Astrid's French fashion magazines, but then again she might be a formidable girl from Ikast with both feet on the ground, and *The Fall of the King* was merely one of her accessories, like the very cinematic and mysterious sunglasses. I felt like a complete fool as I sat glowering at the innocent, frolicsome squirrels. *Was it possible that I hadn't been happy?* Possible, yes. It was long since I had considered the question, and anyway now I was on my own. I couldn't reach out to Astrid and test my feelings. But if I wasn't happy, then what was I? Not, at least, the opposite. Perhaps neither. Was that the secret behind my immoderate irritation at the naïveté of the question? That I was neither cold nor hot, but lukewarm, and so spat the question out of my mouth instead of answering? Had Inés reminded me of something that afternoon in Paris, something I preferred to forget or had actually forgotten?

It was not so much my old unhappy love she had reminded me of, it was rather the way I had loved her, wildly and ravenously, without restraint, utterly exposed and defenseless. Afterward I had told myself it was bound to have failed with Inés and I could not blame her for having protected herself against my heedless passion. No one could stand being loved like that, and if she had let me I would certainly have loved her to shatters. It had been an immature, self-absorbed love, I told myself. It had not been Inés I loved at all, but my own besotted image of her, a gilded icon that shone mysteriously in my waking dreams. No one was so mysteriously and utterly wonderful. My fanatical adoration was almost insulting because she could never have lived up to my exaggerated notions about her. And of course she herself had sensed that, which was why she had decided to hasten the time when she had to disappoint me. But why then had she taken my hand in the café on the Place de l'Alma? Why had she reached out to me so transparently, when I suddenly turned up again as if dropped from the sky, years after she had gone off in the snow? Because it was not so marvelous to be free and without obligations in a one-room apartment in Belleville? Perhaps not only that. Perhaps she had reached out to me without any ulterior motive, merely to touch for a moment the memory of a dream that was too beautiful to be forgotten. It was obvious that my young passion had been an infatuation, that she had never been what I wanted to make her. But all the same she had kept the naive, faded image of this unknown illusory woman I had invented, she had not been able to relinquish that. Perhaps my illusions about Inés were like the images on early Renaissance altarpieces by Giotto and Cimabue, their chaste visions of the Blessed Virgin with the pure, defenseless eyes and ivory white cheeks in the Uffizi, the Louvre, and the Metropolitan Museum, like pieces of wreckage from canceled time. The cruel princes of the Italian city-states were dead, their victims and the victims' bereaved were dead, their sufferings forgotten and the machinations of power accounted for and relegated to the archives. Only the dreams remained, weightless hallucinations of that foul and bloody life, painted with fine brushes and preserved as a greeting from the dead to an unknown future. Perhaps not even a prayer to be remembered, but rather an emblem of interior movements that had disengaged themselves from the flesh of the dead long since turned to dust. The recollection of an imploring glance that had painted the world more beautiful than it was simply to be able to endure it. My infatuated fantasies about Inés were very far from the truth of who she was. But they might have been very close to the truth about the person she would have liked to be.

I myself had become the person I was while living with Astrid. The mature, responsible father and husband she occasionally teased about other women desiring him behind his back. As the years passed and he gradually took shape I had no wish to be anyone else. I no longer felt the gap between inside and outside that had made me so melancholy after I left my self-imposed exile in the ruin and went back to my suburban youth, in which my mother came and went between her changing roles and changing lovers. That gap between my interior world and the world outside which I had believed I could cross with my love for Inés, and which had merely opened wider when I reached out for her with my impatient hands. One day I suddenly found myself on the other side of the gap, and I hardly knew how I had closed it. I had become the man who was married to Astrid, father to our daughter and her half-brother. Our life together filled me completely with all its daily repetitions and moments of sudden lightness when I discovered I had forgotten myself, one with the current of our days. And the part of me that was not engrossed and pervaded with everything I did with Astrid and the children was absorbed in my writing, so there was no break between the two, only the swift, imperceptible transitions which made me feel that my life was unfurling like one continuous gesture. Yes, I was happy, and not least because I just didn't have the time to ask myself such an odd question. I was happy, but I didn't dream that Astrid and I would merge into one single four-legged creature of joy. We were two and we went

on being two who parted in the morning and met again in the
evening, in a continuous rhythm of parting and reunion. I was
happy, but my happiness was not to be fulfilled in special
scenes, weighty from the significance I attributed to them. It
was not the recollection or expectation of a rapt present,
in which Astrid and I were united in the perfect light, and in
which we ourselves and everything that involved us merged in
the glow of mutual passion. My happiness was not so theatrical, it was more patient, more modest. It was a joy that could
withstand daylight, and it didn't matter if it was a little stained
or slightly creased. The current itself, not the surface ripples
and reflections, bore us on, we only had to keep afloat, and so
we never asked each other where we were actually going. It
would have been meaningless to ask. We didn't have to go
anywhere, only further onward together, day to day through
the years, like nomads who make their home in a different
place each night and yet, as soon as they have pitched their
tent, can say they are home again. Only occasionally, at night,
every few months, I would lie in the dark beside Astrid as she
slept and ask myself how I had actually come to accompany
her and whether I had not left anything of myself behind on
the way. Whether it was all I was in the whole world, and
whether it might as well have been another, this man lying
here, whom in the early morning Astrid would regard tenderly and sleepily while she waited for him to wake up and
emerge once again in her eyes, as he stretched out his hand to
her cheek, warm and slightly swollen with sleep. Alone in the
dark beside her invisible sleeping body, in the minutes before
my consciousness wrapped itself up and rolled over the edge,
I would sometimes imagine myself hovering above a delta of
tributaries branching out into meandering streams, which

constantly divided anew the higher up I went. One stream resembled another so they were hard to distinguish, and yet each flowed in its own winding course. Seen from so high up it seemed to make no difference which one you followed on the way to the endless, monotonous sea. But was there something I had forgotten, after all? From my dizzy bird's-eye perspective I couldn't catch sight of myself, I could not tell if I had lost my way among the tributaries of the delta, and whether it made any difference at all, whether in the end it didn't just come down to floating with the stream.

As I sat there trying to see if it was the same squirrel or another popping up among the leaves where the first one had vanished, I saw the Lebanese heart surgeon parking his car in front of the house. He was in his early sixties and had an attractive olive complexion. His curly black hair was smoothed back from his high forehead, and his gray and black moustache covered his upper lip completely, which merely added to the unchanging sadness in his Levantine eyes. He jumped out of the car, surprisingly agile, almost eager, and opened the door for a slender, petite woman with big sunglasses and a yellow scarf tied firmly under her chin. She must have been about his own age. When I had had dinner with him after I arrived he told me very frankly how he had met her on a golf course in New Hampshire, precisely a week short of a year since he had buried his wife. The slight lady in the checked pantsuit had made him want to go on living, that was how he expressed it, the man people lined up for to do their bypass operations. He had insisted on hearing everything about Simon and Rosa, looking attentively at me with his dark, oriental eyes as if everything I told him was of the greatest importance to him. His eldest son lived in Cairo and the youngest had settled in

Dusseldorf. He carried his lady friend's traveling bag for her and gallantly offered her his arm before they went up the steps to the house. Half an hour later there was a cautious knock on my door. He smiled apologetically as if to excuse himself for intruding in his own house rather than leaving it to me from cellar to attic. They were giving a little cocktail party the next evening, he wanted to introduce his fiancée to his friends, I would be more than welcome. There was something touching about the studied American manner in which he pronounced the word *fiancée*. But it was even more touching that he used that word at all. Today I might wish I had spent that evening with him and his frail lady friend, and not only to show him that I valued his hospitality, but as he stood there delivering his invitation, I had not the least desire to appear as the European lodger asked to join in out of politeness, an exotic item in the house's inventory. I could hear in advance the questions people would ask and imagine how I would answer them again when the person who had asked turned away to another guest. I improvised an excuse and said I unfortunately had a dinner date with a Danish artist who lived in Manhattan. He just smiled and withdrew, and as he went downstairs it struck me that I hadn't needed to explain who I was going to see. Obviously she still haunted me, the black-clad beauty from the sculpture garden at the Museum of Modern Art. Suddenly I felt caged in my room. I had gotten used to walking around freely in the large silent house, now I could hear my host and his friend talking and playing music downstairs. The aggressive sound of a juicer drowned out *Das wohltemperierte Klavier*, and just as I had adjusted myself to Bach he was replaced by Ella Fitzgerald. I couldn't come to grips with my notes, but went on sitting by the window because I didn't know what else to do. The afternoon light was as golden as the street name, Orange Street, it spread in beams and fans along the walls and sidewalk, as lavish and luxurious as the sedate brown row houses behind the wrought-iron fences. The air was perfectly clear, with a touch of coolness, sharply outlining the shadows of the lobed leaves against the sun's hard afterglow on the trees' bark.

Now that I had made myself homeless for an evening I might as well try to turn my pretense into reality and call the unknown Danish painter. If nothing else I could then confirm or disprove my naive theory that it was she who had been reading *The Fall of the King* earlier that day. But at the thought of calling I had butterflies in my stomach, and it was not only from my innate reluctance to call people I don't know. I also had felt vaguely guilty because, stupidly or not, I had established this link in my mind between the telephone number the curator had written down and the elegant young woman I had spied on in the sculpture garden. What was happening to me? Had I not after all set my mind to rest with all the good reasons for my never having deceived Astrid with so much as a single affair? And what was wrong anyhow with looking for a short while at a girl who was obviously aware of her attributes and clearly dressed to be looked at, and who furthermore had planted herself right in my field of vision? The fact that she was probably Danish and that for an obsessive moment I was reminded of the telephone number on the scrap of paper the curator had given me with a raffish glint in his eye surely did not fall within the sphere of criminal intent. On the contrary, I convinced myself that the only right thing to do was to call the girl, arrange to meet for dinner, and thus

prove I had nothing to fear either from her or about my ten-
year-old, entirely monogamous desire. When I saw the heart
surgeon and his lady friend get into the car, dressed for dinner,
I went downstairs to telephone. She answered at once. She
sounded neither particularly surprised nor particularly enthusiastic when I introduced myself and made my suggestion. As
we talked I continued to picture the pale woman in black with
the boyish haircut. She was not from Ikast anyway, I could
hear. Her voice was surprisingly deep and she spoke slowly, as
if she had to consider even the simplest words and phrases,
perhaps because her thoughts were elsewhere. It turned out
that she had no plans for the next evening. She suggested a
Thai restaurant on Spring Street and even offered to reserve a
table, perhaps to compensate for her preoccupation. My mood
improved as soon as I had put down the phone. I would have
dinner with her, I could tell her about my book, she would talk
about her painting, we might even share gossip about Copenhagen artists, and afterward I would take a taxi back to Brooklyn. It would have been strange to spend a whole month in
New York without meeting anyone except my host. I dialed
my own number in Copenhagen. It took a while for Astrid to
answer. She had gone to bed, it was after one o'clock at home,
her voice was hoarse with sleep. I apologized and asked how
things were, and if anything had happened. Why do we always
think something will happen when we are away? She told me
Rosa had had her hair cut, and Simon's soccer team had won a
match on Sunday. I said the book was going well, and we exchanged the usual tender nothings before saying goodbye. I
would have liked to go on talking to her. That night there was
something despondent and bachelor-like about going to bed

in my room on Orange Street, where the streetlights shone through the trees with a synthetic glare.

I worked with concentration all morning and managed to finish writing a section in which I discussed the technical and expressive differences and similarities between Jackson Pollock's layered explosions of oil paint and Morris Louis's vertical, thinly flowing veils of color. In the afternoon I went to Manhattan. My dinner date was not for several hours. I spent part of the time at the Metropolitan Museum, although I had already been there once or twice, and afterward sat in the sun in front of the Loeb Boathouse, letting my thoughts wander as I observed the angular silhouettes of the tall buildings above the trees in the park, the folded reflections of the sky in the lake, and the vibrating image of the water along the grooved cliff of black granite towering on the opposite shore. There was still plenty of time as I strolled south on Sixth Avenue. Dusk fell as I walked. Suddenly it seemed hazardous somehow to be on the way to dinner with a completely strange woman, and I almost blushed at the thought that she might think I was "after something." But on the other hand she could have said she was busy. Unknown as she was, I was still visualizing, since I lacked a more concrete description, the reading beauty in suit and sunglasses when I finally reached SoHo. There were ten minutes left before our meeting time when I found the restaurant on Spring Street. I went into a bookstore and looked around. On the way back I caught myself smoothing my hair, as if how I looked made any difference. There was a line out on the sidewalk, and I took my place among the people waiting, gazing around as if I knew the face I was watching for. I observed every woman who passed by. A hefty girl with red

cheeks and a snub nose crossed the street and aimed straight
for the line. She wore a pair of lobster-red nylon pants that
looked as if they were about to split around her broad thighs,
which quivered with each stride she took. Was she the one I
was waiting for? Was that why the curator had smiled so slyly
as he wrote down her phone number? A broad smile lit up her
face when she caught sight of a black woman waiting ahead of
me. Why had I been so terrified at the thought of its being the
cheery girl in lobster-red pants I was to discuss art with as
we ate stir-fried vegetables with chopsticks? What was I actually up to? The next female pedestrian was a tall, leggy girl,
moving with long strides at the side of a black man in leather
jacket and cap. She herself wore a black leather jacket and
shabby jeans, and I concluded they must be a couple. I went
on with my spying, still somewhat ashamed of the appraising
glance I had directed at the girl in the red trousers, when the
black leather man turned into the bookstore I had just left and
the leggy girl walked on hurriedly, moving her gaze along
the line. But she stopped some distance from me, and when
I looked in her direction again she was talking to a stooped
young man with rimless glasses. I looked at my watch. Was the
chic beauty from the sculpture garden keeping me waiting? As
the line slowly advanced I listened to the conversations
around me and glanced covertly at the speakers, the hefty girl
in nylon pants who was laughing loudly at herself, and the
leggy girl in leather, who gesticulated with her long slim
hands, telling the stooped man about a film she had seen in a
nasal New York accent. You could see she had just showered,
her hair was still wet. Her hair was unusually long, about the
same length and color as Botticelli's Venus, and her luxuriant
golden brown locks were a strange contrast to the worn leather

jacket and her narrow, slightly hard and angular face, pale, almost transparent it seemed to me, and completely without makeup. The stooping man held a lighter for her, and as she bent her head to light her cigarette she glanced at me briefly with an indifferent expression in her gray eyes. The man lifted his hand in farewell and crossed the street, and the leggy Botticelli girl looked at me again, her head slightly aslant, then smiled a question and came toward me. I wondered why I had not recognized her deep voice.

If the Lebanese heart surgeon had stayed out at his lady friend's house on Long Island, if he had never given his cocktail party, or if I had accepted his invitation or gone to the cinema instead, if I had never watched a strange Danish blonde in the sculpture garden behind the Museum of Modern Art and by absurd association confused her with the unknown woman hiding behind the telephone number given to me by the curator with a diabolical expression, if he hadn't given me the number, if, in brief, everything had gone differently, I would never have met Elisabeth. That probably would have been better, or things still might have gone wrong in a different way. It's useless to speculate on the ramifications of chance, the budding alternative eventualities that wither one by one as events gradually succeed each other, jostle and push each other on until nothing can be changed again. All the same I can't shake the idea of how easily, how smoothly, everything could have developed in another direction when I think of the importance I later ascribed to an evening in SoHo seven years ago. The events in themselves do not mean anything, they are as weightless as anything that never happens, never unfolds. The story does not take place in New York, in Copenhagen, or in Lisbon, it is not about Elisabeth, Astrid, or Inés. It is played out in my confused head as I travel in my mind between the cities, back and forth in memory, and the figures moving through it are only shadows of the women I am describing, flickering, indistinct and intangible when they glide across the cave walls of my skull. The cities and the women are merely names echoing under the vault of the cave, and it is the echo of my own lonely voice that I hear as I attempt to interpret the bewildering shadow play on the wall at the back of my head. Perhaps I have never known these women, perhaps they, like the cities, are nothing more than the handful of moments I remember, the disconnected and fleeting angles of vision in which the faces and the streets came toward me. I have forgotten so much, and there is so much I have never known, never seen. My story is an interpretation of interpretations, it is no more than my hesitant, irremediably distorted recollection of the significances I have ascribed to certain places, certain faces, and of how the faces and the places changed their significance on the way.

In the years that have passed since that evening I have often asked myself whether Elisabeth was even especially beautiful. Not in the same way as Inés or Astrid, not in the obvious, I almost said universal, way they had always been considered beautiful women. Elisabeth's flowing, unruly Botticelli hair was beautiful, but she herself was no beauty, and when we finally got to our table and studied the menu, smiling formally, I was almost relieved that her appearance had freed me of the sexy, black-clad daydream from the sculpture garden, which had so irritatingly clung to my thoughts. There was nothing in her way of speaking or looking at me that even hinted that she viewed me as a man other than in the strictly social sense. She didn't speak nearly as slowly as she had on the telephone, on the contrary she was rather animated, but she made the same sudden pauses, as if searching for words or lost in thoughts of something completely different. She was easy to talk to, and before the first course arrived I had already told her I was married and had children, as if to quickly transform what had threatened to become an obsession into an innocuous evening. I even told her about the woman reading in the sculpture garden and about how I had wondered if it might be her. That amused her, and when she had finished laughing she asked why I hadn't cleared up the mystery sooner. I said I was too shy, and she looked at me in amusement and said I didn't seem particularly shy, but still without a trace of coquettishness. There was something almost boyish about her as she sat there in her faded T-shirt with the name of a baseball team on it, I don't remember which one. There were moments when she could look like a slim boy with her pale narrow face, though a boy with hair down to the hips. She was rather clumsy, and several times nearly knocked my glass over. When I looked at her I felt very mature in my tweed jacket and freshly ironed shirt, even if she must be about thirty, and there could be only six or seven years between us. It turned out that we liked the same painters and shared the same aversion to much of the art produced later. She was particularly fond of Mark Rothko and Morris Louis, that was why she had left Copenhagen after the academy to live here. Among other reasons, she added, tossing her head and looking distant for a moment. She wanted to be close to the pictures she stole so freely from, she said, and smiled again. It made me think of the curator's expression when he wrote down her name and phone number, smiling his foxy smile. I found it as hard to imagine what he saw in her as I might have to understand what she could see in him. I asked her how she knew him. She explained that he had been in charge of a group exhibition of young artists' work, in which she'd had a painting. She said it casually, without so much as a hint that there was anything I must not know. Later, shortly before I returned to Copenhagen, I asked her straight out if they had been together. No, she replied, brushing the tip of my nose with her index finger in a funny, cheeky gesture, as if she was implying for a moment that I was the one who had been disappointed. But he had tried, she must say.

That evening I had no idea, no expectation that I would ever have the chance to ask her. Just as I had been comical in my own eyes when I hung back from the heart surgeon's invitation before finally dialing her number, now I was composed, sitting talking to her while the Thai food made the sweat moisten our foreheads. She was surprisingly adept at eating with chopsticks, considering her boyish awkwardness. I kept waiting for something to come up that we disagreed on, an area where we had not developed kindred ideas, and at one point I silently debated whether she might be playing up to me, but the seriousness in her subdued deep voice made me reject the idea, her searching gaze desultorily noting the smiling faces in the restaurant when she paused to find the right word. Not until I had paid the bill and we were walking among the old cast-iron facades of the neighborhood did it emerge that she had read several of my articles and essays. That was why she had agreed to meet me. Did I think she went out to dinner with whoever came along just to have the opportunity to speak Danish? My text on Giacometti had particularly interested her, the observations on withdrawal, the point of balance between spatiality and absence. The only thing she disagreed with me about was my enthusiasm for Edward Hopper. How could I be so wrong? He was incapable of painting people, his women's breasts were never of equal size, and he could never get them to stand on their feet so you believed in it. The most she would grant was that his color combinations were original, for example when he juxtaposed grass green and mint green, or strawberry red and aubergine. Moreover, his bloody boring fire escapes and fire hoses in slanting sunlight adorned every other girl's room in the backwaters. I enjoyed her pert arrogance and protested just to get her to go on. We sat on the sidewalk in front of a café on West Broadway. Behind her the World Trade Center loomed, its empty, brightly lit offices glittering in the darkness. I tried to get her to tell me about her own paintings, but she made light of them, and even her modesty seemed sincere. I asked if I could see them. She was evasive, she wasn't sure if she dared. What did she mean by that? She smiled and looked away, she was afraid I would like them as little as she did herself. But she found a pen and wrote the heart surgeon's phone number on the back of her left hand as we rode to her place in a taxi. If she changed her mind I still wanted to see them. After we said goodbye, as the taxi was crossing the Brooklyn Bridge, it occurred to me that the evening had gone precisely as I had expected. If I'd ever imagined anything else it was probably only because I had become a bit strange, sitting by myself in front of my window in Orange Street, with only the scurrying squirrels for company, and I still think I had no ulterior motive in hoping she would not wash the back of that hand too well.

I worked steadily during the next days, and thought only briefly of Astrid and even less of my meeting with Elisabeth. It could still have ended like that, before it ever began, one evening among so many others, without consequences, quickly forgotten. Seven years have passed since I put that story behind me, and it has long proved fruitless to speculate whether the story began because I was ready for it, without knowing that myself, or whether it seized the chance to begin because circumstances presented themselves. Nevertheless, I did speculate over it after Astrid was gone and I was strolling around SoHo once again with the autumn wind pulling at my coat and pant legs. When I looked through the list of exhibits in *The Village Voice* I discovered that Elisabeth was showing in a small gallery on the top floor of a former warehouse on Wooster Street. I had not actually thought of going to see it, but as I happened to pass by on the way back from my walk, I went up, tense at the thought that she might be there. As I stood among Elisabeth's wide, almost monochrome canvases, reaching from floor to ceiling in the bare, shabby space, Astrid might have been standing on the Cais da Ribeira in Oporto, with her back to the crumbling old facades tottering on each other's shoulders across the river. I can't recall which of us said that the district beside the river resembled an Asiatic lake village with its broken, soot-blackened tiles and lines of heavy dripping wash and blinds rolled down over security bars in front of windows broadcasting soccer games and family feuds, separated by narrow alleyways with shops the size of broom closets lit by a single grease-spotted bulb. Black alleys that daylight never reached, where we walked hand in hand past emaciated drug addicts with lusterless eyes and toothless little old women carrying their burdens on their heads. While my eyes slowly separated the faint gradations of color and by degrees called forth the vague, barely visible contours in Elisabeth's flat but only apparently empty fogs of color, Astrid may have been standing on the quay beside the dark river looking up at the traffic high above her on the steel bridge linking the city center with the southern bank. At that time I did not even know she was in Portugal. Perhaps she thought I must be in New York by now, perhaps she hadn't given a thought to where I was that evening a week after she had left me. Until she went away I had been absolutely sure she knew nothing about Elisabeth or about what had happened then.

She never asked me, but perhaps she did guess after all that something must have taken place. If so she gave no sign. Perhaps I had revealed it without realizing, not by anything I said but by something in my silence as we drove through Trás-os-Montes among the solitary villages with gray, crumbling stone houses and kneaded black mud in the alleyways where chickens and cattle were free to roam. Perhaps she had merely considered it as a possibility when late one evening we arrived in Oporto and strolled around the illuminated cathedral. Perhaps the suspicion had grown in her like a small invisible hole in her thoughts that let the cold air in as we stood beside the parapet on the embankment above the river and laughed at the boys kicking a ball against the cathedral wall, or as we smiled at the names of the port wine houses spelled in tall neon letters over on the southern bank, familiar English names that suddenly meant nothing, shining in the night sky.

7

Elisabeth called three days after we had dinner together in SoHo. It was a Sunday. I was surprised to hear her voice. I had thought it was Astrid phoning when the Lebanese heart surgeon knocked at my door in the morning, still in his robe, and said there was a phone call for me. Did I still want to see her paintings? Yes, I did. Her enthusiastic, self-forgetful way of speaking of the artists we both liked had inspired me, and if in weak moments I had doubted whether there was anything new to be said about such a thoroughly interpreted and canonized movement as the New York School, every doubt had evaporated the morning after our meeting. Was I doing anything that afternoon? The suggestion took me by surprise, I had just had breakfast and had actually planned to spend Sunday in Brooklyn, writing for a few hours and afterward perhaps going for a walk in Prospect Park, which I had not yet visited. She lived near Tompkins Square, between First Avenue and Avenue A. It was a quiet sunny Sunday in the East Village. There was hardly any traffic and I enjoyed strolling, with the warmth of the sun on my back, among the low brick buildings with fire escapes painted black on their facades. The jagged outlines of the fire escapes and their twisted, zigzagging shadows on the walls made me think of Franz Kline's dramatic abstract architecture of broad black brush strokes, which I had been writing about that morn-

ing when the heart surgeon knocked at my door. The atmosphere was lazy, laid-back, almost idyllic, although in places
it was still a rough neighborhood. Homeless people wrapped
in their filthy coats basked in the sunshine among their junk-
filled shopping carts. Even the drug dealers stood closing
their eyes against the sun when there were no customers.
Puerto Rican mothers walked their strollers beneath the trees
in Tompkins Square and shouted to each other in Spanish, that
soft, childish Spanish the Latin Americans speak, and the
scruffy punks with their green Mohawks and nose and eye-
brow rings had doffed their leather jackets to sun their thin
white arms. Black guys with dreadlocks sat in the flickering
patches of sunshine beating their drums in a shining, drifting
cloud of marijuana smoke. It was a popular neighborhood with
young people, especially if they were artists or dreamed of
the artist's life. Everywhere there were small theaters and
galleries in basements and vacant shops, and if you sat long
enough in one of the chic alternative cafés you could listen to
grandiose plans for the next exhibition, the next play, concert
or performance. Most of them were hopelessly untalented, but
the East Village crowd formed a closed circle whose members
affirmed to each other that they were cool, and rather than aspiring to a breakthrough on Broadway they seemed to prefer
the studiously ragged Bohemian cosiness in which they could
feel young and subversive, well after they had passed thirty.

I found her building and rang the buzzer. A long time
passed and I was about to go look for a telephone when she
stuck her head out of a window on the third floor. She hadn't
expected me so early. Her long hair hung down around her face
like an abbreviated, golden brown waterfall as she smiled, told
me to let myself in, and threw the key down to the sidewalk.

The staircase was narrow and scruffy, and there were several doors on each floor. Hers was open. I knocked lightly before going in. The apartment consisted of a kitchen alcove and one large room where she worked and slept. She was in the kitchen, opening a tin of cat food while a white cat rubbed against her calves. She had bare legs and feet, very long chalk-white legs beneath a pair of synthetic indigo blue athletic shorts, and her hair hung like a musketeer's cape around a checked washed-out man's shirt with so many missing buttons that her stomach showed when she moved. Was she dressed so lightly because she had not expected me until later? She smiled and made a humorous apologetic gesture with the can before kneeling down and serving the impatient cat. Then she rose again and flung out her arms, suddenly a bit shy. Well, this was where she lived. Would I like a glass of wine? She had already set out the bottle on a tray with two glasses and a bowl of salted peanuts. It was an excellent Orvieto, I noticed, and she carried the tray into the room and put it down on the worn floorboards, almost ceremonially, between a battered sofa and an old striped-canvas deck chair. Her easel stood at the opposite end of the room, on the other side of a rolled-up futon, between the canvases stacked against one wall with the stretchers facing out. I chose the sofa and she curled into the deck chair, pulling her long legs up under her, watching me as if to see what I thought. Again I felt vaguely old, although I was only thirty-seven that afternoon, as I sat breathing in the smell of turpentine and oil paint in her apartment, and fixed her gray eyes slightly longer than I would have otherwise, so as not to be distracted by her folded and, something I could no longer ignore, unusually shapely legs. She rested her glass against her pink knee and gazed into the corn yellow liquid for a moment, turned the glass around, and said she almost had not called me. I cleared my throat and asked why. She blushed a little as she looked up at me. She knew quite well she was not really good, not yet, she still had a long way to go. We had had such a good talk and she was afraid she wouldn't measure up to everything we had spoken about, so I would think she had been spouting big words she didn't really know how to use. Her face didn't seem nearly as sharp as it had a few evenings before in the artificial light, but I was struck again by the contrast between her unruly, romantic hair and her angular features, the prominent chin, the narrow mouth, the pale gray eyes and long nose which was a trifle crooked. Her nose bent a little to one side in the middle, which gave her a slightly degenerate profile and brought to mind certain dukes, astronomers, and encyclopedists of the eighteenth century. Her face, devoid of makeup, radiated an almost ascetic spirituality in contrast to the impractical luxuriance of the hair. The golden brown locks were constantly falling in her face, and she had to keep pushing them back from her forehead as she tried to pursue an idea, to find the words that would take her in the direction of what she was attempting to approach in her thoughts.

She was counting on me to express my opinion honestly. There were so many people who merely patted her on the shoulder for one reason or another, but what I had to say would mean something to her. She had read what I wrote, she was sure that I would at least be able to see what she was striving for. I said I was glad she had summoned the courage to call me, and told her how our conversation had helped allay the doubt I sometimes felt about my project of writing on the New York School. Her enthusiasm had convinced me, I said. She smiled, embarrassed, and took a sip of wine. It had been quite unexpected, I went on, to meet someone who thought the same way about Morris Louis and Mark Rothko, no one seemed to be interested in them any more, they had been canonized and then forgotten. I felt I might be exaggerating my doubt as well as the constructive effect of our meeting on my work, but she looked at me attentively as I spoke, and after all it wasn't totally wrong, only laid on rather thick, for the sake of clarity. Again she supported her glass against her kneecap and gazed into the wine, as if into a crystal ball. It was not only out of shyness about her pictures that she had hesitated to call. I lit a cigarette, and she looked up at me briefly as I blew out smoke. She had also been afraid I would misunderstand her. People talked so much. She didn't know what the curator had said about her, perhaps I thought—no, she interrupted herself, that sounded utterly daft. What did? I asked. She smiled ironically. Perhaps I believed she was the sort who ran after married men. We laughed over that, and I said she didn't give that impression at all, and besides, the curator had said only nice things about her. I didn't mention his conspiratorial smile, instead I said that actually I had had the same thought when I called her, I had been afraid she would misunderstand me too. All considered it was astonishing how much we had talked about us already. When you meet a woman, at first you talk about anything else, anything in the world that may interest you. Later you talk mostly about each other, about your own story and the other's and about the sensational fact that you are together, until you again start to talk about the world outside, unless you stop saying anything at all. Perhaps Elisabeth too thought we had talked enough about us, for she suddenly rose and remarked lightheartedly that she might as well get it over with, and began to pull out canvases from the stacks along the wall.

Her pictures were certainly not as impossible as she had

made them out to be, but her own appraisal of them was actually quite precise. Her sources of inspiration were still visible, but it would be wrong to call her an imitator. There was a huge gap between them and the confidently balanced abstractions I would see in the gallery on Wooster Street seven years later, but the rudiments were already there, the awareness of color and attitude to the material, and above all I could see that she was not satisfied with easy solutions. But there was still something subdued and "felt" about her canvases, a slightly excessive use of sponge and thinner, as if she was afraid of being too obvious, of adding flesh and bone to her compositions, an anxiety that made her weakest pictures overly decorative and eager to please. She had gone into the kitchen, I could hear her washing up, dropping cutlery and pots on the floor in her clumsiness and intimidation at the idea of what I might be thinking about her work. Alone with her paintings, passing from one to another and concentrating on discovering what I thought about them, I felt both serene and crestfallen. What I had repressed during our dinner on Spring Street because I was so relieved at being freed from my futile daydreams of the mysterious beauty in the sculpture garden had announced itself all the more painfully when we were together again sitting opposite each other, I on the battered sofa, she in the deck chair her beautiful long legs tucked up under her chin so the comical athletic shorts, probably without her noticing, rode up along her perfectly arched thighs around the little curve of her sex. I had done my best to censor that part of my field of vision as she told me how her fear of being misunderstood had almost stopped her from calling me, but I couldn't hide my attraction from myself, and it would be hard enough to keep it from her. How depressingly inane it was.

Could I really not meet a woman who thought and talked on the same frequency as myself without getting ideas at the sight of her thighs just because they were lovely, and because she unwittingly exposed them to my voracious gaze? Even when she clearly suggested that the wavelength we had been lucky enough to find in common should be kept free of erotic static. I went to join her in the kitchen. She sat at the table with the cat on her lap, apparently immersed in a newspaper article. I sat down across from her and said what I thought about her paintings. I spared neither my praise nor my criticisms, as far as those were concerned I was even a little brutal in my honesty, and I wondered whether I might have been quite so honest if she hadn't made it plain that our new acquaintanceship was absolutely platonic. Was I even punishing her a little? Or was I merely completing a clarification of the kind of relationship we were to have, leaving no room to make a fool of myself? She looked at me, trying not to blink, and absentmindedly scratching the cat behind the ear. In the silence after I finished speaking the cat jumped down from her lap with a soft thump and stretched before slinking into the next room. Now she didn't even have that to occupy her hands with. She cleared her throat, pushed the hair back from her cheek, and said I was right. She was glad, she said, that I had been so direct, it was almost like receiving a present, and in fact she did know where her weak points were, but it was sometimes easier to realize when it came from someone else, that happened only rarely, so she could really benefit from my criticism. I felt almost too sorry for her and tried to retract a little, but she persisted in her self-criticism until I was forced to praise the best paintings fervently to put an end to so much honesty.

She said she was looking forward to reading my book on

our favorite painters and asked why I had doubted whether it
was worth writing. I wondered whether she was questioning
me about my self-doubt in order to restore the balance between us, now that she had revealed her own uncertainty, but
I couldn't tell whether she was asking because it gave her
pleasure to shake the pedestal on which she had apparently
placed me or because my confession of doubt had touched her
sympathy. I replied that my problem was the same for anyone
wanting to write about artists who were neither academic
nor literary. The paradox involved in writing about the New
York School was that the strength of their painting actually de-
rived from its consistently nonlinguistic character. Their non-
conceptual pictures evaded every description, every verbal
characterization, and you would never be able to contain them
or the effect they had on you even if you used the most sensi-
tive vocabulary. Something would always remain that could
not be expressed in words, and it was this experience beyond
words that made you keep returning to them. An experience
that could only be expressed in painting itself and only unfold
in the meeting between the eye and the purely physical, non-
referential presence of the picture. A combination of consciousness, matter and form that could not be interpreted because it
was unique in the deepest and most unfathomable meaning of
that word, whereas language always had to make use of similarities and contrasts, in other words, of comparisons, in order
to set consciousness in motion. The only linguistic utterances
that came anywhere near what I was talking about were perhaps the paradoxes of the Zen Buddhist sages, because to them
the exercise of disciplines such as archery and calligraphy
elicited the same spontaneous insight as that which occurred
on rare occasions in the encounter with a perfectly achieved

painting. As she listened her eyes had an intensity that seemed to register every movement in my face, while at the same time her thoughts were in a different place entirely, and I must admit I was quite moved by my little paean to pure painting. As I was speaking I even decided that something like this should be the preface to my book. Suddenly she rose, as if she could not take in any more, and suggested we go for a walk. There are only so many ways you can be together with someone in a small apartment. You can sit across from each other on separate seats or you can go to bed, and when the latter possibility is excluded you eventually grow tired of the former, especially when you still don't know each other well and the pauses in conversation should preferably signal a deepening of mutual contact. We had already become quite close through our love for the New York School, and now that was enough, now something else must happen if we didn't want to end up in a blind alley. I scratched the cat politely under the chin while she pushed her bare feet into a pair of worn-out sneakers. She put on a scruffy old raincoat and a pair of scratched sunglasses and lifted her hair up over the coat collar with a shy smile, as if to apologize for its immoderate length. Soon afterward we were down on the street.

She walked fast, with long energetic strides, and as I walked beside her I noticed for the first time that we were the same height, if she wasn't a bit taller. All the same, we must have made an odd couple, she in her beat-up coat, with bare legs and dirty sneakers, I in my tweed jacket and polished shoes. I felt hopelessly conventional, almost like a plainclothes cop, as we walked through the East Village, which seemed to be populated by a cross section of international originals, so that eccentricity had become the norm while the normal was extraordinary. What could she have seen in me, an intellectual bourgeois in a tweed jacket and newly ironed pale blue shirt? I felt like a stranger, not quite myself, and wondered what kind of relationship we were establishing. There was nothing in the least flirtatious or portentous in the way we spoke to each other, and I felt reassured by the idea that at any rate it could not be the start of an affair, now that I had visited her at home and we had gone out again, into public, neutral space. Was it the start of a friendship? I pictured Astrid and the children. They had finished dinner now, Simon was most likely lost in some space invaders game on his computer, Astrid was probably reading a story to Rosa, and I saw her on the sofa with the small figure who had almost disappeared inside the duvet she had dragged with her into the living room. At the same time I was here walking in the afternoon sun on the other side of the Atlantic, beside a girl I knew hardly anything about, far from my life, my town, my daily routine, where every step I took was a step along familiar, well-trodden paths. We followed the Bowery past the dusty stores selling restaurant equipment and then crossed Little Italy and SoHo, walking toward the Hudson. From time to time I would point out an anonymous detail that had caught my attention like a naive tourist, as I described to her how my experience of pure painting corresponded to my experience of the mysterious presence of things when you concentrated on their physiognomy alone, detached from their purpose or significance. I told her about my childhood, when I had moved away from my parents into a ruin to ruminate on the passage of light and shadows across the collapsed remnants of walls and fallen beams. She understood me, she had been like that as a child too, and like me she could fall into a reverie over the pattern in a manhole cover or the torn posters on a wall. We talked about the special though uneventful moments when the sudden lightness of an unconscious, inadvertent movement and the light that falls upon it and the shadow it briefly makes, when all this is united in a mysterious way with one's gaze, as if the movement arose and issued from the eyes that follow it. At one point I accidentally kicked a big rusty nut on the sidewalk so that it rolled over the sunlit pavement, balancing on the edge of its own shadow like a runaway figure eight, and hovering in a diminishing spiral until it toppled over and became a nut again. She bent down to pick it up, then handed it to me with a smile saying it was from her to me so I wouldn't forget our meeting. I still have it in a drawer somewhere. Then she suddenly asked me to tell her something about my wife, as if just to be safe she wanted to remind me of our tacit agreement, in case I might have misunderstood something.

It was strange to hear her speak the words "your wife," and equally strange to talk about Astrid, summarily describing her the way people give a description of themselves in a personal advertisement. Thirty-eight, film editor, narrow eyes, wide cheekbones, slender, chestnut brown hair that curls in wet weather, previously married to a well-known film director, mother of two, the eldest from the first marriage, likes Truffaut, crayfish parties, tramps beside the sea, antiques, Catholic kitsch and trips to southern Europe, cool and reserved in the opinion of others, but in fact intuitive, considerate, and sensual behind the facade. Was that Astrid? She suddenly seemed so remote and small in my inner eye. Had I said too much already, or should I have said nothing at all, because regardless of how much I said it would be too little anyhow? Both. But yet another threatening question hit me when we reached the West

Side Highway and walked toward the World Trade Center on the wide sidewalk beside the sparkling river. There was a cool breeze in our faces as we strolled among the puffing joggers, along the same stretch I would take a week after Astrid had left. It is the same thought that has pursued me ever since the morning she stood in front of the mirror and casually announced that she wanted to go away, so casually I forgot to ask why. The same question that poses itself each time I see her again before me, standing in the bedroom doorway regarding me, minutes before she vanishes. Do I know Astrid at all? Do I know anything about her except what I know about the years we spent together, the things we did together, and the fragments she told me about the time before we met, as summary as the description I had given Elisabeth? And does she know anything more about me? Elisabeth asked how long we had been married. Ten years? So it could be done then! I laughed and kept my voice light as I spoke of being liberated from the impatient and egocentric expectations of youth, of the happiness that could withstand daylight, withstand getting creased, and while she listened and looked at me attentively, I suddenly felt it all sounded so thin and pallid, and it seemed to me that she too could see and hear the faint shadow beneath my mature smile and confident words.

But it was true, wasn't it, that was what it was like. Wasn't it? I asked her about her own situation. Now I was the one who had a balance to restore, I who had revealed myself and awaited a disclosure from her, give and take, just as I had repaid her artistic self-criticism with the account of my occasional writing crises. We had stopped to look out over the deserted quays and the empty river, the wind had freshened and pulled at her hair and her coat, and she pushed aside the locks that blew across her face as she smiled faintly and looked at the pale blue and blue gray and iridescent blue water ruffled by the wind in restless flurries. It was a long time since she had been with anyone. Two years earlier she had found herself pregnant. He was an artist too, back in Copenhagen, it had ended badly. That was when she had come to America. She had grown used to being alone most of the time, she didn't mind, although sometimes she had to ask herself whether she wasn't getting too good at it. Now and then she felt like going home. It was a tough city, nothing was handed to you on a plate, but on the other hand she liked having to fight. She didn't really know what she'd expected. Sometimes she missed being in a place where people knew her. A speck of dust flew into my eye, it felt as sharp as a pine needle and the tears ran down my cheek. She turned to me like someone suddenly waking and held my eyelid open with one finger, but she couldn't see anything, and suddenly the speck was gone. A couple of seconds passed before I said it was gone, during which her fingers still rested against my cheek, and you might say I made use of the moment, that I withheld relevant information, so to speak, as I lightly took hold of her wrist, as if to remove her hand. We stood like that, not long but long enough, I with her wrist in my hand as we looked into each other's eyes, I with my red, tear-filled eye, then she moved her hand and I let it go, and she turned to the river. I mustn't get fond of you, she said. No, I said, and looked in the same direction as she did, over at the Colgate clock reflecting the sun so you couldn't make out the time. We stood there quite close together for a while. A crazy, pointless place to stand, with our backs to the calm, monotonous Sunday traffic and the deserted, sooty warehouses. She turned her face toward me, serious and with a new gen-

tleness. You are strong, she said. Why would she think so? I
said nothing. She said she was cold and wanted to go home, I
could get a train from Church Street, she said. I said I would
walk part of the way with her. She said I didn't need to. I said
I knew that. We started to walk. I tried to find something to
say, something light, anything, but managed nothing except
scattered rambling remarks separated by endless pauses, on
the way back to the East Village. I couldn't make out if she
was the one who had been good at hiding her feelings or I who
had been blind. We had both been clever at misunderstanding
each other. We hesitated in front of her street door, she took a
long time to find her keys. When she had opened the door she
turned to me and said goodbye. I kissed her, she didn't pull
away. I hope you know what you're doing, she said. I said I
knew. I hadn't the least idea.

They are the same things you do, the same motions, and
yet you feel it must be different, must mean something else,
because it is another person meeting your eyes or closing her
eyes as you bend over her. Why did I take it so much to heart?
Was it because for ten years I hadn't slept with anyone except
Astrid? Was it merely what is commonly called a "digression"?
Well, I'd apparently been digressing for a long time, although
unaware of it myself, long before the afternoon I sat staring at
a chic young woman in the sculpture garden at the Museum of
Modern Art, sidetracked by the utterly improbable hypothesis
that she might be identical with this Elisabeth I originally had
no intention of calling, supposedly in defiance of the curator's
raffish expression, as if he had given me the telephone number
of the most luxurious tart of all time, but certainly as much in
fear of what I myself might think of doing. But if it was not a
matter of my being just another weary married man who

wanted a bit on the side on his break from the daily round, in America at that, far from any curious or judgmental eyes, then Elisabeth was merely an extra in my private little drama, the absolutely chance object of my pent-up desperation. That was how I put it to myself later, chafing with shame, but I was more tender as I stood in her apartment again that afternoon and embraced her among her canvases, while the cat rubbed itself jealously around my trouser legs and her bare calves. We remained standing for a long time, she clasping my jacket lapels and resting her head on my shoulder so her hair tickled my nose, locked in that embrace, unable to move, perhaps because neither of us knew where we were going. I thought of another embrace in another apartment, another twilight hour, when I had walked all over town with Inés after she had turned toward me, standing alone in a quiet shadowy gallery among the battered marble portraits of forgotten emperors. And I thought of the chasm that had opened up in me when I left my childhood haunt, where I had lived for a couple of weeks with the mice and the wild cats, lost and happy, and moved back home to my parents' empty, silent house. As I stood holding Elisabeth it seemed as if I had stepped across the same distance a few minutes earlier when I went to her and opened my arms. As if the old distance had opened up again while Rosa and Simon grew between Astrid and me as time went on with us, without my seeing it, perhaps because I had so much more than myself to look after. Was I about to deceive Astrid, or had I deceived both her and myself over the years? Had I after all left the most primordial part of my self when I took the chance that evening in my kitchen, when I caressed Astrid's cheek for the first time, since she was the one who had turned up in my loneliness? I hadn't known exactly

what I was doing then either. Slowly Elisabeth let go of my
jacket, I let my arms fall, and she took a step back and looked
at me, shy and slightly confused. I had no idea what she could
read in my face, but she must have been able to see something,
exposed as I was to her eyes. She let her coat fall to the floor
and undressed before me until she stood completely naked, face
to face with the strange, fully clothed man who had invaded her
life, as if she wanted him to know what he was taking on, see
her as she had been created, with her small breasts and protruding ribs. Then she went over to the rolled up futon and
spread it out, kneeling to straighten the sheet, and I noticed the
grayish dirty color of her heels and missed her already, although she had only gone a few steps away. I could hear the
police car sirens up on First Avenue. A noisy salsa tape from a
car radio echoed among the facades, grew louder and died
away, and through the window I saw the shadow of a pigeon's
flapping wings approach the fire escape's folded, hatched
shadow on the wall of the building opposite, at the top where
the bricks still shone with the low sun's deep glow. The sunlit
flapping pigeon and the pigeon's flapping shadow approached
each other until the distance between them was closed as it
landed on the top step of the fire escape and folded its wings.

To tell the truth it was not at all unforgettable, the first
time Elisabeth and I lay together on her hard futon, watched
over by the white cat, who sat in the doorway with impeccably
folded paws like a household sphinx, to whom nothing human
was strange. I was inclined to believe her when she said it was
a long time since she had been with a man. The angularity
of her body seemed to be transmitted to her movements, and
our endeavor developed into a hectic and hoarsely breathing
tussle, until we had to give up. She lay resting her cheek on my

thigh, regarding my still aroused cock with a dazed expression. I mentioned the famous photograph by Man Ray, in which
a silent film star from the twenties with a sultry pout and long
eyelashes bends her head to regard a primitive African stat-
uette. We both laughed, not only at my comparison but also
because I should have thought of it at all, and we chuckled
again as we drew close together in the dusk, beneath the heavy
woolen poncho that served as her duvet. She asked if I was
disappointed. I wasn't, not at all. I was almost relieved at not
having had to perform brilliantly the first time, after so many
years of having Astrid as the steadily more biased witness
of my sexual prowess. I had never quite believed any other
woman would be as satisfied in her place, whether I thought
she was being modest or overrating what had now become
hers, merely because it was hers. But I said nothing about that
to Elisabeth as we lay close beneath her poncho, nor to my
surprise did I have a trace of bad conscience, perhaps because
there was nothing demonic or especially exotic to be felt in her
long narrow body against mine. It was just another body, different from the one I was used to. I tried to explain to her how
I was feeling, how it seemed like I had crossed a distance inside myself, a distance that had grown through the years I
lived with Astrid without my having noticed it, because it had
opened so slowly and gradually, but she put a finger on my
mouth and told me to stop.

Later we never talked about Astrid. Nor did we talk
about us, about what had happened between us, or what was
going to happen. The future was taboo. We discussed art, our
work, what we saw and heard and what we had once seen or
heard, and we avoided touching on the inevitable day when I
would return to what was my life. We pretended it was not
approaching, and settled ourselves in our soft shining soap

bubble, delighted that it stayed aloft. We counted not the days but the hours, and so the next three weeks became a small eternity. We spent most of the time in her apartment, and took long walks without a destination or went shopping in the middle of the night at the Korean greengrocer's on Avenue A. I cooked hearty Spanish casseroles for her, and she managed to gain a kilo while we were together. We also learned how to make love to each other, but there were nights when we just lay chatting and quite forgot that forbidden lovers are supposed to fuck like mad. Every other day I went over to Brooklyn Heights and slept at the Lebanese heart surgeon's house to work for a few hours the next morning, but just as often I sat writing in Elisabeth's kitchen, while she worked in the next room and the cat went back and forth between us like an affectionate messenger. My book progressed more quickly than I had expected, neither Elisabeth nor her cat distracted me. On the contrary, I found it easier than before to focus on the themes I was developing, and when I read aloud to her the pages I had written during the day I could hear they were better than most of what I had written thus far. The heart surgeon was rarely at home, he apparently preferred his lady friend's house on Long Island, and only once was there a message that Astrid had called. I myself called home a few times and was amazed at how natural I was when I asked what had been happening or talked about my book. She sounded as though she didn't suspect anything. I would not have believed deception could feel so easy and effortless, and I listened to her voice with my usual tenderness, slightly delayed by the satellite link, as if Elisabeth and she really existed in separate worlds and the boundary between them went straight down through myself.

We spoke to hardly anyone apart from the times when we were in one of the cafés in the East Village and her friends came over to say hello, nonchalant artist types who shook my hand politely, stealing curious glances at me as they exchanged news with Elisabeth, mildly wondering what kind of bourgeois specimen she had raked up. She made no special effort to introduce me to her world, and I was only too glad to have her to myself. Only once did she take me with her to a fashionable private showing in SoHo. The gallery was in an old converted garage with glazed glass windows facing onto the street, so the cool white space formed a hermetic abstract sphere around the exhibit and the specially invited guests standing in groups with their backs to the pictures, conversing animatedly while eyeing whoever came and went. Nobody noticed me at my observation post in the far corner, I was temporarily invisible. I was surprised to see how many people knew Elisabeth, and from my corner I watched my graceful ragamuffin of a lover being kissed on the cheek by middle-aged men with ponytails and black T-shirts under their pinstriped suits from Saks. So they too were part of her world, the world I had disturbed and to which she would return when I had gone home. Even the artist was clearly one of her oldest and dearest friends, a little Italian with thinning hair in a white suit and sandals, who had to tilt his head back to look up at her as they stood giggling together. He was the only one who allowed himself to smoke, and he puffed away at a full-size Havana cigar as he told her a story that made her double over with laughter. I couldn't help noticing how he jovially put his little hairy hand with the smoking Havana on her buttock in the washed-out jeans full of holes, as he stood on tiptoe in his sandals to whisper in her ear, totally indifferent to the obviously well-to-do women in pink and lemon yellow Chanel creations fidgeting for an audience. Again I was reminded of the curator and his foxy smile. Was I a laughing-stock as I stood there, stripped bare by love in this antiseptic, droning place?

The day before I left we went out to Coney Island. We had a beer at a bar on the promenade, where elderly men in dented baseball caps were hunched over, silhouetted against the sea. The ugly cries of seagulls echoed inside the bar, which naturally was called the Atlantic, and behind it the Ferris wheel turned in the empty amusement park. The television was on above the bar, and the football field was almost the same green as the walls in that scruffy place. The players jammed together on the field, a confused bunch of numbers on bowed backs, and the next moment spread out again like a flock of heavy, clumsy gulls. One glittering airplane after another approached in the sky over the sea and prepared to land at JFK airport, and the fishermen out on the jetty dropped their lines into the water again and again. They used minnows as bait. Behind them, beyond the park, were some of the last tenements in America, their windows facing the ocean, brown, tall, and square. Elisabeth thought the melancholy apartment houses resembled the thousand-year-old high-rise mud houses in Sana, Yemen. We stayed for an hour on the beach. She rested her head in my lap and closed her eyes in the white cloudy light, her hair fanning out over my knees. I looked at her face and the sea. I asked if she still thought of moving back to Copenhagen. She didn't know. Perhaps. We didn't say much that day or the next in the taxi on the way to the airport. She smiled wryly as we stood facing each other before the check-in counters. It had been great to meet me. It sounded as if we would never see each other again, as if nothing special had happened. Then she kissed me briefly and left without looking back. Six months

later I stood on another beach with Astrid. It was the day after
we arrived at Oporto. We intended to go straight to Lisbon,
perhaps with a stop in Coimbra, but first we wanted to see the
sea. We hadn't seen it since San Sebastian. We followed the
Douro along the increasingly shabby facades with sooty black
tiles, rusty balcony railings, lines of sheets and faded children's clothes, out to the river mouth where the fishermen
stood on a sand spit, small and lost in the mist. We drove all
the way to Matosinhos and walked across the enormous deserted beach with our backs to the derelict beach cafés and
beach cabins and the great oil tanks further away, glittering
dully in the misty sunlight. We walked as far as we could go,
until we could stand before the yellowish surf of foam and
whirled-up sand and look out to where the sea became one
with the fog. I discovered afterward that Matosinhos and
Coney Island lie almost opposite each other, at about forty and
forty-one degrees northern latitude. The beach where I sat
with Elisabeth's head in my lap trying to imagine what it
would be like to leave Astrid, and the beach where I stood with
Astrid six months later, after I had parted from Elisabeth for
the second time. A beach in the old world and a beach in the
new, divided by the sea that so many before me had crossed
full of hope, as if the world were not after all one connected
place that is merely very large. As if it was a matter of separate worlds. Astrid was not waiting for me at the airport
the first time, that spring when I came back from New York.
The memory of Elisabeth was a blurred, unreal afterimage at
the base of my fatigue. It was a great relief. I had been afraid
she would be standing there holding Rosa's hand, with Simon
hanging back a little, wearing his baseball cap and walkman,
restless and impatient because it was rather beneath a sixteen-

year-old's dignity to meet his stepfather at the airport. I had prepared myself so intensively for this reunion in the arrival terminal that I had had no time to foresee what else would happen. Would anything happen? As I dozed in the plane my betrayal had dawned on me in all its incalculable dimensions. I couldn't think of what had taken place in the East Village during the past three weeks as a mere affair, even though I was now many kilometers above the sea, alone again, and should have made the airspace over the Atlantic into an elegant, painless sluice that divided me from my secret and closed again behind me. Of course I knew that an affair like this was something utterly banal when you were an adult who could only smile at your own guileless youth, just as you smile at the old pictures of yourself looking so naive, with your soft cheeks, dressed in clothes long since out of date. I knew very well that it need be nothing more than a harmless diversion without consequences, that there was no reason at all to make an issue of it or to burden Astrid with quite unnecessary pain. But the idea of my own silence was just as painful as the thought of Astrid's reaction if I told her what had gone on in New York. Until three weeks ago I had been the man I had become over the years with Astrid, but I had only been that man because I believed she knew all there was to know about him. I had never wanted to have secrets from her. On the contrary, I had always been afraid of the thought that there might be something I hadn't managed to tell or show her, something she had not seen and seen through. I only dared to believe in her love if I could count on her loving me despite all she knew about me, despite all my faults and failings. Ten years ago when I kissed her for the first time one winter evening in my kitchen, a strange girl I'd picked up in my taxi and given shelter merely to be kind, and ten months after that, when she told me she was pregnant and I replied with my reckless *Why not,* I had seized the chance to escape my loneliness and become some-one in the world, together with someone else, in her eyes and in everything we did together. After Inés left me I had felt struck by a curse that made me invisible. It hadn't been re-motely like the feeling I had when I lay on the moldy sofa in the idyllic ruin of my youth among the heaps of broken tiles, watching the birds flying through the roof as I dreamed of being no one. It hadn't been as I had thought in my childish arrogance, and as it said in the poem I had memorized: *how dreary to be somebody, how public, like a frog...* Rather, Inés had punished me for my ill-fated passion, in the cruelest way, and transformed me into a hideous toad, slimy and mold green with loneliness. Not until Astrid kissed me did I become a per-son again like everyone else, though not just anyone. For I be-came precisely that human being she had met so fortuitously and yet liked more than so many others, and I determined on the spot, in that moment, without hesitation and rather irre-sponsibly, that he was the one I wanted to be, the man she had called forth from invisibility with her gaze. And thus I had closed the door behind me on the innermost room in myself, I thought on the plane as the darkness accelerated over the At-lantic. It was just how I had turned my back on the room in my overgrown ruin, where I had been myself more than any-where else because I had all the company I needed with the mice and wild cats around me, and did not need somebody else's eyes to hold me fast and prevent me from vanishing. I had escaped invisibility, I thought in my airplane seat as I watched the sky turn dark blue above the clouds, but only to lose myself in the visible world's welter of faces and forms and be swept along by the current of days in the labyrinthine delta of coincidences.

I landed early in the morning. The others had already left when I let myself into the apartment. There was a note from Astrid on the kitchen table, she had set out a tray with coffee and rolls, and Rosa had made a drawing of me, a man in a flowered jacket standing smiling among skyscrapers only half a head taller than himself. Atop her clumsy rendering of the Empire State Building stood a chimpanzee in spotted bathing trunks. It too was splitting its sides with laughter, and it had what looked like a Barbie doll under its arm, with long wavy hair. I went to bed and slept all day. When I woke up the sun had set. I was roused by Rosa's hand stroking my stubble, and I heard Astrid call to her in a whisper. I opened my eyes and saw them for a moment in the doorway of the twilit bedroom before they disappeared. I lay still for a little while, listening to their distant voices in the kitchen and the screeching brakes and excited American dialogue in the film Simon was watching in the next room. I felt as if I too was watching a film that had been stopped and now continued again with the same actors, the same plot. I looked at the verdigris, illuminated hands of the alarm clock. It was half past twelve in New York, Elisabeth might be working on the painting I had seen her start a couple of days earlier, or perhaps she was walking along First Avenue with long, quick strides with her hair waving like a shining flag in the sun and wind. I rose and went out into the living room to Simon. He looked at me vaguely, quite lost in the film, then he stood up and embraced me, a little shyly, as if he was really too old for that kind of thing. He asked how it had gone. On the screen behind him a wild-eyed man hung in the air over Manhattan, clutching one of the runners of a helicopter as another man crushed his white knuckles with the heel of his boot. Well, I replied, and told him to watch to the end of the film. He smiled apologetically, it was at the most exciting place, I smiled back and went out to the others. When Rosa heard my footsteps she came rushing along the hallway and leaped into my arms, nearly knocking me over. I kissed her and carried her into the kitchen where Astrid was peeling potatoes. She stood smiling at us with the potato peeler in her hand until I let Rosa slide down to the floor and embraced her. She had lost some weight, I could feel, she looked beautiful, beautiful and unsuspecting as she stood there recognizing me with her eyes, as if she saw all there was to see. As usual when I came back from a trip, I told them what I had experienced and gave them the small presents I had remembered to buy. Later in the evening, when Astrid and I went to bed, it surprised me that she could see nothing, and I made love to her roughly and impatiently, as if I could hide behind my violence, as if I wanted to get it over with, in a sudden rage, as if I wanted to punish her for her ignorance, punish her for my own crime. Afterward she said it had been a long time since it was so good. I kissed her eyelids and she opened her lazy narrow eyes a little and creased her lips into an ironic smile and said she almost wished I went away more often so I could come home and make love to her like that.

I lay awake in the dark beside her until at last we put out the light. For several hours I listened to her breathing and the occasional cars driving by along the Lakes. I thought of Simon's shyness on the sofa, watching his hair-raising video, of Rosa's happy shriek when she reached out her arms to leap into my embrace. I thought of Astrid's eyes in the kitchen when she turned toward me and seemed to make my homecoming face regain its outlines in her memory, and I thought of Elisabeth, who was probably sitting eating a tray of sushi she had bought in the Japanese restaurant on Avenue A, while the cat regarded her with its cool, unparticipating eyes. What was it about her that made her such a watershed? Was it the earnest timbre of her deep voice? Her profuse wild hair and her hectic, breathless way of making love? Was it the cool nonchalance of her appearance and the dust that gathered along the walls of her ascetic apartment, self-forgetfully absorbed as she was in her painting? Was it our mutual love of Mark Rothko and Morris Louis, her way of intuiting what I was going to say about them and about everything else we discussed because each of us had thought and felt the same thing? Was it the remarkable, finely tuned, undisturbed, and noiseless wavelength where we had found each other so easily, because for years we had transmitted on the same frequency without knowing it? Or was she merely an extraneous, incidental opportunity that made me open my eyes to what I had ignored for years and forced me to answer the question I had allowed to remain unanswered amid the fleeting, whirling current? The question Inés had left inside me when she kissed me goodbye on the Place de l'Alma a year or two ago and vanished once again, down into the metro. Had I been happy? Or was it merely a consolation prize, this everyday happiness that could withstand both daylight and the daily chores, this patient and modest, relaxed bourgeois happiness that could be washed and ironed? Had I been off the mark, perhaps a little too quick, when I replied to Astrid's unexpected announcement with my casual *Why not*? Was my real deception that ambivalent reply, when Astrid offered me a child and meaning for my pointless, melancholy life? Had I only grabbed at her out of cowardice, because self-pity and loneliness made me cave in? Had she herself been happy, or had I wasted her time? Did I love her or did it just look that way? Had Inés left an empty room inside me that Astrid was never allowed to enter because I had locked the door and thrown away the key? Had I really believed that I could condemn my own despondency and forget myself in my new life of restless activity, fond duties, and humming, quotidian tenderness? Was it there, in my empty interior, that Elisabeth had suddenly appeared through a hidden door in the peeling, rotten wallpaper? A door that had been so secret that it was possible to hide its existence even from myself?

The next day I thought Astrid had found me out. When I woke up in the morning and went into the bathroom she was sorting out dirty laundry. As I was brushing my teeth I saw her in the mirror removing a white cat's hair from one of my shirts. I rinsed my mouth and told her the Lebanese heart surgeon's cat had kept me company as I wrote. It probably felt as lonely as I was, I said, now that its master preferred to stay with his lady friend on Long Island. It had more or less moved into the guest room with me. As I stood there lying, with toothpaste foam at the corners of my mouth, I was struck by how plausible it sounded, as long as I kept the image in my mind's eye of the white cat sunning itself in the window over Orange Street. Astrid smiled, she thought I didn't like cats, and it was true, I had several times objected when Rosa pestered us to get her a kitten, because I could all too easily see who would end up changing its cat litter and removing its hard, stinking little turds. But this cat had been rather likable, I said, visualizing it strutting around the big old house in Brooklyn Heights or sitting watching me write, arrogant and inscrutable. As the days went by it grew easier to go on skirting the truth. The film continued and I fell into my customary role. Ater all, I did know my lines by heart. I knew precisely when I was in the frame and what was expected of me. Besides, it had always been characteristic of me to be slightly preoccupied, at times even distrait, which Astrid only thought charming, and at most might tease me about in an affectionate tone. Now I had to ask myself if it was the concentration on my work or an unacknowledged awkwardness toward Astrid that had been the cause of my increasing distraction through the years. I still had my book as an excuse for being absent-minded, and I ensconced myself in my study and wrote a great deal in the weeks that followed. When I was not writing I attended to my domestic duties, and in the evening I was even more attentive and available to the children than I was normally, perhaps in an attempt to compensate for my bad conscience. Only when I was alone with Astrid did my fondness become somewhat distanced and conventional, but she was accustomed to that in the periods when I worked intensively, just as she recognized the symptoms of a bad conscience when I spoiled the children, which she attributed to my usual anxiety about neglecting them for my work.

For Astrid my intellectual life had been an inaccessible zone from the outset, and she wouldn't dream of interfering with it, whether out of respect, not wanting to disturb me when I sat at my window overlooking the Lakes bent over my manuscripts, or because my scribblings did not particularly interest her. I was never offended by her lack of interest in what I wrote; on the contrary. When I met her I had in fact felt that she released me from my brooding solitary nature. She had drawn me into a sphere of unworried ease, and even the grayest days had never been ugly or chilling in their inevitable triviality. With all its necessary repetitions daily life had rather been transformed into a light, vibrating mobile turning gracefully around itself, set in movement by the warmth between us. I had never expected her to disturb me in the solitary circles of my work. It was as if only by keeping outside could she remain a counterbalance to my abstractions and prevent me from completely losing sight of the real world. In a subtle way my intellectual loneliness was the price I paid not to be lonely. Therefore I never thought about her when I worked, although Elisabeth was constantly on my mind as I was finishing my book. To think of Elisabeth and write about the artists of the New York School was the same thing, not only because she had thought about them in the same way as I did, but also because for the first time in many years I had dreamed anew that life and work could merge in one unbroken movement. For I had indeed discovered it was possible, in the transient bubble of the days she and I had spent in the East Village. The bubble's thin membrane had broken, but I could not forget its radiance and iridescence, I could not let go of the thought that it might be possible to blow a new and larger bubble that could go on floating. Some dreams are so detailed and lifelike that you go on dreaming them even after you have awakened. I kept returning to what she had hinted at once or twice, that she might think of going home to Copenhagen, and I indulged more and more frequently in idyllic fantasies of us living together in another part of town, of how she would paint while I wrote, and get to know Rosa and Simon. It was all very delightful, and Astrid was always conveniently out of sight when I indulged my hopeful hallucinations.

Even before I met Elisabeth, while I was living at the Lebanese heart surgeon's house in Brooklyn Heights, I had

found it hard to visualize Astrid clearly. I saw the familiar sit-
uations at different times of the day, the same every day, but
she remained indistinct, and when I tried to focus on a close-
up of her it was always one of those slightly stiff, posed, and
far too self-conscious portraits that hide more than they reveal. My recollection of her was not that of a clearly defined,
fast-frozen moment detached from the flashing, unsteady
stream of time, for she had been there the whole time, in all
the years we had been together. I couldn't catch sight of her
because she was everywhere. The recollection of her face
couldn't be isolated into firm, unmoving images, it blended together with my diffuse memory of time itself, the continued
movement through the years, which made the hours and days
flow together in the shining fog of speed, the haste with
which everything had happened to us. On the other hand, I
could see Elisabeth quite clearly, she grew only clearer as the
weeks passed, after we had parted at Kennedy airport. She sat
with her eyes closed and her head leaning back in the sunshine, on the sidewalk in front of a café opposite Tompkins
Square. The cigarette between her lips outlined its changing
calligraphy of blue smoke in the air, and the transparent
shadow of the smoke drew a fine veil over her calm, sunlit face.
She stood before her easel in the backlight that made the color
glitter on the canvas like a metal sheet, herself only a gray silhouette with her hair gathered into an untidy turban of loose
locks, bare-legged, with stripes of chrome yellow and crimson
on her thighs. She sat with her legs apart in a ray of sunlight
on the floor in front of the open window, bent over my sheets
of manuscript, which she had spread out in front of her while
she ate yogurt, absorbed in her reading so completely that
she forgot to wipe away the white stripe over her upper lip

curving upward at the corners of her mouth like a stiffened, unintended smile. I saw her so clearly in my mind's eye as I sat watching the fresh shining green shoots on the trees along the lakeside under my window. Two weeks later I gave in and called her, early in the afternoon while there was still time before Simon and Rosa came home from school. Her voice was heavy with sleep, it was only half past six in New York. I asked what she was doing. She said the cat was lying on her stomach, and was eyeing a pigeon outside on the windowsill. I said I missed her. She said she missed me too. The words were almost like an impediment between us, they did not connect us, only made it all the harder to reach her. She told me she had a commission to exhibit at a nearby gallery, I talked about my book. It all seemed so mundane in contrast to everything I had been thinking after we parted. She asked what it was like to be home. I said it was difficult, that I thought about her a lot. She thought about me too. Was it just something she said? I said I would come to New York, I didn't know exactly when, but I would come. Then we'll meet, she said. There was silence over the telephone, a long, satellite-transmitted silence, faintly hissing, as you imagine the silence in space. I repeated that I missed her, mainly to fill the hissing emptiness with something, kill the silence spread out between us all the way across the Atlantic. Soon afterward we ended the call.

It was not until Astrid left that I began to see her as clearly as I saw Elisabeth then, after I had come home, in calm and clearly defined, easy-to-grasp images. The images are all I have, and I go on looking at them for fear they too will disappear. But the more clearly I see them, the more incomprehensible they become. Her story is not the same as mine, after all. The pattern of my story hides the story Astrid could have told me if she had not left, and I am only telling my own because she isn't here, but the longer it gets the more she withdraws. And yet I have to tell it if I'm to reach the point where my words die away, the boundary where they have to give up, faced with the distance between Astrid as she appears in my self-centered narrative and the Astrid who hides behind my pictures of her. Astrid standing on the balcony on a summer morning, looking over the treetops and the lake with a distant gaze, as if wondering about her life. Astrid in her coat in the bedroom doorway, looking at me silently for a few seconds before she turns and disappears. Astrid in sunglasses, surrounded by the river's glittering snowstorm of reflections, smiling before the view over Lisbon from one of the ferries to Cacilhas. Her inaccessible eyes and her dazzling smile among the minute houses rising up behind one another on the heights of Bairro Alto and Alfama, brilliant white in the low light of afternoon.

8

We spent the summer by the sea, Astrid, the children, and I. While I was in New York she had arranged to rent the house where we had stayed the first summer we were together, when she was expecting Rosa, and where we had vacationed several times. It had originally been a low-ceilinged, thatched fisherman's cottage, enlarged around the turn of the century with an extension on two floors, holding several generations of summer guests at once in its numerous little rooms with faded wallpaper and creaking beds and floors with scrunching sand, furnished through generations, so the place seemed as timeless as the sea outside the windows down the slope. I did all I could to seem enthusiastic. When I stood among the rosebushes again, on the steps that led down to the beach, and looked out over the empty, monochrome sea, time felt longer than it had before, the time that had passed since the night I kept watch after Astrid had been taken away in an ambulance. She had almost lost Rosa, what had become Rosa, the long-legged ten-year-old with brown legs and sun-bleached braids who now ran along the edge of the beach throwing jellyfish at her big brother and screaming shrilly and theatrically when he turned her upside down and threw her into the waves. Here I had sat on the steps among the fragrant rosebushes, looking out at the dark breakers as I lit each cigarette from the butt of the last one and talked to Astrid as if she could hear me where she was in the hospital. As if it could make any difference, my repeating the same inadequate little words over and over again through my clenched teeth, *Hold on, hold on.* And now I was prepared to let go of it all. I thought of Elisabeth all the time, and I had to pretend I was having problems with my book on the New York School, explain to Astrid that was why I was so often absent-minded or irritable. In reality the book had been finished for several weeks, I only needed to write a brief concluding chapter and go through the manuscript, but I spun it out and sat for hours bent over the fair copy by my window facing the Lakes and later by the rickety dressing table by the window looking onto the idle and intemperate blue sea, while the others went swimming or lay in the sun. I felt closer to Elisabeth when I was writing about the painters we both loved, just as I had felt closer to her in Copenhagen, perhaps because it was closer to the airport.

After a week by the sea Astrid was brown and lovely, and scented with wind and salt when she lay down beside me. I was still as white as a skeleton and smelled of nothing but too many cigarettes and far too much black coffee. I was amazed at her patience, and even that irritated me. Elisabeth had come between us, and clearly she had come to stay. It was only by mustering all my concentration that I succeeded in responding to Astrid's caresses at night, now and then performing a half-hearted and routine fuck in order to allay her suspicions. But it was unnecessary, she seemed to think it was my work as usual that distanced me from her, she even tried to comfort and encourage me, which only made me still more morose. When I was not thinking of Elisabeth I thought, for the first time ever, that Astrid had never understood what excited me.

Not only was she ignorant of the fact that I had been unfaithful to her, she had hardly any perception at all of the world where I spent half my life, whereas I had often talked to her about the films she edited and showed her how in their compositional technique the directors she admired had drawn their inspiration from painting. Suddenly it seemed to me that we had not been living together but beside each other, each in our own world, with the children as our chief concern. Was I to stay with her purely for their sake? As I saw it that would only increase my resignation until finally I would shut myself in completely behind my words and my pictures, because in time it would be only the pattern of repetitions we had laced ourselves into that could still call me back to our mutual reality, not Astrid herself and the urge to reach out to her, the spontaneous tenderness, the recurring desire that had earlier set the pattern in movement. Would we just be friends? Could Astrid consent to live with a man who loved another woman?

There I had to stop my self-justifying defense. Did I really love Elisabeth, or had she just become an obsession, a phantom for my frustrated craving for something different, another life, a new beginning? I visualized her in the sun on Tompkins Square, in front of her easel and bent over my sheets of manuscript, with yogurt on her upper lip, quite clear but also mysterious. The sight of her struck me with something resembling pain, but it did not answer my question, and I knew there was only one way to get an answer. Once or twice since my return I had hinted that I might have to go back to New York for a week or so to undertake supplementary research, and my alternately melancholy and sullen introversion only started to abate when Astrid herself suggested that I should go again, since I had worked so well there. She really did say that, and I hated myself as I kissed her, hated myself, because my gratitude could not be distinguished from the silent, patronizing contempt oozing out behind my smile. But perhaps she was not as gullible as I imagined, perhaps she had in fact caught wind of what was happening. Perhaps her unexpected and generous suggestion was just another expression of the refined dignity everyone admired in her, and which made the more insolent arrivistes in our circle wince when she smiled graciously at their intimidating or bitchy attempts to disconcert her and chisel a crack in her cool facade. Perhaps she had already thought things through and decided she would rather set me free than demean herself by holding on to a man whose love she had already lost. It might even be, I thought in my shadowy room looking out on the dazzling summer days by the sea, that she herself had noticed weariness growing like a distance between us, exhausted as I was by the repetition of everything, by no longer being on the way to some indefinite place, but further into a future that was no longer so unpredictable as it had once been. Perhaps she was merely waiting with deceptive passivity for me to take the first step. In my state the idea was almost encouraging, and I sucked at it as you suck a candy until it has melted, dissolved by saliva, leaving only a sticky, sweetish, and vaguely shameful feeling in the mouth.

One afternoon while the others were on the beach I called Elisabeth again. I had almost done it several times but held back, either because Simon or Rosa had come rushing in or because I'd lost my nerve at the last minute. It had become too heavy, too serious to call her compared with the easy, untroubled way we had talked about whatever crossed our minds

in the three weeks we spent together. I held my breath when I
heard her deep serious voice speaking to me on the other end
in its impeccable New York accent, and I was about to answer
her when I realized it was her answering machine I was listening to. She said she was away until the end of August. As
I sat with the receiver pressed to my ear listening to her
voice, I saw Astrid come into view among the rosebushes
outside, naked and sunburned under her open robe, swinging
her wet bathing suit like a child in a cloud of sparkling drops
that made the leaves on the bushes flutter as she walked past.
She didn't see me as she passed the narrow windows of the
low-ceilinged room, her head bent, immersed in unknown
thoughts. The wet sand stuck to her calves and ankles, and her
beautiful breasts swayed softly in time to her strides, slightly
paler than her brown face and legs. Why didn't I go out to
her? Why didn't I carry her off to the furthest room of the
house in this quiet afternoon hour, while the children roamed
on the beach? Why didn't I just forget this hopeless story, why
did I sit there clutching the telephone listening to the message
Elisabeth had recorded, most likely several weeks ago, for the
benefit of all and sundry? She hadn't said anything about
going away. But perhaps she had only decided at the last
minute, after all she was free and independent and could make
decisions from day to day. Had she traveled alone or was she
with someone? Actually, I knew hardly anything about her or
the people she knew. She must surely see others sometimes,
and maybe I was not the only man in her life. "In her life." The
phrase suddenly seemed far too solemn. Wasn't I just a man
she had been with for a couple of weeks in the spring? Had it
ever been "in the cards," as they say, that I should be anything
more? I imagined her at this moment sitting on the back seat

of a motorcycle driving through the Mojave desert, her arms around the hips of one of the aspiring young artists in black leather jackets and narrow sunglasses I had seen leaning world-wearily against the bar counters in the East Village. While I sat here in a thatched vacation house, married and bourgeois and filled with longing. I couldn't even see the comedy or utter distortion of being jealous of the woman I had been fucking behind my wife's back.

A few days later I drove into town to meet my editor. Then I went to look at an apartment downtown that had been advertized in one of the Sunday papers. The owner was a journalist with a beer belly and sweat on his upper lip, who would be based in Moscow starting that autumn, provisionally for a year, he wanted to rent the apartment furnished, he said, as he showed me around. He had exceptionally bad taste, which in a way encouraged me because his smoked glass tables and brandy-colored leather sofas merely dramatized my subversive and brutal determination. If one altered the vulgar furnishings a little Elisabeth and I could each have a room where we could work, hers even had a balcony facing north, and with a bit of goodwill the room could function as a studio. I was amazed at my own boldness as I questioned the owner about heating costs and the shared facilities of the property. I behaved as if Elisabeth had not only decided to return to Copenhagen but was also intending to move in with me, although I had scant reason for believing any of this. When the journalist showed me the bathroom and proudly pointed out that the gilt armatures matched the brown tiles and mahogany toilet seat, he wiped the sweat from his upper lip and looked at me with an approving glint in his eye, as if he had acquired certain rights now that I had seen the way he lived. Was I getting

divorced? Or did I just need a discreet little love nest? He
really did use that expression. I was speechless, and it struck
me as often before that people's heads are probably furnished
like their homes. I mumbled something about a working
apartment now that the children were growing up and needed
more space, but he merely grunted contentedly, it had nothing
to do with him. It was not only his bathroom that was brown,
suddenly I felt brown inside too. He asked for a telephone
number but I said I would be away for the rest of the summer.
I would call back. *Good luck*, he smiled sweatily, and his raffish
glance, man to man, stuck to my flustered face as he closed
the door behind me. As I drove north I tried to convince myself that the journalist's sticky smile and his brown interior
wouldn't need to affect us, and that what had come into being
between Elisabeth and me would be the same regardless of
where we lived. But what had I actually imagined? What
would our new life be like? Would she be "like a mother" to
Rosa, she who was so distrait that she forgot to tie her own
shoelaces? Would she and Astrid become "friends"? Or would
she take Astrid's place at the dinner parties with friends? It
seemed unthinkable that she would sit in her worn leather
jacket and washed-out T-shirt and participate in the worldly
table talk in a villa out in the northern suburbs. As I drove
along the highway in the slanting afternoon light that made
the cars throw long, deformed shadows on the glittering asphalt, I realized that it was not only Astrid but the whole of
my previous life I was about to leave. And perhaps it was not
only the thought of Elisabeth that seemed obsessive, but also
the thought of leaving it all. The thought of being no one
again and leaving everything I was in the eyes of others, like a
snake sloughing off its skin. The thought of feeling the empty

air in my pores again and breathing in the dizzy sensation that everything was still possible, that my account with the future was not yet made up.

It was Midsummer Eve. I had completely forgotten that Astrid had invited guests, they were already sitting with their drinks in front of the house, beside the table among the dog-rose bushes above the sea, the curator, his wife, and my mother. He raised his glass in the air when he caught sight of me, with a cheerful, man-about-town gesture, and an enthusiastic roar came from my mother as if it was Santa Claus himself arriving six months late. I turned around as Astrid came out of the house carrying a tray of various tapas and proffering her cheek with an intimate glance, as if she wanted to palliate my own mother's exaggerated and theatrical joy over seeing me again. She smiled, she thought I had run away. I hastened to laugh at her light, ironic tone and sat down. The sun was setting, everyone had left the beach and the shadows began to flow into the hollows in the sand where millions of heels had trod. I caught sight of two small silhouettes out in the water, black against the backdrop of whirling golden reflections below the horizon. Soon they came up the beach, it was Rosa and Simon. Had I really thought of leaving them? As if the time for new beginnings were not long past, the great shining openness to everything possible. It was theirs, the openness, not mine, as they came running toward us across the beach, their wet bodies glistening in the low light. How would I ever find the words to explain why I left them ahead of time? Before the time when they themselves would leave us to discover who they might become. The curator suggested we go for a dip before eating, and I went up to get my bathing trunks. From the window I could look down on the little group in front of the house. Simon and Rosa stood with their towels draped like cloaks around their shuddering bodies, explaining something or other with frozen blue lips and dripping hair, and Astrid massaged their backs while my mother leaned forward to hear what they said, with the demonstrative teacher's expression she always put on when she spoke to the children, as if conversing with two backward pupils. Astrid looked at me in surprise as I came down in bathing trunks with a towel slung sportily over my shoulder. She creased her lips and smiled with her narrow eyes. Now I must really take care not to catch cold.

The water was actually quite cold. The curator is one of those people who use the city boy's method when they brave the first swim of the summer. He cupped water in his hands and rubbed it against arms and stomach before carefully easing his skinny body under the surface. I enjoyed the breathless moment when the water closed around me like a gigantic ice-cold hand, and I swam quickly out to the sandbar to get warm, dazzled by the glittering drops on my eyelashes. He was puffing with effort when at last he caught up with me. We lay floating on our backs like two club gentlemen in their chaise longues in the smoking room. Had I met any interesting people in New York? He had kept his glasses on and they reflected the sun so I couldn't see his eyes. I replied that I had kept to myself most of the time. He smiled his foxy smile. Had I called Elisabeth? I said we had had a coffee together, and started to swim to the quay of stakes and boulders framing the little bay where the fishermen had once pulled their boats up on shore. I didn't like him calling her by her first name. He swam after me. Charming, didn't I think? I turned to him, treading water. She was certainly very sweet, I replied, doing my best to sound casual. And he was right, I went on, she was certainly talented. I had already said too much. So had I got to see her pictures? I had the sun at my back, I was no more than a silhouette before the silhouettes of the quay's big stones, but he smiled all the same as if he could see my expression. He knew she would be just my type. What did he mean by that? He smiled again. I needn't worry, it would stay between us, we were friends, after all, weren't we? I swam out, he followed and came up beside me. It was nothing to be ashamed of, a good-looking guy like me, alone in New York, of course it wasn't. Besides, I wasn't the only one to appreciate her talent. He had had the pleasure himself, like so many others, from what he knew she had a liking for men. I started to swim in to shore. I could see the others in front of the house but only as insubstantial little figures, my mother's wide-brimmed straw hat, Astrid's dark hair as she bent forward to pour. The curator gave me a chummy punch on the shoulder as we stood drying ourselves on the beach. He was glad I had made myself at home over there. He held up his glasses against the sky and wiped them with his towel, blinking at me short-sightedly. Everyone needed to try something different, eh?

The roses resembled colored Japanese paper flowers in the lavender blue air when the sun had disappeared behind the calm sea, which reflected the evening sky with a faint greenish tinge below the horizon. While we were eating, the curator's wife questioned me about my book, and I chatted on about the New York School painters. Everything I said sounded superficial and conventional, but she nodded eagerly as I spoke, simultaneously asking myself if I had got anything out of the past months' work except this handful of tired, complacent clichés. Like Astrid, she had no idea what her husband was up to behind her back. Nor did she know anything of the hidden doors and trapdoors in her apparently harmonious and comfortable life. Across the table my mother was initiating the curator on the most nerve-racking manner in which she had had to confront hidden and painful sides of herself while preparing for her latest role, and as he listened he bowed his bald head respectfully and smiled his slyest and most ingratiating smile, almost as if he had in mind to seduce her. Spurred by his attentiveness she became even more fervent and hand-wringing in her account of how hard it was to be an actor and to bare one's innermost soul to the audience, out there in the dark every evening. Astrid went in and out with Simon and Rosa, serving each new course, now and then catching my eye and looking at me affectionately, as if she rejoiced that I had finally risen to the surface again after my long period of crankiness and introspection. I looked sidelong at the curator as I entertained his wife with the stages in Jackson Pollock's development. To this day I still don't know if Elisabeth was lying when I asked her if she had slept with him. If he was telling the truth when we were out swimming in the sunset, was that perhaps why a year or two later he felt entitled to place a hand on Astrid's knee when he drove her home after dining with our mutual friends, when I was away? Perhaps he had even told her about Elisabeth and me in order to somehow justify the sudden presence of his hand on her knee. In that case Astrid had been clever at concealing her knowledge from me. But on that Midsummer Eve I was convinced he must be lying. And even if there was a shred of truth in his chummy confidences, they belonged in a pub or a locker room, not in my memory of Elisabeth and our three weeks in the East Village, floating in our transparent bubble outside the world, occupied only with each other and our work. Even if she really had spent a night with the curator, however improbable that seemed, it could not have had the same significance for her as the time she and I had spent together. Or rather, our time together could not have meant so little. Those were my thoughts as I chattered mechanically about Jackson Pollock, alternately observing the curator's shining pate and the canine teeth in his foxy smile, his wife's gentle, gullible cow's eyes and my mother's ravaged, dramatic face, in which every single movement was distorted into an exaggerated caricature, as if she wanted to convince not only the curator but herself as well that she really thought and felt what she said she thought and felt.

Later we went to the Midsummer Eve bonfire that had been lit further down the beach. I carried Rosa on my shoulders although she was really too big and heavy, and she grabbed hold of my hair each time I was about to stumble on the loose sand. She told me to hurry, the flames had already caught onto the witch's clothes, and I heard Astrid and the others laughing behind us when I broke into a run toward the fire with Rosa hooting above my head. There were crowds of people on the beach and I recognized several faces as we passed them. It was almost like walking along Stróget in Copenhagen on a Saturday morning, I thought, as I made my way among the figures with dark faces, in white dresses and jackets that gleamed like the small lines of foam in the blue transparent semidarkness over the sea and the beach. At a distance the faces were impossible to read, they merged with the dark pines of the plantation behind the dunes, so it looked as if the light-colored dresses and suits were weaving among themselves on their own accord like lost, anonymous ghosts, chatting and laughing. We move on sand, I thought, and took my place in the group gathered around the bonfire. The flames shot high into the air, and the flickering reflection of the fire offset at first glance all the differences in the ring of faces, red brown like burned clay, like the statues of Chinese warriors I had seen in a photograph recently, thousands of life-size clay warriors that had been dug up during the excavation of an emperor's grave, each with his individual features and yet alike, with the same red brown, uniform complexion. I felt Astrid's hands on my hips and heard my mother laughing loudly at something the curator had told her. Simon was on the other side of the fire talking politely to a gray-haired man who like me carried a little girl on his shoulders, and a moment later I recognized his father, the film director. Of course he was here too, everyone was here on Midsummer Eve, and it really wouldn't have surprised me if I had seen Inés and Elisabeth among the women in their summer dresses, with red brown cheeks, squinting against the heat from the bonfire. Astrid helped Rosa down from my shoulders and said she would go back and put her to bed before putting the kettle on for coffee. She probably didn't want to confront the film director, who was having a conversation with the son of his second marriage while his little daughter pulled his hair and his new young wife stood smiling shyly in the background. Would I be standing like that one Midsummer Eve in a few years with a new little child on my shoulders, while Elisabeth shyly looked on as I questioned Rosa on her progress at school, slightly awkward, slightly strange, now that we had come across each other by chance?

The next day was overcast. The curator and his wife had already gone when I woke up. Looking out the window I saw

my mother sitting in front of the house reading aloud to Rosa
with clear, dramatic diction, just as she did on the radio, but
she seemed genuinely relaxed in the role of grandmother, sitting on the bench among the dog roses with Rosa on her lap
and a faded scarf around her dyed hair like a Russian peasant
woman. Astrid and Simon went out on the lawn, she asked if
Rosa wanted to go shopping with them, and soon I saw the
three of them go to the car. My mother remained on the bench
with the closed children's book on her lap, gazing at the sea,
gray like the sky, gray and bottle green, dappled with darker
sections where the sand floor was covered with seaweed. I
couldn't recall when I had last seen her sit like that, alone with
herself, passive and unmoving, her face resting slack in its ravaged folds. You could still see how beautiful she had once been,
but here before the sea, where she thought no one could see
her, she did nothing to divert attention from the baggy weight
of her cheeks and the drooping corners of her mouth, which
had kissed so many men and uttered the words of so many
writers. I drank a cup of lukewarm coffee in the kitchen and
went out to her. She smiled quietly when she saw me, but
didn't say anything. I stood for a while looking down on the
empty beach and the tired waves breaking in the offshore
wind. Then she suggested we go for a walk. There were no
people on the beach. We walked at the water's edge where the
sand was damp and firm, past the quay and the charred remains of the bonfire and further on beside the pine plantation.
At first we walked without breaking the silence in the pauses
between the dull beating of the little waves. They skimmed
the sloping extent of sand and withdrew again at once, the
gray light reflected only for a moment before the sand sucked
in the water and again grew lusterless and gritty. We had
walked like this for some time when she finally looked at me.

Time after time over the years I have been surprised that
this vain and superficial woman should have such a sharp eye.
I cannot hide anything from her, and I hadn't been able to this
time either. Her voice was subdued and completely calm, almost gentle, quite lacking in the usual drama when she asked
if I had met someone else. I tried to defend myself, if only for
the sake of appearances. What had given her that idea? She
smiled, but without any sting. I needn't talk about it if I didn't
feel like it. I realized I might as well give up. I said I didn't
know what to do. She said I was wrong, I knew perfectly well
what I should do, that was why I hesitated. What did she
mean? She took my hand and pulled me aside a little, just as a
wave was about to wash over my shoes. She had hesitated as
well, she went on, when she broke up with my father, even if I
didn't believe it. She knew quite well I had never forgiven her,
and from the start she had seen clearly that she would have to
live with that. She had known what she was doing and that
was why she had hesitated. Because she knew what she was
about, and because she knew she would have to pay the price.
It was a pathetic remark, but for once there was nothing at all
pathetic about her tone of voice. She asked me to tell her who
it was. I held back a bit, mostly because I couldn't decide
where to begin. Then I told her how I had met Elisabeth,
about the strangely clear and finely tuned wavelength we had
immediately found, as if for years we had thought about and
experienced the world on the same frequency, without knowing each other. I told her about Elisabeth's paintings and our
weeks together in the spartan apartment in the East Village,
how when I met her I had discovered that a distance had
grown in me over the years, an old gap that had reopened, although I thought I'd put it behind me long ago. That same old

gap I had once more put behind me, together with Elisabeth, for the first time in years completely present, wholly and fully there in everything I was and held. My mother merely smiled as I was speaking, until I fell silent again, because suddenly the words seemed so inadequate, so imprecise and foolish in their impersonality. She took my arm as we walked across the beach and up the sand dunes, in through the pine plantation, shaped by the wind into crooked interlacing. I couldn't decide whether to fasten upon the pine trees' malformation or the stubbornness that kept them growing. We could no longer hear the sound of the waves, only the wind's occasional sigh among the gray green, stiff, sticky needles of the trees.

But what was she like? My mother looked darkly, almost ominously at me as she asked. I told her about the contrast between Elisabeth's Botticelli hair and her angular face and gawky body, about the contrast between her ascetic lifestyle and her almost hypersensitivity to the colors and surfaces of things, whether it was a rusty nut she gave me on the street in SoHo, or a pumpkin she bought from the Korean grocer on Avenue A, merely to keep on her table to look at and feel with her long, nervously registering fingers. I told her how from one moment to the next she could alternate between her cool, consistent, and merciless faculty for abstract thought and her almost childish, spontaneous, and playful whims, as when she woke me up in the small hours because she wanted us to see the sun rise over the Brooklyn Bridge. In fact I knew hardly anything about her, I said, but it was not an erotic obsession in the usual banal sense, it was not even so amazing when we lay grappling with each other on her hard futon. If I couldn't forget her it was rather that when I was with her everything

around me—movements, places and things, light and shadows—awoke my old longing just to be, here and now, in the
midst of the world. As if I had woken up after sleeping for a
long time only to discover that I already was where I had
dreamed of being. I could see from my mother's raised eye-
brow that even she thought that sounded a little over the top.
That was what it was like, I persisted, what it had been like to
wake beside Elisabeth in the morning, as if I had slept for ten
years, from the time Inés left me and I grabbed the first girl
who came along by chance and rushed to make a life with her,
as if it couldn't go fast enough. My mother regarded me for a
long time as she lit a cigarette and blew smoke from her nose.
I said smoking wasn't allowed in the plantation because of the
fire hazard, and she tilted her head to one side as she knocked
her ash onto the rusty red needles covering the sandy path. Infatuation, wasn't it really? Then she stopped. Wasn't Elisabeth
also the first girl who came along, after ten years with a wife
and children? I had to admit it. But then what was the difference? Was it just time? Time and boredom? She smiled sar-
castically. Hadn't Astrid's cheerful nature and lovely face been
just as revolutionary as Elisabeth's Botticelli tresses and her
capacity for abstract thought? I stood for a while looking
down at my shoes. Really, the two of us were alike, she said,
throwing down her cigarette and treading out the stub with
exaggerated thoroughness, looking up at me sideways. Would
the forest ranger be satisfied? We went on among the twisted
pines until the plantation gave way to broad-leaved trees.

I might not believe her, but she had actually expected it to
happen. I was much too complicated for a woman like Astrid,
and she didn't say that in order to denigrate her, I mustn't
think that. She really was a wonderful girl. On the contrary,

she had feared that I would hurt her one day. Ever since I was
a child I had carried a darkness within me, which I concealed
from my surroundings and which therefore had only grown
denser through the years, impenetrable not only to others but
even to myself. It sounded like a speech from one of her television dramas I had always switched off when she appeared on
the screen. At one time she had believed that she was to blame
for my flight into that darkness, where I had hidden for so
long that I could no longer see myself. But eventually she had
reached the conclusion that she was no more responsible for
my closed and secretive nature than she was for the fact that I
had inherited her nose and her eyes. I must excuse her, but she
could no longer reproach herself for having left my father. If
she understood me now it was only because the decision I hesitated to take was the same decision she herself had taken
then. And I should not rely on this Elisabeth to make it easier
to decide. To her it was probably just an affair, what we had
had together during my little holiday from the marital grind.
Oh, she knew me all right, she knew how I always felt everything much more deeply than everyone else. She had not left
my father because she was in love with someone else. She had
gone her own way because she could not stand dissembling
any longer. This Elisabeth, so intellectual and spontaneous
and ascetic and sensual, was merely an occasion, just as her
own various affairs had been, and I might as well realize that
now. But she knew it all right, she had the same problem as I
did, she went around with the same darkness inside her. Of
course I didn't believe her, she knew perfectly well I despised
her for her poses and her airs, but that was her way of endur-
ing. She knew the darkness in which I staggered around like a
blind man. She knew the impatient expectation that someone,

a totally unknown stranger, would open the door onto that darkness, let in the daylight and discover who she really was. But now she had waited for many years, and that person, she had gradually come to realize, didn't exist. You had to go out into the light on your own, at least occasionally, when the darkness within grew too dense and impassable. That was what she had done when she made her escape from my moaning wimp of a father and chose freedom with all its costs. And that was what I was about to do if I could summon the courage to leave my sweet pretty wife and my sweet children and my cozy, comfortable life, where I was on the point of being suffocated. But it was up to me, and now she thought we should say no more on the subject.

I had never talked to my mother that way before, and have never since. Even when we were alone together we did not touch on "that subject." She was right, and so was the Count of Monte Cristo in the chapter I read aloud to Simon and Rosa in the evening: "There are two strong weapons against every evil—time and silence." When we arrived back at the house Astrid had prepared lunch, and my mother overdid it as usual. The fried herring tasted divine, not just good, and Astrid had never looked as *enchanting* as she did that summer. As a matter of course there was invariably something that had *never* been so wonderfully delightful, so shudderingly and ecstatically fantastic, and so her life glided on to still newer, dizzier heights. We were completely exhausted a few days later when she was obliged to go back to "her rehearsals" as she always called them, as if the producers and the other actors only breathed to serve as humble and grateful witnesses to the unfolding of her graceful talent. When later I recalled our conversation that summer day on the beach and in the wood, I was amazed both at how much she had perceived and how little she had understood. Her words had hit me, but I couldn't escape the fact that she was the one who had pronounced them. By insisting that we resembled each other, wasn't she trying to ease her bad conscience by making me her accomplice? Because it would absolve her in my eyes if I repeated her old crime? Otherwise why should it be so urgent for her to get me to leave Astrid and the children? She had boasted of having walked out honestly, not for the sake of some man or other. I reckon she walked out for one or another or a third man's sake, so overall she was probably right, she had merely acted in accord with her restless nature. After she walked out on my father she hadn't spent as much as a fortnight without having at least one hungry worshipper whom she could alternately hold off or let in. Not until age had begun to make itself felt in earnest did she know loneliness, and perhaps it was this new, enforced loneliness that she had tried to transform into something heroic, retrospectively, when she described herself during our walk as another Nora, who had left her Helmer out of sheer inner necessity. Except with the difference that in her case it was Helmer who was thrown out while Nora stayed on in the doll's house and turned it into a brothel. If we had ever again discussed what happened in New York that spring, she would doubtless have criticized me because I actually did stay with Astrid. She would have scorned what she would have seen as my cowardice, but like me she chose to let time and silence solve my little problem, and with the years I think she simply forgot what we had spoken of, that we had ever walked together beside the gray sea amid the twisted pine trees.

The summer passed and with every week I grew better at concealing my uneasiness. Everything appeared to be as usual.

Astrid seemed convinced it was my "writing crisis" that sometimes tormented me and made me melancholy. She even asked
me when I intended to go to New York to finish my book, and
I replied that September would be a good time, it was too hot
in August. I learned to live with my treachery and to neutral-
ize a sneaking contempt for her, which enticed me at the back
of my mind like an offer of relief from my guilt. I made use of
the repellent, covert contempt of her credulity to feel coldness
toward her caresses. I fought against it, fought at least to re-
discover a cool, neutral tenderness for her, for "everything we
had together." I tried to protect my tenderness against my
guilty desire when I made love to her, violently, at times almost brutally, as if I could chase away the memory of Elisabeth, if only for half an hour. And gradually I succeeded in
splitting my interior into separate worlds and prevented them
from touching each other. Perhaps what they say is true, that
you can get used to anything. Perhaps it helped too to think of
the hypocritical way my mother had spoken of Astrid's "cheerful nature" and of how I was far too complicated for a woman
like her, and then fifteen minutes later, when we returned to
the house, had overwhelmed her with her usual sham, exalted
compliments. Her denigration of Astrid almost resuscitated my
loyalty to the woman I had betrayed, and in the following weeks
I was especially considerate to her, sometimes downright affectionate, as if she was ill without realizing it. I rose early in the
morning and let her sleep on, I swam and played with the children while she lay in the sun, and when the weather was gray I
went cycling with them in the forest. There were times when I
discovered that I had completely forgotten to think of Elisabeth,
and not until the evening, when quietness descended on me and

I sat alone on the steps among the rosebushes looking out over the sea in the eternal twilight of the summer night, did the house become a strange place again, where I felt I didn't belong.

The same feeling lay in wait the next time I had an errand in town and opened the door of our apartment. It had been empty for over a month and when I noticed the dusty, close air I thought it was not merely a place we had shut up for the summer; it already resembled a place I had left and would not return to. I dialed Elisabeth's number as I read the headlines of a yellowing newspaper we had left behind the day we packed the car and drove to the country. This time the answering machine was not on, but a long time passed and I was about to put the receiver down when she answered at last. She sounded out of breath, she had been on her way up when the telephone rang. She was glad to hear my voice, she had been almost afraid of forgetting how it sounded. She had come back from Mexico the previous week, she had traveled around the Yucatán peninsula all alone, it had been horrific. She had been ill in a dirty hotel room with cockroaches as big as armadillos, it came flooding out of her at both ends, and she had lain there wishing I was with her and wondering if she would ever hear from me again. I smiled at the thought of my jealous fantasies about her streaking through the Mojave desert on a motorcycle with another man. She told me it was just as hot and humid in New York as in Mexico, she couldn't bear it anywhere, and it was impossible to get anything done, all she could do was lie without a stitch on gasping beneath the electric fan. I visualized it clearly, her voluminous hair spread out over the sheet, the protruding ribs under her small breasts, her long pale legs, her fearless light gray eyes. She was suddenly so close again, not just a thought, an image, but the person she was, all skin and hair. I said we would soon meet again. Was I coming to New York? She sounded glad but also surprised, as if she thought by a lucky coincidence some other reason made it possible to meet. I said I couldn't do without her, I had thought a great deal about what had happened. She had thought about it too, she said after a pause, and she really did sound very thoughtful. When was I coming? In September, I said, sometime in September. I didn't say anything about the apartment I had looked at. I wanted to take one thing, one step, at a time. Perhaps I was afraid of frightening her, perhaps I already suspected it was a castle in the air, that apartment, a mirage with brown tiles in the bathroom. I couldn't yet know whether Elisabeth was only an incitement, a random stranger who had inadvertently opened the door of my darkness, as my mother put it, so the light had suddenly poured in and dazzled me. I had to see her again in order to know, I thought, as I mumbled a few tender words of farewell. As if it would be something that could be seen.

One evening in September I landed again at Kennedy airport. I didn't see Elisabeth anywhere when I walked into the arrival wing, and I wondered anxiously whether she had heard the message I had left on her answering machine before boarding the plane. I stood still in the stream of impatiently pushing passengers, looking around me in disappointment, when a smiling young woman approached me. It was the smile I recognized first. She had had her hair cut, her wavy, golden brown hair reached only halfway down her neck, and she was dressed in a black tailored jacket and a short black skirt and shoes with heels that made her half a head taller than me. I had never seen her in a skirt, altogether I had never seen her so well-dressed, and as we embraced I was reminded for a moment of the elegant woman in black I had secretly observed one afternoon in the sculpture garden at the Museum of Modern Art. Was it for my sake she had dressed like this, to offset the contrast between the Bohemian slattern and her well-dressed bourgeois lover? To show me she could move in my world, and was prepared to go with me wherever it might be? Or was it someone else who had taught her to make more of her appearance? Was it to make herself attractive to another man's expectant eyes? We stood there in a long still embrace amid the confusion of people and luggage, and I caught the unexpected, strange scent of perfume on her neck. In the taxi she laughed at my surprise, and I caressed her naked, delicate neck as she questioned me about my book and told me about the exhibition she had had, and about her trip to Yucatán, which suddenly sounded like a long exotic adventure without any stomach problems at all. Suddenly it was very real to be sitting in a taxi on the way through Brooklyn talking about this and that, far too real. She was almost frighteningly beautiful to look at, and her new cool elegance made me uneasy, as if it was a first warning that all might not go as I hoped, even though she pressed against me and leaned her head against mine. But at the start there was a euphoria about our reunion, as if we had cheated the whole world and everything that had prevented us from being together in the past months, and we could hardly wait for the taxi to stop in front of her door. We did not let go of each other until far into the night, sweating and breathless. She went into the bathroom, I stayed in bed, exhausted by the flight and our hectic reunion. The cat crept around soundlessly on the bare floors, sniffing cautiously at our clothes, which lay jumbled together in contorted heaps. I heard the water running in the bathtub, at first with a hard metallic sound, then a soft splashing as it filled up. The rusty taps creaked and then there was silence. I listened to the faraway police sirens, the voices calling in Spanish down in the street, and the cars now and then passing with techno-pop beating out through the rolled-down windows. It was a warm night and the windows were open in the building opposite. Behind one of them a man was shaving, even though it was past three o'clock, from another a slow tango was playing, and I recognized Astor Piazzolla's passionate *bandoneón*. It was many years since I had heard that recording. When I went into the bathroom Elisabeth lay in the bath with a washcloth covering her face. The greenish water distorted her body slightly, so it seemed flat as photography, and the damp terry stuck to her nose and eye sockets like a mask. I sat down on the edge of the tub. I said I had thought of what she had talked about a few times. That she had considered moving back to Copenhagen. The tap dripped, and the drips measured out the silence as they struck the water. The little rings made the surface tremble and blot out the image of her motionless slender body. I said I loved her, that she was the one I wanted to be with, and that I had decided to leave Astrid, but the drops merely went on measuring the seconds, *plop, plop,* one second at a time. Cautiously I took hold of the edge of the cloth under her chin and pulled it until her face came uncovered. Her eyelids were closed, and she lay still for a long time before opening them and looking at me with her light gray eyes.

So after all, our hours together, even the most precious, had not had any special consequences. The surprising understanding, the spontaneous intimacy of each single moment had not, then, been a pact, a promise of future moments. They were not to be linked together, they were not a story, or were only a story that constantly ended and constantly started again, until one evening it was broken off in the middle of a sentence, as unexpectedly as when I seized her hand five months earlier as we looked over the Hudson River. Seven years later, when I stood pondering Elisabeth's cool, mono-chrome abstractions at a gallery in SoHo, a man of my own age came up and asked if I knew her work. I said I was an old friend but we had lost touch. He introduced himself as her art dealer and we started to talk. She lived in Vermont now, in a house way out in the country, with her husband and their small son. He was a sculptor, very talented. I nodded with in-terest. The art dealer showed me a photograph hanging on the bulletin board above his desk in the back room. The pic-ture had been taken in the evening in front of a white-painted wooden house, just after sundown, with a flash. There was a strange contrast between the white flashlight and the sulphur glow in the narrow section of sky behind the corner of the house. I thought of Hopper's lonely American houses backed by the evening sky. Their eyes shone red, the black-haired boy with suntanned arms, the swarthy man with a black beard standing behind the boy resting his hands on his shoulders, and Elisabeth, standing beside them in an old-fashioned flow-ered summer dress, lowering her face so her cheek touched the man's. She still had short hair and looked only slightly older. She smiled as she gazed into the camera with her red pupils. She looked like herself, the smiling woman, and yet it wasn't the one who had lain in her bath one September night seven years before, looking at me with expressionless gray eyes. It amazed me that I should have been prepared to turn my life upside down to be with her, even though we didn't really know each other and had only spent a few weeks together one spring. It had needed nothing more, so flimsy had been my idea of who I was and where I belonged, as weightless as images and words.

Of course it hurt, but not as much as I would have believed, when she considerately explained to me that was not quite what she had in mind, not because there was anyone else she would rather be with, but simply because she felt good living alone. Moreover, she had decided to stay in New York. She even shed a tear for my sake as a little sacrifice to the beautiful story I had made up about us, and I kissed her tear away and pulled myself together. Had the curator been right after all? Was I just another man in the string of men I visualized standing in a long, impatient line all the way to First Avenue? I never found out, it is of no consequence now. The next day I checked into a cheap hotel in Little Italy, but we did go out to dinner a couple of times, and we talked as we had from the beginning, about the New York School and anything else that we hit upon, on the same wavelength as before. And if I had not upset the balance between us with my inopportune, drastic plans for the future, I am sure we would have romped around on her futon for another week, observed by her completely indifferent cat, for she really was fond of me, there was a real flow between us when we were together. It was just what it was, nothing else, nothing more. I was not particularly unhappy when we parted, I was paralyzed and in a way also relieved. On the day I left we had lunch together on Spring Street where we had first met. Then we stood for a while looking at each other on the corner of West Broadway, before I hailed a taxi. If at that moment she had reconsidered, everything might have been different, but she only patted my chest affectionately and told me to take care of myself. I felt like saying the same, but made do with an adult smile and a kiss on her forehead, before getting into the taxi. Nice lady, but very thin, said the driver in his winning Pakistani accent, as he drove up West Broadway. Yeah, very nice, I replied, turning around to get a last glimpse through the back window of her tall slim figure, moving with long quick strides among the other pedestrians, a moment later impossible to distinguish from the other moving shapes.

9

Astrid had only stayed a single night in Oporto, then she continued south. According to the bank statement she used her Mastercard again at a gas station outside Aveiro, and later in the day had lunch in Coimbra. The same evening she checked into the hotel in Lisbon where we had stayed for a week, in Graça, with a view over the city and the river, that autumn seven years ago after I came home from New York for the second time as if nothing had happened. Before she left Oporto she may have driven out to Matosinhos, out to the empty beach with the oil tanks and the closed, dilapidated shacks with concessions and changing rooms. She may have walked where we walked together in the wind, in the smell of salt and seaweed, out to the surf that broke on the beach in deafening waves, yellow with whirled-up sand. It might have been misty that day too, so she could not see the horizon, only the dull restless sheen of the waves, shining like copper further out where the sea and the mist blended together. I had made the suggestion as soon as I got into the car when she met me at Kastrup, that we should go to Portugal together, alone together. I don't know why it had to be Portugal, perhaps because we had never been there. I had hit on the idea in the plane as I leafed through the airline magazine and studied the world map with its two half spheres like the wings of a butterfly cut and spread out, like separate worlds connected only by the company routes drawn in criss-crossing red lines, converging from their junctions in the big cities. I had placed my finger on New York, outside Coney Island, and drawn a straight line across the Atlantic between forty and forty-one degrees north, until I hit the coast near Oporto. It had been a stressful year, I said, with my book and all, and we needed some time to ourselves. Perhaps we could get my mother to stay at the apartment while we were away, and Simon was big enough now to look after Rosa when my mother was at the theater in the evening. Astrid smiled in surprise as she steered through the traffic. Why not?

In the plane, while the sky grew dark over the cloud cover's dazzling, bumpy wilderness, the paralysis gradually passed, and I wondered at myself. How had it all happened? How had I come to put my life in the long, slim hands of an almost unknown young woman and let her shape it? Had Elisabeth after all been only a pretext? Had I, without knowing it, for years been preparing to leave Astrid? I thought back to the conversation with my mother as we walked along the beach and through the twisted pine trees. Perhaps she had been right, perhaps I should sit down and consider my unanswered questions on a brandy-colored leather sofa in a rented apartment with brown tiles in the bathroom. But that would not make either Astrid or myself any happier, I told myself. Was it really those brown tiles that made the idea so depressing? The prospect of becoming a gloomy recluse who heated his frozen meals in another man's microwave oven as he stared forlornly out at the rain? His homeless solitude, drifting in the swirl of empty days? But would we be happier going on together? Once again I recalled Inés's question to me in the café on the Place de l'Alma. If I was happy with Astrid. The question had stayed in the background ever since, as time just went on. It had accompanied me as the moon accompanies you when you drive a car at night, its pale, pockmarked face never moving an inch in the side window behind the roadside trees rushing past. It was that indiscreet, stiff question about happiness that had led me to believe it was time to cut and run. But who had asked it? Had Elisabeth been anything but a substitute for Inés, now that I was questioning the whole of my adult life? Had she been more than just a delayed revenge for the ancient, festering defeat of my youth? Or had I in reality cast Astrid in the role of Inés, to have someone to avenge myself on? Was he my true self, the unhappy young man who had stood at a window watching Inés disappear into the snowflakes one long-ago winter? Had I never been myself again after I betrayed him and took Astrid's face between my hands for the first time? Or was my biggest illusion making him into my original, uncorrupted self? And in that case was I no more than the sum of the fleeting, distorted shadows I had cast on the retinas of various women behind their inscrutable gaze? Was I nothing but this constant metamorphosis? Perhaps it was my fatigue, perhaps it was the turbulence over the Atlantic that made me dizzy and gave me the sense that all my thoughts were just so many masks that tumbled one after another, spiraling down into the darkness over the Labrador Basin without my ever penetrating behind all the layers of self-delusion and interpretation.

Astrid must have reached Lisbon in the late afternoon. If she had a room with a view she probably would have gone out on the terrace and looked down over the tiles on the staggered roofs between the parapets of the citadel and the river, which is so wide that the opposite side is only a blurred, bluish band when it rains. I imagine her standing for a while with closed eyes, her face lifted in the white light as the rain settles in her hair and pricks her forehead and cheeks and soaks through her blouse, a sensation reminiscent of the light touch of cool fingertips on one's shoulders. She may have stood and breathed in the scent of dust dissolved in the dampness. She may have stood like that once more before going in and lying down on the bed fully clothed. I left the door to the terrace open even though it was cool, and eased the shoes from her feet before lying down beside her. We had still not unpacked. I put an arm around her and hid my face in the shadow between us. We were not going any further, it was Lisbon we had been heading for, the last city in Europe, as she said with an exhausted smile, when at long last the highway led us in among the suburban tenements of crumbling concrete. She lay on her stomach with her eyes closed, I covered her with the bedspread. She stroked my hair calmly with slow hands, and the warm air from her nostrils brushed my face with the faint scent of sweat and perfume. Then we both lay quite still, I with a hand on her back, and I could feel her breathing against my palm, a slow movement in the small of her back, beneath the warm skin between her blouse and her tights. I didn't know whether she had fallen asleep. Had she noticed anything in my silence after all? Had a little split opened in her thoughts into which the cold air seeped? The air from an alien world that only on its surface resembled the one where she lived at my side, as we had done for so long? Her world could be inside mine, but there was no room for mine in hers, this difference had arisen, so we no longer knew the same thing. How could I avoid making her less than she needed to be? Shouldn't I leave her, now that we lived in separate worlds? Hadn't I already wasted far too much of her time with my melancholy egotism? I could at

least have told her what had happened so she could decide
whether she would be able to breathe in the other world from
which I watched her face, so close to mine, with her closed
eyes as if she slept. I could have told her on that October
evening in Lisbon, as I lay listening to the rain on the tiles of
the terrace, the metal blinds being rolled down in front of the
shops, and the scooters pushing their way up the Rua Senhora
do Monte. I did not say anything, and that was my greatest
betrayal. Not that I had been on the point of leaving her to live
with another woman, but that I had come home and driven all
the way to Lisbon with her. That I had come slinking back
with my secret, suppressed defeat, as if it had been nothing but
a little short circuit, a little technical malfunction. That I lay
here at the end of the road and kept silent, as if there was
nothing to say. How did it happen that I didn't leave her? Why
did I come back so feebly when my adventure ended up like an
abortion, washed out like all the other possibilities one misses
or is cheated of on the way through the years? Did I come
back for pure convenience? Out of fear of the old, despondent
loneliness I still remembered so well? No doubt. But not only
for that.

When I lay there in Lisbon that rainy evening dozing in
the dim hotel room beside Astrid, exhausted after the long
drive, I could not decide whether I had woken from a dream or
had fallen asleep again after being awake for a few months.
When I met her it had been like waking up from my young
dream of Inés. When I met Inés it had been like waking from
my dreaming childhood. When I met Elisabeth it felt as if I
had been asleep for years. And when I returned to Astrid, I
had realized that my dreams of another life had been nothing
but dreams set in motion by a pair of light gray eyes that had

never seen me as other than the person I was. A married man who reached out to her, perhaps out of boredom, perhaps out of desperation, perhaps because she happened to be there. Perhaps I had spent my whole life dreaming, perhaps that is how we all spend our lives until the moment comes, early or late, when we awake to pure nothing. Perhaps it cannot be otherwise, perhaps we breathe through our dreams, in separate worlds, as we clasp each other in sleep. That was how I thought of it as I lay beside Astrid one evening in Lisbon seven years ago, as the rain eased and the blue dusk spread around us and I felt her body's warmth against mine in the evening chill. She had fallen asleep. She furrowed her brow and mumbled something I could not hear, then her face relaxed again. I couldn't know what she was dreaming. My hand tingled, it was numb after resting so long on her back. I pulled it away cautiously and rose from the bed. Her face was indistinct, blurred in the dark and hardly recognizable. I went out on the terrace and lit a cigarette and looked down on the streetlights and car lights that rose and fell in the darkness. I could no longer see the river, but I saw where the lights tailed off in the opaque darkness.

I must have stayed a long time looking at the photo of Elisabeth and her husband and their little son, smiling with red eyes from the flash in front of their white-painted wooden house in Vermont. A little too long, I think, for I remember that the art dealer cleared his throat and asked if I would like their address. I said no thank you and left the gallery on Wooster Street. I went to the cinema, just to be in a place where there were other people, without having to say or do anything. Later I had a meal at a Japanese restaurant, and in the evening I took a taxi back to the hotel on Lexington

Avenue. Who knows, perhaps that glimpse of Elisabeth's life
would have made a deeper impression if Astrid had been waiting for me at home in Copenhagen, if I had been able to call her
from the hotel room, if I had been able to count on her answering the phone, because it was the time when she usually came
home. Now it was just an amateur photograph of a woman I
had once known, almost as much a stranger as the unknown
man who had become her husband. Perhaps the truth is as dis-
gracefully banal as that. It is obviously so perishable, the significance you ascribe to a face for the time that its features lend
their outline to your tender hopes. The sight of Elisabeth had
been as painless as the sight of Inés years ago when I was leaving the cinema with Astrid. If I was a little sad at the sight of
my old flames, however, it was not only because they had been
transformed into ash but also because they had been extinguished so easily. I had nevertheless been burned, and although
I couldn't remember the pain I did remember that it had once
hurt. Now it was my images of Astrid that seared me. I picked
up the receiver and dialed our number, you never know. As I
listened to it ringing I caught sight of myself in the dark television screen, a gray, hunched silhouette sitting on the edge of
a bed in an anonymous hotel room. I grabbed the remote control and switched it on, just so as not to see the lonely anonymous figure in the curved glass of the screen. I turned down
the sound and absentmindedly watched the short news clips. A
river had burst its banks, I couldn't see where it was. Trees,
road signs, and roofs rose up from the muddy water. Why
didn't I put the receiver down? I visualized the empty apartment, the dark windows onto the Lakes and the facades on the
other side, the rows of lit windows. Suppose Astrid had come

back after all. A military helicopter hovered in the air, the rotor blades whipped up the water in small waves, and the waves spread in all directions around a rowboat that had moored at the top floor of a house, from which a covered, mummy-like figure was hoisted up on a stretcher, twisting slowly around. Suddenly the receiver was picked up, it was Rosa. I had woken her up, it was six o'clock in the morning at home. I could hear she was glad I called. I asked if she had moved back home. She laughed, she was a bit tired of boyfriends for the moment. Did she have several, then? She laughed again. Wouldn't I like to know! I asked if she had heard from Astrid. The reporter stood looking earnestly into the camera as he spoke soundlessly into the microphone. She had tried to call Gunilla in Stockholm to find out when I was coming home, but there had been no answer, so they were probably still out in the Skerries. She thought it was great that we could think of traveling separately and giving each other space for a bit. The reporter was wearing waders and stood in water up to his waist, moving his lips. But Simon had called home from Bologna, where he had met a girl he was sold on, so we shouldn't expect to see anything of him for a while. She said she would meet me at the airport, and I got out my ticket and read out my flight number and arrival time.

I stayed in front of the television screen's incessant stream of people speaking or moving in amputated clips jumping between places in the world. It was late and I was tired, but I knew it would be no use going to bed. I thought about the old idea that time is a river, apparently unchanging and yet never the same. I tried to recall the seven years that had passed since Astrid and I drove to Lisbon and wandered side by side through the narrow streets of Bairro Alto and Alfama, between the scruffy old rattling trams and the sooty, geometric or organic ornamentation of the tiles on the facade. Nothing particular had happened, time had run on with us, the children had grown and we ourselves were slightly older, while Astrid edited her films and I wrote about my painters. I couldn't catch sight of us. The months and the years flowed into a formless, changing foam, and I only saw us in disconnected shreds of hours and days, which doubled up and turned quickly around themselves like withered leaves on the whirling current before vanishing. When I thought of Elisabeth and our story, I would do so precisely the way you think of an incredible story you have been told, first with a shake of the head, then with a shrug of the shoulders. As if there is no great difference, as time passes, between what we have experienced ourselves and what we have merely heard or seen on television. Was it really me, or had I just been slightly out of my wits, seized by a six-month-long passing fit, a last rebellious, ungovernable gesture, before at long last I grew up? When a few months had passed I was relieved that I had shielded Astrid from learning about my escapade. Why should I hurt her unnecessarily when I myself conquered my fantasies of a new and quite different life? Thus I soothed my battered conscience. I could still feel awkward at times when Astrid's narrow eyes responded to my gaze. I was ashamed not only of my treachery but also that I had actually believed I could escape from myself and become someone else, different from the man I had become over all the years with her and the children. Who should he have been? If I wasn't in the right place at home with Astrid in the apartment by the Lakes, where then? As the children loosened their grip on us and began to manage by themselves, the days became longer, not so full, and when we met in

the evening in the quiet apartment we were almost shy sometimes, as if a little puzzled that time had passed. We fell into a
looser, calmer rhythm of parting and reunion, suddenly free
now to immerse ourselves separately in our own pursuits, and
by and large we did as we pleased, because it was no longer so
important precisely when we came home.

Eventually I had stopped asking myself if I was happy.
It had become unnecessary, but also futile to ask. After all, you
can't be happy all the time, gasping and salivating in one
trembling spasm of happiness from the time you get up until
you finally fall asleep with an idiotic smile on your wet lips.
I thought of my mother, who always tried to make it sound
as if she was living on a volcano. Maybe she was, but it was
an extinguished volcano, with a barren crater of dried
lava. Perhaps the question had been wrongly put from the
start. Was I happy? Had I reached out to Elisabeth because
I thought she would make me happy? More probably I had
reached out to her to escape my happiness, in an attack of
claustrophobia. Even as a child I had been irritated when I
heard what, according to the Bible, Paradise looked like. I
thought it must get boring with all that sweetness and light,
and perhaps it was the same bland taste of eternity that had
made me restless. The impression that I could see my own future before me with Astrid and the children, and later on alone
with her when we would no longer have Simon and Rosa as a
daily, mutual bond. The defeats and victories of work, the marital boredom and the passing moments of revived marital desire, Sunday outings, dinner parties with friends, profound or
superficial conversations about this and that, vacation trips,
museum visits, film, and everything else you have time for. The
whole abundant and yet strangely disappointing catalogue of

"interests and activities" that all the lonely but nonetheless cheerful and economically independent wretches list in the Sunday papers' personal ads, perhaps in an attempt to seem dependably normal. A perspective of repetitions, as when you are in a Parisian café with mirrors on the walls and see the interior repeating itself in an endless corridor of reflections where you lift the same glass of wine, hold the same cigarette between your fingers, and where you yourself are the same, nauseously the same, vanishing into the perspective. Fortunately that had been yet another illusion, after all it was never the same day I awoke beside Astrid, even though sometimes it seemed that way. Nor were she and I quite the same from year to year, but the change was no longer a question of covering distances, of other worlds, another life, as I gradually came to understand when I had returned to Astrid after my abortive attempt at flight.

The change did not mean we were on the way anywhere, it played itself out in our bodies and minds. It evolved slowly and imperceptibly out of the monotonous spirals of repetition, so that only occasionally, at intervals of months, would I notice that Rosa's flat, gawky torso was becoming shapely, or that a faint shadow had appeared on Simon's upper lip, that another gray streak had appeared in Astrid's chestnut brown hair, or that one morning as I was shaving the furrows between my nostrils and mouth suddenly seemed deeper and longer than I remembered. We did not feel time as it passed with us, perhaps because we lived in several times at once. Astrid was still the young woman who had sat in the back seat of my taxi one winter evening comforting her little son. I was still the young man who one summer night had sat among the rosebushes above the sea repeating *Hold on, hold on.* She was at once the woman I had wanted to leave and the woman I had gone back to, and I was the man who had seen her alternately as my salvation and my warden, as an unexpected, liberating lightness in my life and a burden that chained me to the eternally grinding treadmill of days. When she was on the phone exchanging gossip with Gunilla in Stockholm I might shake my head and ask myself how she had ever become the woman in my life. And when she came into the living room still wearing her coat and placed a bunch of white tulips on the windowsill, the stalks squeaking lightly against each other, and she stood there at the window looking thoughtfully down on the rippling lake, I might wonder how I could ever have thought of leaving her. When I went into the bedroom and she lay naked in bed looking at me with an unequivocal, encouraging look, I sometimes felt like lying down with my back to her and falling asleep. And when we arranged to meet at a café, and I caught sight of her crossing the street in the rain a moment before she saw me, brushing the damp hair from her forehead with a casual movement of her hand, I could be overwhelmed by a desire so violent I had to fold the newspaper over my lap. It was not only the gossip or the tulips, her nakedness and inviting gaze, or the hand through her damp hair that made the difference, and it was certainly not anything in me. It was the constant exchange between what happened around me and what stirred within me, between a present that was never the same, when we saw each other afresh, and my restless, changing memories, always announcing themselves in a slightly different light, with a slightly different meaning.

But how did I get from one thing to another? How had I been able to sit in an airplane flying over the Atlantic, convinced that I would have to leave Astrid to save myself from the odious perpetuity of repetition, only to get the idea a week later, in an identical plane flying east, that she and I should go to Portugal together? After I lost sight of Elisabeth among the other pedestrians, a silhouette among the silhouettes in the backlight on West Broadway, my tenderness was still there, the silent, searching tenderness I felt for Astrid one night in Lisbon a few weeks later when I lay holding her, listening to the rain. Tenderness was there, the way her mouth and skin somehow summoned my lips and hands, and there was the old familiarity of just lying and breathing side by side as it grew dark outside. It was a tenderness that prevailed of its own volition and made its way regardless of what I was thinking about her, about us, at any given moment. The palms of my hands knew each hollow of her body, each swell, as if through the years they had formed each other, her body and my hands, her hands and my body. My caresses were more like inscrutable but indisputable facts than questions waiting for an answer. It did not matter why we loved when we made love to each other. I could not know how much or how little she knew, and I no longer knew myself what to think about all that had happened, and everything that had moved within me on the way through the years, my perpetual dizzy wavering between doubts, unanswered questions and faint hope. Perhaps she had discovered as I had that the roads and the faces do not mean anything in themselves, the roads that branch out toward the unknown, the faces that come up to you with their alien eyes, where you might be anyone. Perhaps she too had been forced to admit that to begin with it does not matter which road you take and who you walk along with because your love does not care who you love, provided it is allowed to run freely along the path you walk, through the eyes you hold fast with your gaze. Perhaps she too had understood that you are not presented with your story, that you must tell it yourself, and that you do not know the story before it has been told. That you can never know beforehand what it means, or how much. That the story must be told one day, one step, at a time, whether you tell it in a hesitant or firm voice, confidently or plagued with doubt. And yet, then she too had wavered, she too had stopped to ask herself if she had lost her way, if she had allowed herself to be carried along the chance ramifications of the years in the arms of the wrong man, pulled along by her love's blind desire to run where she had smoothed its path with her patient steps. And then one morning she had packed a bag and stood waiting for me to wake up, in the bedroom doorway, with her coat already on.

Did she notice at some moment that she had shrunk in my eyes, where she had accommodated herself as if she belonged there? Did she have to leave me and be alone, she who had not been on her own for almost twenty-five years, because she had grown so small in my distant glance that she was about to vanish? Or did she feel that the space my gaze had once opened around her, where she had thought she would be able to run as fast and as long as she wished, had grown too narrow? Had she come to see that I had shaped her too, until she was no more than the one who lived at my side? When did it dawn on her that there was still an unknown woman trying to draw breath through her nose and mouth, a woman I had never set eyes on, behind her familiar features? When did she discover the eyes of that woman in the mirror, through the narrow chinks in her face where she was accustomed to meet her own familiar glance? Eyes that looked at her in subdued

wonderment at how her life had taken shape, as if it had happened in her sleep. Perhaps she had seen them in the mirrors
of hotel rooms on her way, those unknown, wondering eyes.
Perhaps they had waited for her in the mirrors of San Sebastian, in Santiago de Compostela, in Oporto, and in Lisbon. On
her way through those towns she may have looked at me with
the same wonderment, asked herself if this man really was the
one she had loved, and if she still loved him. But why had she
waited so long? Why hadn't she left me before, to meet the unknown woman behind the mirrors? Did she doubt whether the
other one would be able to draw breath alone, without the pro-
tective mask of her familiar face? Had she expected me to tell
her what she had already noticed in my silence, until she felt
she had waited long enough? Had she expected me to admit
that I too was not exactly the person I pretended to be? Or
had she already made her decision? Had she stayed for the
sake of the children, until they were old enough to cope? I
cannot tell what she read in my face, from my glances as we
walked up and down the steep alleys of Bairro Alto, slightly
uncertain and hesitant, in the desultory way that tourists walk
around a strange town. She may have seen and sensed more
than I thought. The town always came between us, with its
trams and sooty tiles, its sparkling river and its smoke from the
chestnut vendors' charcoal braziers, the town where I hoped to
find her again. We had nothing to hold on to there, so far from
the place where we belonged. We had only each other's words,
and they ran out quickly in the strange, greedy silence. We had
only each other's bodies in the anonymous hotel room where
I held her like a shipwrecked mariner as I listened to the rain
and watched the light fade and felt the chill air from outside.

Had she been happy? Did I make her happy? I think so, at
the start, when I replied to the disturbing news of her preg-

nancy with my young, reckless *Why not?* When with my rash *Why not?*, after months of circling around in my taxi like a solitary astronaut orbiting the earth, I took the chance and leaped into the unknown, and to my surprise discovered I had landed on my feet. I think I did make her happy in the years that followed, after I sat above the sea one summer night on the steps among the rosebushes adjuring her and our unknown child to *Hold on, hold on.* For a few years, when Rosa was small, I was completely attentive. Perhaps that is why I remember them so indistinctly. While she was learning to walk, while she was beginning to talk, I was nothing but a happy, tired man who had consigned himself to the hours and the days, adrift in their unthinking current. I felt in the midst of my life, and I never came closer to that middle than at that time, when we were on our way, Astrid and I, from day to day, heedless of where we were going. I think she herself must have thought like that about those years, later, when she felt the cold air of something strange come oozing through an invisible crack in her knowledge of who we were. When I began to be preoccupied, when she began to notice my doubt as an awkward silence, a flicker in my gaze, a sudden clumsiness when I lay beside her at night.

I must have fallen asleep. It was pitch-dark when I awoke in the hotel room in the Rua Senhora do Monte. The sheet was cold where I had felt her warm side against my palm. I called to her, she wasn't there. I sat for a while on the edge of the bed, looking out at Lisbon's glimmering chains of light beneath the terrace. They could be the lights of any city. I put on my shoes and went down to reception, they told me she had left the hotel half an hour earlier. It was in a quiet residential neighborhood with steep narrow streets. I thought I might find her if I walked around a little. Surely she could not have

gone far. There were only a few people around. Two middle-
aged women in aprons stood in a doorway talking quietly, a
young couple passed on a scooter, the girl leaning her cheek
against the young man's back. Suddenly I felt a thin cold
stream of water running down my hair and neck. When I
looked up I caught sight of an old man on a balcony watering
potted plants. He raised his hand in a gesture that was both
greeting and apology, and said something I didn't understand.
Some boys were kicking a ball on the gravel among the peeling plane trees in a small square. The gravel shone with an
unreal light in the glare of the orange streetlights criss-
crossing through the trees' crooked shadows, and the blotched
facades resembled stage sets in the garish light. Behind the
closed blinds above the balcony railings I could hear energetic
voices from television sets and softer, more scattered voices
blending with the sound of clinking china. I sat on a bench beneath the planes and lit a cigarette, listening to the boys'
shouts, the dull thump of the ball on the gravel, and the foreign yet homely sounds from the open balcony doors. Of course
she had merely gone for a walk, as I had, yet still I missed her
in the same lonely way as when I had traveled alone to a foreign city and left her at home with the children.

I tried to imagine I had left her. That instead of suggest-
ing this trip I had told her what had happened in New York
when she met me at the airport. I imagined saying it in the car,
or later, in the bedroom, when the children had gone to bed. I
don't know how she would have reacted. Whether she would
have broken down, or just listened and looked at me with the
expression she would have when she stood looking at me the
morning she left. As if she already knew everything. I imagined telling the children. I imagined Rosa weeping and Simon's

slightly embarrassed silence. How I would have hesitated a bit, embracing Rosa, before disengaging myself and leaving. I would have rented an apartment, perhaps the one where I had imagined Elisabeth and I would live. I would have furnished the room I had envisaged as Elisabeth's studio as a room for Rosa. I would have picked her up from the apartment beside the Lakes, just as the gray-haired film director had once picked up Simon, when he tried for a weekend to be what he had once been. She would have been ready with her little bag and a doll under her arm, and there would have been a moment when she stood between us before she kissed Astrid goodbye to go downstairs with me, a brief moment when Astrid and I would have to look each other in the face. What would we have thought? That Rosa was all that was left? The only proof that we had once loved each other and believed we had arrived at our life? The place from where everything could be seen and told about? Would I have sat in a rented apartment with brandy-colored leather sofas and smoke-colored glass tables reading aloud to Rosa and at the same time thinking she was in fact the result of a mistake, a misjudgment, a rash move? In the seven years since I sat in the little square in Graça where the boys ran about playing soccer, I have sometimes asked myself if I stayed with Astrid only for the children's sake. In that case I should have been relieved when they left home and Astrid packed her bag one morning and handed me over to the silence they had left behind them. But when she left me I had begun to feel that the dizziness and doubt had gradually been offset by the weight of time in our changed bodies, and by the puzzling gentleness of the unexpected moments when we suddenly caught sight of each other again.

If I had left Astrid I would probably have gone to Lisbon, alone for the first time in ten years, alone in a town I had never seen before. I would have sat looking at the boys kicking the ball over the gravel, their small shouting silhouettes in the orange streetlights, and I would have listened to the scattered sounds from the houses around the square, the sounds from televisions and clinking plates and laughter, of the lives of strangers. It would not have mattered where I was, in which town, it would have made no difference. I don't know how long I sat on the bench amid the plane trees, perhaps five or ten minutes. Behind me I heard the yelling, barking staccato sounds and the deep, distorted, electronic man's voice from a loudspeaker. I turned around. A boy of Simon's age was bending over a flickering video screen behind the beaded curtain at the entrance to a small bar. Behind him, at the bar counter, I caught sight of Astrid. She waved. I went to join her. She had been watching me. Where had she been? She shrugged and smiled her crooked smile. Here. I stroked the hair back from her forehead and let my hand slide down her cheek and recognized the gesture, the same as when I stood face to face with her in my kitchen long ago, the first time we touched. She too must have recalled my caress, for she smiled again as she slowly bent her head to one side and leaned her cheek against my hand. I moved my hand to her neck and drew her toward me. I could feel her low voice like a faint, warm puff of air against my throat. What about you? she asked. Where have *you* been? Here, I replied. She looked up at me with a searching glance and smiled again, not so broadly, as if she had forgotten the smile on her lips while thinking over what she saw.

Rosa laughed when I said goodnight. She would go out for some bread, now that I had woken her up, and I smiled at the thought of all the time there was between us, she in the apartment beside the Lakes, I in my hotel room on Lexington Avenue. I leafed through the catalogue of the Edward Hopper exhibition at the Whitney Museum and paused at the picture of the young woman sitting on a bed in the sunshine from the window, looking out over the rooftops with a distant expression, perhaps pondering the self-evident thought that the world is what it is, beneath the boundless sky. That it is nothing else, there is no more. I lay down on the bed and switched off the light, observing the dim, colorless outlines of things in the glimmer of the television screen and the lighted offices in the building opposite. It helped to lie there in semidarkness, I could picture Astrid better, the faint afterglow of isolated moments that faded as I looked at them because they shone with the light of long-vanished days. I thought of the images of the helicopter and the river inundating houses and trees, flowing over fields, through forests. I mused that time is not only a river, but a river that constantly breaks its banks so you must flee from it as it covers everything behind your back, flee into the future, empty-handed and dispossessed, as the river obliterates your footprints with every step you take, your every passage from one moment to the next. It is only our own helpless lack of synchronicity, the inertia of our senses, the illusory power of memory and habit, that shields us from facing the unknown when we open our eyes in the morning, washed up on the shore of yet another alien day. Every morning we tread an unknown path, and we have only faint and failing memories to tell us who we might be. Disconnected, frayed memories, that no longer distinguish between the world we passed and the shadows it cast in our hollow, clean-swept head as we fled onward, on and on. Now and then we overcome our fear of

stumbling and turn around to look back one last time, and
again one very last time, because we do not understand the
strangeness that approaches, and the words we have to name
it will be hopelessly inadequate, and so we flee from the havoc
of time, backward, until we are nothing other than the story
there is to tell of all we have lost.

I thought that by writing my story I would come closer
to the point when she went away from me, but all my sentences have only been a way of withdrawing, while she withdrew in the opposite direction. I thought I was writing about
Astrid, or about Inés and Elisabeth for that matter, but in fact
I was only writing about myself, and when conversely I tried
to recall my own thoughts and feelings through the years, I
merely interpreted the fleeting shadows that an Elisabeth, an
Astrid, and an Inés in turn threw on the vault of my skull's
mumbling loneliness. I thought I knew Astrid, but she may
have begun to disappear one winter evening in my youth,
when I rose and walked into my kitchen to the young woman
who had paused in the middle of washing up, with a shining
wet plate in her hand as she looked out into the darkness
through her indistinct reflection. That unknown woman with
narrow eyes and a crooked smile I had taken into my taxi and
into my apartment because neither of us knew where else I
should take her. Perhaps she only became more unknown, as
she turned toward me and I lifted my hand and stroked her
cheek as a first sign that I wanted to get to know her. Perhaps
I got in the way of my own gaze, perhaps my words drowned
out the silent breathing, the living silence, that more than any
words is the sound of another person. Perhaps she herself
drowned it out in the days and years that followed, when she
told me details of her story in casual, summary, and incom-

plete fragments, the way one talks about oneself as life goes on, so the whole of it is already another story. For her words were addressed to me before they were spoken, already included in the story we were together engaged in telling about each other and ourselves, about those people we were becoming. Just as there are things I never told her, there must be things she never told me, and just as I acquired a secret to keep, there must certainly be people and events that she kept secret from me. When she had released me from my dreams of Inés, long before I dreamed that Elisabeth would release me again, there was a time when I believed she knew everything there was to know about me, more than I could know myself. That she could see me as I was, just as I felt I knew her when I awoke beside her and whispered her name. But perhaps we were never so blind as when we looked into each other's eyes in order to be recognized. We had a story, and our story ended up containing all previous stories, so that in the end they were only extraneous, backward-looking digressions in the continued narrative of our life together. But there must still be so much else, so much more in a human being than what is told, and what can be told at all. Most of it disappears between the words. It only reveals itself as a hesitation before you speak, a silence when you look down at the floor or out the window without really knowing what to say. When you have gone for good only the story remains, but when Astrid left she also left emptiness and stillness in me, which I have filled up with words, although perhaps I should have tried to keep the empty space open by keeping quiet. But I only have words, and without them I would not be able to hear her silence in the pauses between the words, the cracks and hollow places in my narrative, from which she has withdrawn, just as she came into sight

out of nowhere one winter evening, holding a little boy by
the hand.

Rosa met me at the airport as she had promised when I
came home from New York. As we left the terminal I was
about to walk over to the line of taxis, but she laughed at me
and rattled Astrid's car keys. She had passed her driving test
while I was away. Now she was really grown up. She drove
hesitantly and uncertainly, and ground the gears when she
shifted, but I didn't comment. She asked if I minded her bor-
rowing the car for two weeks, I didn't use it much, did I? She
had arranged to go to Berlin with her boyfriend. Everyone is
on the move these days. Had she found a new boyfriend already? She smiled and shook her head. It was the same one,
she had decided to give it another go. I thought of the shaven
installation artist who had sat in my kitchen a week ago, looking at me in despair as I ironed my shirts. But was it all right
about the car? Astrid had said OK. I looked at her. Astrid? She
smiled as she overtook a bus and swung back again hard so as
not to hit the approaching car coming at us with murderous
speed. I was shaken, both because I had looked death in the eye
for a second and on account of her casual reply. Had Astrid
called? She smiled patiently as if she thought I must be very
tired. Yes, Astrid had called the day before. She thought I had
come back. Where had she called from? She didn't know, from
Stockholm she supposed, where else? Had she told Astrid
when I would be back? She wrinkled her forehead as if stopping to think about it. No, she hadn't asked, and they had gone
on to talk of something else. Had Astrid said when she was
coming home? She hesitated a moment. She had forgotten to
ask. She dropped me at the door. She had to be on her way, the
installation artist was waiting. She kissed my cheek, and I

stood anxiously watching as she turned into the traffic again. You could hear it a long way off when she changed gear. Astrid had called, she would surely call again. Perhaps the last word had not been said.

I picked up the pile of letters from the hall floor and took them into my study. My eyes ran over and over the statement of places and times Astrid had used her Mastercard, a laconic narrative of her movements in names and numbers. She had left this trail, leading me back to Lisbon by our old route. There she abandons me, left to my memories. As I sat at my desk before the view of the Lakes, with my coat still on, she has been waking up at the hotel on the Rua Senhora do Monte. Perhaps she sits for a while on the edge of the bed resting her gaze on the view, the random slice of town and river. Perhaps she lingers a little longer before getting dressed and walking out of the picture. I imagine her sitting in a ray of sunlight as she looks out over the roofs of Lisbon and the wide river and its opposite bank, where the invisible car windows catch the sun for a fraction of a second and send its reflections back across the river to her shadowy room like abrupt and disconnected Morse code. Perhaps she ponders everything being as it is, as if it could not be otherwise. As if everything was not still undecided. When I remember Astrid in Lisbon seven years ago, I see her walking alone. I cannot see myself. She walks alone where we walked, with narrow eyes in the clear afternoon sunshine that makes the tram lines glitter in the steep streets in front of her. The sun shone the morning after our arrival, and we walked through Graça, past the market-place where the stalls were already being dismantled. We walked without any particular purpose, down toward the blue river, which kept appearing between the rooftops when the streets dropped suddenly. I am not present in my few photos from Lisbon. I only see Astrid, as if I were not there. Sitting in the Rossio in front of a café on the square, where the trams screech close by our table and the sun shines in the thin smoke from the chestnut sellers' braziers as she bends her head and looks down into her coffee cup, lost in thought. Walking in front of me on a path in the botanical garden, beneath an arch of trees that filter the sunlight so that both the path and her light-colored coat are spotted with yellow, her face in profile looking up alertly as a bird's wings flap against the plane trees' thick foliage. Standing at the rail of the little ferry taking us over to Cacilhas, in sunglasses, smiling her white smile in front of the distant white town. She took only one picture of me, in the ruined church at Largo do Carmo. It had no roof, the sparrows flew around freely between the bare moss-covered walls. I am standing on the grass beneath the Gothic arches, outlined like gnawed rib bones against the sky. I am smiling at her, the invisible photographer, but she has taken too long to focus, the smile has stiffened. There is actually no smile left, only a forced, fatuous grimace as I meet my own gaze, as if I am looking straight through her. As if by looking myself in the eye I open a void into which she has already vanished.